SIA

SIA

DARK CITY ROYALS
BOOK 1

EDEN O'NEILL

BOOKS BY EDEN O'NEILL

Court High
They The Pretty Stars
Illusions That May
Court Kept
We The Pretty Stars

Court University
Brutal Heir
Kingpin
Beautiful Brute
Lover

Court Legacy
Dirty Wicked Prince
Savage Little Lies
Tiny Dark Deeds
Eat You Alive
Eat Your Heart Out
Pretty Like A Devil

Standalones
Sia

SIA: Dark City Royals Book 1

Copyright © 2025 by Eden O'Neill

All rights reserved. No part of this book may be reproduced or transmitted in any form, including electronic or mechanical, without written permission from the publisher, except in the case of brief quotations embodied in critical articles or reviews.

This book is a work of fiction and any resemblance to any person, living or dead, any place, events, or occurrences, is purely coincidental and not intended by the author.

Cover Art: Ever After Cover Design

Editing: A. Jane Dove

CONTENT WARNINGS:

SIA is a dark mafia romance recommended for readers 18+. Please see the author's website at www.edenoneill.com for all the book's content warnings.

A MESSAGE FROM THE AUTHOR:

This story was previously published on Kindle Vella as a serial, but nothing major has been changed. It's now been completed in its entirety for your enjoyment. Please note this book is inspired by Anastasia but is not a literal retelling. For a list of tropes and content warnings please see the author's website www.edenoneill.com.

PART ONE
THE BEGINNING

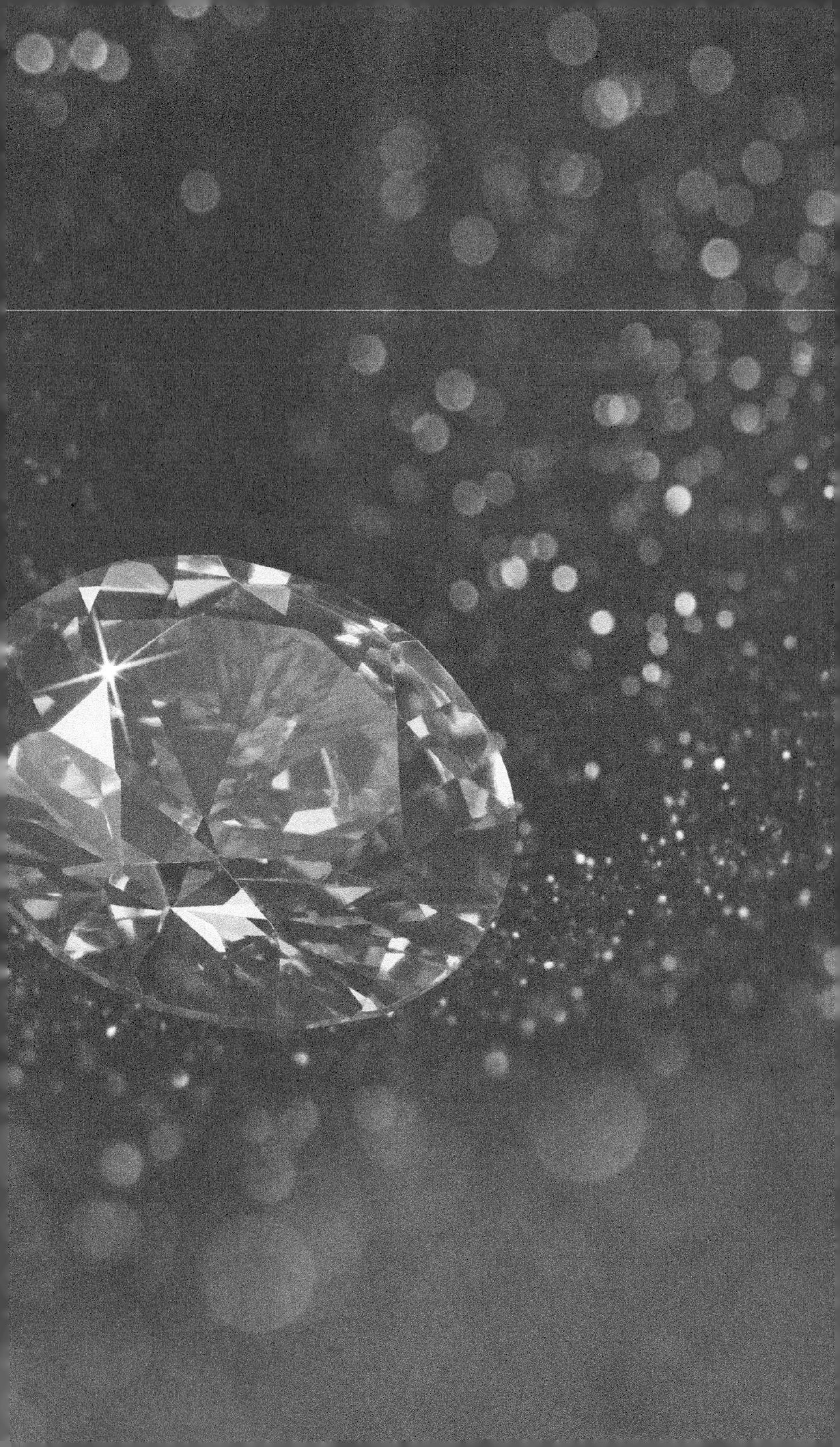

CHAPTER ONE

Sia

Swift chirps came honking down the street, and I lifted my head.

Oh God.

The white Jeep bumped down the street, arms flailing in a wave inside. My friend Lettie never said what she'd be driving, but I wasn't surprised that it was literally the car from Clueless.

Lettie…

I tried not to cringe when she parked it in front of a legit halfway house: my halfway house. The majority of the girls were inside, but they weren't the ones I was concerned about.

The guys who lived in the house across the street leered in Lettie's direction, and when the leggy blonde in high-waisted shorts and a bra for a top got out of the car, those leers became feral.

"Eh!" I stood up from the stoop I'd been waiting on. "Don't look at her."

They smirked in my direction, making kissing faces, and I

flipped them off. Meanwhile, Odette "Lettie" Petrov was none the wiser. She was too busy hugging me.

"Ah! Look at you. You look *good*," she chirped, appraising me, and I smirked. I was in a pair of ripped shorts and a long-sleeved flannel, all of which I'd gotten out of the donation bin.

Someone stole my stuff.

Shit like that happened. I was lucky I came out with the rest of my stuff: a few pairs of jeans, a couple tops, and some underwear. All of which I planned to replace once I got my first check at my new job.

"Thanks." I took the compliment. Mostly because I wanted both her and myself out of here. I'd spent ninety days at this crap shoot and I was tired of feeling like a drug addict.

You are a drug addict.

That reality was not lost on me as I shooed my friend back into her Jeep. I tried to hold my things in my lap, but Lettie insisted on putting it all in the back.

It was hard for me to get used to that shit. People wanting to help me instead of taking things from me. I tried to tell myself it was because I'd spent the last three months in a halfway house.

"Holy shit, I can't believe you're here, girl." Once inside, Lettie kissed my cheek. Another weird thing. She was the touchy-feely type and I wasn't. She held my face. "How are you? They treat you well?"

"Fine." And I'd be better if she got this car off this block before we caused any more attention.

I urged her to do so, completely aware the guys across the street were standing now. Before they got any ideas, I got Lettie moving this flashy ride and finally relaxed when she got us off this street and onto the freeway.

"Seriously, though. You all right? Well, besides the obvious," she said, my friend literally putting a joint in her mouth in front of me. Lettie knew the details of my last few months, but the girl could definitely be a bit flighty. She pulled it out of her mouth. "Oh, shit. Can I do this in front of you?"

I laughed, waving her off. Weed obviously wasn't allowed in rehab, but I wasn't going to tell her no. I mean, she was about to do me a huge favor. "It's fine."

"You sure, dude?"

I was, but she probably shouldn't. I smirked at her. "Are dancers supposed to be smoking?"

"Hell, no." She chuckled. "Why do you think I'm doing it? I'm trying to get what I can in before I head off to school."

I'd only heard about Lettie's dancing and schooling. Lettie was technically a new friend, but I knew she was going to some ritzy dance school in New York City soon. That left a room open in her house and since I needed a place to stay…

I actually hadn't asked her for help. She offered once she found out my situation. If I didn't get my act together, stay clean and get a real job and a place to stay, I was going to prison.

And that was it.

The judge had been pretty harsh that day considering I hadn't gotten in trouble for a while.

I shoved up my sleeves. "You sure your dad's okay with me coming?" I swallowed. "And the job?"

Lettie was helping me out with both. Apparently, her dad was like a workaholic or something. He wasn't around much, but he probably should care more about having a drug addict living in his house.

I was surprised when Lettie said he didn't. She also said he didn't care about the random job she was giving me on his behalf. Apparently with her going away to school she thought getting her dad a dog was a good idea. He was a single dad, and I guess Lettie had been taking care of him her whole life. Well, in the social sense.

Clearly, Lettie was the one being taken care of financially. I could probably buy this car with the purse she had on the center console between us.

Anyway, the dog was for her dad, and I was for the dog I guess. She knew I had some experience with handling animals.

I shifted in my seat. "Because if he changed his mind…"

"Why would he change his mind?"

"I don't know. Because I hit a cop on top of having a drug related charge." It wasn't one of my finest moments and definitely wasn't something I planned to do again.

But who planned things like that?

In my silence, Lettie flicked her blue eyes in my direction. She put out her smoke. "Yeah, and that was like a one-time thing."

"How do you know?"

"Because you told me, and I trust you."

She probably shouldn't. I mean, we were friends, but we kind of barely knew each other. There was also the circumstances in which we met and became friends, and that *definitely* should put her dad off.

I really wasn't trying to literally bite off the hand that fed me, but I had made some mistakes, and it was kind of unusual I was getting a chance at all from someone I hadn't even met.

"I vouched for you," Lettie continued. She flicked her joint out the window. "You told me it was a one-time thing, and you also literally just spent time in rehab for the drug stuff." She peered over. "Which was also a one-time thing according to you."

I mean, I hoped so. But again, best laid plans.

"You told me something, and I believe you." She nodded. "Also, my dad trusts me wholeheartedly. So if you're good with me, you're good with him."

It was nice she had that: someone who cared and someone

she obviously could trust if he trusted her. "I guess if you're sure."

"I am sure, and my dad is cool. He actually thought it was kind of funny you hit a cop."

I shot back in my seat. "Funny?"

"Well, not funny *per se*, but I told him you were like my size so, yeah, he had a laugh."

She was being a bit generous there. We may be the same height, but Lettie had the svelte form and toned definition of a ballet dancer, which was exactly the dance style I heard she did. Even if she hadn't told me I would have known it. The girl was skinny as a rod, but also looked like she could crush wood with her thighs. Or her calves for that matter.

She chuckled another laugh. "If anything, I say that put you more in his good graces. Dad's not a fan of cops, and he certainly doesn't have room to judge anyone's legal history. He's a businessman but doesn't always work inside the law."

"What do you mean?"

"I wish I could say, but a lot of what he does is need to know. Meaning, he doesn't even tell me a lot of it."

"You make it sound like he's in the mafia."

Her eyes hit the road then and, before I could question her more, we were pulling off the freeway and merging into traffic.

The culture definitely changed, re: the vehicles. There were Mercedes and Audis everywhere. Bentleys. I suddenly felt like I was in a car commercial. The nice rides continued as we veered into a neighborhood with some of the biggest houses I'd ever seen.

I honestly didn't know houses like this existed in the crap town I'd called home my entire life. I definitely didn't live on this side. The parts I lived in were either run down or boarded up.

Whoa.

Gates open for Lettie's Jeep, literal gates. I turned to see an attendant waving outside of a little security booth at us. He told Lettie to have a good day.

And he called her Ms. Petrov.

I turned back around and a sea of woods were in front of me. It was like we were in some storybook land. It was all green and lush. We traveled within it until suddenly the world opened up to a large brick home.

Double whoa.

The place looked like a castle: old school, with ivy and rich greenery running down the side. There were also people everywhere. They cut grass and trimmed hedges. The area was huge and definitely needed people to upkeep it all.

"Home sweet home," Lettie chirped, and though I assumed this was where she lived, my jaw dropped. She faced me. "What do you think?"

I think I felt like a scrub in my tattered clothes and military duffle in the backseat. I'd gotten that out of the donation bin too.

"Lettie, this is insane." I did a full 180° pivot in my seat. They even had a friggin' fountain! "You didn't tell me you were like princess-level loaded."

I mean, I could assume by the way she always carried herself and this expensive ride, but this was Duke of Cambridge rich.

Lettie chuckled. "It's my dad's money. Not mine."

Also something rich people said. My eyes lifted, and Lettie pulled us around to an airport hangar, not a garage. The space legitimately was a car factory, mostly sports cars of a rich and handsome black. Lettie's white Jeep certainly stood out, and when we got inside, someone actually took the car from us and helped park it the rest of the way.

"Come on. I'll show you around," Lettie said jovially. She immediately linked arms with me—the girl definitely the touchy-feely type. I didn't think I'd ever get used to it, but I did smile when she tucked me close and pointed out all the points of the property on our way inside. She had a guy following behind us with my duffle and her purse.

Again, princess-level rich.

Before we went inside, she pointed out the general area of where the pool, tennis courts, and basketball courts were. They even had a mini winery farther up the property.

"Dad likes to make his in-house," she said, fusing me into her at this point. I honestly liked how open she was with her personality and general optimism. She obviously hadn't been jaded by anything in this life, and I tried not to resent her for that. It'd be nice to be trusting, open.

I lost track of all the rooms she pointed out on the way to her bedroom. She showed me the kitchen and some bathrooms, but I'd never remember all of it by the time I needed it.

"And my room." She opened the princess palace—literally white everywhere, from the chiffon curtains to the four-poster bed. The curtains on the bed were tied back, and the girl had so many pillows on her mattress that one could easily drown in the sea of them.

"Sophia will turn the bed down for you every night," Lettie said, noticing me eyeing all the pillows. She laughed. "There's a chest for all that. The pillows?"

I saw that too, and I'd already met Sophia. She actually took the bags from the guy who followed us on the house tour. She was the head of the house, and I was to go to her if I needed anything.

Stepping in behind us in a black dress, Sophia took my stuff and Lettie's and disappeared into what I assumed was the room's closet. I faced Lettie. "I'm staying in here?"

"Uh-huh. You can keep my stuff warm for me." Lettie sat on the bed, but frowned when she saw my face. "What's wrong?"

"Uh, nothing. It's just a lot." I pointed back toward the

door. "Wouldn't you like me to stay in one of the guest rooms?"

There were like a million in this house, surely.

Her eyes lifting, Lettie got up. She took my hand. "My space is your space and, like I said, you can keep my stuff warm until I get back."

But she'd need it for school breaks and stuff, and when I told her that, she waved me off.

"We'll work it out," she said, grinning. "So you like it?"

She asked me like it was possible *not* to like it. "It's kind of like a dream."

There was no kind of. This place *was* a dream, and I eased a look outside when Lettie turned to speak to Sophia about something. There were lots of people out there tending to the property, and the vineyard Lettie spoke about stretched in a length of rows well beyond where I could see.

It was truly amazing, really. I folded my arms. I'd never seen a vineyard before, but my attention escaped it when I noticed a guy a level down on the phone. He faced the vineyard, but I saw him when he pivoted.

He had his sleeves rolled up, thick arms tatted down to his knuckles. Literally, the guy had tattoos down the length of his fingers, and his hair was an inky black. He worked his tatted fingers through it. He was dressed in well-fitted trousers and a stark white shirt. The dress shirt hugged his brawny build and was a sharp juxtaposition to all those tats.

And the messy hair.

Tousled, it fell in interesting ways over his jet black sunglasses, and I blinked when Lettie bumped my shoulder.

"Who's that guy out there?" I asked casually. For some reason, Lettie laughed.

"Oh God, not you too," she said, borderline cringing, and when I didn't understand, her eyes lifted. She faced outside. "That's my dad."

Her *dad*...

I blinked again. "*That's* your dad?"

My jaw was basically on the floor at this point, and Lettie's eyes rolled again. "Yes, that's my dad. And please spare me any thoughts you have of him being a zaddy, or a daddy," she paused, pretty much shuddering in front of me. "Or a DILF. I've literally heard it all since I was thirteen from any friend I've brought to the house."

She left my side, but I didn't follow. "But he's, like, young."

Like really young. At least, young-looking. He didn't look as young as me or her, but he couldn't be like more than thirty.

"He's thirty-six." Lettie was on the bed and obviously wanted to be done with this conversation. Her head cocked. "He had me when he was eighteen, which literally blows my mind because I couldn't imagine having a kid at my age."

I mean, same. I was a couple years older than her at twenty, but still I couldn't imagine.

I glanced outside. Her dad was off the phone now and yelling at someone. I mean, he wasn't yelling but was strongly commanding someone with a bunch of grapes in their hands. Her dad had his hands posted on his hips while he spoke, and though the guy speaking with him didn't look intimidated, I would be. Her dad was huge.

And all those tats...

Lettie kicked her feet. "You can wipe the drool off your face because I'm legit about to be sick."

My eyes rolled. "I'm not drooling. It's just you don't look like him, and he is young." I pushed my sleeves up, hugging my arms. She may have been uncomfortable with the conversation, but I was too. I mean, that was her *dad*.

I pushed off the window, distancing myself, and Lettie smiled.

"I've heard I look more like my mom. Not that I know since she's a deadbeat." Lettie shrugged. "According to my dad, she left me on his doorstep. Some stripper he hooked up with."

I blanched that she said that so casually. "Well, that sucks."

"Not really. I don't need her, and my dad definitely doesn't need her." She lay back. "It's always been just the two of us, and we're cool like that."

It sounded like it, but what I wouldn't give to have some kind of family. I had no one.

"In the car, you mentioned your dad not exactly working inside the law," I said, remembering the conversation, and she sat up. I chewed my lip. "It's just I don't have, like, any strikes, and I can't mess up."

My next stop was prison if someone in a uniform even got a whisper about me getting into trouble.

And judging by the look of her dad…

I was seriously questioning the mafia thing at this point, and looking around at the life these two had going was definitely giving me some…vibes. I couldn't judge of course and wouldn't if that was the case, but I just couldn't have any part of anything that might have the cops sniffing around.

Lettie got up. "I'm being honest when I say I don't know everything he does. He keeps me pretty sheltered from all that."

She did give off those vibes, and when I mentioned that, she shouldered me.

"Seriously, though. I don't know a lot. But what I do, I'm not exactly allowed to talk about."

Yeah, definitely giving off sketchy here. "I can't get into trouble, Lettie. That's the whole point of all this."

A permanent place to live, a job, and no criminal activity. The judge was pretty clear on her rules, and I told Lettie that.

She smiled. "Believe me when I say this is the last place you'll find trouble. Actually, I've brought in more over the years."

I laughed when I did think about how we met. She'd been doing a stint of community service for hitting a cop...with her car. She didn't physically hit the guy, but his squad car. I'd been doing my own stint of community service but for other reasons.

Again, I had no more strikes.

I fingered some of my curls and she grabbed my hand.

"You're good here, Sia," she said. "You won't find any trouble, and you'd be doing me a huge favor by staying here and working for my dad. He acts like it's not a big deal, me leaving tomorrow. But it's only just been the two of us for so long. I worry about him."

Hence his need for the dog. I sighed. "You'd be doing me a favor too."

"So you'll do it? You'll stay?" Her eyes lit up. "Pretty please with sugar on top?"

I laughed. "Where's the pupper?"

"Ahh! You're the best." She grabbed me, squeezing. This girl really had no boundaries at all, but something about her had me not minding so much. At least, I wouldn't have to worry about that when it came to her dad. The guy seemed intense.

I actually hugged Lettie back. I would miss her too.

She was my only friend.

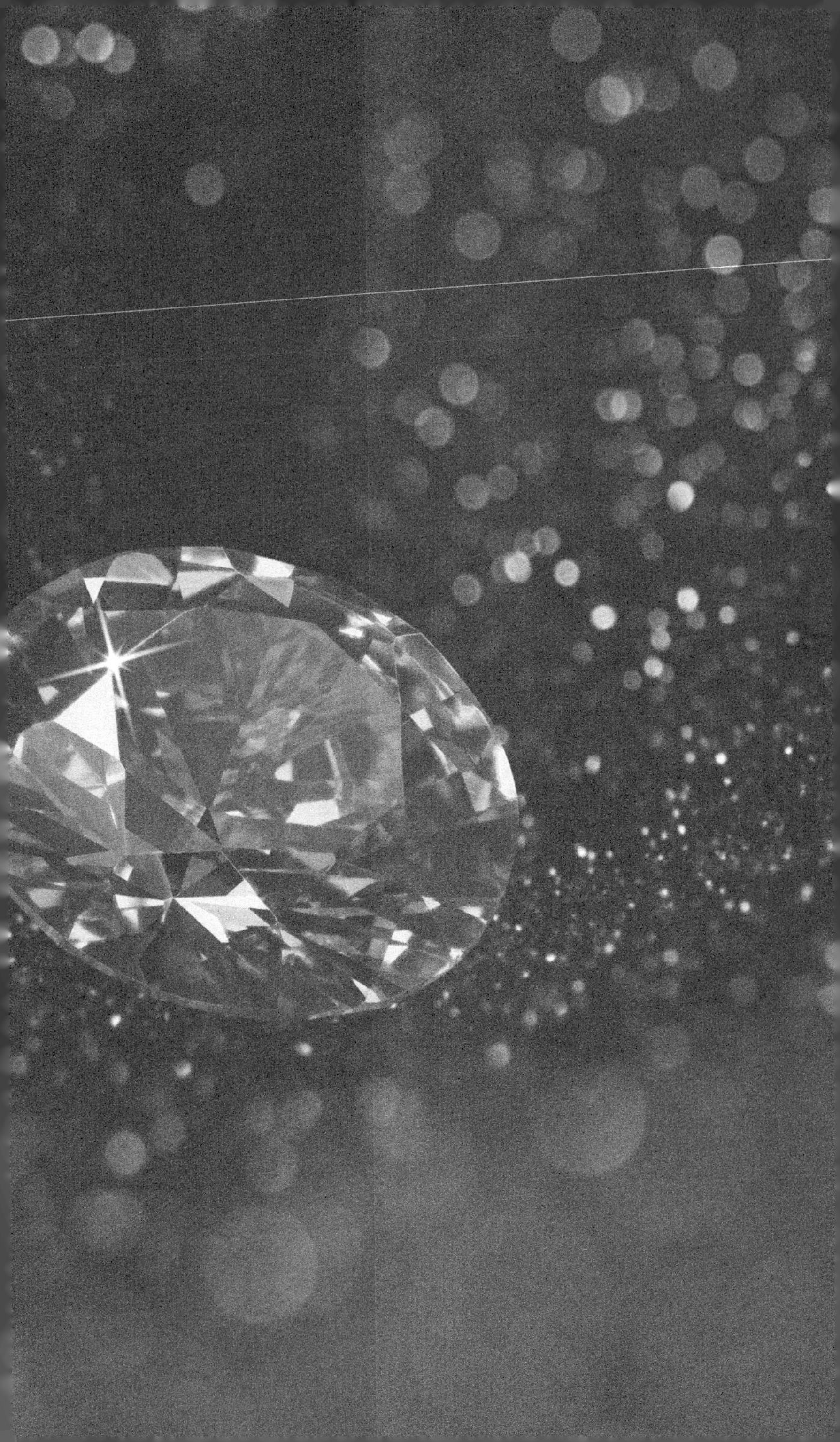

CHAPTER TWO

Maxim

I was fucking annoyed. Work kept me out all day, people in my fucking face when all I wanted to do was to be at home with my kid. It was her last day before she went off to college, and here I was showing up at five AM, basically hours before her flight took off.

Cursing, I unbuttoned my shirt, stripping it off to take a shower. It was early, but I planned to take Lettie to breakfast. I'd been home today but briefly and hadn't gotten to see her.

I grunted as I stalked through the house. The sun wasn't out yet, the house and the world still dark. I made my shower quick, dressed, then tapped on Lettie's door. "Sweetheart?"

I used to call my daughter a wallflower, but that stopped being relevant the moment she found dance. Ballet really brought her out of her shell and now she was even going to school for it. I had a Juilliard girl and was very proud.

I pressed a hand to the door. "Lettie?"

She was no doubt trying to get some sleep before her flight, but I needed to see her. I didn't have a lot of time.

Trying not to think about that, I cracked the door, letting sconce light from the hallway into the room. Her small form rose softly in slumber beneath her bedding. "Lettie?"

The air felt different in here, smelled different. I stepped inside, aware something felt...off.

Passing it off as working late, I sat on Lettie's bed. I put my hand on her shoulder. "Hey. I know it's early, but what do you think about getting some breakfast before your flight takes off?"

It was the least I could do, but my daughter didn't move when I spoke to her. I shook her a little, and the moment I did, the scent of something hit me. Something soft...

Foreign.

My nose lifted at something sweet and delicate. It distracted me, and the form beneath my hand scurried away.

It hit the headboard.

A girl with brown skin and wide eyes brought the sheet up over her body, a fury of vibrant curls surrounding her face. She clawed desperately at the sheets, trying to keep them over her body. I rose to my feet. "Who the fuck are you?"

Right away, I flicked the light on the end table and, where I'd normally go for my knife, I stopped upon seeing the girl's terror. She looked horrified, but she still didn't answer my question.

"I'm going to repeat myself, *malyshka*," I said, low, menacing, and it did the fucking job. She shrank under the sheets. I snarled. "Who. The. Fuck. Are. You. And where is my daughter?"

And why the fuck was she in Lettie's bed?

This little one wasn't speaking fast enough, and I leaned forward. Her brown skin flushed, the fear radiating off her.

I could taste it.

My blood heated, my eyes rolling back a little. My hand moved for my knife, but my kid's voice had me pivoting around.

Lettie had her purse on her shoulder. "Dad, what's going on?"

I blinked before I could see her by the door, well aware of the haze I'd placed myself in. It happened sometimes, but I was fully out of it by the time Lettie made her way inside the room.

And this girl went to her.

She was about my daughter's size, same height but fuller, curvier. She scrubbed her hand through all those brown curls, her eyes dark and light brown cheeks flushed with color. I'd scared her, clearly.

Good.

I pointed at her, then looked at my kid. "Explain."

The petite little thing next to Lettie rocked on her toes, doing everything she could to hide the fact she wasn't wearing a bra. She had a big shirt on that ran down to her knees, but her hugging on herself and fidgeting the way she was didn't hide the fact she had tits.

My eyes narrowed at her, but then, Lettie was at my side.

"Relax," Lettie said, her voice in the background. I leaned down when she hugged me. My daughter was a hugger. "This is Sia Reynolds. She's caring for Polly."

"The fuck's a Polly?" This *Sia* was at the door now, looking on the verge of retreat. I smirked at her. *Scared, little one?*

She *was* scared. My mouth lifted a little, but when I looked at my daughter, she was frowning.

Her head cocked. "Polly is your dog, Dad. The dog I got you?" She rolled her eyes. "I hired Sia to take care of her. Don't you remember?"

Faintly. Hardly. I looked at Sia. She was at the doorframe now. "Nowhere did I hear you say she'd be staying in your goddamn bedroom."

Which isn't appropriate. There were places for staff.

I'd been quite observant of Sia during this exchange. She'd

been well on her way out of the door but stopped. She stood solid in the doorframe and, where she'd been scared before, she wasn't now.

Now, she just looked pissed.

Her little lips pouted like she *was* pissed, pissed at me, and I laughed.

This only made her scowl deeper, like she knew my thoughts and was mad at me. Her head cocked, she puffed up like the man I had bleeding at my feet earlier this morning. He'd had a lot of fight in him before he gave up information.

They did that sometimes.

Ignoring this Sia, I faced Lettie. "We're going to breakfast. I expect you downstairs in ten."

And this wasn't a negotiation. My daughter had a lot to answer for. The first question I had was why the dog trainer was in her bed and not down the hall with the rest of the staff.

I left, passing Sia. She didn't move for me, and I smirked again.

"Dad—"

"Downstairs in *ten*, Lettie," I barked over my shoulder, still walking. "And maybe you'll convince me to actually let you go to school now seeing as how you're clearly sneaking back into this house."

She was probably out with that reject boyfriend of hers.

Growling, I slammed the door behind me, my steps quick. I had ten minutes to cool down.

So I didn't say things to my daughter I'd regret.

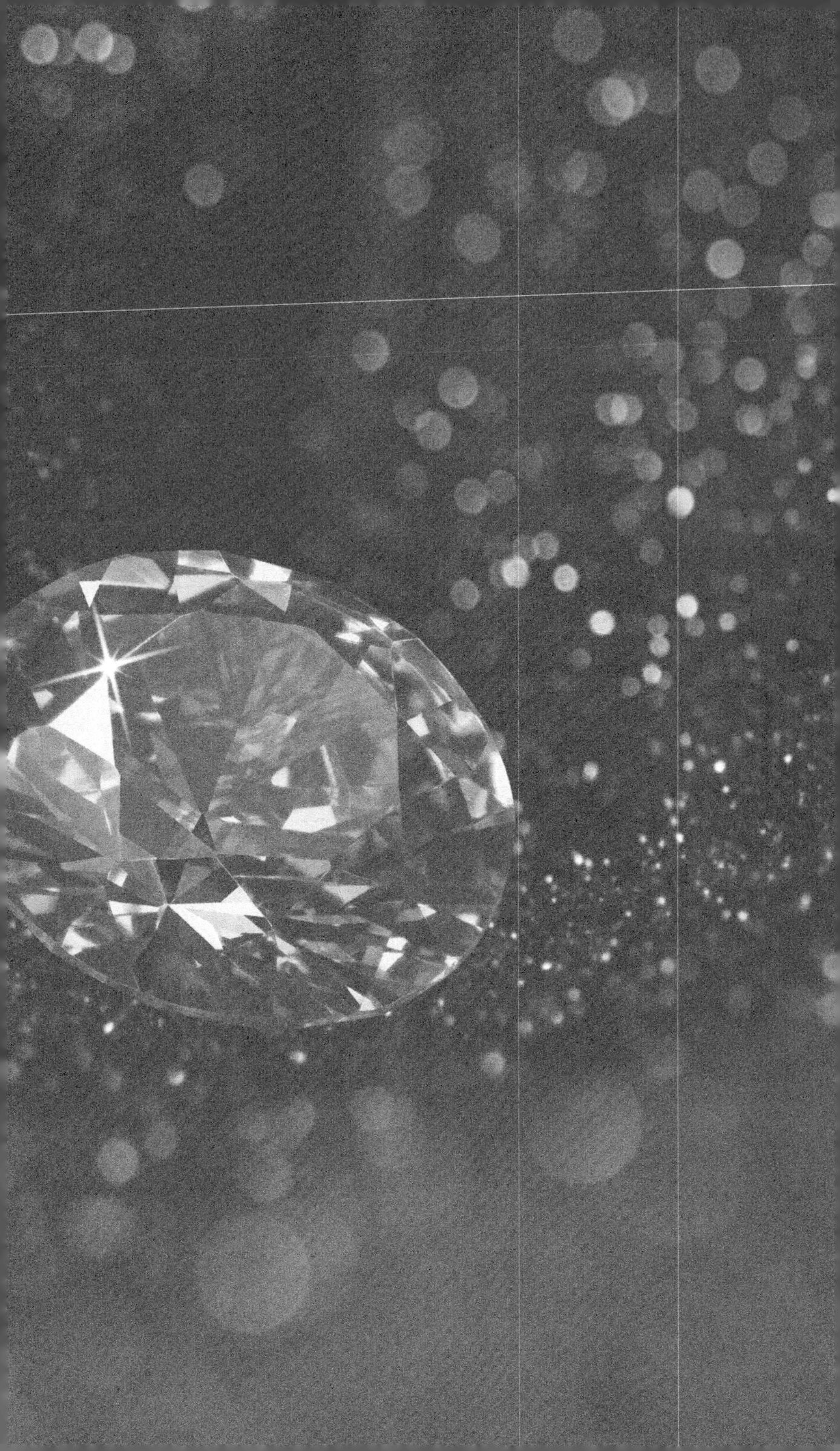

CHAPTER THREE

Sia

So, Lettie's dad was terrifying.

And an asshole.

I'd never met an adult male who cursed so much. At least in front of someone he just met. I mean, I cursed but again, he just met me.

What. The. Hell.

He'd been completely foreboding, *dominating*, and if I hadn't been questioning the whole mafia thing before, I was now.

Especially considering what he'd called me.

I didn't know if that had been Russian or what, but since Lettie's last name, Petrov, sounded Russian I could assume he spoke Russian to me.

What was this place I was staying at and who was that crazy, scary dude who pretty much ripped me out of Lettie's bed? I told Lettie I shouldn't have been staying in there yet, but she insisted since she said she'd be spending her last night before leaving with her boyfriend. I guess they dated all throughout high school or something.

They'd been gone all morning, Lettie and her dad, and I hadn't really known what to do after that, so I waited. They'd basically been gone for hours, and when they did come home, Lettie apologized profusely. She felt really bad about how her dad acted toward me, but that wasn't her fault.

It was the asshole's.

He'd looked at me so unusually in Lettie's room. Like I'd been an insect he couldn't wait to dissect. While apologizing, Lettie said she'd at least reminded her dad about who I was. By the end of the conversation, it sounded like they were on the same page finally. Goody goody gumdrops for me.

I needed my jellybeans.

I found a bag of them in the closet with my things, and I immediately munched on the yellow ones. They all technically tasted the same, but I liked the yellow ones best. I did that after Lettie and Mr. Petrov left for the second time that morning, and Lettie must have been able to convince her dad she could go to school because that's where they headed off to.

I took the opportunity to leave my room.

At least, I thought this was still my room. I *thought* I worked here. I didn't really know now. Lettie sounded like everything was fine.

But with her gone now...

I tried not to freak out about that, eating my jellybeans while I tried to find my way around the Petrov manor. Manor it was. The place was like an old school palace out of some fantasy novel. It had paintings everywhere and the ceilings had even been painted like ones in an actual palace. There were flying cherubs and Greek gods up there.

The place was completely foreboding, dark. What little light there was came from flickering wall sconces that gave the illusion of candlelight. The manor definitely held its place in the haunted castle territory.

About the only place I was familiar with was where the dog, Polly, was staying. Her residence wasn't even technically in the house, but the wing off the side of it. It was bougie as fuck like the rest of the place but, apparently, Lettie's dad wanted the dog in there until it was properly housebroken. This was my job, but I wasn't too keen on the fact that Polly was just out there by herself.

It was lonely.

I knew a little something about that and, while I met Polly yesterday, she still had a bit of hesitance when I entered her space. This wasn't surprising since she was out here by herself.

I grumbled at her owner's doing. Mr. Petrov was something else. I put him out of my mind while I got Polly out. Another job of mine was to make sure she was fed, watered, and walked.

Polly was a German Shepherd that was about twice my size and nearly as tall. She was a hella intimidating dog and probably the best breed to get if someone wanted to look tough or like they didn't give a fuck. She definitely looked like she'd take a bite out of someone, but she was basically still a puppy at one year old.

"Come on, girl." I met her only briefly yesterday, but when I held myself in a position to let her know I wasn't a threat, she came easily.

Big softy.

I nearly had her on her back at one point, rubbing her stomach. Grinning, I worked on a couple commands to get her alert before taking her out onto the Petrovs' property.

And property it was. The place was friggin' huge. I wouldn't take Polly far since I didn't want to get lost.

We traveled through the Petrovs' gardens a bit, and I worked on keeping her walking with me rather than tugging.

She was a fast learner, so I didn't have to give her too many reward treats, which was good. Dogs could get reliant on those.

"Good girl." I rubbed her as I got a text from my phone. I pulled it out.

Lettie: I'm so sorry again.

I smiled.

Me: Aren't you supposed to be like in the air or something?

Polly started tugging again, getting impatient. I rubbed her again while Lettie's text message bubble came up.

Lettie: Still waiting. Just wanted to message before I took off.

Lettie: Also, to make sure you weren't going to run. I know my dad can be intense.

Well, that was the understatement of the year.

Me: Honestly, I was waiting for the ball to drop and you or him to tell me I couldn't work here anymore.

Which would suck. I needed this job and the place to stay. I was desperate.

Lettie: Oh thank God you still want the job. And I know my dad can be gruff, but he will soften up. He's just not quick to warm up to people.

Yeah, I got that.

Lettie: I'm so glad you're staying though, and I know I'm far away but always text me if you need something.

She definitely didn't need to worry about me when she was about to be in her first year of college.

I glanced around then, a prickle on my neck. I wasn't sure why I decided to turn around in that moment, but when I looked up, I realized why.

A man stood in the wide window facing the Petrovs' gardens.

Mr. Petrov had a glass of something brown in his hand. Something he tipped back before staring at me. He saluted me with it and his tatted fingers, his eyes cold and dismissive before he gave his back to me and walked away.

Yeah, that guy was a barrel of laughs.

But then again, so was I.

Lettie: I appreciate you being there, and I know this is a lot to ask and completely out of the job description, but would it be too much if you could keep an eye on him for me? I mean, like just be around and present. I really don't like him in that big house by himself.

He technically wasn't. These people had so many staff. I'd probably be interacting with him a lot since I needed to train him as much as the dog.

But could Mr. Petrov be trained?

I wasn't sure, but it wasn't my job to question. It was my job to train and that was what I'd do.

I assured Lettie I'd be around, but I wasn't sure about looking out for her dad. That guy seemed like the last person to need someone looking out for him.

After wishing Lettie good luck on her first semester, I took Polly inside. I rewarded her with treats for staying by my side. I was so distracted that I jumped when someone cleared their throat.

"Miss Reynolds, could you come in here please?"

Even *his voice* gave me chills, pricked goosebumps on my skin.

Standing tall, I rerouted myself and Polly into the dining room I'd apparently passed. That was where I heard Mr. Petrov's voice. He sat with his liquor and lunch at a large oak table.

King of his castle, he sat back, watching me from basically a throne-like seat. All the seats in the room had high backs, but his was the tallest.

I fought my eyes from lifting, trying to be respectful. Despite that, my fingers itched to get the jellybeans in my pocket.

He's not going to intimidate me.

I made myself a promise years ago I wouldn't be intimidated when it came to strong men. I could take care of myself and had been for a long time.

"Sit, Polly," I said.

The dog sat at my side; something I'd been working with her on all morning. Mr. Petrov seemed less than impressed, a newspaper in his hand while he ate his lunch. The man had a large T-Bone steak in front of him and, like, who ate that for lunch casually?

"I'm sure you know dogs aren't allowed in the main house," he said, peering over his newspaper. He actually appeared a semblance of normal with reading glasses on, but when he lowered the paper the fact this man wasn't normal rang through the air. Another white dress shirt strained over his bulky body, the buttons laboring at the seams. He had tattoos on his chest too: black, the ink faint like prison tats.

God, what was I getting myself into?

Mr. Petrov's head cocked. "Miss Reynolds?"

I realized then I'd been staring at him—at all those tattoos in particular. I peered off. "Lettie told me, but I lost my way in this house."

He was smirking when I finally looked at him, something I totally remembered upstairs. He had a cocky smile, like he ruled the world and I was just honored to be in it.

He pointed with his newspaper. "The dog's quarters can always be accessed from the foyer."

"Polly."

"What?"

"The dog's name is Polly," I corrected. "You should call her by her name. She needs to know you and your voice."

"Is that right?"

"Yes, and my name is Sia. You can call me that, or Ms. Reynolds, but I just wanted to let you know."

Because he had problems remembering things and all that.

Mr. Petrov's smile deepened, and for someone who probably spoke Russian, I noticed he didn't have an accent. Nor did Lettie. He might be second generation or something.

"I remember, *Miss* Reynolds." He sat back. "And while we're on the topic of names, you will call me Mr. Petrov while you're here. You're staff, and that's what staff calls me."

I wondered what his first name was. I hadn't asked Lettie.

His lips thinned. "And the dog *and you* are my daughter's idea. If I had it my way, I'd be free of both of you."

At least he was honest. Jesus.

"I don't need a dog to babysit me," he snipped, obviously having figured out Lettie's plan. He peered over me. "As far as you, I'm aware how you and my daughter met."

"Community service, yes. Lettie hit a cop."

"It seems you guys share that in common."

True, but not in the same way.

Mr. Petrov had obviously looked me up, and Lettie mentioned he found that particular detail of my past funny.

"But what you don't share is your own rap sheet," he continued, and though I knew this was probably coming, my stomach still soured. "In and out of juvie since you were thirteen, and at one point, you set your foster family's house on fire."

He really did look into me. I stood tall. "I have a history."

And that was all I'd say about that.

Lettie said he was cool...

I felt really sick now, real fucking sick. Especially talking about my history in the system.

"What you've gotten up to most recently is light in comparison," Mr. Petrov said, obviously referencing the drugs and the cop. He frowned. "But I'm also aware that my daughter trusts you, and when I heard what you did for her during her community service stint, I'm finding that hard to ignore. It seems a thank you is in order there."

"It was nothing." It *was* nothing. Lettie was green when it came to breaking the law, clearly. So she'd been a target of some of the more seasoned kids. I stepped in when some of them were giving her a hard time one day when we were picking up trash. We had to work at a zoo together cleaning up.

Mr. Petrov smiled a little, as if at a thought. "I'm sure you and I both know Lettie doesn't typically get into trouble. She's a pampered princess," he stated, and I almost laughed but didn't dare. This guy was so fucking serious. "But that's no fault of hers. I've raised her not to need anything."

Well, he definitely achieved that.

His eyes narrowed. "I do thank you for what you did, and you obviously impressed my daughter with your knowledge of animals that day cleaning the zoo. I remember she couldn't stop talking about that. She said the girl she met during her community service was a genius."

"Hardly. I just used to work in a vet clinic." I shrugged. "So I knew a few things."

He scanned me after I said that, and I found my cheeks more warm from that than the memories. My heart raced too, and I reached for my jellybeans.

"That being said, there are rules in this house. Rules like keeping the dog in its proper quarters. And I'm having your things moved. I understand my daughter was being generous, but you are staff, and I don't think it's appropriate for you to stay in her room."

He'd probably have me out with the dog since he clearly wanted nothing to do with me, and it made sense now why he was letting me stay.

He felt he owed me something. A guy like this didn't seem like the type to like owing someone anything.

He rubbed his knuckles. "Staff quarters are in the west wing. That's where you'll be. As far as general house rules, there are places you—or anyone else for that matter—aren't allowed to go in this house if you're not me. If you have any questions about those places, ask Sophia. I'm sure you've met her."

I had. I nodded. "Is now a good time to discuss my own rules?"

His head jerked up. He'd gone back to his paper at this point.

"Rules for the dog?" I stated. Polly was still sitting quietly, the sweetie. I looked up. "After all, I'll be training her as much as you."

So...originally that was just a thought in my head, and I definitely hadn't intended on actually voicing my annoyance.

He'd talked down to me.

I swallowed upon watching his face. His handsome features managed to darken, grow colder. He placed down his newspaper. "Are you sure you're twenty, Miss Reynolds?"

More facts he'd looked into about me. My throat flicked again. "Yes. Why?"

His shrug was subtle, passive. It accompanied his cocky smirk, and I fought myself from voicing another quip. He chuckled. "Because I've had grown men not dare say such things to me."

I didn't want to say I was grown because then I'd sound like a child. I didn't like when people talked down to me and, most especially, not because of my age. I'd taken care of myself my whole life, and *he* was a grown ass man that had people no doubt making that fancy lunch he ate.

Who was the child now?

I didn't say who. Instead, I gripped Polly's lead when Mr. Petrov stood.

He approached, a hand in his pocket, and I definitely noticed his appraisal of me. I was always aware when men looked at me. His eyes narrowed. "Remember your place in this house, *malyshka*," he said, and when I backed up a little he grinned. "Your stay in my home and working for me is provisional."

He lifted his tatted fingers, like he'd touch me but, instead, he gestured me away.

I turned quickly, but not before noticing his head cock. He also chuckled lightly before going back to his lunch. Perhaps this Mr. Petrov got off on making people squirm and fear him but, newsflash to him, I didn't scare easy.

I hadn't for a long time.

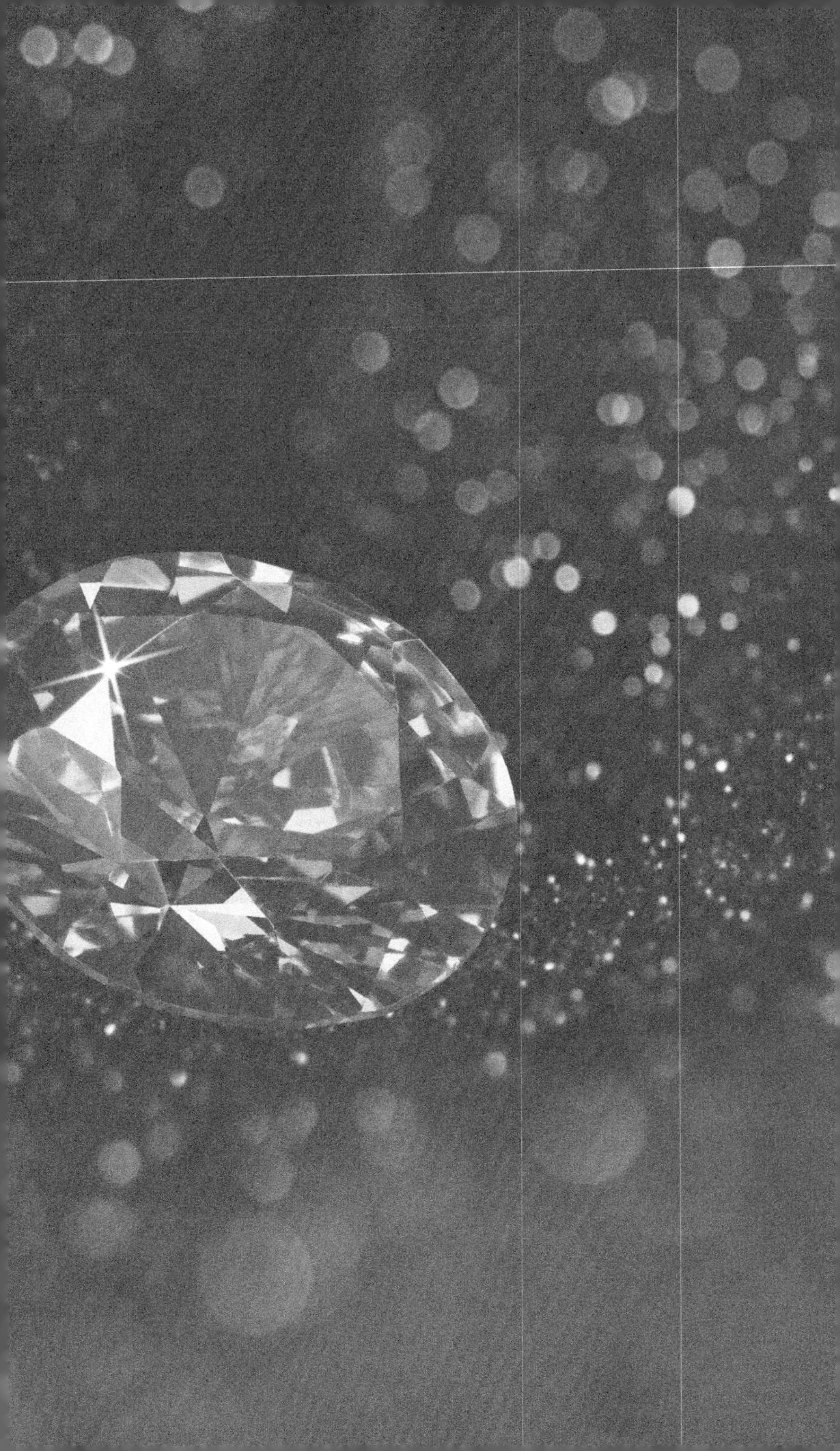

CHAPTER FOUR

Maxim

I tossed my keys to Gleb on my way into work that evening. He was one of few I trusted with my Mercedes, a car man like myself.

"Good evening, boss," he stated in Russian. I wasn't fluent, but I knew phrases. In any sense, Gleb spoke zero English so we had to communicate in some way since he did a lot of the menial tasks around here.

I didn't always get a say when it came to my men, but Gleb was a good worker so I didn't have any complaints. I nodded at him before taking the back door down into the basement. There was an actual funeral at Peters & Burg going on upstairs today, and I didn't want to disrupt it. Things like that commanded respect.

"*Boss*," Val, my head of security amongst other things, signed when I got downstairs. She had a clipboard in her hand. She signed around the clipboard. "*Nice night.*"

"*Is it?*" I signed back to her, and when her head cocked, I looked away so I wouldn't see her hands. I didn't need her sympathy.

She knew what today was.

Eventually, I had to turn around, and her clipboard was gone.

"*How was Lettie's flight?*" she signed, and I let her know what my daughter said when she checked in with me a few hours ago. Lettie had texted she made it to New York just fine. She arrived without a scrape.

That didn't mean I wouldn't miss her.

Needing to work, I intended to get into it, but Val, short for Valerie, was there with her prodding.

"*You know her leaving wouldn't have been so bad if you had a social life, Boss,*" she signed. She was one of the few people who could get away with saying such things to me. She escaped my blade when we initially met, and it took several men to find her when she did. I'd been assigned to kill her.

And now, she was the closest thing I had to a friend.

I didn't do friends—dumb—and I especially didn't do relationships. The only reason Val found herself in any semblance of the former when it came to my life was *because* she'd escaped my knife. That was no easy feat back when I was doing that kind of work, and I respected her for it. I'd gone to the *pakhan* about her after, asking for her life and if she could work for me. The Brotherhood could use someone like her, and our *pakhan* agreed with me back then.

As it turned out, Val did too. The man she'd worked for previously had sliced her throat in anger one day. He also cut out her tongue, silencing her for the rest of her life. At least when it came to her audible voice.

There was no silencing Val. She was quick to speak her mind, especially to me.

"*I didn't ask for your opinion,*" I signed back. I stripped off my coat. "*Anyway, I fuck. I don't do relationships.*"

Something she knew about too, since that was her MO

when it came to women as well. I told her that, and she smirked.

Val laughed. *"I didn't ask for your opinion, Boss."*

With the two of us in agreement about that, I nodded, and she followed me deeper into the basement. The place was deliberately sterile, which was the way I liked it. I needed it clean so I could concentrate, and it was to the point where it'd probably make most people sick.

I didn't give a fuck, knowing my own triggers. I got off on the sight of blood and even worse on the smell. It heated my own blood and triggered the killer inside.

My animal.

I called it my vice, my demon. It could control me, but I didn't give it control. I didn't give anyone that.

"It's a brother today."

Val's hands were moving when I turned around, and I saw her frown. The frown deepened. *"Might be hard."*

I wished I could tell her it was hard for me to kill, but it wasn't. Sure, there was some disappointment when it was supposed to be someone loyal to the Brotherhood, but that only egged on the killer inside me. I didn't do well with betrayal.

I nodded twice, then found my way to the two-way mirror. I had to pass it in order to get into the interrogation room, but stopped immediately upon seeing who was already bleeding and sweating behind it.

He'd even pissed himself. A yellow puddle pooled around his feet on my stark white floor, but I was more unsettled by the man in the chair.

Ilya...

Blinking away, I faced Val. *"What did he do?"*

I signed normally: not rushed, nor fazed. Val was a killer such as myself. She knew tension.

She knew when something was off but, currently, she was distracted by the earpiece cuffed on her ear. She communicated with the rest of the staff from far away by using clicks or sometimes by playing text-to-speech from her phone. She let go of her ear. *"You know Natan. Never says,"* she stated, referencing our boss. Natan was *pakhan* of the Bratva here in Chicago. *"Must have been something bad."*

Ilya hadn't even come to me clean. He was already beaten, bloody. I worked in a certain way, and Natan knew that. I didn't like my work messed with before I got it.

I moved my hands. *"What does he want from him?"*

Meaning, what information did Natan want. I wasn't a hitman. We had underlings for shit like that. No, the work I did was different and only on high profile targets. It was an art really, torture.

I was the one that the head of the Bratva went to in order to get information from our enemies. I didn't do bitch shit and hadn't since I was in my twenties.

I earned that right.

"He doesn't want anything," Val admitted. Dampening her lips, she faced Ilya. *"He just wants him to suffer."*

Suffering I could do. I was good at it. *Great* at it.

I nodded, again not fazed, and the moment Ilya spotted me he pissed himself again. The room also reeked of vomit and the stench burned through my lungs. I was highly sensitive to any type of smells and tastes.

I fought from gagging in the pungent room. The moment I was in Ilya's presence, the fear emanated off him, his eyes wide.

He quivered down to his piss-soaked feet. Ilya had the look of a man who was seeing the Grim Reaper in physical form…

His executioner.

I went by many names in the Bratva, and that one was the most common. When men or women came to me, they didn't enter back into society.

There was never anything left to go back.

Ilya knew this. We have both been in the Brotherhood for many years. Though we'd seen each other few and far between them. In actuality, I hadn't seen him since I was a young man.

That had been on purpose.

I think it'd been on both our accounts. We'd had to do a job and, after, neither one of us made a point to see each other again. It wasn't necessary.

I headed to my tools. Ilya's moment of shock and awe had passed. He was screaming now, testing the limits of the soundproof room. We were deep underground where no screams could be heard.

Not even to the funeral upstairs.

"No! No! No!" The tears and sweat dripped in thick trails down his face. "Maxim, please no. Natan... Natan made a mistake."

Our leader made no mistakes.

My tools in order, I headed toward the sink. I scrubbed my hands.

"You have to explain it to him, Maxim. You have to. Brother, please!"

There was no use in pleading here, and my brother knew this. There were no final chances. This place, *my house*, was where one went to die at the hands of the executioner.

I dried my hands then opened my tools.

"Maxim, I just couldn't!" he shouted, his voice thick and charged with emotion. "The little boy..."

I turned, approaching. "Little boy?"

Ilya cringed. "I couldn't, Maxim. I couldn't."

My mouth parted, words on my lips. Though, in that moment, I didn't know what they might be.

They didn't have a chance to form.

Val entered the room and, though she didn't often watch me work, she was here now. Her expression was curious, her arms folded, and I could imagine that she'd watched me speak to Ilya from the other side of the two-way mirror.

I never spoke to the people I interrogated on a human level. I tortured for information only and didn't care to do more. Didn't see the point.

Val knew no talking needed to be done today. Only work. Her head cocked. She was finding something unusual about this situation, and I knew her well enough to know that.

"Brother," Ilya started to say, but I lifted a hand.

I faced Val. "*Get Gleb in here and some others. I want this one strung up.*"

Val brought her hands forward. "*Sure thing, Boss.*"

"What are you saying? What is she doing?" Ilya pleaded, but Val was quick. She had men outside the door, then in the room within seconds. Gleb was amongst them. I stood back as they bound Ilya by the wrists, then hung him by them from the ceiling.

Ilya screamed. "Maxim—"

"We have to make it hurt, brother. I'm sorry." And I was, truly. I didn't know what he'd done, but it was always disappointing when this happened to one of our own.

I ignored Ilya's continued pleas while I had someone secure some bats. They were baseball bats with spikes, nails. It wasn't often I had my men do something so barbaric. Actually, this particular form of torture was one I hadn't done before.

I had to make a statement.

Many eyes were in here tonight, and I was fully aware of that. That was a big reason I wanted so many in here. They had to witness that I had made this hurt for Ilya before his ultimate death. Natan had to know his orders were being carried out.

One set of those sets of eyes were Val's. She'd watched as the brothers strung Ilya up like a caught fish and didn't turn away when I commanded them to swing to their heart's content. Natan said the punishment needed to hurt.

And so it would.

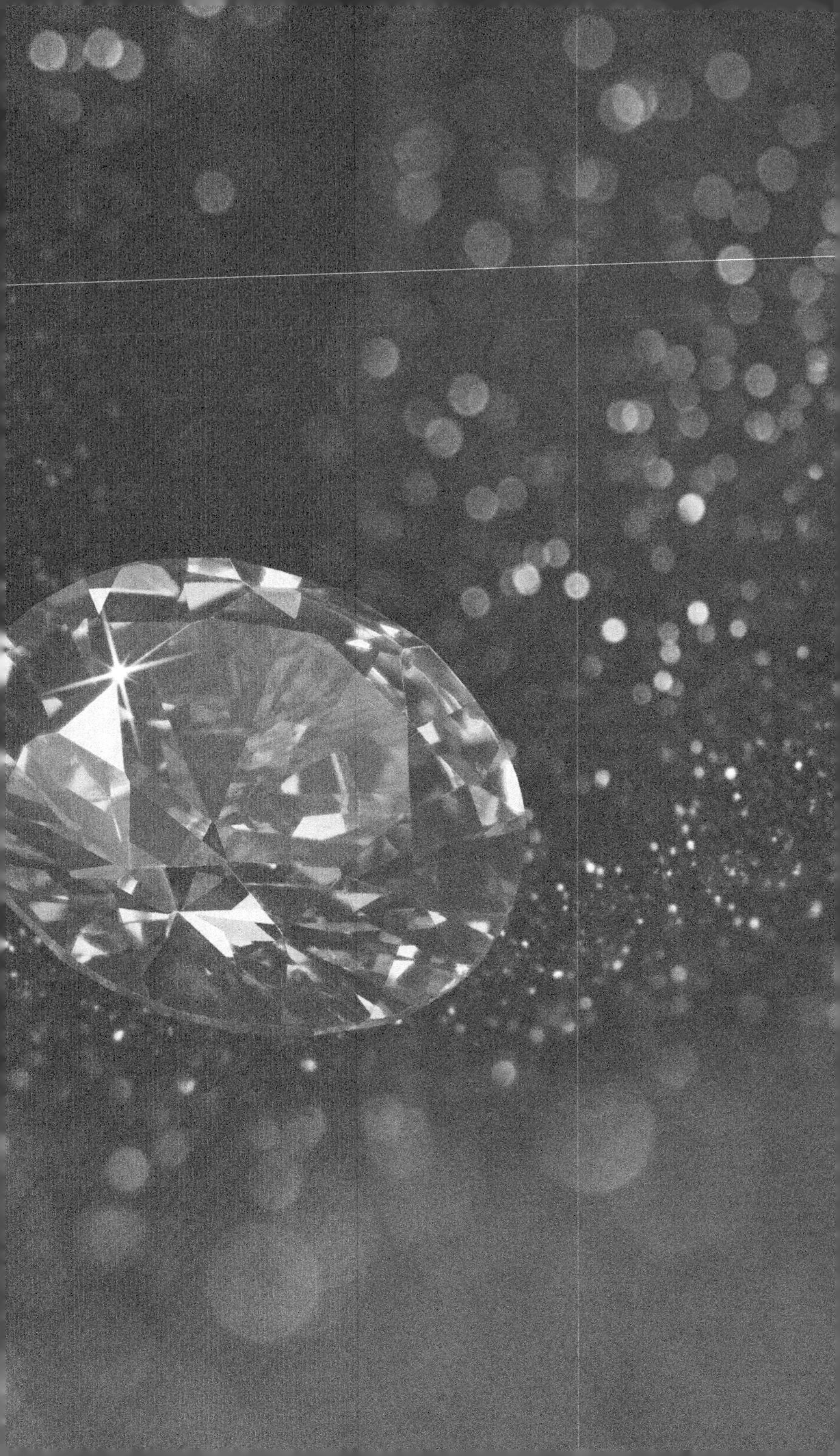

CHAPTER FIVE

Maxim

My cell phone rang while striding across the threshold of my home office.

I answered quick. "Natan."

"Is it done?" came a deep voice with a Russian accent.

He was straight to the point, always was.

"Of course." I unbuttoned my shirt, taking a seat. I took a shower at work, but the labor in my limbs resisted.

The same went for my back. I needed a deep massage in the morning, which I already made arrangements for. Val actually did that for me, and she didn't typically do bitch work.

She knew it was a rough night.

I tossed my jacket on my desk, listening for Natan. He must have been at some kind of club. Russian jazz music played in the background.

"I know tonight was hard for you. Betrayals are often difficult." He breathed harshly into the phone. "I'm glad it's done, and thank you."

I pulled the scotch off the bar behind my desk and a tumbler. It was late—well, early—but I needed one.

"Not really," I said, pouring more alcohol than I probably should at the hour. I plugged the bottle, and Natan laughed.

"My executioner. Always so cold. It's always been just work for you."

I said nothing, aware that calls about my job rarely came. I didn't get calls because I didn't need them. I always got the job done.

"Ilya mentioned a boy tonight," I said, swirling the liquor. "What exactly did Ilya do to cross the Brotherhood?"

"Why do you ask?"

"Just curious." I stole a drink, the burn shooting hard down my throat. Before I thought better, I poured myself another glass.

"I asked him to do a job and he didn't," Natan said, and I placed down my glass. "And I don't believe I have to tell you why I do what I do. Even if you are like a son to me."

I leaned across my desk. "You don't, and I'm sorry for questioning."

"Don't be sorry. You know I don't shed unnecessary blood. We are not the Novikovs, Maxim. You and I are not. *I'm* not."

He spoke a name that had me downing the rest of my alcohol and, before I could do more damage, I pushed the bottle back. "We're not, and again, I'm sorry for questioning."

There was silence on his end, then movement. He was speaking to someone, but probably socially since he was at a jazz club. Important meetings were saved for bathhouses and other places where someone could speak candidly. A man couldn't hide when there were visually no places to hide anything. He couldn't hide when he was stripped bare.

"You've had a tough night, and I do know today wasn't easy for you. I was more so referencing my goddaughter when I said that by the way. And how is Lettie? She get to school okay?"

"She did," I said, trying not to think about that either. "She said to tell you she'd send pictures."

Amongst other things. I was two seconds away from not letting her go to school at all with the shit she pulled yesterday. At breakfast, she'd mentioned seeing that asswipe boyfriend of hers, and about the only good thing coming from her going off to college and leaving me was that she'd also be leaving him. I only wanted the best for my daughter and some reject who did nothing but play video games all day wouldn't be doing that. He couldn't protect her, care for her.

"I'll be expecting them then," Natan continued. He had been in both my life and my kid's life for so long. He was like a father to me, the only one I currently had. I had been so young when my father passed. "And you'd do right not to miss her so. She'll be home for breaks soon enough and spending your money."

I laughed a little. "You know her well."

"I know you both well," he said, and he did. He looked after both of us for many years when I'd been a snot-nosed kid *who'd had a kid*. The only reason Lettie turned out to be anything at all was because of him. He taught me how to be a good man, a good father.

Remembering that, I eased up a bit after our call but did sit there for quite a long time. I was thinking, stewing. I ended up getting another drink before checking on the surveillance of the house. Val ran security here at my home as well, but I often checked the monitors. It was less paranoia and more like this was my goddamn house. I checked all the cameras but stopped at one.

Sia Cam.

I had my people install that while I was at work. I may

have let my daughter's friend work in my home, but I wasn't a fucking idiot.

I clicked around, sitting back. She was up and moving despite the late hour.

What are you doing, little one?

She had a towel in her hands, a bathrobe on. It seemed a late night shower was in order for my new dog trainer.

I clicked the next camera, following her into the steaming bathroom. She had the shower going and the anti-fog on the lens gave view to her stripping off her robe.

My eyes narrowed. Her ass was plump, round. I sat back as she stepped inside the shower. She closed the opaque door, cutting off my view.

I tapped a button, behind the glass with her now. It may have been obsessive, but I didn't give a fuck. I didn't know who the fuck this girl was, and if she was staying in my home, I was keeping an eye on her.

My fingers scratched the stubble on my jaw. Sia's brown skin was sleek, flushed. She had a caramel-toned complexion that hinted at a myriad of races. She could have been one or two or several.

I zoomed in, the camera right behind her. She glided in and out of the water, the thick streams soaking her full curls. She wasn't up to anything particularly intriguing so I started to close my laptop.

That was until her fingers found themselves between her legs.

A little more intrigued now, I watched, curious how she pleasured herself. She had quite a mouth on her that was for sure.

Little *malyshka*.

She could be trouble, this one, a handful. I zoomed in again, my head cocking when she turned around. She massaged her flushed tits with her hand and arm, her other hand between her legs. She toyed with her sex, her hand moving over the dark curls on her snatch while she tweaked her dark nipples.

I took a drink, swallowing. I quickly downed the rest, then closed out the footage before Sia finished. I found I didn't care enough.

Especially since I had another call to make tonight.

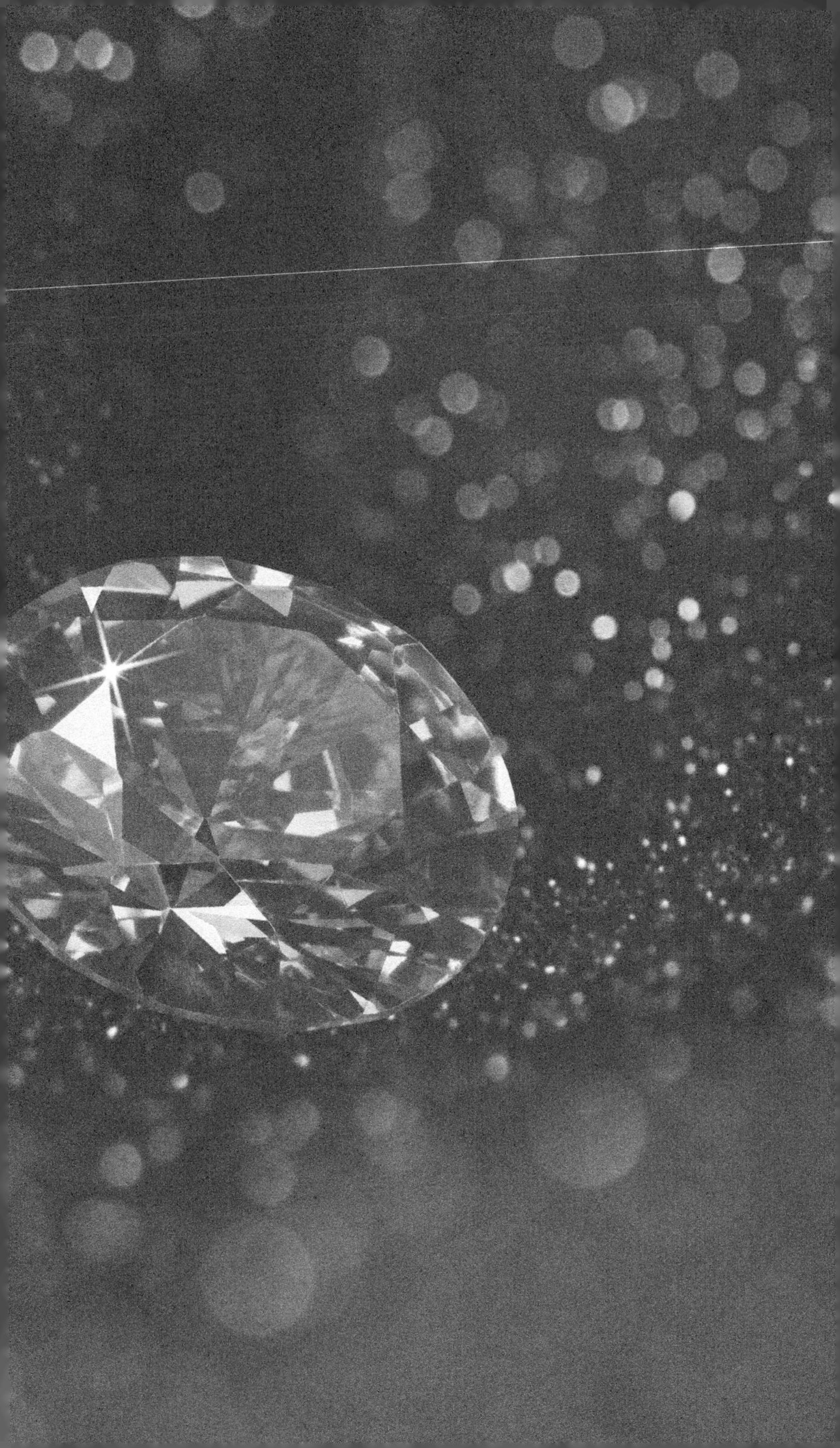

CHAPTER SIX

Sia

I jogged with Polly nearly a week after arriving at the Petrovs', working on keeping her at my side. She was doing *very* well with that and had stopped tugging almost entirely. It got to the point where she might not even need a lead soon on the property.

I was happy that she was socialized enough where every person on the property didn't take her interest. Many dogs with little interaction tended to have squirrel energy: they barked at basically everything and chased just as much.

Polly was pretty good about not doing either, which was good. She was a huge dog, and I had almost lost her lead a couple times when we first started.

These were things we were working on, as well as her house training. She had an accident overnight, which wasn't good since she was a year old.

It just meant she hadn't been trained and, though I didn't know who came before me, I did know that her excitement for me and the few issues she did have could be directly linked to her owner.

Her dad.

Lettie may have gotten this dog for her father, but he'd also accepted Polly, and that came with some responsibility. Polly was a dog and couldn't take care of herself. Shit like that annoyed me, and I planned to tell Mr. Petrov about that today. I believed that I'd done a good job telling him what I needed from him the week prior and hadn't backed down.

Even though he was scary as fuck.

I was bracing myself for another interaction, but I hadn't expected it to be when I came across the pool with Polly. He was in there swimming laps.

And he was naked.

His tatted back streamlined through clear water, each powerful stroke roving the thick muscles in his chiseled arms and legs. The man had tattoos everywhere.

Even on his ass.

I saw that well. It was firm, toned. I tried to glance away, but Mr. Petrov stroked up to the side of the pool quickly.

"Good morning, Miss Reynolds," he quipped, catching me. He lifted out of the pool, and the gasp hit my throat.

I turned around right away. Because like, what the fuck? I glanced over my shoulder to find him grabbing a towel from a stack near some lounge chairs.

"Miss Reynolds?"

He repeated my name and something of an annoyance now laced his deep tone. It made me look up and, though I was completely aware he was naked, I didn't give him the satisfaction of looking at anything but his face. He had dark stubble on his cut jawline, those eyes of his steely gray. He was a beautiful man from his dark eyelashes to his full lips.

Too bad he was a dick.

My face hot, I didn't let my eyes move away from his. Even when he approached.

"Have you never seen a cock before, Miss Reynolds?" he asked, casually toweling himself off. He dried his forearms. "Miss Reynolds, I'm speaking to you."

He was speaking to me like I was an idiot or a child. My nails bit into Polly's lead. "I've seen a cock. It's just rude you're showing yours."

Not to mention inappropriate. I mean, I worked for him.

He was making me uncomfortable standing there so confident in front of me, cocky. He still hadn't covered himself and, by the time he had, my face was still on fire.

"Is that how you really feel?" he questioned, cinching the towel tight at his waist. He had tats on his defined hip bones as well. "That I'm being rude to you. That I am rude?"

This felt like a test, and, though I wasn't sure I could take it, I had a hard time keeping quiet when it came to guys being assholes. They thought they could just do whatever they wanted when it came to girls and women in general. I stood tall. "Yes, that's how I feel."

He got closer, smelling like heat and aftershave. He had a different smell than most guys I'd been around. Mostly because he was older.

"Good girl," he said, and for some reason, my skin buzzed, my face. His smile hiked right. "You should always say how you feel."

I should?

I wished he'd step back and put…distance between us. I didn't like him being this close, and that had nothing to do with the fact that he was only wearing a towel.

Though it should.

Thankfully, Polly saved me. She pushed between us, and Mr. Petrov gave me a wide berth. He backed up immediately, and his sight averted to the glistening pool.

His expression cooled. "But this is my house and I do whatever the fuck I want in it," he said, and my eyes widened. He smiled. "So as long as we have that understanding?"

Christ.

"Anyway, if you don't want to see my cock I suggest refraining from being around the pool area between the hours of whenever I want to fucking swim." He took a glass bottle of water out of the cooler beneath the stacked towels, his eyes dancing. My heart slammed against my chest, and my tongue definitely itched for a retort. I *hated* cocky men.

I forced myself to nod. "Are you ready to train then?"

"Train?"

"For Polly." I brought her close. "I need to show you what to do in regards to interacting with her. I mentioned we'd need to train."

This looked like the last thing he wanted to do. He had a newspaper by the pool, and he drank his water while studying it. "Unfortunately, mornings don't work for me."

I had a feeling no time worked for him. I kept my growl low. "This afternoon then."

"Not good either." He tucked the newspaper under his arm, and I sighed.

"Well, when then? She should be on your schedule."

His grimace was full on both me and the dog. Like he held disdain for us both, which made zero sense since I was supposed to be here for him. It was my job to work around him and help him.

An attendant came through, one of many he had walking around this place. This one in particular gave him a bathrobe like a king, and I fought my eyes from lifting.

"Be downstairs in a half hour," he said, shrugging the robe on. He tied it. "I'll have someone get the car ready."

He toed on some thong sandals before starting to walk off, but I followed him. "The car?"

He maneuvered around. "You wanted to train, right?" Annoyance laced his deep tone, the same in his eyes. He frowned. "I have to work. You want to train. We do it on the fly."

He snapped his fingers at the attendant, gaining his attention and telling the man to get his car ready. He left me standing there after that, dismissing me, and I did growl.

It wasn't like I could do much else.

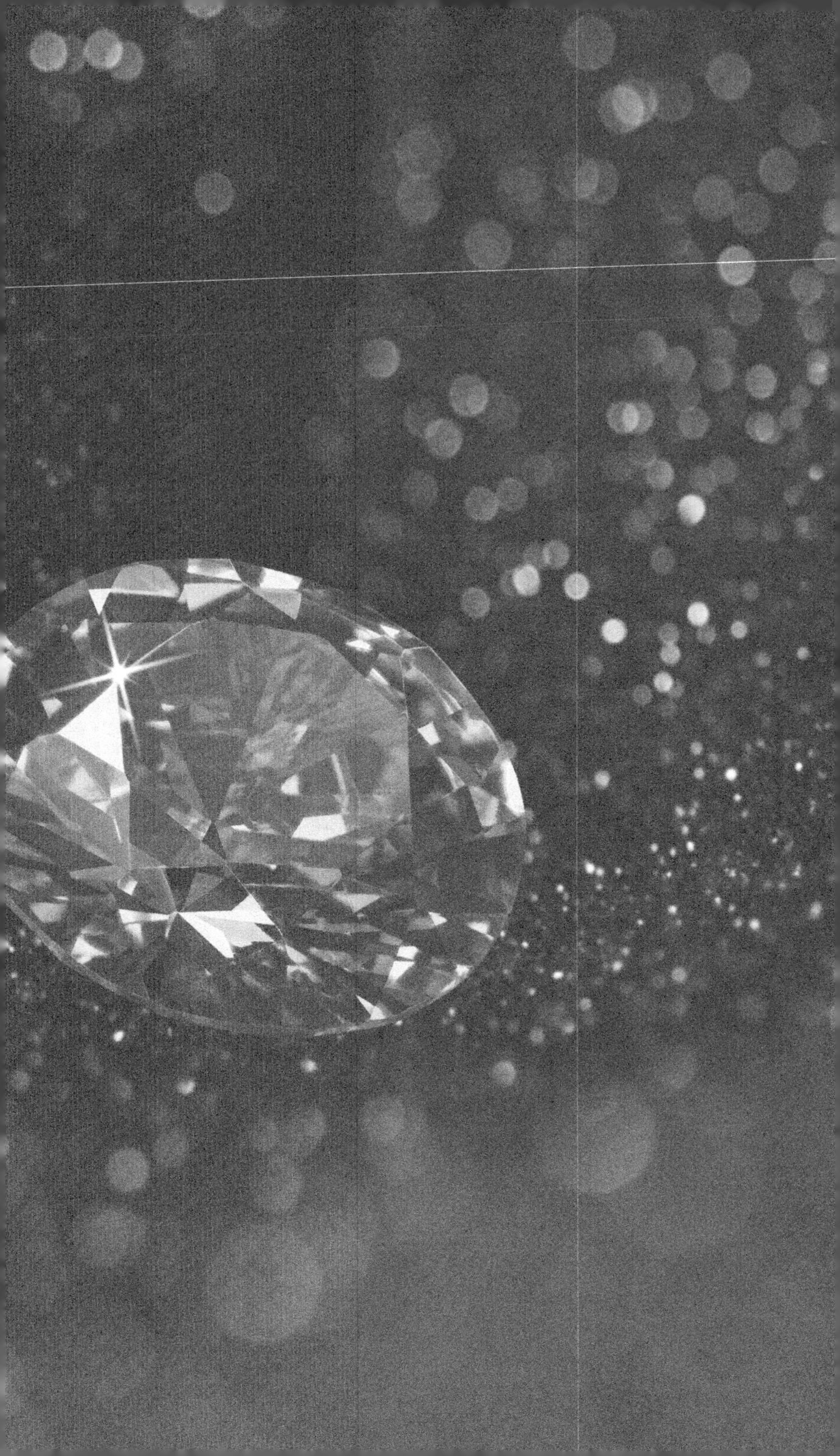

CHAPTER SEVEN

Maxim

The dog trainer fidgeted in my car.

Especially when I revved it up.

I deliberately hit sharp turns and zipped through traffic in my Mercedes, annoyed she was here, but even more annoyed she had *the dog* on my million dollar leather.

Growling, I focused on the road, smirking every time my daughter's little project gripped the seat or sucked in a breath. At one point, Sia started eating jellybeans, which was unusual.

"Have a sweet tooth, Miss Reynolds?" I questioned, completely aware when she set the bag of sweets on her brown thighs. I'd been watching her in the shower more than once this week and felt I knew her body better than herself.

I needed to keep an eye on her.

If she was in my home, I was keeping a goddamn eye out, and when she noticed *I noticed* her jellybeans, she tucked them further into her lap.

"I just like them," she said. She was eating them like a

fiend. Especially when we rolled up to the funeral home. Peters & Burg had several locations, but this was the main one I operated out of. Sia swiveled on my leather. "What are we doing here?"

Annoyed again, I stayed focused behind my shades as I typed my code into Peters & Burg's entry gate. One of my guys buzzed us in, and I rolled my Mercedes forward. "I told you, if you want to train, you're working around me today."

"But you work here?" she asked, surprised. Her brown cheeks flushed, and I smirked again. She studied me. "At a funeral home?"

She looked confused, which was nice. It meant my daughter hadn't really told her what I did for a living.

And how I loved surprises.

"I own them. Several," I said, parking in my designated space. I shut off the car. "Mind being around dead bodies, Miss Reynolds?"

The response I hoped for didn't come when all Sia did was bunch her arms over her chest. Her shoulders hiked. "Not much different than being on the streets," she said, surprising me. "Drive-bys are a thing that happen every day in my world."

Sia unstrapped her seatbelt, feigning badassery when she confidently got out of my car and headed to the back. She finally got the dog off my seats, holding the dog's lead. "And I don't know if Lettie told you, but I want to be a surgeon. So no, dead bodies aren't a thing for me."

Maybe she wasn't feigning confidence after all.

We'll see about that.

Lettie hadn't told me that little detail but no matter. I gestured toward the funeral home. "I'll let you lead the way then."

Miss Reynolds certainly had some bite in her and, though I knew some of her history, I was sure that being around dead bodies on the regular was certainly different than what she'd seen.

Especially here.

Bodies weren't always dead when I got them. I followed Sia inside, holding the door open for her. If she wanted to see some dead bodies, I'd let her.

Sia

So I was about 99.9 percent sure Lettie's dad was in the mafia at this point.

People who worked in funeral homes didn't look like this.

Big guys…freaking huge guys were everywhere and just about all of them had the same physical demeanor as Mr. Petrov. They had massive arms and legs the size of tree trunks, their thick necks tatted in dark tattoos down to their fingertips.

Fuck Almighty.

I kept Polly close, surprised that Mr. Petrov said that I could bring her in here. The place was creepy as fuck with all the caskets but, despite Mr. Petrov's warning, I didn't see any dead bodies anywhere.

Mr. Petrov stopped a guy. "Dog stays here," he said, gesturing to a man nearby. The dude came over, and I kept hold of Polly. Mr. Petrov frowned. "This is a funeral home, Miss Reynolds. Dogs can't be in here."

And I suppose that was where Mr. Petrov's goodwill ended. I frowned now. "You said we'd train with her."

The patience on his face ran thin but, despite that, he calmly pushed back his hair. "We will after. Gleb?"

He'd summoned one of the burly dudes. He then proceeded to rattle off something in another language to the guy, and I blinked. That definitely sounded like Russian.

Though I'd really never heard the language in person. It had sounded like Russian though, and Mr. Petrov had spoken something to me in the language before. The single word made me lock up and heat rush to my face.

Not thinking about that now, I watched as Gleb made his way over to me. Mr. Petrov nodded for me to hand off Polly's lead to Gleb, but I held it tight.

Mr. Petrov posted his tatted hands on his hips.

"The dog will be fine," he said through gritted teeth, and I had half a mind to think she wouldn't be. I didn't know this Gleb guy, and I definitely didn't know Mr. Petrov. At least outside of the mean ol' grump he clearly was.

Mr. Petrov scratched his head, annoyance ticking at his eyes. He put his hands together. "The dog—"

"Polly."

His eyes narrowed at me. "Polly will be fine. Gleb has dogs. He annoys me every time he has to take off for a vet appointment for them."

That certainly made me look at Gleb in a different away, and though he exchanged his attention between both Mr. Petrov and me, he did so with confusion. He held a questioning look about him that made me think he didn't quite understand what was going on.

Mr. Petrov faced him. He mumbled something in a different language again, and I was surprised that it took him a second. The phrase was broken, and he kept looking up like he had to find the words. In any sense, whatever he said brought a smile to Gleb's face, and the next thing I knew, the big man was getting on one knee. He spoke Polly's name and she left me so quick.

Gleb started playing with her then, rubbing her. She quickly forgot about me, and my stomach settled a bit.

I guess he is *a dog guy.*

Even still, *I* didn't want to be without her. Being alone with Mr. Petrov didn't sound ideal...

"Now, Miss Reynolds, if you'd follow me." Mr. Petrov had his hand out, gesturing in another direction. Polly really *had* forgotten about me. She quickly trotted off with Gleb, and the man rewarded her with a treat from his pocket. Dude even had dog treats with him. Mr. Petrov pursed his lips. "Miss Reynolds—"

Rather than have him call me again (like a dog), I caught up to him. I was unsettled about having to be alone with him and annoyed myself that I had to, and when he clearly noticed both, he smirked at me.

"You all good, Miss Reynolds?"

"Fine," I said. I didn't look at him, but I could smell him beside me. He smelled of sweet cigars and something spicier. It was sharp and rough.

Masculine.

I didn't like either smell. Both were triggering but for completely different reasons. I had no business being around anything that could be smoked at all, and as far as the latter scent, I didn't like the way my skin buzzed after my nose took it in.

I walked a bit slower then, giving Mr. Petrov and me a bit more space. It felt necessary, and the man clearly hadn't noticed. He strode ahead with his long legs, taking us to an elevator. We got inside and, within the close proximity, he keyed in a code. We rode for a little while before the door opened and, once it did, I didn't move right away.

It was a completely different world down there, a dark world. Everything was in black brick and dungeon-like. Upstairs was all floral wallpaper and sandy-toned carpets like a grandmother's house. *Here*, there was a medicinal smell that made my nose burn. The whole place reeked like a hospital, but it looked like the Batcave.

Freaky.

I didn't really know what to think at this point, and I noticed Mr. Petrov's stupid smirk again. As he strode in his dark suit, he had it on me. Like he found my reaction funny.

I fingered the inside of my pocket on instinct, but I knew I'd come up empty. I ran out of jellybeans in the freaking car.

What. The. Fuck.

An open casket passed by me, but it wasn't filled with a body.

Guns... Lots and lots of freaking guns were in there. About two dozen assault rifles lay innocently in the maroon-colored fabric. When Mr. Petrov shot a look to the man standing next to it, the guy closed the casket.

I swallowed and was watching the spectacle so hard that I ran into an immovable force.

Mr. Petrov didn't move an inch upon the collision. Meanwhile, my face hit a broad back that smelled like sharp spices and sweet cigars. I quickly regained my footing as Mr. Petrov glanced back slowly at me.

His eyes cooled. "You need assistance staying on your feet, *malyshka*?"

There was that word again. I didn't know what it meant, but it did make me swallow again. "No, I just didn't know you stopped."

"Obviously."

Asshole.

My finger inched to seriously flip this guy off, and I did *not* like that.

Seriously, who is this guy turning me into?

I normally liked everyone, and people generally liked me. I was nice to everyone, respectable.

But around this man...

He was just mean. Terrible.

Mr. Petrov wet his full lips, a quick motion before he faced a woman who had her head cocked. She strode down the hallway in a black pantsuit. Her skin was a deep brown, and she had a tight braid that was wrapped into a clean bun behind her head.

Mr. Petrov immediately started signing to her once she was in front of us. His hands moved quickly. Another thing I didn't know about him: he was fluent in ASL.

The woman signed back, and I studied their exchange. I didn't think I'd ever seen sign language up close and personal before, and as I watched the woman, I noticed her neck.

She had a scar right across her throat. It was a dark, bubbled wound, but I gazed away when Mr. Petrov started signing in my direction. It was aggressive and almost angry. Then, he glanced back at the woman.

"This is as far as you go," he stated while signing. "Val will take you now. She's my head of security. Both for here and my home. She'll keep an eye on you while I do a couple things."

Do a couple things.

I didn't know what that meant, but then he was leaving. He hadn't even introduced me to his head of security. He clearly didn't care, but I suppose he probably did tell her who I was. There was a lot of aggressive signing.

Left with Val, I wasn't sure how I'd communicate with her, but she seemed to know exactly what to do. She waved me on, so I followed her down the hallway.

There were so many rooms in this literal dungeon. I curiously wondered what was behind these walls and if there were those dead bodies that Mr. Petrov spoke of. I was morbidly curious since I *did* want to be a trauma surgeon. I wasn't sure why I was so fascinated with how the human body—or really any organism—worked and, growing up, I did freak people out a lot when I asked questions about death. I was kind of fascinated with it. Where did we go after we were gone and, most importantly, how did it feel once we were?

These were thoughts I kept to myself. I had a period of my

life where I sought those questions more often than not, and that really did bother people.

Val escorted me into an office. There was nothing weird or freaky about it. She headed over to the desk, retrieving a clipboard from a drawer.

I watched her scrawl down something on it, feeling awkward. Eventually, she tucked the clipboard under her arm and pulled out her cell phone. She typed quickly before showing me the screen.

"So where should I forward your check?" her screen displayed, and when I clearly appeared confused, she typed again. She showed me the screen. *"I'm assuming this is your last day working for Mr. Petrov."*

Why would she assume that?

She thumbed her screen again. *"I can forward the check to anywhere you'd like. I just need to know an address."*

Again, I didn't understand.

She frowned before tapping the screen, then flashing me the phone again. *"Look. Boss could have taken you to any of his funeral homes, but he brought you here."* She glanced up, then typed. *"He obviously wanted to make a statement."*

"So his funeral homes don't typically look like this?" I asked, then closed my mouth. I assumed Val wouldn't be able to understand me vocally, but then she showed me her screen.

"I can hear you speak just fine, darling, and even if I couldn't, I can read lips." Her eyes were warm before she typed again. *"Really comes in handy."*

She laughed after that, but it was silent. It seemed she just wasn't able to use her voice.

"But no, they don't typically look like this," her screen said. She typed again. *"I'm supposed to take you to a few more places around here, but rather than show you the boss's circus I'm just going to give you a way out. You seem like a nice girl, innocent."* Her smile left. *"I figured I'd spare you the morbidity."*

Morbidity.

I was angry now, my head lifting. Apparently, Mr. Petrov had no intention of training with Polly at all today.

He just wanted to freak me out.

This guy's asshole meter was ridiculous at this point, and I was really starting to question Lettie's relation to him. I didn't know her well, but she always came off super nice and was so bubbly. How a man like that raised a girl like her blew my mind.

I folded my arms. "I'm assuming the dead bodies were coming next on the tour?"

"Amongst other things," Val's screen said. She nodded before showing me her clipboard. There was a check there with my name on it. She pointed toward the line where one would put in a monetary amount, then glanced at me.

Wow. He really *did* want me to leave. The guy was freaking paying me off!

How easy it would be just to give this guy what he wanted—I didn't really want to work for him either. I could cash the check then move where I wanted. I'd have a roof over my head and food.

But you'd have no stability...

Nor a job. Neither of which was good. Eventually, whatever I asked for would run out, and then I'd be on the streets again, alone.

I didn't do well alone.

This was ironic since I'd essentially raised myself, but whenever I was left to my own devices I did get into trouble. At least I had recently, and I was so vulnerable right now. I didn't trust myself.

I pushed back my curls. "Actually, I think I'll stay on," I said, clearly surprising Val. Her dark eyebrows nearly hiked to her hairline. I shrugged. "And not a whole lot freaks me out. You can let Mr. Petrov know that."

I'd spent a lot of time expelling demons from my life; whatever Mr. Petrov had around here was child's play.

At least, I hoped so.

Lettie promised there'd be no trouble for me if I worked for him, and I was starting to think that was completely true. The only trouble—the only *danger*—appeared to be Mr. Petrov himself. He was both arrogant and cruel.

A small smile quirked Val's lips. She typed something on her phone, and when she lifted it, I smiled.

"I'll let him know," her screen said, then she nodded before mouthing, "Good luck."

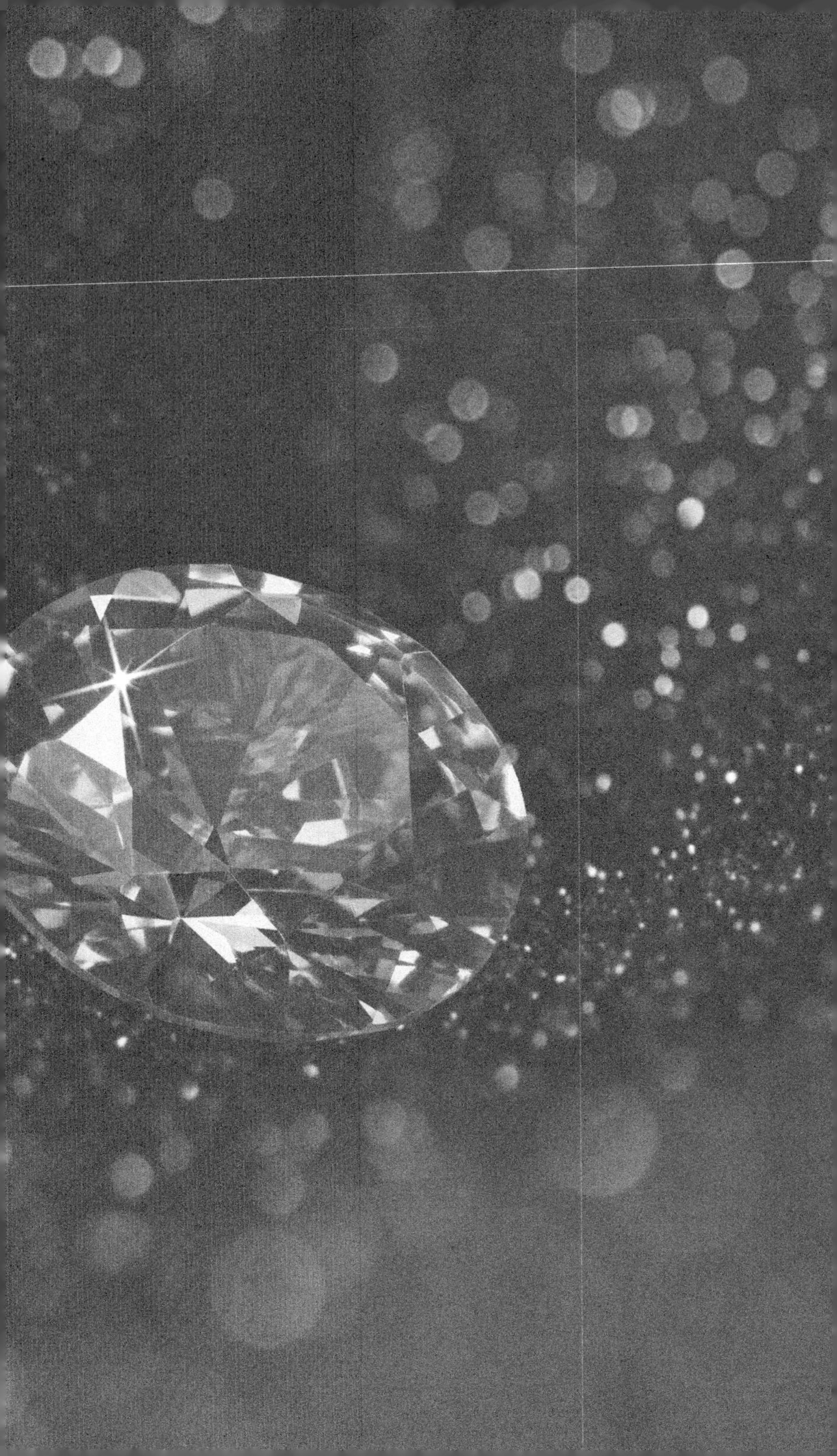

CHAPTER EIGHT

Maxim

"The fuck you mean she's not going anywhere?"

I even forgot to sign, pissed, but Val could obviously hear me. Even though she could, I made sure to communicate with her in the way most people never bothered. It also came in handy as she was my closest confidante and sometimes people didn't need to hear what we were talking about.

Val moved her hands through FaceTime, her phone positioned somewhere back at Peters & Burg. *"She's not going anywhere."*

"And you offered her the check?" I rolled up to my desk in my home office, doing a speaking/signing combination. "You did and…"

"She said she's not leaving." She even smiled. *"She also said to tell you not a lot freaks her out."*

I grunted. The dog trainer didn't know the half of what I could arrange in order to "freak her out".

I ended the call quickly, then sent Sophia off into the

house to go get the thorn in my ass. Miss Reynolds had been quiet the whole ride home this afternoon, and I'd mistaken that silence for a win.

I thought I'd gotten rid of her. Apparently not. A soft knock announced her arrival.

"Come in," I barked, rolling back in my chair. My daughter's project was about to swiftly get the fuck out of my life.

I smelled her before I saw her, the air changing. Like in my daughter's room, Miss Sia Reynolds had a particular scent.

Most people did. All people did. I took notice of the aroma/aura people left around them as well as how they carried themselves. Sia Reynolds put off confidence and self-assuredness, but she had the underlining disposition of a fragile lamb. She tried to come off as brave around me. But I saw right through her.

I pointed toward the chair in front of my desk before lacing my fingers together. "Take a seat please."

I intentionally had Val show Sia around to let her know what she was getting into by working with me. I didn't necessarily have qualms about my daughter hiring staff for me, but Sia Reynolds had a mouth on her. She was also young, and young people tended to be stupid and reckless.

"This feels like being called into the principal's office," she said, watching Sophia exit and close the door. Sia faced me. "Am I in trouble?"

She thought herself cute, didn't she? I gestured toward the vacant chair again. Her and that mouth. I didn't appreciate people talking back to me and had no patience for it.

Sia finally took the seat, and my attention shifted to her thick curls and the flush in her cheeks. Again, that faux confidence. She also had a scar on her left eyebrow, something that told me she'd either fallen or been attacked.

I didn't care about either. My eyes narrowed. "Why are you still in my home, Miss Reynolds?"

"Excuse me?"

"My head of security offered you a check to leave."

"I know, and I said no."

"Why?"

"Because I need a job." She shrugged, folding her little arms. "Not to mention a roof over my head."

"Money could have rented you an apartment while you looked for another place of employment." I analyzed her, confused as fuck. "You could have written in whatever amount you saw fit."

Anyone would have taken that offer for a few hours of work. I liked being able to read and understand a person's actions. Sia Reynolds wasn't readable.

And that made her dangerous.

"The money would have eventually run out, Mr. Petrov." She studied me now and, like in my dining room, her bottom lip popped out with her frown. "You offered me a job and a place to stay."

"My daughter did."

"But on your behalf, right?" Her head tilted, her curls gliding across her shoulder. "I'm supposed to help you. You know my history—getting a job's not easy with a record and…" She scrubbed her hands into her curls. "I need this job and I need a place to live."

Even after what she'd seen? I instructed Val to give her a nice tour of Peters & Burg to showcase my work area. Needless to say, the tools I used weren't just to ready bodies for a casket. People that came directly to me didn't *get* funerals, actually.

There wasn't much left worth viewing.

Again, I didn't understand this girl. I leaned forward. "I don't know what my daughter told you, but there are things in my life that must remain secret. Private." I studied her. "You might see things you don't want to see, and I'm not sure I want to take on the liability when it comes to you."

"Liability?" Her face screwed up.

"A young girl with a criminal history such as yours... There's, well, temptation to do stupid things."

Her little pout transformed into anger. "Care to elaborate?"

"Sure." I sat back. "I have enemies, Miss Reynolds. I have a life that requires discretion and loyalty. I need people around me I can trust and aren't easily susceptible to the first person that offers them something of interest."

Her anger softened, but only slightly. "I'm clean, Mr. Petrov."

She was today, but today wasn't all days. I had no judgement and, frankly, didn't care about her history with drugs. But I *did* need loyalty and people who couldn't be easily broken.

The fragile lamb across from me scanned my desk. I had to say, considering the fact I told her I had enemies, she didn't appear too put off. In actuality, she seemed more interested in calculating her way through this conversion. Surely she still didn't want to work for me?

Sia's fragrant smell hit the air again, and I assumed this was something she put in her hair. She smelled tropical, like coconut and the beaches I took Lettie to on vacations.

Sia played with her hands in her lap. I made her nervous, as I should. I could end her before her next breath.

"I understand the need for discretion, loyalty." She lifted her head. "And if you give me a chance to prove myself, you will have that from me. I need this job, Mr. Petrov. Lettie told me you're not exactly honest in your business, but I swear I don't care what you do. I don't. I need this job, and I won't say anything to anyone about anything I see while working here."

There was no faux bravery behind any of her words. No waver. Intriguing. I placed my hands on my desk. "What exactly do you think I do?"

I dared her to say, and she expelled a breath.

"Like I said, I don't care." She shrugged and her passiveness, her ease, appeared genuine. "Anyway, Lettie said you keep all that to yourself."

My daughter was aware of my business, but not the particulars. I tried to protect her from the more dangerous aspects of my life as much as I could.

"I'm going to call a car for you," I said, intrigued by the conversation yes, but certainly not convinced by it. "I want you to have your things packed. You may think you're brave, Miss Reynolds, but you don't know the half about my life."

She sat up. "Mr. Petrov—"

I lifted a finger. "Consider this a gift, Miss Reynolds. You're being given an out with fair compensation. I'll make sure you get a check before you leave for your time here."

I'd still honor payment and whatever amount she deemed fair to leave from the premises. Sia shook her head. "I'm sorry. What do you mean by you're giving me an out?"

I'd been dialing for that car, but stopped. I grinned at her. "It is an out because if you were ever to break your word to me, I wouldn't just hurt *you*, but everyone in your life."

And I'd do it with little more than a thought. Fuck, I'd enjoy it.

So very much.

My head cocked, my demon excited about the prospect. I started to dial for my driver to get a car ready again, but Sia said something. I glanced up. "I beg your pardon?"

I heard her words, but wanted her to say them again.

"I said that'd be a short list," she said. Her expression hardened. "I don't have anyone, and nobody would care if I was gone."

She hadn't even said what she had in a sad way. Through my research, I learned this girl grew up in the foster care system and, after reading what happened with one of her foster families, I knew why. She had a history of arson, amongst other things.

A fire starter.

I definitely saw that and, though I had no place in my life for it, I was intrigued once more. It was her lack of emotion when it came to her background this time. "You think you can handle my world, Miss Reynolds?"

"I don't know your world, but if you're looking for someone who won't ask questions, that's me. I just ask that I'm not a part of whatever you're doing. I can't be. I won't go to jail." She shook her head. "I just need a chance. As far as loyalty, you'll have that too. I want to start over. Legit. I'll keep my head down. If you want, I won't even leave this house."

I wasn't the guy to give a chance to her, but again, I was intrigued by her and what she was willing to do for that chance. I settled into my chair. "There is the matter of loyalty, but I'm not joking about the environment you'll be in while working here. There might be things you see in this house that you can't unsee."

Though I did try to protect Lettie from that, it did happen. Sometimes my personal life and business crossed over; even though I kept certain things from my daughter, she wasn't a child anymore. I was sure she could guess some of the things my life entailed.

I wouldn't protect Sia from anything in my life. In fact, I'd go out of my way to break her.

"I need the job," she merely said, and she didn't look happy that she did. It seemed she had no choice but to take the options available to her here. I understood that. Sometimes our choices weren't left to us.

I rubbed my knuckles, fingering over brass rings. "If you stay here, work here, you won't leave this house. Not at first anyway." She had a good idea there with her proposal. I nodded. "You won't until I know what I'm dealing with when it comes to you."

"Fine," she said, and even though she'd proposed it, she didn't look happy about that either. Those brown cheeks filled with red color and I smirked at her.

We'll see how long this innocent little lamb lasts.

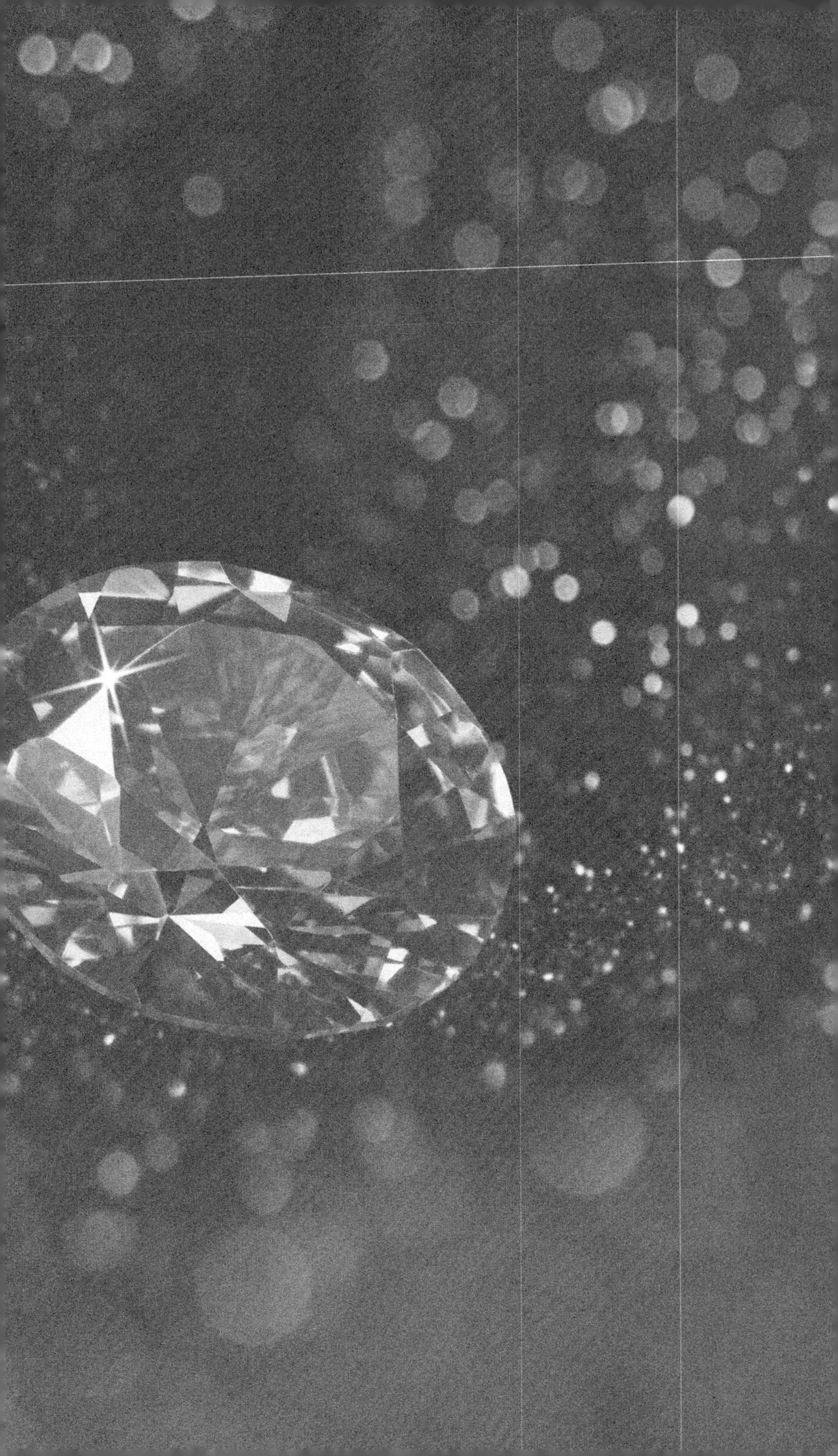

CHAPTER
NINE

Sia

Today was the first day Lettie's dad came home covered in blood. He wasn't covered *per se*, but I definitely noticed the red splatter on what was usually a crisp, clean, *white* dress shirt. He made sure to look up at me from the ground floor when he'd come home.

He'd been smiling.

It'd been a cheeky one, and I would have scoffed if not for the red I noticed. I'd been on the second floor and wandering through the brick prison he'd confined me to. I know I suggested it, but had no idea he'd actually say I couldn't leave the house. He hadn't been joking that I wasn't allowed to leave the Petrov property.

He apparently wasn't joking about a lot of things.

He made sure to look at me every time he came home after the day I saw the blood. He'd come in at random hours and, each time he spotted me, I noticed blood splatter. Sometimes he'd be wiping it from his hands, a cloth working over his tatted fingers.

He was obviously trying to scare me out of this place, but *I* wasn't lying when I said I didn't scare easily. Growing up on the streets wasn't easy, and *I* hadn't been joking when I told Mr. Petrov that.

I wished I had. I wished both the things I'd seen and been through hadn't affected me in such a fucked up way. *I wished* what I saw at the Petrov manor sent me running for the hills and not morbidly wondering what he'd done to get that blood on his hands. It was weird to have those thoughts. Freaky.

I'm a freak.

This was something I'd known for a long time and I stopped questioning eventually. If I didn't, I ended up down dark paths.

I hurt myself.

In actuality, seeing Mr. Petrov in such a way every day pissed me off. He thought he could treat me like that and abandon me in his large home. I wasn't his friend so he didn't owe me anything, but I was employed by him and he certainly wasn't around enough to let me do my job. It was basically just Polly and me day in and day out. Good news for her was that allowed me to get her properly trained. She had no more accidents in the house. She was completely house broken and responded to each and every command I gave her. She didn't even tug her leash anymore.

Not that my boss knew that.

I had a trained dog with no human to interact with. Polly and I were the same a bit in that way. I didn't consider myself a social butterfly, but I did like to be around people. I didn't do well by myself generally.

I rubbed my arm, another lonely day in the Petrov house. I texted Lettie from time to time. Well, she texted me. This was mostly to check up on Polly. Of course she asked about me, but we were new friends and a lot of her questions surrounded her dad and how he was doing.

She was worried about him.

That man had no reason for anyone to worry about him. He obviously took care of himself.

His bloody hands told me that.

I found myself traipsing through empty halls again one day. I ended up stopping in the middle of the hall, distracted by sounds. They came from Mr. Petrov's study, so I stopped in front of it. The door was ajar.

He wasn't in there a whole lot, but he was today.

There were a few men with him, all of them were as beefy and tatted as Mr. Petrov himself. Mr. Petrov sat on the corner of his desk in front of them, his head cocked while they all stood. He had his arms folded like he was the boss dog and the rest of the men were his flunkies. He started to say something to them but, suddenly, his head turned in the direction of the door.

I froze, obviously not as silent as I thought I'd been.

Familiar eyes of a steely gray cooled in my direction, and my heart thumped. This man looked at me in two ways, generally. One was when he poked fun at me or was being an asshole.

And the other was this.

Hatred, pure and venomous hatred was currently aimed in my direction. His hands gripped the desk, and that's when his friends faced me as well. Having Mr. Petrov's attention was already bad enough but having several dudes who were just as jacked looking at me too?

I backed up, so confused as to why Lettie's dad looked at me in that second way at all. I could only gather that he associated me with Polly, who he also wasn't a fan of. Polly obviously represented his daughter's belief he needed companionship.

Mr. Petrov clearly didn't want that, and he definitely didn't want me.

I basically sprinted down the hall, and I was so confused

as to how he heard me. I swear to God I hadn't made a noise. The man reacted with skill like a silent predator stalking his kill.

Which made me the prey.

Mary Sunshine that one.

I wasn't headed toward the kitchen after pretty much running down the hallway. Actually, I'd been heading up to my room.

My jellybeans were up there.

They were my lifeline, but I stopped my pursuit when I again heard noises, rustling. They were coming from the kitchen, and I spotted a familiar face around the corner.

Val.

She was by the counter with several grocery bags in her arms. I hadn't really seen her since that day at the funeral home and immediately went over to assist her.

"Oh, let me help you," I said, the urge to get my jellybeans tapering off a bit with the distraction. I wanted to help Val, and she heard me, swiveling around. She probably didn't need help, jacked just like Mr. Petrov's men. I hadn't noticed it as much that day at the funeral home, but her clothing was more casual today and displayed the muscular definition in her arms. This woman definitely worked out.

Mr. Petrov clearly surrounded himself with powerful people, and even though Val probably didn't need the assistance, I wanted to help. I even found myself asking Sophia if she needed anything these days. If anything for something to do with all the spare time I had now that Polly was trained.

Val had a glimmer of a smile on her lips as I helped her with the bags. There were a ton of them, and together, we placed them down. I suppose I technically *had* seen her around the Petrov property, but only through windows. Most of the staff around the Petrov property signed, but they weren't as experienced as Mr. Petrov himself. The language was clearly second nature to him in the few times I'd watched him with Val.

Val placed her fingers near her lips and mouthed, *"Thank you."* I made a mental note of the sign after she showed me and nodded with a smile. I looked up a few signs on my cell phone since I'd gotten here. I learned *"yes"* and *"no"* and a few other things just in case I did see Val and got the opportunity to talk with her again.

"No problem," I said, and she smiled. Her hands free now, she pulled out her phone.

She showed me the screen. *"Still here, are you?"*

I laughed.

I nodded. "Still here."

Maybe, like Mr. Petrov, she thought I'd run for the hills. She might have hoped I would. I remember how she hadn't showed me the more graphic elements of Mr. Petrov's business, and I wondered about those too.

I was pretty sure Mr. Petrov's funeral home wasn't just a funeral home and *so* wanted to know what he did there. Especially if he did work for or was in the mob. I knew there was a Russian one, but didn't know much besides its existence. I basically confirmed he and Lettie were Russian. I'd looked up their last names when I'd been searching for ASL signs.

Grinning, Val typed on her phone again.

"If you could let Sophia know these are here?" it said. *"I'm just dropping them off. I am security, but Boss likes to treat me like his glorified assistant sometimes."*

Her eyes lifted at that, and though I laughed, what she said didn't make me happy. Was there anyone he treated with respect? He was like a grumpy beast without the grizzly exterior.

Though maybe he just wore his scars in a different way.

Going through the bags, I started to put some things away. I'd gotten to know the Petrov kitchen pretty well too. There wasn't much else to do.

"You doing okay around here? I am surprised you're still here."

Val stepped back after letting me read her phone, and I shrugged. I noticed there were jellybeans in the bag, which meant this shopping list came from Sophia. I asked her to always get some for me if she remembered.

I held the jellybeans, and Val smiled at me.

"I should have known those weren't for Boss," her phone said. She typed again. *"He hates sugar."*

Her boss seemed to hate a lot of things. "I'm okay," I said, answering her previous question, then chewed my lip. "You think you could teach me a few signs? I looked up a few on my phone and would like to practice."

She looked surprised that I'd asked but nodded. She typed on her phone. *"Maybe next time I come. If you're still here that is."*

She eyed me a little before winking, and I laughed.

"I will be," I said because I would. Mr. Petrov was definitely prickly but, lucky for me, he wasn't even around enough for me to feel the sting.

At least not much.

Val tapped my shoulder before leaving the kitchen. I broke out the jellybeans. I chewed with a quick mouth before chewing more. It was true Mr. Petrov was an asshole, but at least he didn't pretend he wasn't one. He wore who he was on his sleeve and definitely wasn't the first monster I'd met in my life.

At least he didn't hide behind a mask.

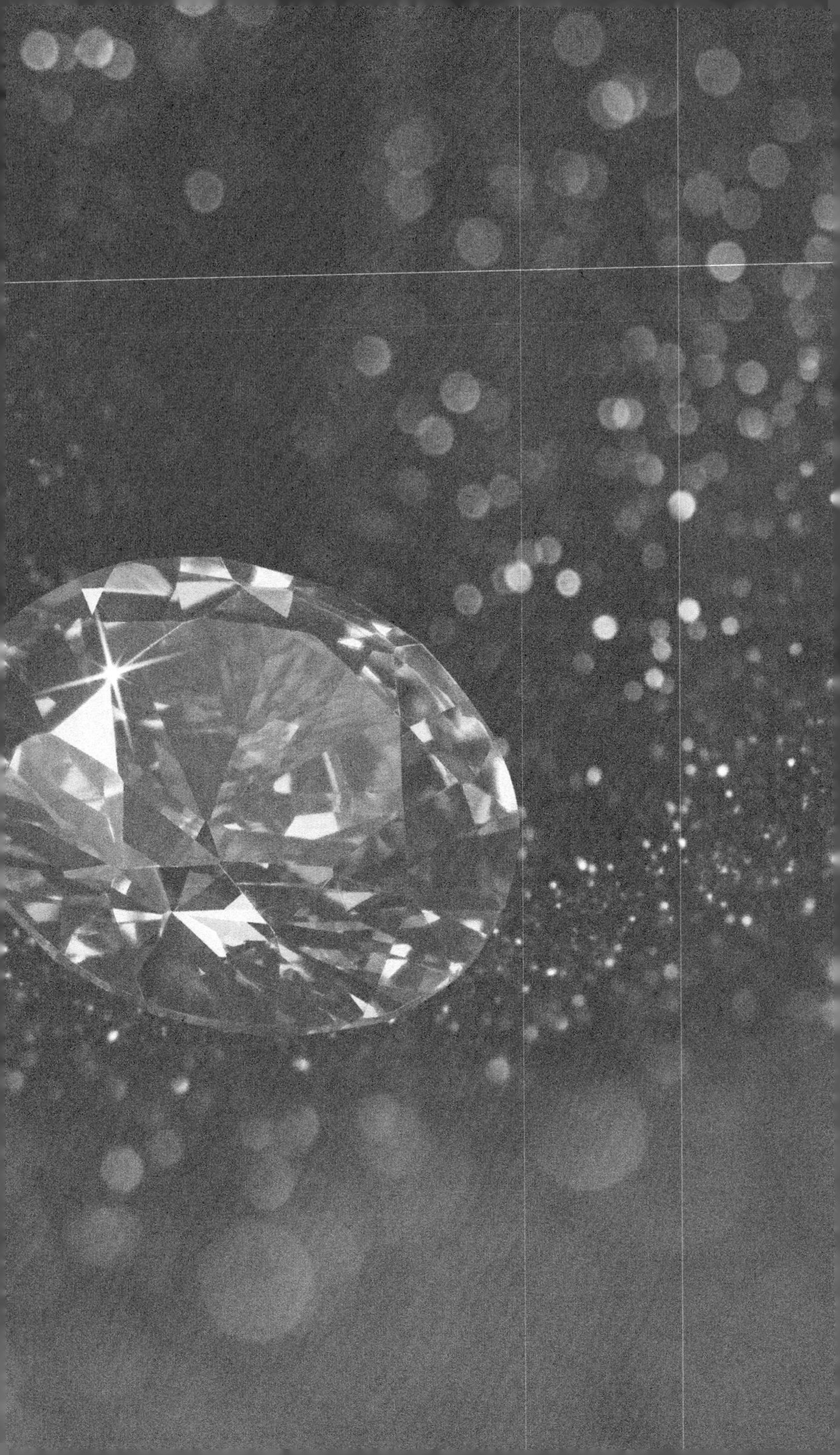

CHAPTER TEN

Sia

"Hey! How've you been, girl? Haven't talk to you much. You okay?"

I sat on my bed and laid back. "Yeah. Sorry. I guess I didn't want to bother you at school."

"Oh my God. You're not bothering me." Lettie was bopping around where she was. I could hear about a million people in the background, all of whom she shouted at to shut up so she could talk on the phone. Suddenly, things were quiet on her end like maybe she left the room or closed the door. "And, believe me, hearing from you is a relief. They've been working us to the bone every day. I feel like I'm icing my feet every night."

I smiled, trying to picture Lettie on stage in a pair of ballet shoes. She definitely had the body of a dancer, but her overall bubbly exterior was the complete opposite of the serious ballet dancers I'd seen in the media. "Are you having fun though?"

"Oh, loads. Dancing is my life. It's just hard AF, and I'm feeling a little bitchy. Tired."

I laughed.

"Anyway, how are you? Glad I caught you."

There wasn't much to catch up on in my life considering I didn't go anywhere. I got up, then went through my drawer for some bed clothes. "I'm good. Just working with Polly."

"Sweet. She been doing okay?"

"Amazing actually." I grinned, thinking about what I taught her today. "She can stand on her hind legs and do a little dance. It's funny."

Especially since she was so huge.

"Oh my God. I love that. Has Dad seen her do that?"

He would have if he'd been around enough to see anything, and when I told her that, she sighed.

"I'm sorry. I warned you he works all the time."

He did work a lot, but he was home some of the time. Like today, when he'd once again come home covered in blood.

I pulled my things out of the drawer. "I'm kind of thinking I know what he does for a living. Or at least part of what he does?" There was silence on the other line, and I swallowed. "You obviously don't have to tell me details, but I have a feeling working outside the law is a vast understatement."

I waited for her to say something about that, anything. Regardless of what she said though, I intended to keep my promise to her dad. I wasn't going to say anything about what I saw here to anyone. I made a choice to stay here, and since I did, I was going to keep a lock on what I generally thought Mr. Petrov was a part of regarding his job.

Or I guess I should say the organization I believed he might be a part of.

"God, Sia, I'm sorry," Lettie said, and I sighed. "I very much don't know the details like I told you, but... I've suspected things. Lots of things over the years."

"Don't apologize." I sat on the bed with my stuff. "But I do feel a little blindsided."

The girl told me I had nothing to worry about in regards to her dad when it came to the cops. But *being in the mob* meant the police could come sniffing around at any time, and I just got out of all that.

"You just..." Lettie paused. "You know, seemed desperate."

I laughed, *still* desperate.

She sighed. "Are you going to quit? I completely understand if you do, and you can, you know."

Her dad would welcome that. "I said I was going to stay. I need this job, Lettie. No one will give me work with my record."

This still remained true, and when Lettie released another breath through the phone, I did too.

"Well, maybe you can look for something else while you work for my dad. Being there can at least buy you some time?" she stated, and I hoped so. She huffed. "But you are safe there. The place is literally Fort Knox."

She wasn't lying about that. Whatever security Val set up came with loads of armed men on the regular. Mr. Petrov literally had people everywhere and eyeing the situation. When it came to his home, things weren't a joke, clearly.

"Are you mad at me?" Lettie asked, sounding worried. "If I thought you were in any kind of danger, I never would have suggested the job."

I scrubbed my hands into my hair. "I know. This place is safe, and Val is cool."

"Oh, you met Val? She's great, isn't she?"

She was and was also just about the only social interaction I had outside of the household staff.

I told Lettie that too, and when I did, she huffed again.

"My dad is...a special breed," she said, and I laughed at

that. She did too. "I guess that's putting it lightly. He's just really focused. He has a lot going on with his job so, yeah."

I got that, wondering every day the reasons why he was covered in blood. Was he torturing people like they did in the movies? Was he doing worse?

I pushed my hair out of my face, deciding to move the conversation on. I didn't want to alarm myself that I did want to know more details about what he did no matter how morbid and disturbing. That was unusual, and I knew that.

I blamed my intrigue on the fact that I wanted to go into the healthcare field. The art of putting things back together fascinated me. I wanted to help people, make things not so broken like they had been for me most of my life.

I ended the conversation with Lettie by hearing about her classes, and she asked *me* if I was thinking anymore about school for myself. I dodged the question though. I couldn't focus on that right now. I was just trying to keep my head above the water.

Swallowing hard, I stripped down and put a robe on. I took my bed clothes into the bathroom, then started the shower. I had a long day out with Polly today. We'd explored the Petrovs' vineyard.

I threw water droplets off my hand after testing the water. I needed a towel so I headed to the closet to get one. That's when I spotted Mr. Petrov. The pool was right below my bathroom window, and he was in it.

He was naked again.

Tanned, tatted skin cut through clear water surrounded by pool lighting. I hadn't caught him in the pool since he exposed himself to me, but then again, he was never home.

I pushed out of the window curtains, angry that he just did shit like that. I mean no one wanted to see his junk, but there he was, naked and doing a freestyle swim. He was so cocky, arrogant.

I put my towel on the toilet and hopped into the shower.

Mr. Petrov was getting out of the pool by the time I finished. I was passing the window when I spotted him again, and I thought he'd towel off, then head inside, but he didn't. He waltzed over to the outdoor shower, turning it on, then cutting into the water. He did this naked too, but when he'd been in the pool, I'd only been able to see the back of him.

I saw *all of him* now, his perfect body chiseled and completely tatted. There were very few areas he didn't have tattoos. He turned, facing my window full on when he pushed fingers through his inky black hair.

I watched him despite myself. The moon hit him just right, the pool lights doing the rest. I couldn't look away.

I mean, he was beautiful.

He was, despite how arrogant and godawful he was. I hated I found guys in general intimidating. Especially if they were older. I didn't trust men because nearly every one I came across in my life had an agenda. Because of that, I didn't date a whole lot, which was why I had to get myself off in the shower just about every night. My hand didn't betray my body, nor did the adjustable shower head when I used it between my legs.

Christ.

Mr. Petrov closed his eyes under the water. He guided the water down his body, fisting himself at one point.

My heart hit my chest. My legs eased apart, and I found my hand moving between them.

What are you doing?

I told my brain I touched myself because he did, but he wasn't doing it in the same way. Truth be told, he only touched himself briefly. He was *taking a shower* and cleaning off, but that wasn't what I was doing.

My fingers picked up between my legs when he got soap and moved it over his cock. Again, he was only there briefly before washing his hair, but that didn't matter.

My folds were so wet watching him, slick. I was spying on

this guy...this older man while he washed himself and here I was touching myself like a pervert.

But I didn't stop.

My lids hooded, my body panted. Mr. Petrov guided his head beneath the stream of water. He stood there still like a marble statue, his hands laced behind his neck while he enjoyed the warm water. He let the steady stream hit all those dark tattoos, and my fingers strummed my clit in quick time.

Stop.

I couldn't stop, my fingers suddenly moving in and out of my body. I clenched the curtains with my other hand. If anything, for stability. I couldn't breathe and was hot everywhere. I touched my breast, pinching my nipple.

Oh, God.

Oh God was right as I didn't just hit that peak but tumbled over it. My walls vibrating around my fingers, I closed my eyes, my thighs shaking. Letting go of the curtain, I touched my head to the wall.

Why did you just do that?

I didn't know. I didn't like that man at all and him being Lettie's dad only made things worse. I literally got off watching my best friend's dad, but not only that...

I liked it.

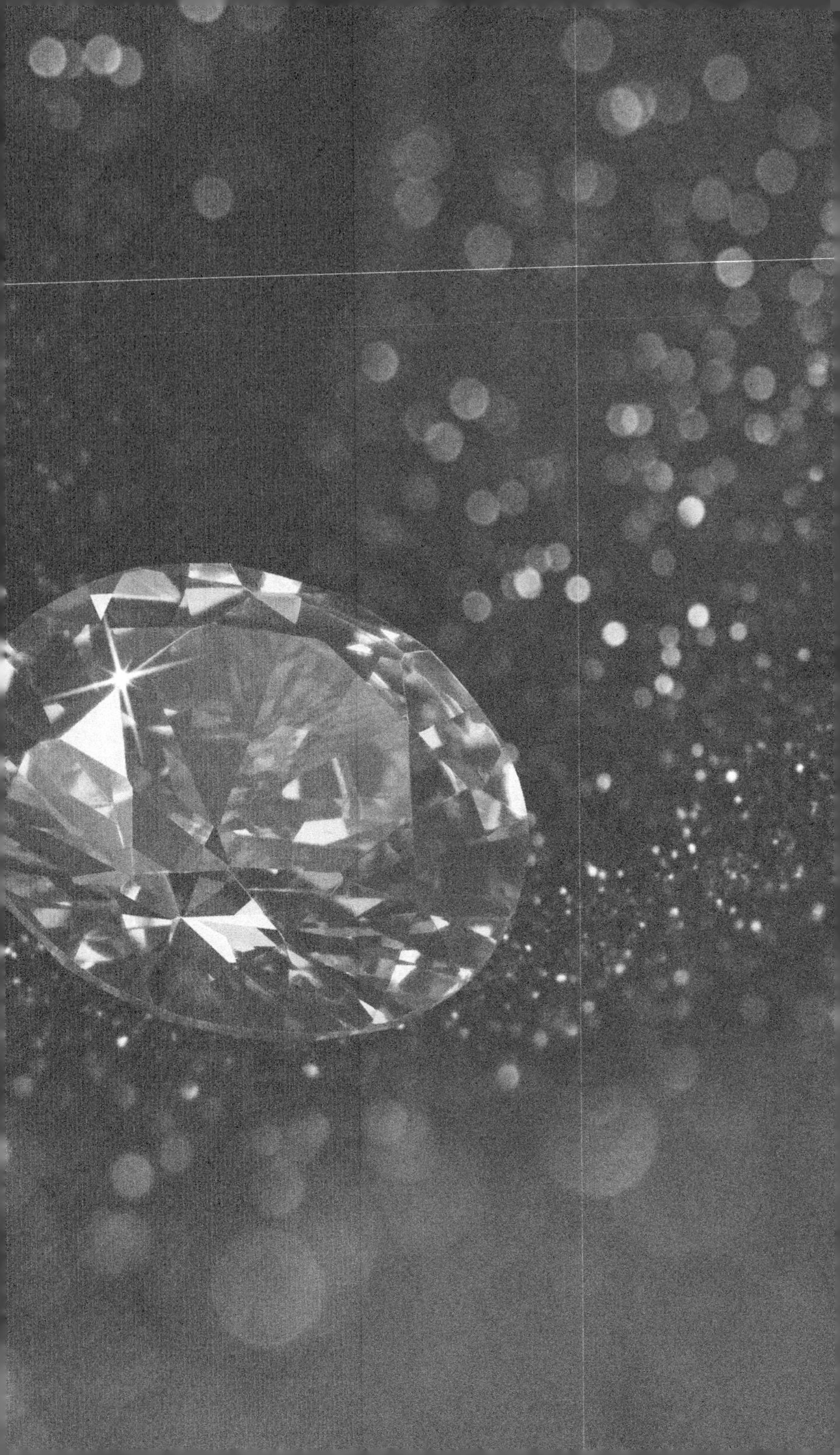

CHAPTER ELEVEN

Maxim

My fist slammed into Miss Sia Reynolds' door, and when she opened it, her sweatshirt hung off her shoulder. Flushed, her creamy brown skin radiated just like the rosy color in her cheeks. She had sleep in her eyes, and her bed shorts barely covered her thighs.

I wet my lips. "Get your clothes on."

I didn't give her a chance to speak.

I stepped away, and little steps padded down the hallway after me.

Malyshka…

"What are you talking about—" she started, but shot back when I pivoted.

"I said get your fucking clothes on." I was in her face now, and she shrank in front of me. I growled. "Get them on *now* and bring the fucking dog."

I charged down the hallway before I could do or say something else.

I could smell her.

Her soft scent maddened me, and I was pacing by the time I saw her again, clothed now. I didn't look at her. "Get in the car."

I already had my Mercedes running and had actually gotten it ready myself. I'd been impatient and hadn't bothered asking any of my staff to do it.

I didn't like who I'd turned into in the last hour. What I was capable of...

I felt unhinged and on the brink of doing something stupid. Something like taking my blade and gutting the first person I saw. That person could be Miss Reynolds. It might be if I couldn't control my demon.

Sia was shaking by the time she got in my car, and I only knew that because of the state of her legs. She'd covered them, wearing too-tight jeans, and they were shaking in my seats.

"Where are we going?" she asked, attempting to strap in. She had the dog in the backseat, but only Sia yelped when I shot off like lightning. She hadn't had a chance to get her seatbelt all the way on. "Hey—"

She didn't dare speak to me, and my gaze was hard in her direction. I revved up, and her panicky hands got her seatbelt on.

She gripped the seats. "You're going really fast."

"Yeah?" I laughed, feeling manic. I faced her. "Well, it's my fucking car."

Her fear had me dizzy, choking me with adrenaline. It was amping me up. Especially with all that flush coloring her cheeks.

Her neck...

She was rosy everywhere, an innocent little lamb I could easily break.

I charged forward again, the dog unaffected. In actuality, the beast of a thing was laying down on my leather seats like it was having a joyride. Apparently, I'd disturbed its slumber.

Well, that made two of us.

My hand on the wheel, I propelled the car in the direction of Peters & Burg. Val was already on standby. When I came home earlier today, I left some work behind at my place of business. I'd already had a long day and believed it could wait until morning.

That was until I caught Sia on surveillance tonight.

Growling, I shot into the first parking space I saw. Gleb was there, and I didn't even greet him before launching myself out of the car.

I was too busy grabbing Sia.

I brought her too close, and I realized my mistake right away. I could see that fear right in my face.

I could smell her way too close.

Her aroma changed the air just like the first day I came across her in my daughter's room, and I think the only reason I was able to hold onto her without losing my fucking mind was because she didn't smell like sex. Arousal…

She had earlier tonight. I knew because I *saw her*. I hadn't noticed her while I'd been swimming, but I had after I'd gotten dressed and gone into my office. I played back footage and watched her fuck herself earlier tonight.

To the sight of me.

Hard as a fucking rock, I directed her to get the dog out of the backseat, but she hesitated. She frowned. "Why?"

She was panting while she asked, sharp, rapid breaths expelling in front of me. It caused more of her scent to waft into the air and shoot straight into my fucking nose. My cock. I got her arm. "You and the dog are going into work with me, and whatever you see…whatever you hear, you do nothing. You understand?"

Shocked, her eyes twitched wide. "See?"

I put pressure into her delicate flesh, managing to bring her closer to me. She was weak like a twig and would be so easy to break. "You're not to react to anything you see," I said, then jutted my chin toward the dog. "And make the dog look tough when you bring her."

"Why?"

"Just fucking do it," I ground out, and she closed her mouth. I was losing control here. Hell, I'd already fucking lost it. I'd taken this twenty-year-old girl out of bed to teach her a lesson. She'd crossed a line tonight. She fucked up.

And now, she was about to know it.

Sia got the dog out of the car and quickly brought her close. She managed to keep up with my long strides, and I noticed she stayed closer to the dog than to me. Perhaps she thought the dog would protect her from me.

I fought myself from grinning, too angry to give into the sick pleasure I felt from her fear. I passed a shocked Val on the way. Her eyes were wide on both the situation and me. She'd been surprised to hear I was coming back to the office when I called. She knew I'd had a long day.

Well, her surprise managed to grow upon seeing Sia *and the dog* with me. She lifted her hands. *"What's going on?"*

I ignored her question but lifted my hands. *"Bring the girl into my workspace in five minutes. She and the dog come alone. Don't allow anyone else in with her."*

Val's head shot back. My workspace was sacred unless I called for others to assist, and she knew that. She shook her head. *"But..."*

"Five minutes, Val." I left her. I left Sia.

My client sat in the same chair and state I'd left him in. He was bleeding but not broken. He was a former member of the organization, but abandoned the Brotherhood to work for one of our enemies.

He smirked upon seeing me coming into the room. I worked him long and hard today, but again, hadn't managed to break him yet. He had a few teeth missing from my labor, which showed after he spit blood at me. "I told you. I won't say shit to you or Natan, you son of a bitch."

I'd been called worse, and though he thought he was getting the better of me, he actually made my job more fun. I always liked it when they didn't break easy.

It meant I could use other ways to break.

When breaking someone physically was harder, I often looked toward other means. Psychological fears could be just as effective, and people always gave away what they were scared of when interrogated. One just had to ask the right questions.

And I had tonight.

I waited for Sia and the dog to come into my workspace, and when she ultimately did, she was guarded and not that spitfire I'd come to know.

Perhaps it was the sight of my toys.

I had tools…torture devices everywhere. This space was my candy shop, the tools my candy.

Sia backed up a little upon seeing them and even more so when she witnessed the bleeding man in front of her. The man was filthy, and though he greeted Sia with a gleeful smirk, it faded away the instant he noticed the large as fuck German Shepherd at her side. He instantly bucked in his chair, the legs hitting the floor again and again. I supposed I was correct when I guessed his fear.

I always guessed correctly.

"No! No! No!" The traitor was blind to his fear now. All he could see was the dog. He simply gave me too much information today during our interrogation. Things about his childhood. Of course, he didn't say he had a severe phobia of dogs, but it was easy to discern considering his reactions to certain questions I had.

In all honesty, I had something more gruesome planned for him after he gave himself away. I'd actually arranged to have other dogs come in first thing in the morning. I planned to let them slowly tear him apart until he gave up the location of a Bratva brother. He and our enemies knew the location, which was why he was here with me today.

Plans changed though, and Sia appeared to be just as freaked out as this man. She gripped the dog's leash, the man in front of her full-out screaming and crying. The dog at Sia's side barked at him because of it. I told her to make the pooch look fierce, but she didn't even have to try with all the man's carrying on. He had streams of tears flying down his face, and when Sia looked on the cusp of running away, I took a step in front of her.

She froze, her escape blocked, and didn't dare move from where she stood. I told her to do nothing once she was in this room.

She wasn't now, not that she had a choice. The man and his noise were clearly freaking out the dog because the hound started jerking at its leash to get to him. This of course made the son of a bitch scream louder, and a pool of piss flooded the floor beneath him.

"No, please. I'll tell you!" he shouted, facing me. "Just get the dog away. Just get it away. Please…"

He didn't have my focus at this point. Instead, I studied Sia. This whole display was more for her and less for this pathetic piece of shit in front of me. She fucking pissed me off.

She crossed a line.

She made me lose control, and not a lot of things did that to me.

Deciding to make this quick, I headed over to my tools. My client was still crying, and the dog still barked. This was all becoming a bit much and more drama than I cared to endure at the present.

"Please. He's with my boss, Bortnik. At his home uptown. He's got him chained in his basement," he cried, and when he rattled off an address, I turned around.

I smiled. "Thank you."

He didn't get to say you're welcome. He didn't get to say

anything. I pulled the trigger, the bullet from the gun in my hands landing between his eyes, smoking. The traitor's screams stopped, and the impact of the bullet sent him flying back. If he hadn't been secured to his chair, he would have easily landed in the piss on the floor.

I lowered the gun, and at this point, the dog's barking stopped. I had a silencer on my pistol so that didn't surprise me, and since the man stopped screaming, the dog was no longer unsettled. It was completely silent in that room and Miss Sia Reynolds was a part of it.

She stared at the floor and the bleeding man in front of her. She was shaking, but I noticed she had her head cocked. Almost like she was studying the man before her.

She and her intense stare were frozen like her eyes couldn't leave. I thought she might actually approach the guy at one point, but then her hand shot to her mouth.

She raced from the room after that and took the dog with her. Val was at the doorframe and had to maneuver away from it to make way for Sia. Once Sia cleared, Val headed after her, but not before she shot a look at me. My head of security could say so much with her eyes. She'd appeared confused when I initially brought Sia here.

Needless to say, there was no confusion now.

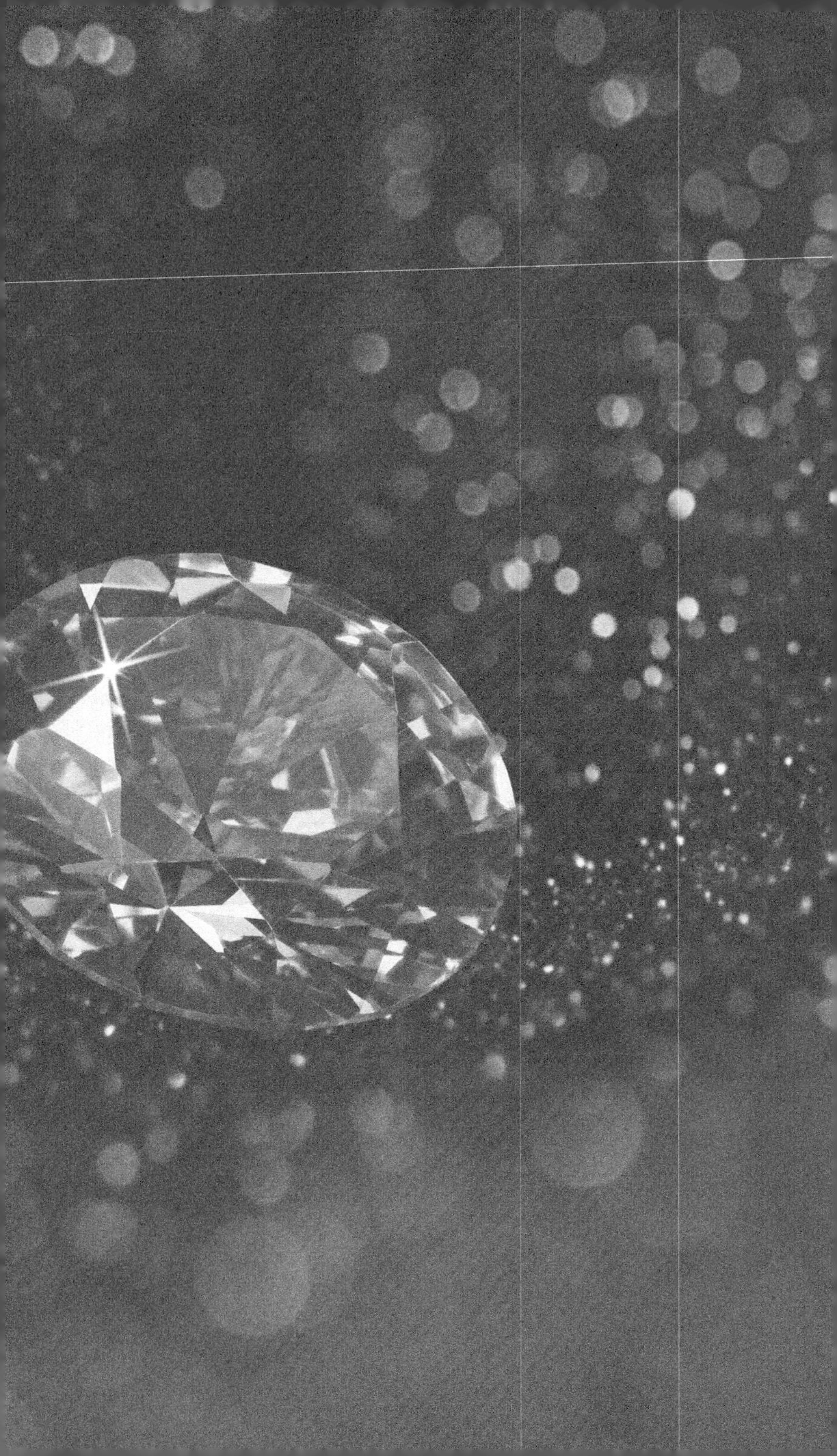

CHAPTER
TWELVE

Sia

I flinched as steps approached me.

I gripped the porcelain bowl.

A phone screen slid in front of my face next, and I didn't bother reading it before flushing the toilet. I wiped my mouth.

The phone screen hovered in front of my face again. *"You okay, kid?"*

Val had first asked that before I threw up. After all, she was the one who led me to the bathroom.

I mean, she knew I wasn't okay.

My eyes averting from her, I got up, and when she tried to help me, I shrugged away. I grabbed Polly instead. Val had taken her leash so I could vomit.

Val started to type something on her phone again but, once more, I didn't bother reading it.

I just wanted to get the fuck out of there.

———

Maxim

Val was silent with her approach, but I always heard her.

I heard everyone.

I couldn't *not* turn off my senses sometimes, and I continued cleaning knives as she raised her hands. I liked my tools thoroughly clean even if I hadn't used them.

I ignored Val's signs beside me before I asked, "Where's the girl?"

Val smirked. *"I put her in a car home,"* she signed, and I returned the clean knife to its appropriate place. Val forced her hands in front of me. *"And her name's Sia."*

I was well aware of the girl's name. Val lingered at my side, her hands folded. She clearly had something to say but wasn't saying it.

"Is there something else?" I dared her. It wasn't her job to question me.

Val shook her head but, regardless, raised her hands again. *"You could have just fired her if you didn't want her around."*

Annoyed at being questioned, I growled. I lifted my hands. *"What I did was necessary."*

Mostly. Sia Reynolds had no place here and definitely not in my life. She was a foolish little girl with foolish emotions, and I had no time for *little* girl crushes. She clearly had one on me, touching herself…

My grunt low, I strode across a clean floor. Gleb was quick with his men and moved the traitor's body on to the next phase. We disappeared people here after getting information. We did through my other places of work.

My network of funeral homes was the perfect cover for the Brotherhood. It'd been my idea to use the facilities for tortures and body disposal. The Bratva owned half the funeral homes this side of the state thanks to me.

Val started to sign again, but I started first.

"And it's a good thing I don't care about your opinion. And you should get back to work."

The anger that emanated off her I could visibly see, but I gave zero fucks about it. Again, it wasn't her job to question me.

Val put her back to me, but signed over her shoulder. *"She's not a part of our world."*

Then she stalked off, acting like a child herself. Perhaps my head of security was getting too attached to the girl who worked in my home.

I faced my knives, well aware Miss Reynolds wasn't part of our world.

That was exactly why what occurred here tonight had been more than a gracious favor.

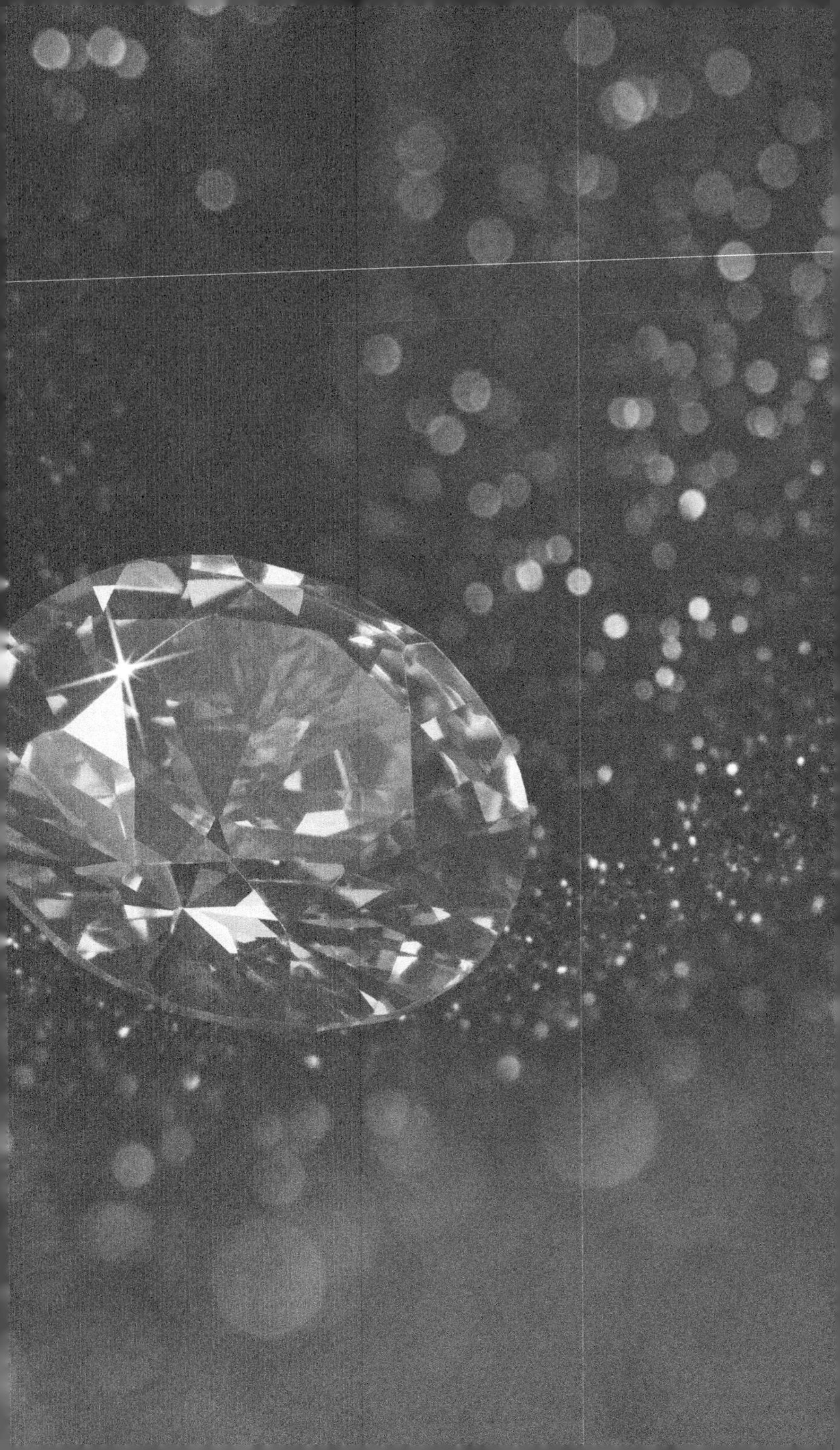

CHAPTER THIRTEEN

Maxim

I got home twenty-four hours later.

It was like I'd never left.

Of course I *had* left and all signs of that came when I'd still been at work. I was told Miss Sia Reynolds requested to leave the Petrov property.

I allowed it.

I'd more than allowed it. Hell, I was fucking relieved by it. Sia hadn't told the gatekeeper why she wanted to leave, but I didn't fucking care.

Good riddance, Miss Reynolds.

She didn't belong in my world, and Val was right about that. And Sia most certainly didn't belong around me.

I washed my hands later that night in my master's bathroom. Well, it was more so morning. It was around 3 AM, and I was ready for fucking bed. It'd been a long day, and I'd chosen to work in my office at Peters & Burg after Sia left, doing a little bookkeeping. I liked to know where my money was.

It also gave my mind something to do, and, after drying my hands, I left the bathroom. I started to unbutton my shirt for bed when a call hit my line.

I squinted at it before deciding to answer. "What?"

This was my usual greeting. Only close confidants had my line, which was why the lack of an immediate answer put me off.

"Who the fuck is this?" I barked, realizing now only a number came up on my phone and not a name. This person calling wasn't in my contacts. I started to threaten the caller again, but hesitated when faint laughter hit the line.

"God, you're such a dick," slurred into my ear, the soft voice sloppy and messy. Whoever was on the other end of the phone sniffed before laughing again. "And God it feels good to say that."

I knew right away who this was. I mean, I knew her voice. "Miss Reynolds?"

Why was she calling me, and why in the fuck did she have my line?

I didn't get a chance to ask either question. Like airy wind chimes, Sia's light laughter flowed into the line again, and my eyes narrowed.

"It's Sia," she slurred again, and I growled. How was she not even *here* and still defying me? "And you'll call me that because I don't work for you. I quit, asshole, in case you didn't know."

"I know," I said. I tucked a hand under my arm. "Were you able to get all your things? If not, I'll have someone gather anything you left and bring it to wherever you're staying."

More of that soft laughter, and I ground my teeth.

"I have everything," she bit out. "And I have Polly. I took her with me in case you hadn't noticed."

I actually hadn't noticed. My people hadn't informed me,

but that was fine. I'd wanted to be rid of both her and the dog anyway.

"Very well," I said, now wondering where she was. There was chatter in the background, loud talking somewhere in the room with her. It was multiple voices, and I found myself analyzing the carpet as I attempted to filter through conversations. This was just instinct and had nothing to do with her. I didn't care where she was.

"You don't deserve her you know," she said, chuckling and clearly drunk. "She's a good dog. A great dog."

"Miss Reynolds?" I didn't have to cut her off. She'd done that herself as she suddenly threw herself into a fit of giggles. I gripped the phone. "Miss Reynolds, are you listening to me?"

"Miss Reynolds. Miss Reynolds," she singsonged, but anger laced her voice. She huffed into the phone. "I said it's Sia."

"Sia then." I dampened my lips, patience not my strong suit. "Sia, why would you jeopardize your sobriety?"

I had no idea why I asked her this, but found the words tumbling out of my mouth.

And I was listening hard again, my ears searching that background noise. It sounded as if she were at a bar with all that ruckus, and there were many in the area that would serve a minor. Especially, if they were young like her, vulnerable...

"I was in rehab for drugs not alcohol you ass wipe." She laughed, and my teeth gnashed. "And I wouldn't have been drinking if you actually kept jellybeans stocked like I asked."

I had no idea what she was talking about. None, but she sounded like a little kid barking at me. She *was* a kid a young, *vulnerable* kid.

Where was she?

"I guess Sophia forgot," she continued on, her voice suddenly sad. "I don't ask you for anything, you know? That was like the only fucking thing. It was the only thing I wanted from you while being there, the only thing I needed…"

Emotion touched her voice, making it thick, defeated. She sounded nothing like the girl who gave me hell on a regular basis. I scanned the floor. "Sia—"

"Anyway, why do you care about my sobriety?" she questioned, trying to downplay the emotion in her voice. She was doing a terrible job. It bled through completely. Especially with the last thing she said. Her breathing was soft. "You don't care about it."

She was right. I didn't care.

I forced my attention back on the call instead of where she could be. I ignored it all and that went double for the emotion in her voice. "Forward your new address to the house line, and I'll make sure you get your last check." I had no idea how she'd gotten my personal line, but with how upset Val had been with me I wouldn't put it past her to share it with Sia. I could trust Val, but she was obviously getting attached to this girl.

This was another reason she needed to go. My jaw shifted. "I wish you luck in all your future endeavors, Miss Reynolds."

It was the proper thing to say, the decent thing. I started to hang up, but heard yelling in the background. Sia called someone an asshole next, and my hand dropped from under my arm. My eyes narrowed.

"Miss Reynolds?" She didn't speak to me, too busy yelling at someone else. "Sia, where the fuck are you?"

Again, it sounded like a bar, but I wasn't sure which one. The closest was Rasputin's Pub, and if she was on foot (with a dog), she'd probably go there. There was a motel next door.

"Shut your filthy mouth and back off, dick!" Sia shouted. Then, the line went dead. In fact, it went eerily silent, deathly silent. I could hear the blood pulsing in my ears but not for long. I was too busy analyzing the different ways to kill someone with what I had on my person. I could have stopped by my personal armory in the house, but didn't before getting to my car. I honestly hadn't even thought to go there I was moving so quickly. I just acted without thought.

I never acted without thought.

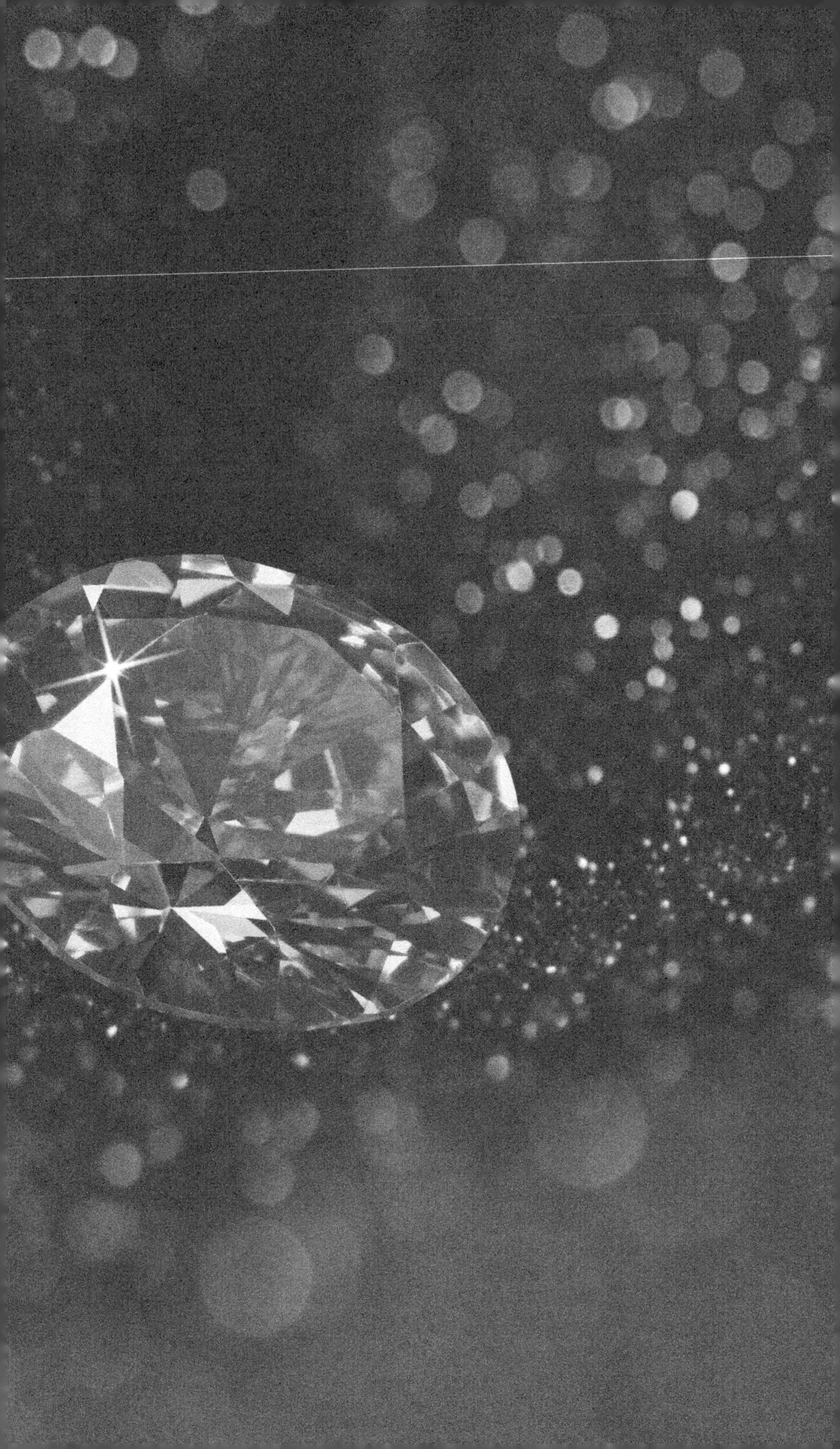

CHAPTER FOURTEEN

Maxim

I threw open the door of Rasputin's.

They knew me well here.

No one questioned me as I stalked my way to the bar. They just moved.

And what I saw...

One of my Bratva brothers had his hand lifted. I didn't know him well, but I did know he frequented this bar just like the rest of the brothers here.

His hand reared back, swiftly striking it down in the direction of the curly-haired woman beneath him.

Sia went flying upon impact, hitting the floor and landing in a heap before his feet. She grabbed her face where he'd struck, and the fucker drew back to hit her again.

He didn't get the chance.

My blade was in my hands only seconds before it left my fingertips. A flash of silver cut through the crowd before the knife sliced precisely into the palm of my Bratva brother. The blade stayed, and the brother howled. He gripped his hand, and everyone whipped around in the direction the knife came from. Many reached for their gun holsters.

They stopped when they saw me.

Everyone stopped. *Everything* stopped. People took notice when I entered a room.

I supposed being the adopted son of our leader did that.

It wasn't official, but Natan had basically raised me. Everyone here knew that, and even outside of that, they knew who I was. Natan's executioner got respect.

They even stopped the bar music, the room parting for me. Goal-oriented, I only headed for one place.

Sia was on the floor holding her face. She had her eyes closed, her body locked up in anticipation of another hit. I assumed this because everyone in this bar had eyes on me, but she cowered beneath the bar, her small frame shaking.

Little one...

She had no right to be here, obviously thinking she could play with the big boys. This behavior was completely in her nature, but was foolish. One couldn't dick around in my world.

Eventually, Sia realized she wouldn't be struck again because her eyes opened. The first thing those brown eyes spotted was me standing above her, and they widened immediately. She scooted back, her back hitting the bar and her hand still on her face. She'd been brave in front of me before, but that didn't seem to be the case now. Now, I clearly scared her with my presence.

The reason why was evident, considering the last time we'd been together, and her fear and shock was only exacerbated upon seeing the bleeding man in front of her. The brother had stopped screaming, but I think that was only because I was here. He'd silenced himself in front of me and definitely noticed the second blade in my hand.

I'd pulled it out only seconds after I'd thrown the first. I toyed with it, his eyes and everyone else's on it. He swallowed. "Maxim."

My eyes still on him, I lowered my body in Sia's direction. It was instinct to keep him in my line of sight. I glanced toward Sia, the young girl still cowering. My eyes narrowed. "You struck this woman?"

He obviously had, and he knew I'd seen it. During this exchange, Sia's gaze passed over my shoulder. Her eyes shot large again upon seeing all the attention in our direction.

"Maxim," the brother said instead of answering my question, and I growled.

"Did you strike this woman?" I repeated, and though the man was bleeding profusely, he let go of his hand. Tears were in this fucker's eyes, but he was clearly trying to be brave.

He nodded once. "Yes, but I didn't know she was yours."

"She works for me," I said, and I was proud of myself. I was actually still cordially speaking to this motherfucker and didn't allow a shred of emotion to enter my voice.

I wanted to tear him apart. I wanted him to *bleed*, and the demon inside only goaded the urge. I was a hunter by nature, but I didn't hunt animals.

I hunted people.

The chase brought me life, enlivened me. My jaw tight, I fought my natural instinct. Especially when the brother started to speak again. I was sure anything he voiced would surely set me off, and it was only Sia's sudden movement that kept me from acting. She took my attention, her cheeks flushed. Her hand lowered from her cheek, and I noticed a cut on her brown skin. The brother must have been wearing a ring when he struck her.

The sight of the blood had my demon growling, the metallic scent of blood growing in the air. It was potent, but, instead of wanting to draw more of it out, I wanted to stop it. I didn't want Sia bleeding.

My demon redirected toward the brother, my blade heavy

in my hands. I gripped the handle but resisted the urge to use it. I forced my attention to Sia instead. She was quivering like a leaf. "Are you hurt?"

Besides her cheek, I meant. Her eyes scanned mine, and a quick shake of her head forced the scent of coconuts into the air. It was light, airy.

I wet my lips. "What did he say to you before I got here? On the phone I heard yelling."

I heard her tell someone to shut their filthy mouth which meant he said something to her.

"What did he say to disrespect you?" I asked, and movement occurred behind me.

"Maxim, I swear to God I didn't—"

I lifted a finger toward the brother who still had my blade lodged in his hand. I was waiting for Sia to speak, but she suddenly had no words. She was usually so quick to voice them.

Come on, malyshka. Use your voice.

I'd coax the words out of her if I needed to. Someone would pay today for hurting her. I had no idea why I suddenly felt protective over her. I was always a man who believed in justice. The innocent should never be punished.

And Sia Reynolds was an innocent. Especially in my world.

Eventually, Sia took her attention off the crowd and focused on me. She wet her full lips. "He called me a bitch for not wanting to suck his cock. He explained how he wanted it...in detail."

Good girl.

I gave her my hand then, and though she was shy about taking it, she did let me help her stand. She was unstable with her footing. This might have been because she'd clearly been drinking earlier.

"Go to the car," I told her, nodding. I left it running

outside because I was going to get her out of here. She had no business being here.

Sia gazed around, everyone's eyes still on us. Her expression changed as she looked at the bleeding brother who disrespected her, her eyes cold. Her gaze found me. "What will you do?"

She didn't want to know, and what I was about to do wasn't for her to know. I folded a hand on her arm. "Car, Sia. Now."

That was all I had to say. She didn't question me anymore before touching the blood on her face. It was dripping down to her mouth now.

I fought the animal inside me, and I studied her back as she left the bar. The crowd parted for her easily. Even the brother who hurt her gave her a wide berth.

After she was gone, he studied me. "Maxim—"

That was the last word he'd ever say, but not because I laid him out. The punishment always fit the crime in the Brotherhood.

And it did today.

I studied the second blade in my hand after I used it to slice my Bratva brother's windpipe. A deep red dripped down from it to the floor, and I glanced up to hear gurgling noises.

Blood gushed around my Bratva brother's hand as he fell to the floor, and others quickly crowded around him. I'd been precise with my strike. He wouldn't die tonight, but he'd never speak another word.

Again, the punishment always fit the crime.

I made my way outside after retrieving both my blades. They'd need cleaning, but I wrapped them in a handkerchief in the meantime. I didn't enjoy the smell of blood. It was triggering.

I got into the car.

Sia didn't speak for a while, until the question I knew was coming finally came out. "What did you do to him?"

"Best you not speak," I said, accelerating. I headed toward the house. I frowned. "Not after what you did."

Her head shot back. "What I did? You're kidding."

I cut her a look, not kidding. "Your actions have consequences." And in this case, they had me acting against a brother. It wasn't that that didn't happen, but it was the way in which it did. The confrontation shouldn't have happened at all.

Grunting, I faced the road, and Sia huffed. She was all puffed up and trying to appear like a badass again. This was the exact opposite of how she'd been at the bar. She'd known her place there, but clearly didn't now.

She sighed. "Look. I get you're pissed, but that guy came onto me."

"And are you going to be the one to tell his family that?" I didn't even look at her at this point, too angry. The fact I didn't know whether that was more so directed at her or myself pissed me off. I forced back my hair. "That man will never speak again because of you."

"What?"

I glanced her way, my expression serious. "He's forever silenced for disrespecting you."

She didn't say anything. Not at first.

"I never asked..." she started, then pushed back her curls. It sent a waft of that coconut scent flying into the air again, and I gripped the steering wheel. I'd always been sensitive to smells, the only reason I was affected by hers. She shook her head. "I never asked you to do that. Be *crazy* like that. Fuck."

She had her feet up on my leather seats, her hands in her hair. Her panic reminded me of how she'd reacted when I shot that traitor point blank in front of her.

"And then there's what you did to his hand," she continued, rubbing hers. She was right about his hand. If he regained use, it'd never be right again.

He was lucky I didn't remove his fingers.

I would have if others hadn't been around, if I'd been allowed to give in to my rage and what the fuck did that mean? I didn't lose control.

For some reason, this dog trainer was making me. Sia hugged her arms, but let go once she glanced out the window.

"We need to stop," she said, studying the motel I quickly cruised past. She sat up. "That's my motel. The one I'm staying at. We need to stop."

"We're not going to stop."

"Why?"

If she didn't stop asking me fucking questions... I squeezed the wheel. "You're going home. To *my home*."

And I noticed she'd sobered up a bit. Her words weren't slurred or anything, but I bet she'd had a hard time getting into the car on her own.

Her mouth parted. "Why are you taking me there?"

To do something about her face for starters. "You're bleeding. You need care."

"And you're going to give that to me?" She sounded shocked, and when I said nothing, she laughed. She shook her head. "I need to go back to my motel. My stuff is there and Polly."

I almost asked what a Polly was, but then remembered. I'd been calling the dog, *Dog*. "I'll send someone for her. You're going home."

She didn't argue with me this time. She just opened the door, and I was forced to wheel my Mercedes in the opposite direction. The door closed right away, and Sia screamed.

I bared teeth. "The fuck you think you're doing!"

"I'm going to get Polly. Now, you either stop this car, or I'm rolling out of it."

The look she gave me was deadly, and she didn't let up. Rather than risk scraping her off the pavement, I doubled back. I was silent all the way to the fucking motel, but only to keep myself in check.

Because if I had it my way...

There wouldn't be any taking her back home. There'd be me letting her out on the side of the road and telling her to run. There'd be me *chasing* her, punishing her...

"You get that dog, and you come right out," I said, my car still running. She was outside of it now, but actually listening to me as she stood with the door open. My eyes narrowed. "Don't make me come in there after you."

She really wouldn't want that and slammed the door in my face like the kid she was. She was inside too long, but came out just shy of me doing something about that.

Sia strode quickly with the dog, a bag on her arm. She told me she'd gotten her stuff, but this was all she owned? Once she got the dog inside, she returned to her seat and didn't dare say another word. Neither of us did.

We got to the house quickly. The bar wasn't far from my home, and once we arrived, I shut off the car. I got out, and when Sia started to do the same with not just herself but the dog, I walked around the car. I gripped the door. "Dog stays here. I'll have someone take it to its room."

"*She* comes with me." Sia had the dog's leash in her hands and was acting completely petulant. "I'm not leaving her."

She then proceeded to direct the dog around me and into my fucking house. "Miss Reynolds..."

I went for her arm, but the dog got in my way. It blocked my reach, and I could do nothing but watch Sia walk away from me. She was still a bit off kilter (I assumed from the alcohol), and at one point, I attempted to get her arm again and stabilize her.

She recoiled from my reach, and I shook my head.

"Let me help you, goddammit," I gritted. Though I

wondered why I was trying to help her. I was wondering about a lot of things tonight.

Sia felt the same way, judging by the way she analyzed me. I was hoping she'd leave the dog at the foot of the stairs once we got inside, but hell if I was getting any favors tonight.

Sia kept the dog close to her, and it stayed with us all the way to Sia's room in the servants' quarters.

I opened Sia's door, and when she took the dog in there, she dropped her stuff on the floor. She started to sit on the bed with the hound, but that was the last fucking straw.

"Dogs don't belong in this part of the house, let alone on my fucking sheets," I cut, striding toward them both. "Dog stays at the door."

"I told you: Polly stays with me."

She started to amble onto the bed with it, but I got the dog's lead.

"The dog is fine by the door," I stated, begging her to test me on this. "Now, sit down so I can do something about that cheek."

She may not be bleeding anymore, but it could still get infected. Who knew where that fucker's hands had been and what was on his ring?

Sia's head tossed back in laughter. "You know what? No, and I'm done with this conversation now."

She ripped the dog's leash away from me. She moved to get by me, but at this point there were no fun and games. There was no more of me saying something and her refusing me.

There was no more.

"I said *sit*," I stated, looming above her. She attempted to distance herself, but I took a step for every two she had. Before she knew it, I had her against the wall. I peered down at her. "Back. *Down*."

The words radiated in the room and even the dog sat at

this point. I found that curious since it hadn't listened at all when Lettie had been looking after it.

I watched Sia, studied her response, and I noticed she wasn't as brave when the flush hit her cheeks this time.

Right away, she told the dog to go to the door, and it did, surprisingly. She must have been able to teach it something. Sia sat on the bed, her arms crossed. "I'm sitting."

She thought she was cute.

"Stay there," I said, putting my back to her. I left the room and dared her to leave it.

She didn't.

I passed the dog, still in its place by the door, now playing with a toy, when I returned with a medical kit.

"Surprised it listened to you," I said. I pulled up a chair from the armoire and informed Sia to sit on it.

She did, begrudgingly. She also had a hard time walking to it but once again refused my hand when I offered.

Stubborn girl.

She was stubborn, headstrong. I didn't do well with either. I cleaned her wound first, and she cursed. I assumed because of the sting from the antiseptic.

"She'd listen to you too you know," she said. I stopped dabbing her wound. Her eyes narrowed. "If you bothered to take the time to train with her."

I smiled that she was still on that. I cleaned away the blood from her cheek. Her cut hadn't been that deep, and she didn't need stitches. I glanced back at the dog. "I don't need a dog, and the only reason I have one is because of my daughter's meddling."

Sia propped her feet up on the bed across from the chair. She hugged her legs every time I touched her wound, and when she sucked in a breath, her lips puckered. A soft breath expelled into the room after she released it and the smell of coconut touched the air.

"Well, maybe she feels like you need something." She

closed her eyes when I touched her this time. I assumed from the pain. Her chin touched her knees. "Some*one*..."

She was wrong about both and cursed again when I dabbed at the wound. My jaw clicked. "None of this would have happened if you hadn't done something so foolish tonight."

Her lashes fanned open, her frown hard. "It's my fault I got hit on?"

No, that was the asshole at the bar, his arrogance.

The rage lassoed me again. Not enough blood was spilled tonight for what he'd done. Men in my world tended to think they owned women. They were nothing but objects, trophies...

"I meant your sobriety," I stated, and when her eyes flashed my way, I nodded. I sat back. "I don't know why you'd do something so dumb. You're a drug addict for fuck's sake."

"Oh, and you care about that?" I handed her a cold compress for her cheek. It was still red from when that fucker struck her, and she held it to her flesh with a pout. "You don't care."

I didn't. "I just know what it's like to have an addiction. Something you can't control."

She eyed me. "You do? In what way?"

Well, that was none of her business.

I turned, avoiding her question when I told her I'd be right back. I had to pass that infernal dog again, but it kept playing with its toy and didn't follow me.

Regardless, I grunted at it. I left the room, returning with a bandage. The medical kit I grabbed had been out of them.

I gestured for Sia to remove the compress, then placed the bandage on her wound. "What you did was just dumb."

She glanced away. "Well, I wouldn't have gotten drunk if I hadn't run out of jellybeans." She'd mumbled under her breath. Her hands gathered in her lap. "That's what the jellybeans are for. They take the edge off."

She was obviously referring to her addiction, and though I understood the need for the candy now, I also thought about what would trigger her in the first place. She'd certainly been through some things recently, seen some things.

My jaw shifting, I peered away.

"Anyway, thanks for everything, and this," she said, pointing to the bandage. She got quiet after that, and that was different for her. It was different for both of us.

In her silence, she started to get up. I waved my hand.

"You're staying here tonight."

She frowned. "What?"

"You're not going back out drunk." She'd barely been able to get up here in the first place, for fuck's sake. I shook my head. "Not until you sleep off whatever you drank."

And there'd be no discussion about that. Zero.

Her arms folded. "You can't tell me what to do. Or have you forgotten I don't work here anymore?"

"You don't, but you're in no condition to be wandering anywhere." Especially not this late. My jaw clicked again. "You're going to stay here for the night. You can leave in the morning. You're safe here."

I was surprised to hear that come from my mouth. I wet my lips, starting to turn away, but the dog got up. I watched it stride over to Sia and, though I should tell her to put the thing downstairs, I didn't.

Sia rubbed the pooch, smiling a little. My head cocked as I watched her. In fact, I hadn't moved and didn't really know why.

Sia caught me in my observation. She chewed her lip. "Did he deserve it?"

I didn't know what she was talking about so I didn't answer. Instead, I continued to watch her and how gentle she was with the dog. Not a lot of things in my world were gentle. Sia Reynolds was too pure of heart to be in my world, my home.

Regardless, here she was, and, after a beat, she told the dog to lay on the bed. It did right away, and, for some reason, I once again didn't stop her.

She continued to stroke the hound. "That man you killed. Did he deserve it? Did he deserve what you did to him?"

What a curious thing for her to say. "Why would you ask me that?"

She'd been repulsed by what she saw, and that was natural. But now she wanted to know if he deserved it? Again, curious...

Sia once more guided a hand over the dog, and I noticed she wouldn't make eye contact with me. She shrugged. "I guess I just wondered..."

"If his death was justified?"

Finally, those brown eyes lifted. Her nod was subtle, and I angled further into the room. "Would that make it easier for you? Knowing that he deserved it?"

She remained silent, and I decided to push her.

"Are you saying some people deserve what's coming to them, Miss Reynolds?" I asked. "That what you saw was okay as long as the person deserved it."

Something feral awoke my demon at the thought. It caused excitement to pulse through me.

It made me hard.

This was a dangerous line of questioning, and, eventually, Sia stopped petting the dog and looked at me. "Some people do deserve what's coming to them, yes."

I went to sleep with those words in my head that night, but not before watching images of Sia Reynolds. I studied the Sia Cam. She did nothing out of the ordinary. She simply slept, but my mind raced. Not many people would say such things out loud to someone else. They may feel that way but never say them.

Perhaps Sia Reynolds wasn't most people.

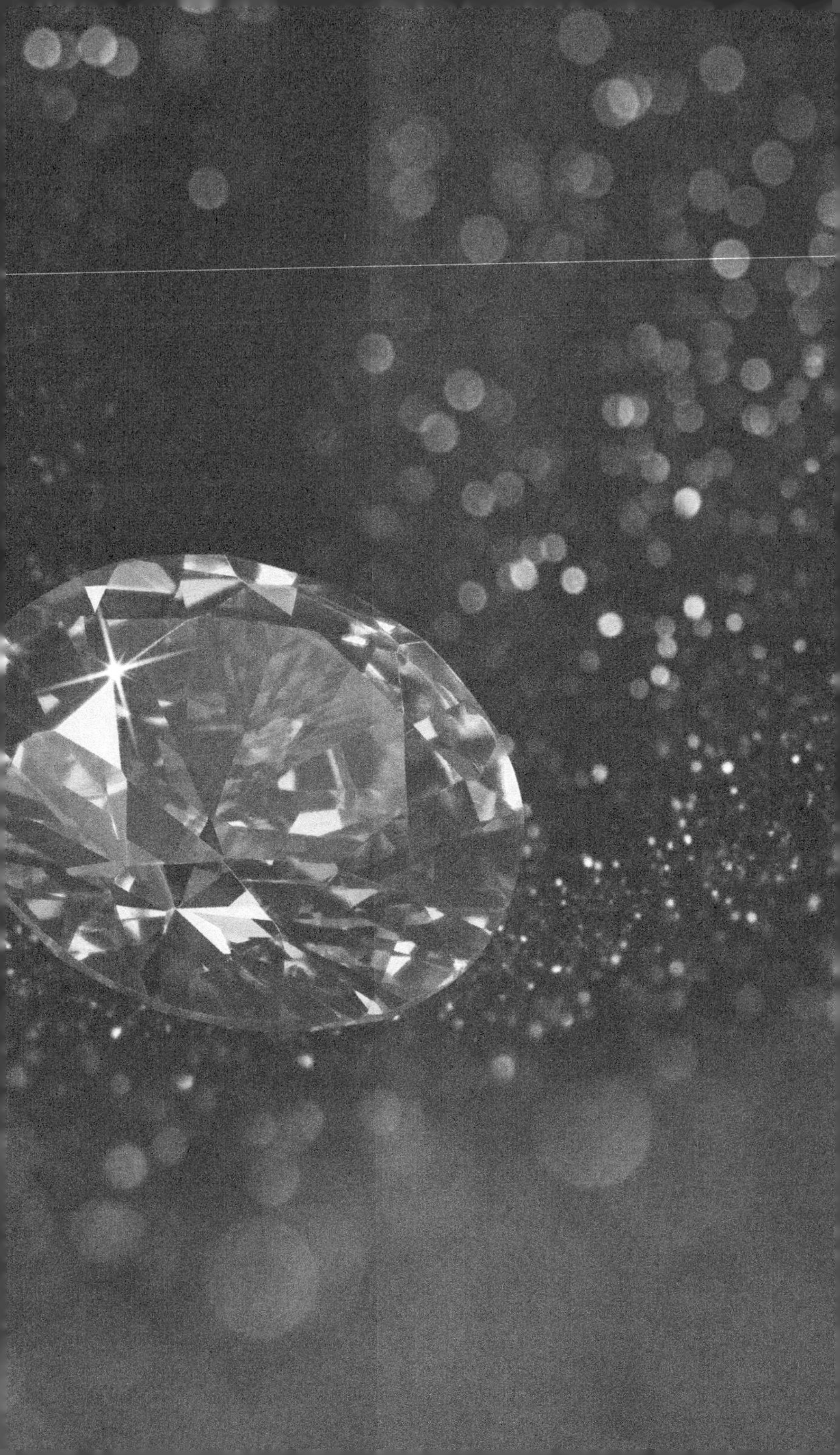

CHAPTER
FIFTEEN

Sia

My head *throbbed*.

Groaning, I opened my eyes, then immediately shut them.

So drinking last night wasn't a good idea.

Honestly, I didn't know what I'd been thinking. But I guess, considering I'd run out of jellybeans, I hadn't been thinking. I'd let my addiction get to me.

Damn.

I pressed my palms to my eyes. My whole body ached and felt heavy. I whistled and patted the bed for Polly, but when she didn't come I opened my eyes. She'd gone to sleep by the side of the bed, but she wasn't here.

I sat up, immediately freaking out. It was no mystery that Mr. Petrov didn't want her in the room with me last night.

I started to shoot out of bed but stopped upon hearing the jingle of a dog collar and leash. I rerouted to the window, and when I gazed outside I blinked.

Polly…my Polly had someone else walking her today.

Or he was at least *trying* to walk her.

Mr. Petrov had Polly by the lead and was wearing not a suit but a dark robe and matching bed pants. Both silk, they draped in a fluid motion over his large body. The robe was slightly open and revealed the bare skin of his broad chest. His dark tattoos were there too of course, stamped like badges of honor across his muscular frame.

I leaned against the window frame, shocked and, well, kind of confused. He wasn't really doing anything out there with Polly. In fact, they both stood there, Mr. Petrov staring curiously at her. Meanwhile, Polly sat in the stationary position I taught her. She was to remain like that until commanded, and, of course, Mr. Petrov wasn't giving her any commands.

Maxim…

That was what that man called him yesterday, and Mr. Petrov, well, he saved me.

Yeah, by hurting someone again.

I swallowed, but then nearly laughed when I saw him tug Polly. He didn't do it in an abrasive motion, and his frustration rang when she didn't do anything. He pushed a hand into his inky hair, and I did laugh then. He had no idea what to do out there, this dog foreign to him. He had a drink in his hand too, but from here it didn't appear to be alcohol. Orange juice in hand, he looked like a man who couldn't handle (of all things) a dog.

I chewed my lip, pushing off the window frame. I slept in my clothes last night so I didn't have to change before leaving the room. On the way out the door, something gave me pause though. There was something on the end table that definitely hadn't been there before.

Reaching over, I picked up the bag of jellybeans. They were the brand I liked, and they were also all yellow…

I gazed out the window again but didn't see Mr. Petrov this time. I didn't see *Maxim*.

I placed the jellybeans down and went to the bathroom.

After freshening up, I found myself outside, and the sun *killed* my sensitive eyes, even through my sunglasses. Sharp rays immediately stung my irises, and I cursed myself again for doing something so stupid. Maxim had definitely been right about that. Though I hated that he was.

I found him outside with Polly. They were both right outside the rows and rows of grape vines. This wasn't far from where I'd seen him when I'd been at the window.

"I see you've risen from the dead," he quipped, taking a sip of his drink. It was orange juice from what I could see. He lowered it. "How's the headache?"

"Feels like death." I rubbed my head and just about groaned but didn't. I didn't like appearing weak in front of this man. I shielded my eyes before jutting my chin at him and Polly. "So who's walking who this morning?"

"What?"

"I said who's walking *who*," I stated, laughing a little. I whistled, and Polly sauntered over to me. Needless to say, Mr. Petrov was more than ready to hand over her leash.

"I told you that dog doesn't listen to anyone. Well, anyone but you." He eyed Polly and me under an observant gaze. "She seems to take a liking to you."

I noticed he called her *she* and not *it* or Dog. I stroked Polly's fur. "I've just taught her basic commands, and I'm not scared of her which helps."

His frown was evident. "I'm not scared of her."

He could have fooled me. He didn't appear to just be put off by her but kept his distance. That was usually a telltale sign of fear with most people.

I continued to stroke Polly, and, though Mr. Petrov approached, he was cautious about it.

He folded his big arms. "Where I come from dogs tear people apart." His look was a curious one on the dog, which I found funny. This big strong guy who clearly had a handle on his world and the people around him was scared of a *dog*. I mean, Polly was a big dog but this was Mr. Petrov.

Maxim.

He was so commanding, large. Even with feet between us, I could feel his dominant energy, and I'd seen when he'd done to that man last night.

And the one from the funeral home before.

My fingers gathered in Polly's fur. "And where's that?" I asked, not knowing why. "Where do you come from, I mean?"

I chanced a look at him, and he was running his tongue casually across his full lips. He wet his lips all the time, and I kept noticing things like that, his mannerisms…

His smell.

His masculine scent ghosted the air and sometimes held a hint of smoke. Like he might smoke cigars sometimes.

"Don't know why you'd ask about that," he said, watching me with Polly.

I shrugged. "I guess I just want to understand." Maybe it'd make more sense what he did at the funeral home and why he'd done what he had last night to that guy at the bar.

He did that for you.

I was well aware of that, and though I didn't want anyone hurt, I had a feeling that guy would have done something bad to me if Maxim hadn't shown up. It'd be something I wouldn't have wanted done.

And that justifies it?

Conflicted, I studied the ground. Right and wrong confused me sometimes. I couldn't help it with the things I'd seen in my life.

Maxim's head cocked. "And I don't know why you'd want to do that either. After all, you're leaving."

"I don't have to go. Well, not right away." I shocked myself saying this and certainly shocked him. His dark eyebrows twitched up. I wrapped Polly's leash around my hand. "Polly is technically for you, and I did tell Lettie I'd help you with her."

It was the only way, frankly, that I'd let Polly stay with him. He needed to learn how to respect her.

I thought he'd come at me hot then. He always did when it came to Polly. He was the first to say he didn't want her, and that all this with her (and me) was Lettie's doing.

"I supposed it wouldn't hurt to learn a few things about her," he said, surprising me this time. He studied her. "But if you stay, no more drinking. Worse things can happen than what occurred last night."

Worse than that?

His jaw moved. "And I'll make sure you have your jellybeans. If that helps, I'll make sure you have them."

He seemed to care about my sobriety for some reason. I really didn't understand why. I suppose maybe he could have struggled with the same, but of course he didn't say. He had admitted an addiction though...

I nodded. "I saw you left some for me upstairs. That *was* you right?"

"It was." His eyes narrowed. "It won't be my fault you mess up your sobriety."

Again, why did he care? I chewed the inside of my cheek.

"Okay, but if I stay, I will have my own rules." He started to say something, but I wouldn't let him. I smiled. "You train with Polly and cooperate. If anything, it will get Lettie off your back. You can be honest when you speak to her about Polly and your progress with her."

I heard the hitch in my voice as I spoke to him, and when I realized that, I rubbed Polly. He made me nervous sometimes.

He remained silent beside me, and aware I was under his probing gaze, my skin buzzed suddenly. This unnerved me, but I wouldn't address it. I didn't address a lot of things like how I touched myself to the sight of him the other night. What I'd done wasn't right, inappropriate...

I mean, he was Lettie's dad.

Again, I wouldn't and *couldn't* address such things, and it took me a beat to realize Mr. Petrov still stared at me.

His gaze averted. "Very well. I'll get you my schedule. We'll work it out."

He couldn't really look at me after he said it and kept rubbing his mouth. I guess I could assume he was still nervous around Polly. I smiled. "Let's start now then."

"I don't have time now. I have work and—"

"We're already outside." I walked off a few steps, and his lips parted. My head cocked. "Come on. We'll get a quick walk in with her."

I suppose he could tell me no, but he didn't. His hand in his robe's pocket, he met my few steps, then strode beside me. It'd be interesting trying to teach him about Polly. It'd be interesting to be *around him*.

I guess we both were about to be put out of our comfort zones.

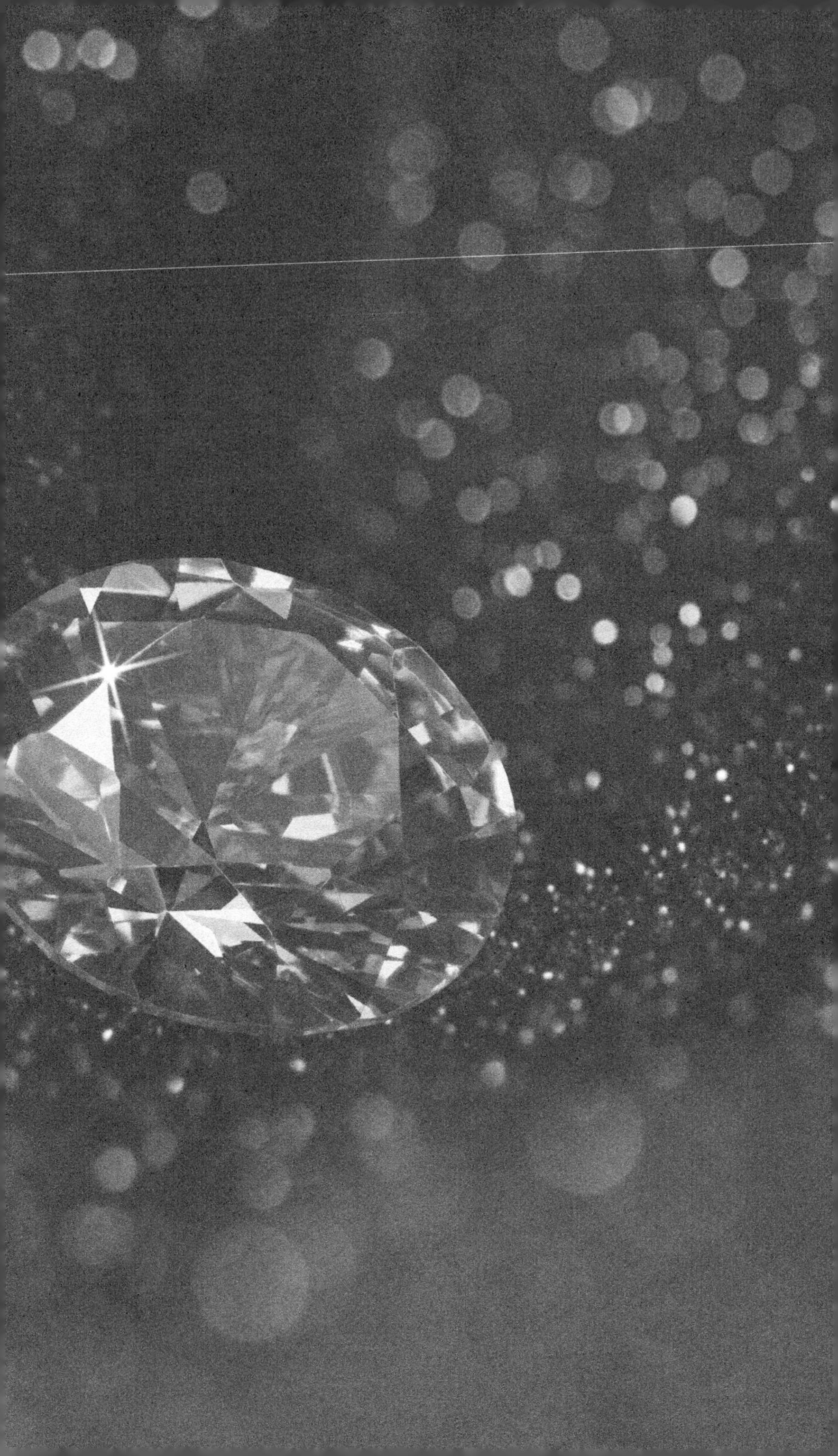

CHAPTER
SIXTEEN

Maxim

She had the damn dog...in my pool.

Sia splashed around with the animal. Rather, it splashed her. She was laughing with it, laughing with...Polly.

I was trying to be better about that, acknowledging the dog had a name. This was mostly to appease her trainer. Sia waved her hand, gesturing toward the pool. "Come on. Get in."

Yeah, that wasn't happening. I folded my arms. "I'm good up here."

My location was the pool's deck, watching the two with a drink in my hand. It was too early for liquor unfortunately, even for me, and leaving Polly, Sia waded toward the side of the pool.

She lifted herself out of it, a bikini on her little frame. She was certainly more developed than my daughter's other friends, more curvy.

My eyes narrowed, I paid more attention to the dog than

her. Polly was dog paddling while Sia crossed her arms in front of me.

"Come *on*," she urged, sitting on the side of the pool. The sun hit her glistening skin. She held a natural tan, and it took the sun nicely, made her glow.

I averted my eyes again as she huffed and got back into the water. It covered her up to her shoulders, and her grin was wiry when she shielded her eyes from the sun. "You said you'd cooperate."

I said I'd train with her and nowhere in that plan was a dog being *in my pool*.

Sia explained it was best that the pup and I shared each other's spaces. Apparently, my space was the pool I'd now have to clean out in order for me to do my morning laps tomorrow.

Sia's grin transformed into a frown, and she eyed me until I sighed and worked my robe off.

"Fine," I cut, bunching it up. I tossed it on a lounge chair before taking the stairs into the pool. "And you owe me for a pool cleaning."

She obviously wouldn't be able to pay. There was a reason she was desperate enough to work for me, and I studied her when I got into the pool. Her dark gaze appraised the length of me, unashamed across my shoulders and down my abs...

To my cock.

Dangerous, malyshka.

That was another reason I didn't want to get into the pool with her, be *half-naked* with her. She obviously developed some kind of little crush on me, and I didn't want to entertain it. That certainly wasn't unusual with one of my daughter's friends, but... I eyed her. "Dog trainer?"

Well, that zapped her out of her fascination with my cock and abs. Both still had her attention and at one point wetting her lips.

My cock hardened, but then I watched my dog trainer

click her little tongue at me. She huffed, putting distance between us. Perhaps, she didn't enjoy being called by her title. That was her position in this house, and she shouldn't forget it.

"Over here, *Mr.* Petrov," she said, and I tried not to smirk at her terse tone. I enjoyed getting a rise out of this little one, playing with her.

I came over, keeping my own distance. The dog hadn't attacked me yet, but who knew what the fuck could happen. Animals went rogue so I didn't fuck with them. People were easier to read.

Usually, people were. Sia appeared to be a recent exception. There's no reason she should still be here in my home, not with the things I'd subjected her to. She also surprised me by what she'd said about that traitor possibly deserving death. Young, *innocent* girls didn't say such things so openly.

"Come closer to Polly, closer to me," Sia said, observing me for a different reason now. She studied my cautious approach. "You don't need to be scared of her. She won't hurt you."

She didn't know that. My eyebrow lifted. "I'm not scared."

"I'm sure you're not."

The words had been under her breath, bold. I got close to her and the dog, but kept what I felt was a comfortable distance. "I'm close enough. What next?"

Her eyes rolled, dark brown, deep. She also had this mark above them, a scar cutting her eyebrow into two parts. I'd seen a lot of animal bites, and that appeared to be one of them. It could have even been a dog bite. I'd seen lots of those as well, and the scar had that same shape.

Regardless, Sia didn't appear to be scared of Polly. She obviously loved dogs and was good with them. Sia smiled at the pup before eventually having the dog swim around me.

I stiffened. "What are you doing?"

"You have to let her into your space. How can you train her if you can't even relax enough to be around her?"

"Easy. Fear." I studied the animal, its circle around me. "Speak to anything directly enough, and you can get them to break for you."

"Is that how you treat everyone in your life, Mr. Petrov?" she questioned, wading backwards. "Maxim?"

My head shot up and away from the dog.

Sia didn't correct herself, but I noticed the column of her throat shift. I wasn't sure if she always knew my name, but never dared to call me by it before.

Studying her, I waded close. I got about a foot away from her and noticed the red tint the tops of her ears, her cheeks.

"Many, yes. Most," I said, answering her question but also enjoying the fact I still maintained the power in this relationship. It would be so easy to break this girl.

Malyshka.

I got closer, probably dumb because at this point her soft scent absolutely radiated in my lungs. I caught a whiff of her within moments of being outside with her actually.

I'd been ignoring it.

Blood flushed her brown skin all over, her neck, her tits. If I had to guess, she was a mixture of races. Her tone light, the flush across her body could be easily seen.

How I affected her could be easily seen.

My growl was low.

"That's enough water fun," I said, drawing back. The dog approached me, but I ignored it. I cut around it. "I have to work."

"You said we had until 8:30."

"Well, I'm saying I have to work," I basically barked, rerouting. I swam to the side of the pool and immediately got out.

I was drying off by the time Sia waded over to Polly. After commanding her, Sia took the stairs out of the pool with the dog beside her. She had Polly by the collar, the dog trainer dripping wet down to her pert little toes.

Growling again, I picked up my phone. I had a few missed texts from Val. I responded to one, then noticed over my shoulder Sia had covered herself and was starting to dry Polly off with one of my good towels.

Christ.

Was there anything this girl did that didn't annoy me?

Grumbling, I started to chastise her but noticed her phone illuminate. She placed it right near mine before getting into the pool earlier, and when I picked it up, I bared my teeth.

Sia had a message. Actually, she had *a match*. I couldn't swipe the phone open, but I was well aware of the notification from a familiar dating app.

I used it to find a good fuck.

I had specific needs. As a man yes, but also as someone who had specific kinks. This particular dating app catered to both.

What are you into, Miss Reynolds?

Some cocksucker named Derek matched with her, and before I thought better of it...

I slammed the phone against the stone table on my deck. I managed to muffle the sound beneath my palm, but after, I dropped the phone on the deck.

Sia heard that, and when she looked up, I was picking up her phone.

"Damn," I said, showing her the shattered screen. She came over, and I shrugged. "Sorry."

Her mouth parted, she took it. "Fuck."

"Must have been on my robe when I went to pick it up," I lied, then held out my hand. "I can get you a new one though. I'll have someone take care of it before I go to work."

She didn't look like she wanted to, but she did give it to me. She sighed. "Okay, thanks."

She said this but didn't look okay. I could imagine the

phone was the only thing she had to connect her to the outside world since she didn't leave my property.

You don't let her.

I wrapped my towel around my waist.

"Do you need anything else today?" I asked for some reason. I forced out a breath. "I mean, besides the phone."

I'd made sure she had jellybeans, and once she got through the ones in her room, she had about ten pounds of them downstairs in the kitchen pantry. I'd asked Sophia about the ones Sia liked.

"No, I'm okay," she said, and for some reason, I was disappointed. Odd. She rubbed her arms. "Actually, can you get me a pillowcase?"

"Are the ones in your room not sufficient?" I found that hard to believe. I had the best sheets flown in from overseas to the house.

"No, they're fine. I just need a special one for my hair." She waved a hand to her damp curls. "Helps with my texture."

I nodded. "What kind do you need?"

She proceeded to tell me silk, and I bobbed my head twice in acknowledgement. That shouldn't be an issue.

"But if you can't find it, whatever." She waved it off, and I didn't know why. Did she not feel she was worth catering to or her needs met?

I tossed the towel on the lounge chair, replacing it with my robe. "I'm sure I can manage, and I'll work on the commands."

She taught me a couple for Polly before getting into the pool, and it was like I was seeking approval from Sia by telling her I'd work on what she instructed.

Again, odd.

I watched Sia go. She took Polly with her, and before I knew it, I was getting Val on the phone. I had a few questions for her.

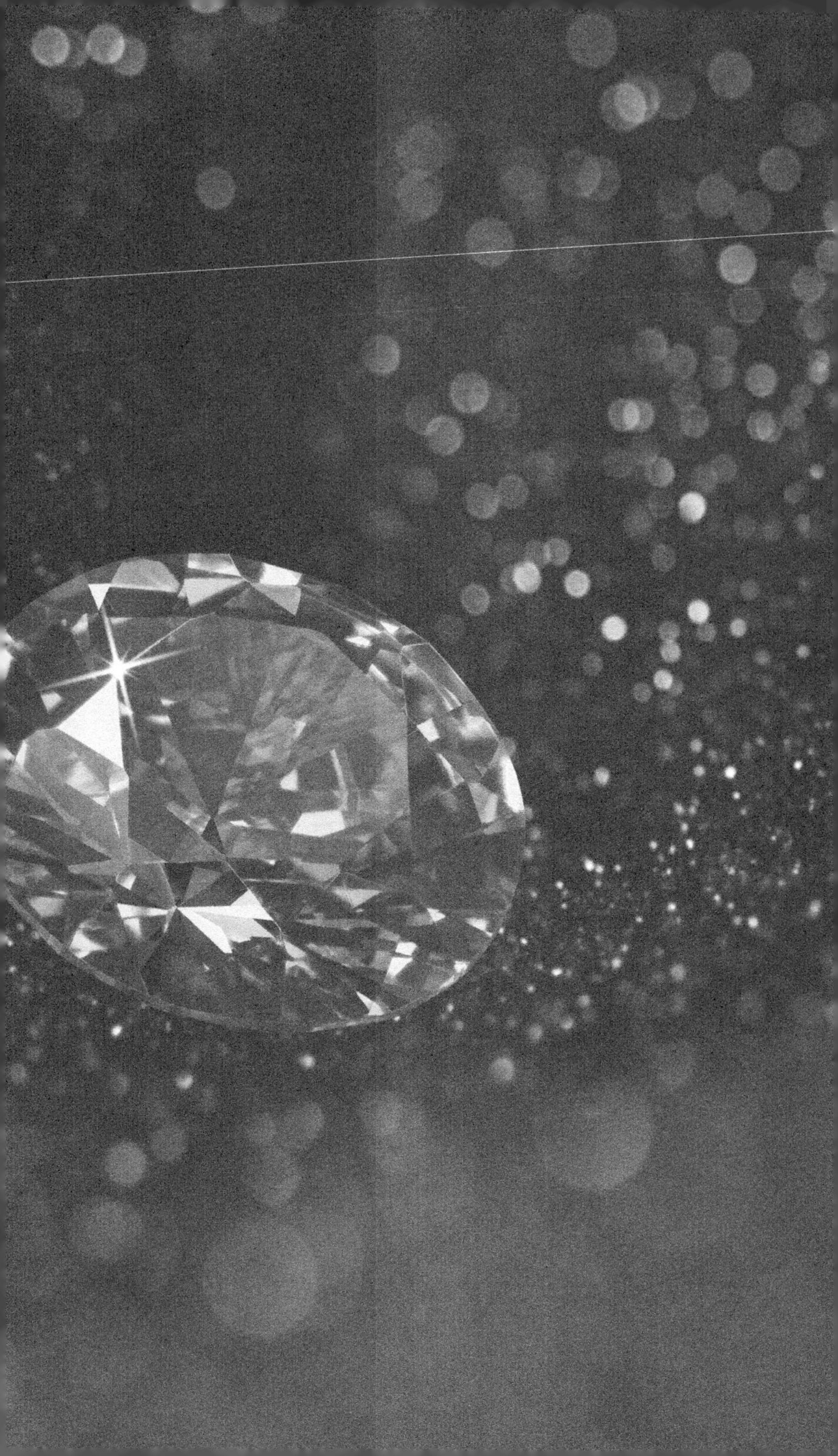

CHAPTER
SEVENTEEN

Sia

Thankfully, I didn't have to go without my phone for long. It was literally the only link I had to the outside world so I was appreciative that Lettie's dad got my phone back to me by the end of the day. He had Sophia get it to me, but what was curious was the only contacts that were in there were Mr. Petrov himself, Val, and Lettie when I got my phone back.

I texted him asking about that, and he said Val had an issue at the wireless store. Apparently, he sent her to get the phone which made me laugh because she did say he treated her like his assistant sometimes.

Anyway, Val informed him the wireless people accidentally deleted all my contacts. It wasn't like I had many. I mean, I basically had none but a few people I met through the years while growing up in the system. Actually, my lack of contacts was kind of pathetic, and the new ones I did have were from dating apps.

Of course those were gone now and something I couldn't recall from memory. I was kind of bummed about that. I hoped eventually Mr. Petrov would let me out of this house so I could actually have a social life soon.

And get laid...

That'd been getting bad, the itch. I was human and needed it. I wasn't terribly active in that department either, but I was well aware of the lack thereof since I only had my hand to do the job. I'd literally been getting off every night in the shower.

Mr. Petrov had been getting laid enough for the both of us.

I noticed something after that day at the pool, and that was all the *women* he brought through the house. Mr. Petrov apparently had an active social life and over the next few weeks, he seemed to have a new girl come through every night. Many of them wore designer silks and all of them were beautiful, mysterious...

I tried not to pay too much attention to them with the exception of the night I actually ran into one.

It was hard not to considering the way she looked.

The woman was filthy. She was still beautiful but *dirty*. Like grass and leaves in her hair and dirt on her face. She'd had it on her shins as well and her clothing had been torn. Her lipstick had also been smeared when I passed her in the kitchen.

She'd acted like she'd been in the most sophisticated of states when I spotted her through. Like all the dirt and leaves had been designer, and I'd been the one looking weird in my PJs. She had a glass of champagne in her hands, her look smug before she tipped her chin and strutted out of the room.

It'd been a very weird interaction, and I tried to put it out of my mind as I went to bed that night. I didn't want to think about what she and Maxim had been up to.

I kept referring to him in my head by his first name more and more. I wasn't sure why, but I was. I never called him that. Referring to him by his first name in person felt weird for some reason so I never did when we trained together with Polly.

He was in my head a lot unfortunately, too much. He was basically the only person I saw on a regular basis besides the household staff. Because of that, I thought about him a lot, and that was the only reason.

Yeah, keep telling yourself that.

I *would* keep telling myself that. Maxim was my employer, and I was his employee. Not to mention his daughter's friend.

I kept myself busy with Polly on a Friday night. The two of us often chilled by the fireplace in the Petrovs' grand living room. At least, I thought it was a living room. There were so many lounge areas in the huge manor.

Many times I found myself in the library. The Petrovs' had a huge one of those too, and I was an active reader. I enjoyed getting lost in fantasy worlds, and it was easy to do in such an old and mysterious home.

Tonight, though, I was rubbing Polly's back while going over my financial situation. I got paid weekly here, and my checks were adding up quickly. I could easily get myself a permanent place to stay for several months if the money kept growing.

I thought about my inevitable departure more and more lately. Especially since Maxim was doing so well with Polly. It'd get to the point where I knew he'd tell me he didn't need me anymore, and I needed to be prepared.

"Staying in tonight, Miss Reynolds?"

His tease came from the southernmost corner of the room. It was a tease because I never went out anywhere. He didn't allow it, and since my check-ins with the court could be done virtually over the computer, I really did have no reason to leave.

I opened my mouth to say something smart. He knew I didn't leave, and I had a habit of shooting off at the mouth when Maxim was being a jerk. The words paused in my throat when he entered the room though, his hair slicked back and a tuxedo on his brawny frame. Most of his tattoos were covered but not all. The ones on his fingers were exposed. He appeared so clean-cut, handsome.

My mouth closed, almost forgetting he was the same man who silenced a dude forever and killed a guy point blank in front of me. I found myself fearing him less and less as I interacted with him every day, and I wasn't sure how I felt about that.

I sat up, pushing my hair back as he entered the room and the fireplace light glided across his body. Some of his tattoos could also be seen from his neck collar, and that only made him more fine.

Shut down those thoughts.

It was so weird I saw him as anything other than my friend's dad. Granted, he was hot, but it was completely inappropriate. Then there was the fact that he was so dangerous.

I mean, he murdered a man.

Again, the fact I wasn't thinking about that right away whenever we were together freaked me out a bit. I stood, and when Polly did the same with me, Maxim raised his hand.

"Sit, Polly," he said, getting rather good at that. He smiled at her. "Can't get any hair on the tux, can we?"

Him joking with her meant he was bonding with her, and even though she did sit down, he reached down and petted her. It was a few gentle pats, brief, but that was progress. He used to be so scared of her, but he wouldn't ever admit that.

Now, he was a man with a dog, but there was also respect there. He respected her, and dare I say, enjoyed having her around. Anyone could see that even though he often tried to hide it. He wasn't fooling me though, his smile warm on her before he stood.

My stomach clenched that I really would be leaving this house soon, and I didn't know why. I mean, I really shouldn't want to be here. I was nothing but an employee, expendable. I chewed my lip. "So, I see you're going out tonight."

"Yes, to an event. I'll probably be returning late." I noticed he didn't have a date on his arm, but that didn't mean he wouldn't have one.

And why do you care?

Not caring, I folded my arms. "You know, I might go out if my owner said I could."

I said this with some sarcasm, and my jokes with him certainly were inappropriate. I didn't like being told what to do, and though I abided by his rules, I often voiced how I didn't like them. They often came out as jokes or something smart.

Again, not appropriate.

I found myself often testing this man who employed me, and the thing was, he rarely shot it down. If anything, I saw something electric hit his eyes whenever I did, and that often sent activity between my legs just like that day I spotted him naked at the pool.

I kept testing both of our boundaries, Maxim's grin wiry as he looked at me. I wasn't nearly as fancily dressed but for some reason my exposed shoulders caught his attention, my thighs in my terry cloth shorts that paired with my tank top… His head tilted. "I think you and I both know you can get anything you want around here. Like how you tested the estate's boundaries when you took Polly on a walk through the vineyards the other day."

Of course he knew about that. I grinned. "What can I say, your staff likes me."

I had a lot of time to get acquainted with everyone here, and he was right. If I wanted, I probably could go out. Attended, but I could. I walked right past his people when I walked Polly and all they did was smile and shake their heads at me before following along. I could go places if I wanted to.

I think maybe I was scared to, that Maxim would actually let me and once he did, the next move would be him telling me to leave.

Maxim's expression changed. I didn't know why, but something had his eyes narrowing.

"Maybe you should FaceTime with Lettie," he suggested, and I shook my head. I normally did chat with Lettie, but with her being in school I didn't want to bother her.

"It's Friday night. She should have a social life." I sat on the arm of a couch, happy when Polly got up and went to Maxim instead of me. He didn't deny her, petting her again, and I hated to admit it, but I loved seeing him with her. He'd really let his guard down and their sweet interactions were becoming the highlights of my days here.

That and Maxim's nightly swims.

It was terrible, but I still watched him. I mean, he did it *right* within view of my window, and I couldn't help it. I blamed it on the fact that I hadn't gotten laid lately, and Maxim was nothing but a visual object I saw before going to bed at night. And if I happened to put my hand between my legs as I fell asleep…

I knew I was a terrible person for this, and probably would be going to hell. I always felt super guilty whenever I did it since he was my friend's dad, but at least Maxim was never around after my fingerings for me to face that guilt. He always seemed to be gone the mornings after. He'd go into work early or have some other engagement.

As if he knew what I was thinking, his eyes smoldered in my direction. The connection was brief before his attention transferred to Polly. At one point, he tried to stop petting her, but she wouldn't let him. He laughed. "I will say, Miss Reynolds, you are a miracle worker. I believe this dog actually likes me."

And he liked her. I laughed too. "That's all you. You did the work. Showed up and trained with her."

"Yes, but without your instruction it wouldn't have been possible."

He was doing that more and more lately: being kind. I never thought I'd see it. Especially in my direction.

"You're good with dogs, but also with people," he said, standing. "I'm honestly surprised you're not attempting to do any classes while you're working. I wouldn't mind if you did. You have a long road to becoming a doctor, and you might as well get started with some of your prerequisites now. There's a local community college here. I can speak to someone about getting you set up."

I was surprised he offered. Again, being kind.

I rubbed my arm. "That's okay. I'm in no rush."

I really wasn't, my eyes averting.

"Well, when you're ready I'm sure you'll shine. You have a gift of putting things back together that's for sure. You'll make a great surgeon."

I didn't know what he meant by that, and by the time I glanced up, he was looking away.

"Anyway, don't stay up too late," he said, teasing again. I probably wouldn't. Actually, I'd probably retire soon after taking a bath.

I mean, I had enough bath products. I came back from a walk with Polly with a closet full of stuff. There was stuff for a bath yes, but also stuff for my hair. There were shampoos, hair lotions, and all for black hair. The bath products had also been for medium and darker skin complexions.

I'd been shocked seeing it and mentioned it to Val in passing. She often circulated the house and said she'd had Sophia buy things for me, but this had been at the request of Maxim himself. He apparently asked Val what I needed after I requested the silk pillowcase. I got that the next day of course and the bath and hair products came soon after.

This had been the first instance of outward kindness he'd showed toward me outside of what he'd done at the bar, and I think that was why I hadn't been able to get over this little feeling I got whenever he was around. My stomach would do things, a flutter or something.

It came back when he nodded at me before leaving the room. He left Polly and me to our own devices, and I really needed to get over this little crush I had on a man almost twice my age.

Because that was all it was.

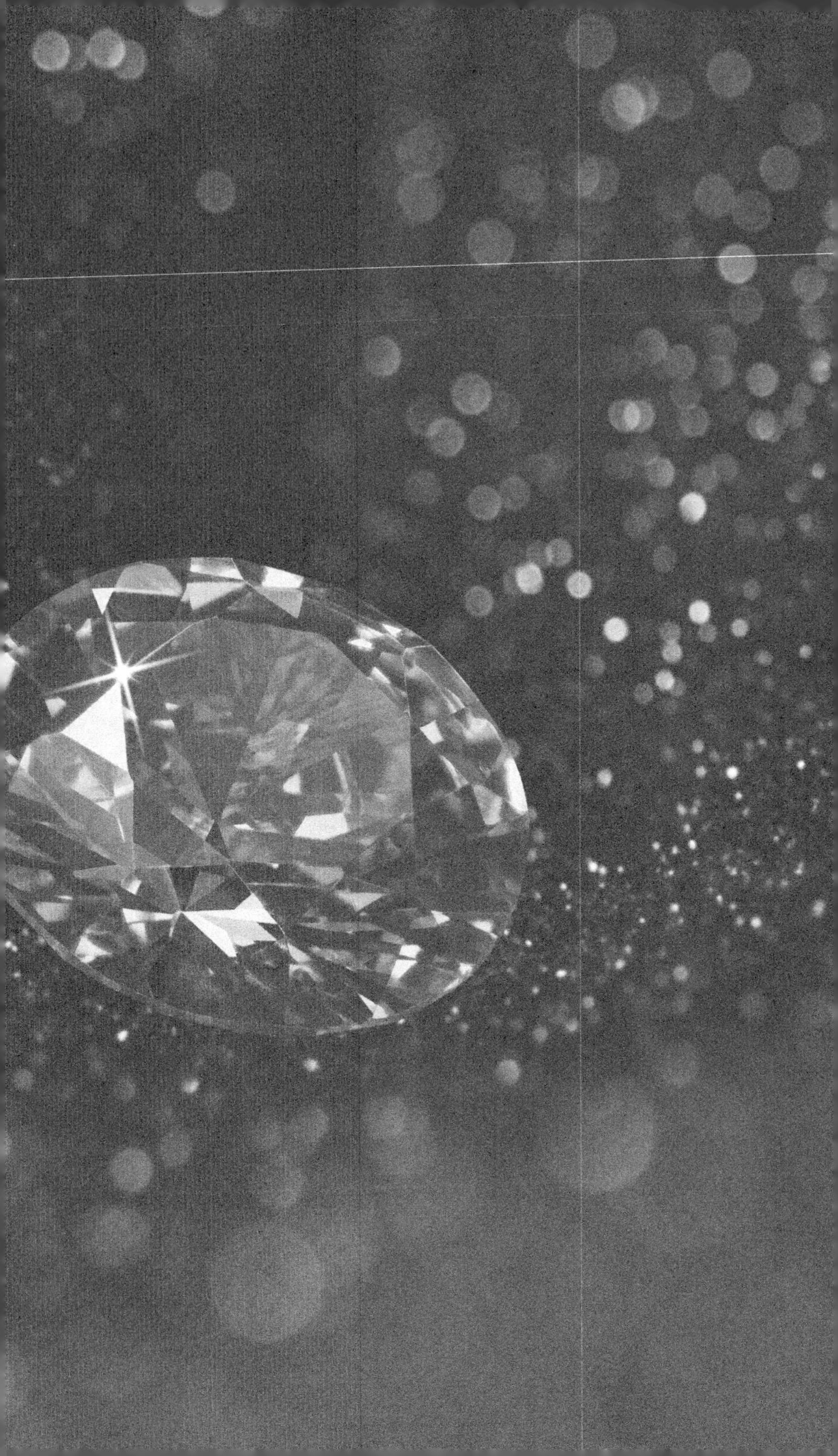

CHAPTER EIGHTEEN

Sia

My head lifted from the couch.

I'd fallen asleep.

Yawning, I sat up, unsure of the hour, but it was still dark outside. I gazed around and immediately stiffened.

"Polly," I said, well aware she was gone, and I was in this room by myself. I never made it upstairs last night. I'd fallen asleep, and she'd definitely been laying on the couch with me when I did. I pushed my hair out of my face. "Polly?"

I whistled for her, but she didn't respond.

Why the fuck had I fallen asleep?

Or rather why had I left her unattended while I slept. She was a good dog, but if she heard anything in the house she'd go running. She'd be curious and still did that.

I got up, calling her name through the room. She was big enough so it was obvious she wasn't in here.

"Polly?" I called out, heading into the hallway. She'd clearly left the room. The door was ajar. "Polly?"

I only heard my own voice as I padded quickly down the

hallway. My phone told me it was just after two and who knew if Maxim had gotten home yet. He may be getting along with Polly, but I had a feeling her being loose in his home wouldn't sit well.

I picked up my pace, calling for her, but she didn't show herself. She must be out of earshot because she'd definitely come if I called her. I'd trained her to do that.

Christ.

I peered in every room I could find in my path, even the areas she probably couldn't get into. I was paranoid though. She was a really good dog, but she hadn't had a lot of temptation to get into anything. I kept her pretty close so if she was free she could certainly get into something.

"Polly," I whisper-shouted, my voice low. If Maxim was home, I didn't want him to catch me calling for her. "Polly, where are you?"

She didn't answer, and I felt like an idiot. I was calling out for her as if she'd respond like a person.

I closed the door of the last room I looked into. I headed around a corner and spotted another room with a door that was ajar.

I gazed inside, and right away, I knew what room this was. I passed Maxim's office every day when I came downstairs.

But normally, the door wasn't open.

I cursed, pushing it open more. Immediately, I assumed Maxim may be in there, but he wasn't. That didn't make me less anxious about going in there though.

"Polly," I whispered, gazing around. Maxim had a wide office, built-in shelves and a fireplace he probably used when he was actually here. Tonight everything lay dormant, and rather than be caught in here by anyone in the Petrov household, I immediately headed toward the door after confirming a certain German Shepherd hadn't made her way in here.

At least, I would have if not for the *sounds*.

Steps occurred outside in the hall. It was a heavy cadence, and I backed up into the room, cursing again. There wasn't really anywhere to hide.

I decided to go for the desk with a single MacBook and portable mouse on the top. The computer was closed, and I got beneath the desk.

"I don't care how much the information costs, Val."

Maxim signed while he said it, gazing at his phone screen. I'd peered around the desk and could see him. His tuxedo tie was undone, his jacket off, and his dark hair was strewn about as if he'd been dancing or socializing all night.

I tucked myself deep under his desk and covered my mouth.

I tried not to breathe.

I had no reason for being in his office that he'd be particularly happy to hear about. For some reason, I cared that he'd be upset that I lost track of Polly and was in here. When I first got here, I wouldn't have given a shit. I would have told him the facts and dealt with the consequences.

So why did I care about disappointing him now?

It was this stupid fucking crush I decided to get on an older man, and I knew that.

Sighing, I placed my hands on the floor, attempting to remain as quiet as I could until he left.

"Just get it *done*," he urged, speaking while I assumed he signed. He sounded agitated more than angry. He shut off the phone, and I knew because he tossed it on his desk.

And then he sat down in his chair.

He wheeled it under the desk, and I backed up as far as I could. He had a pretty large desk, but still it was tight quarters.

I hugged my legs to make myself smaller. I placed my hand on my mouth again, so scared to fucking breathe.

Maxim cursed before stamping his powerful legs out

under his desk. I heard him click around his computer for a bit, and his next move was to reach beneath the desk.

He went for his fly.

He ripped it down, and his hand slipped inside. He pulled his cock out, and his heady scent filled the entirety of the space beneath the desk.

My mouth watered, his hand massaging a steel cock as he pleasured himself like a foot away from my face. I'd seen him do this before, after his nightly swims, but he was often just washing himself.

This was different, him being this close, him *getting off*. His cock was perfect, and I couldn't help getting closer.

I wanted to taste him.

Resisting, I just watched in fascination as his strokes picked up pace. This wasn't like outside. This wasn't a guy just taking a shower. This was *a man* pleasing himself, the veins of his cock thick and pulsing in his hand. Some precum dewed at the tip, and my mouth opened.

I got stupid.

I got so close then and could almost...taste him. I closed my eyes and might have...

Had he not said my name.

My eyes shot open as a charged *Sia* left from his lips. His cock jerked, and he met the sensation by blowing his load into a tissue. He caught it all, his legs spasming, and I was jealous I didn't actually get to taste him.

He said my name.

I was still in shock when he balled the tissue up. He quickly zipped his pants, and the next thing I knew, he exited the room. The door slammed behind him, and I just sat there for a moment, not really knowing what just happened.

But then, I looked at his computer.

He left it opened, and I noticed something right away. I was on his computer screen, a still image of me. There were actually several images, different angles of my room, but the still image of me was in the shower.

I pressed play, seeing me move around in warm mist. I was pleasuring myself too, but I didn't know what day. I lost track of how many times I got off lately after watching Maxim swim outside.

I covered my mouth, my heart beating fast. He'd not only been recording me, but he got off to the image of me. I should be horrified. I should literally find Polly and get the fuck out of this house ASAP. I shouldn't be fascinated that he watched me, pleasured himself to the sight of me...

And I definitely shouldn't be disappointed that he came into a tissue instead of on me.

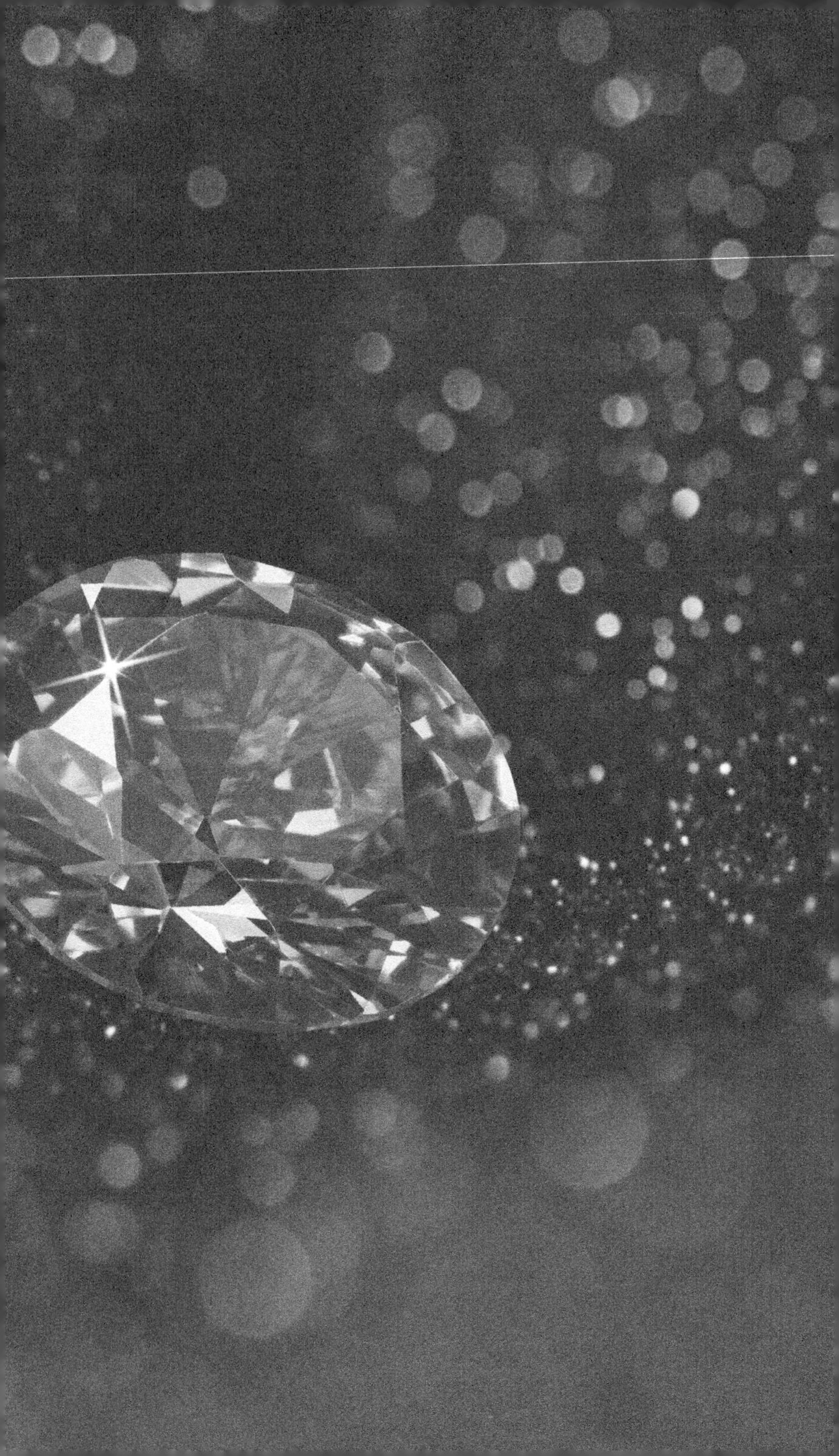

CHAPTER NINETEEN

Maxim

"Would you like to go to work with me today?"

Sia dropped her fork in response. It hit her plate with a clank before toppling to the floor, and when she bent to get it, I lifted my hand.

I snapped at Sophia, who jumped into action. She got Sia's fallen fork, and one of my butlers came in with a fresh utensil.

Sophia placed the fork down in front of Sia after receiving it from my butler, and Sia's nod was curt in response.

"Thank you," she said. She placed her napkin on her lap again.

That had also fallen to the floor.

Sophia had gotten that as well before returning to her position by the wall.

My brow lifted. "Sia?"

I'd been trying to call her by her name more. I only called her by her last name when I was teasing her lately, and these shared mealtimes were new as well. In all honestly, we'd both kind of fallen into them. This was the best time I had to discuss Polly with her before going to work, and since she needed to eat...

Sia usually *did* eat, but that seemed not to be the case today. She appeared to be a little nervous this morning, unsettled. Polly must have noticed this too because she approached Sia from the corner. She'd been sitting on her dog bed.

That was also new, Polly eating in the same room as myself. She often had her breakfast while we had ours, and I didn't scold Sia when she gave Polly a piece of bacon off her plate.

I never did.

"Everything all right?" I asked, curious why she was unsettled. Not to mention, she still hadn't answered me.

"Sorry, uh. What did you ask?" Wiping (what I assumed) was bacon grease off her hands, she picked up her fork again. She started dancing it around the eggs on her plate, and I smiled a little.

"I asked if you wanted to come to work with me?" I repeated, and finished with my own breakfast, I wiped my mouth. I cleaned my plate. Sophia prepared eggs and toast for me this morning. I leaned forward. "I just hired a new embalmer. He used to be a surgeon. Anyway, I figured you might want to ask him some questions."

This made sense considering her ultimate goals for herself in regards to employment, and I still didn't know why she wasn't in school. She was a very smart girl, and that was easy to pick up on since I'd been working with her closely. She had knowledge when it came to Polly, yes, but was quite intelligent in so many other ways. It made me wonder about some of the choices that landed her here in my home, but I was the last one to judge about someone's past.

I'd had a lot of time with this girl my daughter had forced on me. I actually found myself showing up to work late some days just to have more time to work with her and the dog, and that was something I was definitely aware of.

"He's a surgeon, but he came to work for you?" she asked, poking at her eggs, but she also poked at me with her question. She liked to do that, and it used to annoy me.

Used to...

It still annoyed me, but in an entirely different way. I gave into that annoyance last night, and I wished it were the first time. I placed my hand on the table. "I pay him well."

She nodded, hiding beneath a veil of her vibrant curls. I wasn't sure what was wrong with her, but eventually, she nodded again. "Sure, I'll come."

"Are you sure?" I didn't want to make her do anything she didn't want to do. I used to not care.

Again, used to.

"Yes, I'd like to go," she concluded, and I ignored how that made my chest feel. Like boulders had been lifted, and I was now seeing fucking clouds like a legitimate asshole. Like a right fucking idiot who was damn near *excited* that she wanted to come to work with me.

Shaking my head, I watched her get up from the table. She got Polly's lead. "Just let me take her back to her room."

"I can do it." And in all honestly, she usually made me. She wanted me to bond with Polly.

I called her, and when Polly came right over to me, I didn't miss Sia's smile. Nor how it made my insides feel (again) after I clearly pleased her.

I cleared my throat. "I'll have someone get the car ready."

Sia was out in my Mercedes when I arrived outside, her petite body tucked into the seat. She had on a short leather jacket, and her legs were crossed while she waited for me. The white cigarette pants she wore hugged the expanse of her shapely legs, and I wet my lips.

"You look nice," I said, causing her to jump for the second time today. Apparently, she didn't hear me open my own door? I got inside and closed it. "No shorts and a ketchup-stained t-shirt I see."

I was obviously teasing her, and I did sometimes. Normally, she dressed more casually. This reflected her age, but today, she appeared years older, her hair up and her neck exposed.

Her face turned red. She shrugged. "Sophia got me some new clothes," she said, rubbing her arm. She glanced up. "I wanted to look nice."

My head tilted. She did look nice, older. I put my sunglasses on. "You okay?"

It was fine she wanted to look nice, I guess, but we were just going to my place of work where there were clearly dead bodies (and sometimes parts) lying around. I wasn't going to allow her to see any of that today, but still. Those were the facts.

She was fidgeting now.

In her seat, she wriggled beside me, and I hesitated moving the car.

"Yeah, I'm good," she said, which prompted me to finally start the car. She faced the road as we started to move. "Just anxious I guess. I get to meet your doctor friend so I'm anxious."

She was anxious as in excited or uneasy? I frowned. "Are you sure you want to go? You don't have to, and I don't want you to if doing so will trigger you."

Messing with her sobriety wouldn't be a good idea.

"No, I'm okay. I swear." She started to laugh now, and that fucked with me in a different way.

Gripping the wheel, I headed us toward Peters & Burg, and on the way, Sia informed me she'd been doing well in regard to her triggers. That came up from time to time. Like stated, I'd been spending a lot of time with this girl, and it was natural to hear about what she was going through in her day to day.

I kept my own life closer to the cuff, but I enjoyed hearing about hers. It kept my mind off other things I was dealing with lately, and I had noticed the jellybeans in the cabinet hadn't been going as frequently. It was good she was getting a handle on things. Really good.

It took effort, but I fought myself from asking Sia more questions during our drive. She did seem nervous, but I needed to lay off. Frankly, I was battling my own triggers at the present. Like the incessant pull I had to look at her every five fucking seconds, or the shit I had gotten up to last night.

Again, it hadn't been the first time.

It had been a while since I'd given in though, into her. I was dealing with some shit at work and...

Peters & Burg couldn't come into view soon enough. Sia's *scent* kept hitting the breeze, and I thought I might do something stupid like forget this girl was nearly half my age and my daughter's friend.

"Sia, this is Dr. Barinov," I said once we made it inside. We were downstairs with the doctor, but nowhere near where I'd previously taken her. The place where bodies were embalmed was in a different part of the facility. We had legitimate operations around here, even though the funeral homes themselves were just a cover.

Sia never asked about that during our time together. Not that I would inform her about the logistics regarding my business. She did like to poke though. I did as well, but I noticed we'd both been doing that less and less.

"Nice to meet you," Sia said, shaking the doctor's hand. His assistant, Greta, was with him, and when she winked at me, I lifted my head. I normally didn't dip my quill in the office ink, but lately, I hadn't wanted to fuck with the dating apps to get my fix. I had specific needs that sometimes women on the kink apps couldn't even handle. Greta was aware of my...needs and was very accommodating.

I was seeing my mistake by mixing business with pleasure now though as the woman came over to me. She was older, more mature and certainly fit my type. Not to mention, she was age appropriate...

Glancing away from an approaching Greta, I studied Sia. She was chatting with the doctor. We'd all started to walk the facility a bit, but she and the doctor were in their own conversation so they got behind.

"I had a good time the other night," Greta said, distracting me from the clear joy Sia was getting by conversing with the doctor. Her whole face was lighting up, but the simple joy *I got* from her joy was stolen by Greta. Greta grinned. "A real good time."

I made the mistake of letting her stay at my home recently. I did with my partners from time to time, but I worked with this woman and knew better.

"Hmm," I said, once again distracted by Sia. I think it was those fucking pants, and unlike Greta, I hadn't had a good time. In fact, I'd jerked off (after I hadn't gotten off) following our play session, and that was easy to do once I'd gone downstairs to my computer. I had hours and hours of footage to pull my dick out to, and I was aware of how fucked up that was.

But it certainly hadn't stopped me from doing it.

This *thing* with Sia was getting out of control and was turning into a borderline obsession. Breaking her phone and clearing it of all contacts but myself and my staff was one thing, but jerking off to the image of her was another...

I decided to ignore my recent (indecent) time with my computer, and I was forced to engage with Greta when she got close. "I'd love to see you again, Maxim."

"Unfortunately, I find myself very busy lately," I said, certainly more politely than I normally would have. "I'll let you know if that changes."

Something else I noticed was I wasn't an asshole when it came to people's feelings lately. This was obviously Sia's doing again. Her patience, her kindness...

At this point, Dr. Barinov was leading Sia inside the area where he normally worked. Again, it was clear. I had no intention of exposing her to anything graphic, and when I caught sight of Val, I gestured her over.

Val waved at Sia on her journey over, and I couldn't thank my head of security enough for helping me find what Sia needed for her hair. I had no idea about even the most basic things she needed. Val definitely had schooled me on things.

"Sia, I'm going to leave you with the doctor, and he can answer any questions you have from here," I said. I spoke to her, but signed for Val.

Sia's back had been turned while I was speaking. She'd still be chatting with the doctor, but turned. She might have had a response for me, but rather than wait for it, I headed off with Val to start work for the day. This was partially to avoid Greta, but also to put distance between myself and Sia. We needed distance.

I needed distance.

My head was starting to cloud lately with thoughts of the girl who worked for me, and that was dangerous. It was for many reasons, but the main ones had to do with distractions. My head couldn't be fucking clouded right now.

"I'm sorry, Boss, but I couldn't find anything," Val signed as we walked through the facility, something we often did. She'd brief me on interior operations, but lately, I had her working on something else.

She handed me a folder today, and I stared at it. It was a log of children both adopted and not adopted during a certain time period I was interested in. Nothing Val had contained the information I was looking for though.

Acting unfazed, I snapped the folder shut.

"Who is the girl to you?" Val signed before taking back the folder. She popped it under her arm. *"Is this something for Natan..."*

"This is beyond Natan," I admitted. Val was as good at

catching bullshit as myself, so it was best to stick as close to the truth as possible. *"The girl's father owes me a debt."*

This wasn't a lie either, so my signs came easy. I told Val to keep hunting, but kept my instruction casual. I even told her there was no rush on getting me the information.

There might not be need for a rush, but that didn't stop me from asking her to pursue the endeavor. I couldn't help having her look into certain things for me, paranoid. It might not be warranted, but I didn't leave loose ends. Never in all my years in the Brotherhood did I do such things. I, Maxim Petrov, didn't make mistakes.

Except for the one time I had.

I left Val to do her work so I could check in with people who required my attention on the actual business side of, well, my business. There were a lot of moving parts I oversaw for the Bratva, and most of our operations were legitimate. It kept the police from sniffing around and the city's officials from breathing down our necks.

I was with staff when Val found me.

"You have to see this," she signed, and after excusing myself, I followed her. My head of security didn't appear alarmed, but she didn't look at ease either.

"What's going on," I started signing, but stopped. I saw right away what was going on the moment we made it down into my personal workspace.

The room wasn't empty.

A curly haired woman stood by my knives, a wall of them in front of her.

She'd opened the case.

"What is she doing in there?" I signed behind a two-way mirror. I could see inside the room, but those inside couldn't see out here. That was its purpose. Sia couldn't see me.

But I could see her.

She was analyzing my tools under a curious eye, but she

didn't appear frightened. Her hand hovered, not quite touching anything.

I braced the mirror's frame. I should go in there and rip her out, but for some reason, I was waiting for Val's response. Sia was in there alone, and Dr. Barinov wasn't in sight.

"From what I understand, she left the doctor and excused herself to go to the bathroom," Val signed. *"When she didn't come back I was alerted."*

Sia's hand lowered, and I did nothing but watch her. Her head cocked at the metal I used to filet skin and saw limbs. But again, she didn't appear as if she was scared.

I wet my lips.

"What should I do?" Val's signs were slow, and it wasn't often I saw one of my most trusted hesitant. She didn't want to act, but she would if I needed her to. Sia had crossed a clear line by going in there, and in my world, I didn't allow that. I'd cut off a hand just because Sia got close.

Instead, I had my hands on the mirror frame. I debated how to act as well and definitely tried to ignore certain things. Like how my cock was just as hard as it was when I watched this girl in the shower. I enjoyed watching her touch herself, explore herself.

But her hand around one of my knives...

Envisioning such a thing had me dismissing Val to handle this invasion of privacy myself. I entered the room and got behind Sia, her coconut smell making me want to take one of those knives to her delicate throat. She deserved to be punished for being in here, tempting me... "What are you doing in here, *malyshka*?"

She jumped a little, but, curiously, only slightly. The tension was mostly in her shoulders, but she didn't turn around. Her head tipped, her sight on nothing but the knives.

"What's this for?" she asked, gesturing to one. She finally faced me when she did, and I noticed the width of her eyes.

How big they'd gotten, how fascinated... Her throat bobbed. "Besides the obvious."

The obvious being I used it to dice and filet? My eyes narrowed. "Why are you in here, Sia?"

It was dangerous for both of us, her being in here, and she didn't answer me. Instead, she raised her hand as if she would touch one of my tools, and my back straightened.

It did the same time my dick pulsed.

"Each one," she continued as if I'd never spoken. She resisted the urge to touch and test me further. "What do you use each one for?"

Surely, she knew. Not the specifics of course, but...

I was unsure what she wanted from me in that moment, but I certainly knew what I wanted from her. I wanted to touch her, take a blade and study its gleam against her skin. I wanted to *test her* and see how far she'd let me go. My demon begged for it, maddened by it.

Reaching around her, I took one of the knives she pointed toward and her breath hitched. She didn't back away though. Was she not scared? My nose glided along the space above her ear.

"This one is when I don't want to make it quick," I said, unsure of why I was saying this to her in my space. There was something about her being here though. It excited me, enlivened me. A noise rumbled in my chest. "When I want them to suffer."

I did want my clients to suffer sometimes, and not just for the job. It was because I got off on spilling blood just as much as playtime with submissives. I didn't consider myself a dominant, but I enjoyed a scene in which I got to chase my prey from time to time. I hadn't always been this way, but once I went that way, I easily found what I liked.

Control.

I was finding it hard in this moment, the blade now against the column of Sia's neck. I was aware Val could be watching, but for some reason, I was testing boundaries. The thought of spilling Sia Reynolds' blood disgusted me as much as it drove my cock toward the brink of splitting my fucking pants I was so hard.

I pressed it against her, and the breath she took in fogged the glass door of the knife case. She hadn't opened it all the way. Her eyes closed. "And when you do want to make it quick?"

What the fuck?

I had her throat in my hand so quick. I *could taste* this girl she was so close, and my mouth opened. "This one," I stated, directing her eyes that way with a glance. My hands didn't dare leave her. I didn't trust myself not to hurt her or indulge in what I really wanted.

What I'd been wanting for a long time.

These were dangerous thoughts, and though I didn't know how long I had them, I did know they existed now. I could see Sia in a scene of play, in my bed cut up and spent after I chased her, fucked her. I'd tend to her, one of my favorite parts, then fuck her again once she was ready.

I had to physically keep my monster at bay. I wasn't ashamed by it, but I didn't like losing control of it either. How easily I could let it take over.

It *was* taking over.

I had my hands on a twenty-year-old girl who was my daughter's friend, and I may have acted on the desire to do more had not my phone rang.

And my daughter's ring tone sounded.

The soft chirp was like a slap to the face and my cock, sobering me. I pulled away from Sia and took the device out. I answered on a breath. "Hi, love."

Sia just stood there, blinking too. I was doing the same to come back to myself and was definitely trying to focus on what my daughter was telling me. It took me a moment, but once I heard her, *I heard her*.

"I'm upstairs, Dad," she said, laughing. She had a great laugh. Like her mother and the only good thing she got from her. The woman abandoned her child, but at least I got my daughter. Lettie was one I never saw coming, but once I had her, my life was forever changed.

"Sorry, love. What?" I questioned, still trying to get my head back, and by now, Sia was facing me. So much red had hit her cheeks. I wanted to lick it, then spread her out on my bed. It made me sick that I had these thoughts.

She was so innocent.

I had no idea what this was today, but whatever it'd been was a bad idea.

"I'm home. I'm here at your office. Upstairs. Can I come find you?" Lettie continued. "I'm here for the weekend. It was supposed to be a surprise."

I was definitely surprised, and I think Sia was too. I put Lettie on speaker because I really wasn't hearing her.

I was now and I immediately left Sia. I literally left her standing there and passed Val on the way. She had been watching us behind the mirror.

I couldn't determine the look Val was giving, but that was in the back of my mind as I went to look for Lettie. I never allowed her into the burrows of where I worked, and she was the most important thing.

She was all that mattered.

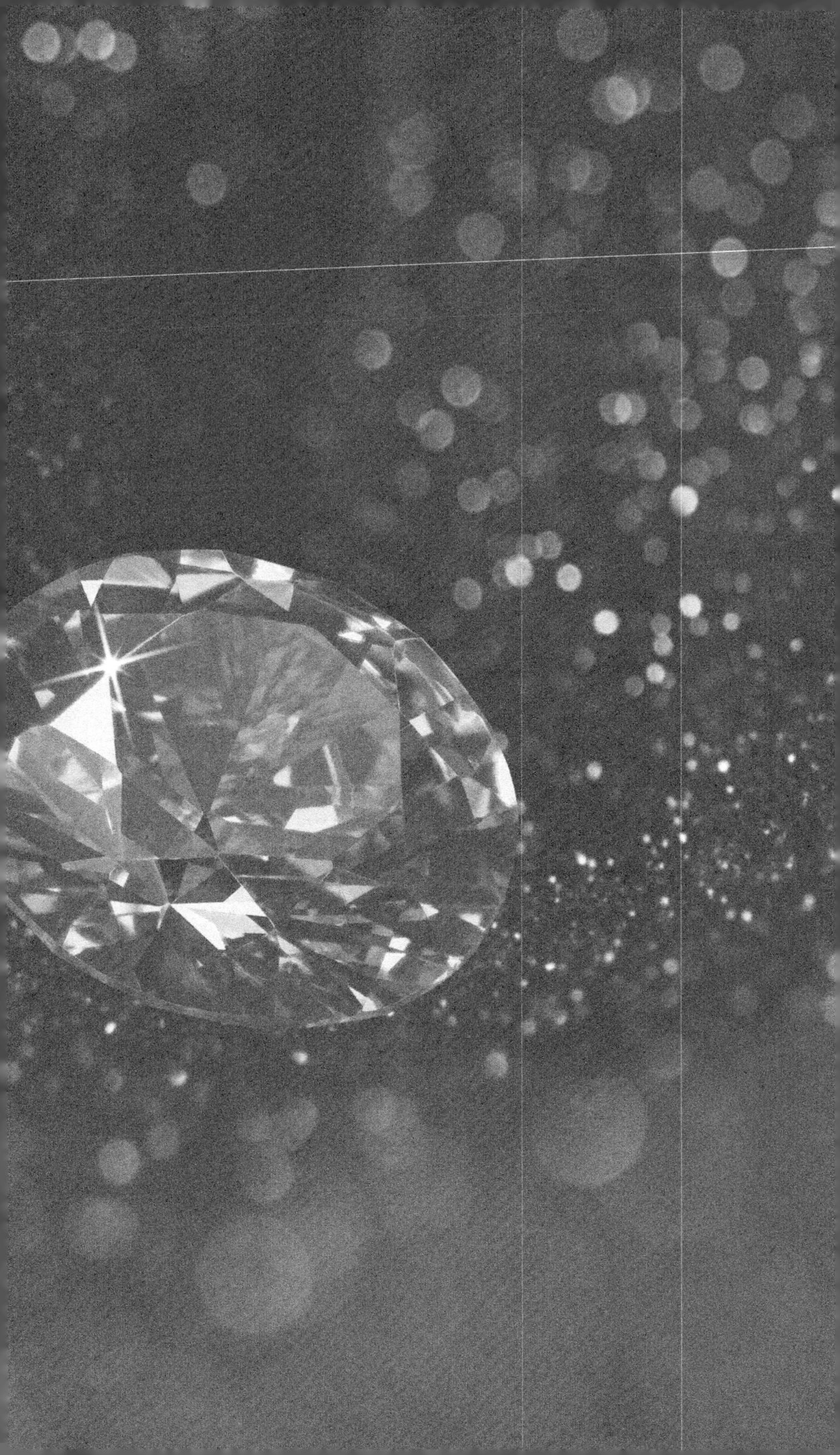

CHAPTER TWENTY

Sia

"So you and my dad are obviously getting along," Lettie said, and my head shot up. We were in her room, and I watched as she unpacked her things. We'd all come back to the Petrov manor after her impromptu visit to her dad's office. She smiled. "I mean, he let you come to Peters & Burg with him. He doesn't even let me do that, usually."

My heart settled after she clarified her statement, and I hugged one of her many pillows. I sat on her bed as she unloaded three bags worth of stuff for what she said would be a weekend stay. She'd literally just come to surprise her dad. She came to surprise *me* and said that.

The guilt sat heavy that I was here and just…silent. Truth be told, I had no idea what was about to happen before she'd called, but Maxim and I had been close before he stopped, *his cock* close…

Mr. Petrov.

He was Mr. Petrov, and I'd been stupid. Odds were nothing was about to happen. It was true I'd come onto him after what I'd seen him do in his office, and *yes*, he grabbed me, touched me, but he also had a knife to my throat.

It'd been hot.

It got to me on a primal level, and I...loved it.

He'd probably been about to turn you down.

He no doubt saw me as a young, *naïve* girl, and yeah, he'd gotten off to a naked video of me, but he could have done that with anyone.

But the fact he took the video...

I couldn't so easily write that off. He had taken a video of me, and he used it. He'd done that in his most intimate moments, and I couldn't get that out of my head.

Lettie's look was curious. Probably because I was just sitting there silent and had been since we got to her house. I answered all her questions about how I was and what was going on with one or two word answers. I was too in my head.

She stared at Polly on the bed and grinned. "Also, he knows Polly's in here and hasn't said anything."

He definitely knew because Polly followed us upstairs. She gave me a fright the night she'd gotten lost, but I obviously found her. Anyway, Maxim had taken Lettie's bags up here for her after we got home and hadn't minded when Polly followed us. He even hadn't said anything when Polly had gotten on the bed, and Lettie nearly fainted when she saw that. Things had certainly changed since she'd left for college.

You've changed.

I felt like I betrayed my friend by gaining a crush on her dad. Not to mention coming on to him. God.

Maxim had even come to check on us at one point and hadn't made eye contact with me at all. If anything, he ignored me, which told me everything I needed to know. I made a mistake and probably was just a body for him to jerk off to. I mean, how could I be anything more? I was around his daughter's age, and how did I even feel about him? Weeks ago, I hated him.

I chewed my lip. "He and Polly have been getting closer."

"And that's obviously because of you," Lettie said. She looked great of course *and strong*. I thought she'd had a dancer's body before, but she'd come home jacked. She was lean and chiseled like a fitness model. She sat on the bed in her white dress. "I'm glad it's worked out. Dad even seems happier."

Did he?

Stop it.

These were the thoughts of a kid, and I wasn't being fair to my friend. I should have never acted on a crush, and it was a betrayal after she'd gotten me a job and let me live in her home.

"How's your semester been so far?" I questioned, wanting to talk about anything but my naïveté. I rubbed my arm. "Fun?"

"Well, fun is subjective with how hard they're making us work and midterms were shit, but I think I did okay."

That was good. I nodded. "I want to hear all about it. I'm sure it's been way more exciting than my time here."

I felt like I was lying to her, but it didn't stop me from asking the question and wanting to get certain thoughts out of my head. Thoughts about her dad and how exhilarating it'd been to have his hands on me today. How I wondered if he'd hurt me, but in the back of my mind knew he wouldn't. I'd wanted to test him and feel the danger of him around me. It'd been a different kind of drug. It'd been...

"Sia?"

I blinked, and Lettie laughed. She lounged on her arm, petting Polly. "I was saying we should go to a party tonight. I want to see my boyfriend. His frat is having one."

I couldn't remember the guy's name, but I knew she was seeing someone. It was nice to know they were still making things work with the distance. She'd said he stayed here and went to school at the local college.

I didn't really want to go to a party.

Perhaps that's why you need to go.

"Sounds fun," I said, and Lettie hugged me. She had always been affectionate and maybe a night out with her would get me over this little fascination I had with her dad. I highly doubted what happened today was what I thought it was.

It was time I acted my age.

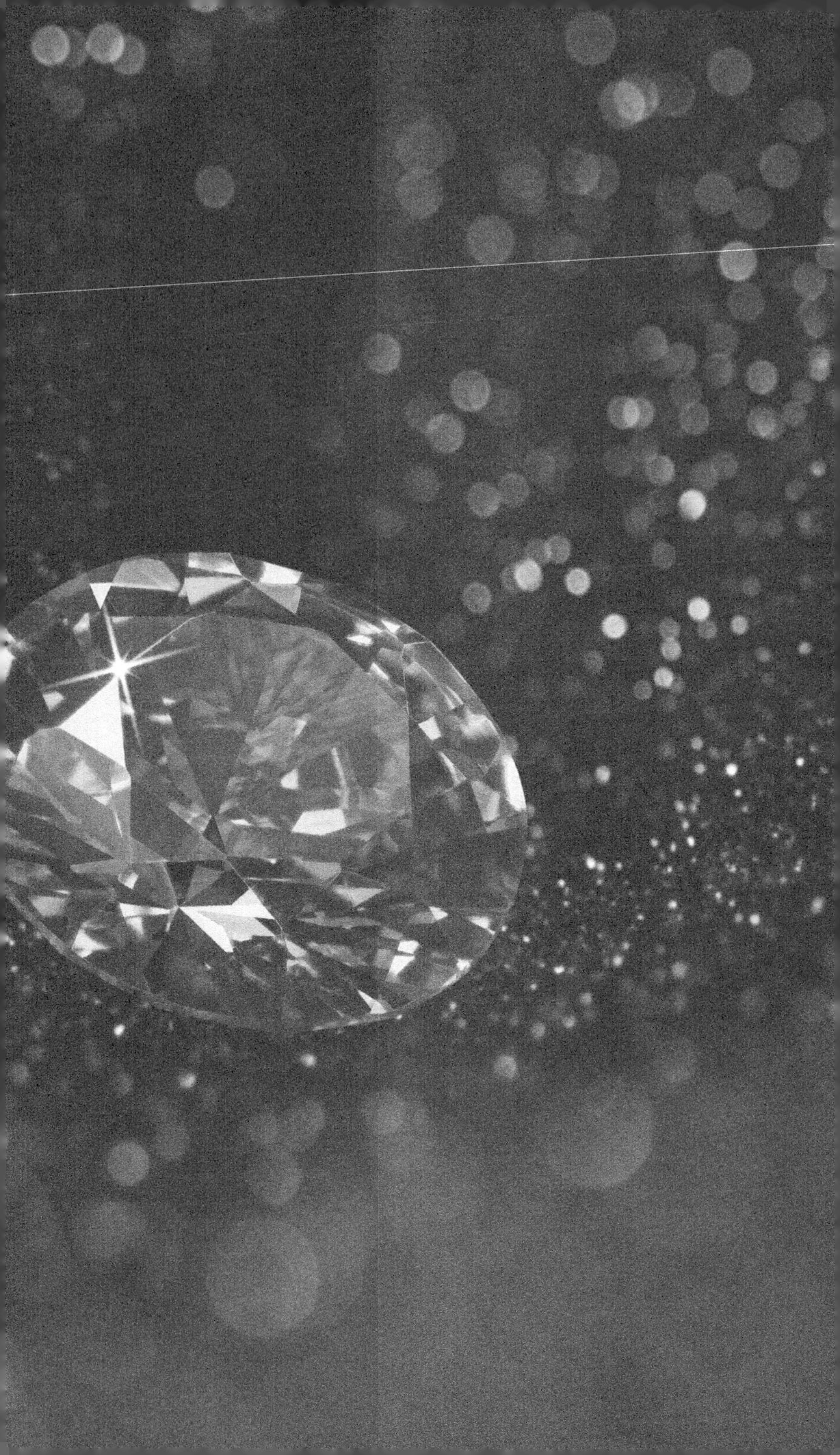

CHAPTER
TWENTY-ONE

Maxim

I tossed my phone on my fucking desk, growling. My daughter had taken Sia to some party.

And Sia had some guy on her.

Some random fucker *had his arm* around Sia, and it took all I had not to blow up my daughter's phone and ask her where they both were. It'd been against my better judgement to let Sia go with Lettie at all. She wasn't allowed off the grounds.

I told her that.

Of course I couldn't enforce that without hearing it from my daughter. She'd fight and tell me I was being unreasonable when it came to my staff. *My* staff…

Mine.

I wet my lips, blocking out the fact that I'd stalked Lettie's social media for the better part of an hour. That was how I found out Sia was being touched. It was a group shot with Lettie and her friends, but even Lettie's *boyfriend* hadn't been hugged up on her as much as that dude was on Sia. He had his hand on her bare shoulder, his fingers on her brown skin...

I needed a run.

Recently, I'd been taking Polly with me on my runs. She was good about trotting beside me, and after getting into shorts and a cut-off tee, I took her out into the vineyard.

I ran us both ragged. In fact, the property turned dark around us as the sun set, the grapes changing from dark purple to black. I made wine in my spare time when I had an iota of it to do leisurely activities.

That was before Sia and what was clearly turning into an obsession with her. My hobbies had completely fallen by the wayside lately, my evenings spent with her instead. I still watched her on the Sia Cam, but stopped watching her take a shower. I'd been trying to give her privacy.

That was, until I couldn't fight it anymore.

There'd been a period where I hadn't been jerking off at my computer to the image of a certain girl living in my home. I *had been* respecting her and things had been completely platonic, but then Val told me she'd been having a hard time locating the information I needed. She'd been having zero luck in fact, and that was the first time I pulled my dick out. Normally, I'd call up a fuck buddy to release some tension, but I didn't want to touch another girl.

I was too obsessed with my daughter's friend.

Polly was tired, and though I was too, I only headed back to the house so I didn't exhaust her. I made sure she was in her kennel with plenty of water, but after, I needed to tire my fucking body out.

I ended up swimming.

I glided into my pool. Naked, I did long and seemingly endless strokes. Eventually, I ended up in a flow state, and it took me a moment to realize I was exhausted and needed to slow down.

Even still, I kept swimming. It wasn't until I caught a whiff of coconut that I stopped mid stroke. I was so fucked up I thought the soft smell was a phantom scent in my lungs, but then, I spotted a woman standing off to the side of the pool.

She was bathed in its light.

"Sia?" I started to say more but stopped. The young woman wasn't in her oversized tee or even a bathing suit. She wore a nightgown.

It was see through.

Dark nipples revealed themselves beneath white material. The same went for her snatch, the curls dusky, unshaven.

My breath expelled in the night. "What are you doing here?"

It wasn't so much that she was here. It was more her lack of clothing.

And mine.

I was hard under the water, steel, and as if she could see, her attention ventured in that direction.

What are you doing, malyshka?

"I wasn't having fun I guess. At the party?" she explained. Barefoot in front of me, she chewed her lip, and in that white nightgown, she was like an innocent lamb ready for slaughter.

Step away.

I glided backwards in the water, not able to trust myself. I kept my eyes on hers. "Where's my daughter?"

"She's still at the party."

I continued to follow her dark irises.

She moved. Light footfalls carried her toward the pool's steps. She dipped a toe in, but soon was up to her ankles.

She didn't stop.

Soft brown skin glided into the pool, and I stiffened when the water reached her thighs.

"What are you doing, Miss Reynolds?" I asked, my demon

waking up. I wasn't just hard. I was fucking feral. My eyes narrowed. "Sia, stop."

She didn't, the water passing the dark curls between her thighs. It drew above her nipples, and I didn't fucking move.

I didn't know what I'd do if I did.

"Or what?" she questioned, causing me to blanch. It wasn't unusual for her to talk back, but in this capacity, the both of us naked... Her head tilted. "What will you do if I don't stop?"

I didn't know what had gotten into her, but flashes of before came into my head. Flashes of her in my most intimate of spaces. She nearly had her hands on my tools today, tempting me then.

Deciding to play her game, I drew in closer. I was well aware I should stop whatever this was, but the next thing I knew, I was up on her.

Neither one of us breathed.

Her lips were the color of a soft rose, pink and pouty. I studied them, a breath away. "For starters, I'd take you into my vineyard," I said, reaching beneath the water. She sucked in a sharp breath, and I'd bet money she thought I was going to grab her.

Instead, she watched me fist myself.

It was like my quiet time in front of the computer but the image in front of me was in real time. I indulged in slow strokes, leaning in toward the trembling girl in front of me. "I'd run you down, then *fuck you raw* for letting that guy put his hands on you."

I was admitting to her things I did in private, my hunts, and it was more than inappropriate, the activity I was engaging in beneath the water. But if she came here so boldly...

This was a test. I wouldn't put hands on her. She was my daughter's friend, but I wanted to show her she was playing with fire. I wanted to frighten her with real thoughts I was having about her. I wanted to show her she couldn't go toe-to-toe with me and needed to *back away*.

"What guy?" she gasped, and I nearly did taste her. My mouth hovered over her throat, her scent maddening.

My nose glided along the curls at her neck. "That fucker at the party Lettie took you to. I saw you both on social media. I saw *him*, his hands on you…"

Our chests nearly touched, and her nightgown was so wet it was pointless she even had it on. She was completely exposed to me.

Her eyes closed, and I grinned.

"I'd make sure you knew you belong to no one but me," I explained, testing myself now. I had no idea what I was saying, dizzy…drunk off her smell and the situation. "Could you handle that, *malyshka*?"

She said nothing, and my mouth did touch her neck. Her gasp caused her delicate skin to touch my teeth, but I didn't dare do anything else.

"Could you handle that, baby girl?" I questioned, my nickname for her in English this time, and her lashes fluttered. She was mine and had been since the day she entered my home and first stood up to me. I had claims on her.

It was inevitable.

I knew this now, and whether she wanted it or not that was the case. If she denied me now, I didn't know if I had the strength to let her walk away.

"Yes," she whispered, and it was like a switch went off. There were no more tests. There was no more will we or won't we. There were no more games and zero thoughts, at least on my end.

My hands molded around her hips, and I drew her close to my cock. I rubbed it against her just as I had in my workspace. I thought she'd collapse she trembled so hard, and I questioned my own stability in that moment.

I questioned my sanity.

For how sane could I be with my hands on this girl way too young for me. My hands on *my daughter's friend*.

The fact only made her more tempting.

My teeth tugged her ear. "Then let's see if you can handle directions."

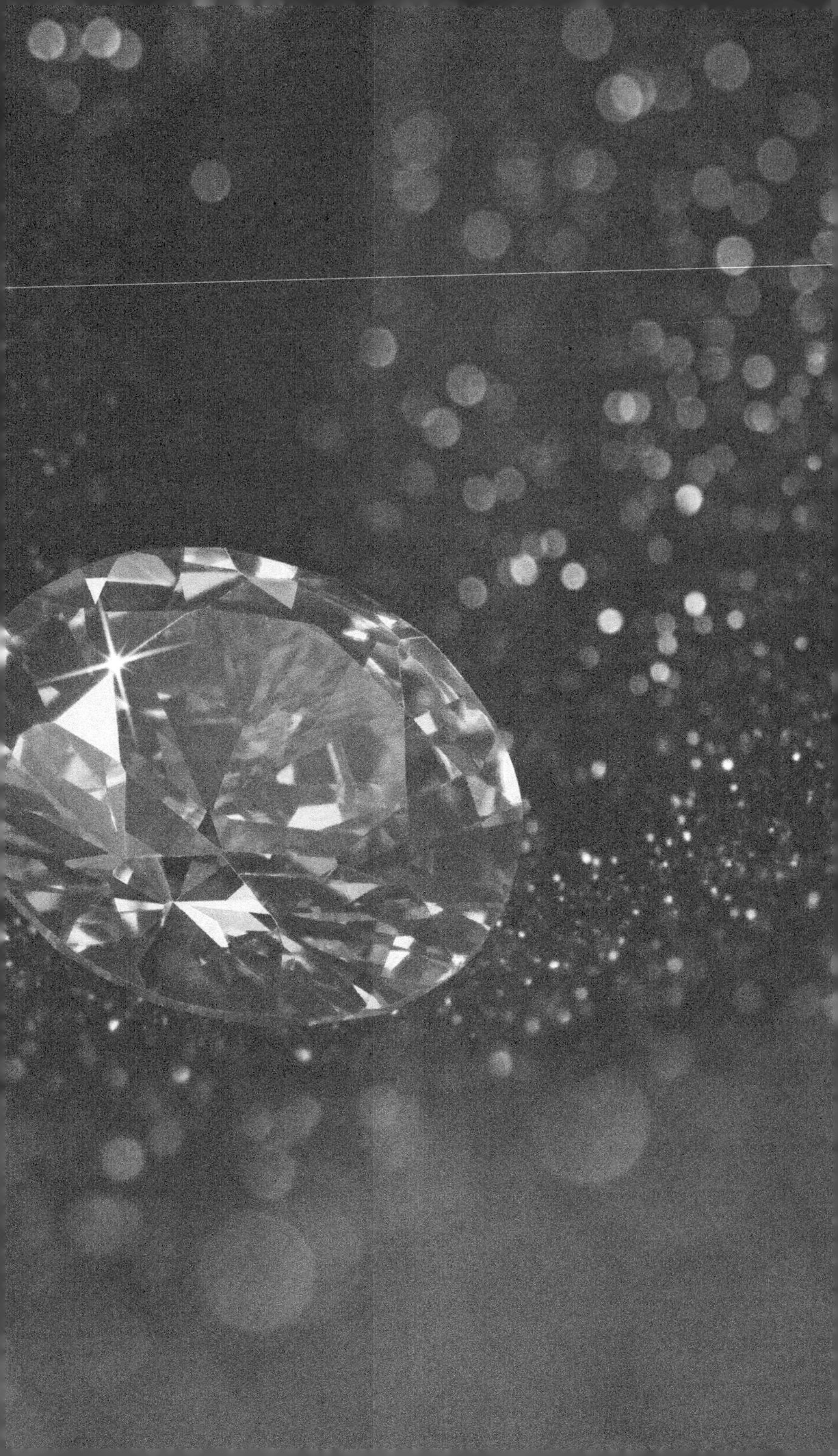

CHAPTER
TWENTY-TWO

Sia

Maxim took my hand and guided me out of the pool, but he didn't dry me off. He let us both drip and left me exposed in my damp nightgown.

Is this really happening?

My heart beat like a jack rabbit. I was only partially sure he'd be receptive to my advances. When I came home in a ride share, I wasn't exactly sure if he'd want to continue where we'd left off in his office. I had no confidence at all.

There had been something there between us though, and I think I only denied that earlier because of my own fear. I was scared of him. I was horrified actually, but not in the way I should be.

He took me to his room.

I'd never been there of course. He didn't let go of my hand once we were inside.

It was gorgeous. He had a fireplace that casted a glow on his dark bedding and matching curtains. It gave his room a dungeon look and matched his personality.

Is this happening right now? Really?

I should be thinking about other things. Not just his age in relation to mine, but the fact he was my friend's dad.

But that was the last thing on my mind.

Perhaps it had something to do with his touch when he placed his hands on my face. He fingered my curls away from my eyes in the dim light of his room, and I thought he may kiss me, but he ultimately stepped away.

"I want you on your knees, *malyshka*," he said, still naked in the dark room, wet. His dick hung heavy, his abs surging with heavy breath. Did I turn him on? His eyes darkened. "I want you on your knees for me."

I normally didn't like being told what to do. Especially by him. But something happened once I dropped to my knees, and he stroked my cheek. There was approval in his gray eyes, and that sent something wild soaring into my heart. I loved defying him.

But I loved pleasing him more.

His rough digits pulsed awareness beneath my skin, but he didn't do anything more as he touched my cheek. His eyes scanning mine, he appeared to have something of a debate in his eyes. I wondered if he'd stop this, but then his hand guided my chin up.

"I need to know if you can follow directions," he said, repeating what he had downstairs. His mouth formed into a firm line. "I will push you to your limits. I'm going to fuck you, but in ways that probably won't be ordinary to you. They can be sadistic, depraved, and once I get going I won't stop outside of the hard rules and boundaries we have in place."

Tremors hit deep into my knees, but I didn't move. I was taken back, but wasn't scared by what he said.

Why wasn't I scared?

I nodded. "Okay."

He stroked my chin. "It will be intense, Sia, and I could

very well break you. Often times you probably won't even like what I do to you."

He was talking like he was some kind of a dominant, and though I didn't know anything about BDSM, it felt like that might be what he was talking about. I swallowed. "Will you hurt me?"

"It's a given I'll hurt you," he said, not ashamed. He let go of my chin and was hard in front of me. He'd been hard before but was steel now. Like this conversation was doing something for him.

It was certainly doing something for me.

Maybe I was just as dark and depraved as he was.

He wet his lips. "But anything that happens between us will be agreed upon before and completely consensual. Anything that is done will be because you've allowed it, *malyshka*, but it will be intense."

The rough pads of his fingers stroked my jaw again, and something odd happened. Instead of being fearful, *running away*, I eased more into his touch. I almost felt…comfort in his touch and words when I certainly shouldn't. Honestly, as soon as he said what he had I should have gotten up and left. But I didn't.

I closed my eyes in the warm heat of the room and his calloused fingers. I liked that he was being honest about what he wanted. I liked he wasn't a *liar*, and though he was saying some dark and depraved things, he was saying them. He wasn't hiding who he was from me.

And that meant something.

I think that was where the comfort came from, and I opened my eyes in the fireplace light. "If I say yes, will we be going outside next?" I asked, and he blinked. I wasn't sure if it was because I was considering this arrangement or what I mentioned about going outside. I assumed some of the things he was talking about would be out there. He brought women through this house that were physically dirty like he'd chased them.

Hunted them.

After Maxim's initial shock, his grip on my chin intensified. A dark gleam rimmed his gray irises, and I questioned if he'd make me leave.

"You're not ready for that," he said, confirming some of my theories about the things he was into. His eyes narrowed. "I'm not ready. I don't want to hurt you. Not like that. Not until..." He shook his head. "We'll take things slow tonight. It will be good...for both of us."

I didn't know what he meant by that, but soon my cheeks were in both of his hands. There was a kindness in his voice and words, a tenderness I didn't normally see, and that fluttered something in my heart.

"I want you to say 'red' if I do anything tonight that takes you past your limits," he instructed. "You say that and everything stops."

Something about him saying that had emotion hitting my eyes, tears. I didn't know why.

Yes, you do.

I did but said nothing about it and fought the tears when I nodded. I wouldn't cry and hadn't in years. I'd taken back my power long ago.

Even when it was taken from me.

"Okay," I told him, the emotion thick still in my throat. I nodded again. "All right."

"Okay." He guided me to look up at him once more. "Can we proceed? I'd like to touch you now."

My head bobbed twice in acknowledgment, but he didn't move.

His expression intensified. "I need you to tell me I can touch you intimately. Give me clear permission, and I will proceed."

His voice was borderline feral. Like he was on the brink of testing his own limits.

I trembled. "Yes, you can touch me."

A noise hummed in his chest when his fingers escaped my jaw.

They moved to my nipple.

He outlined my areola softly through my wet nightgown. Unable to take it, I made my own noise, and he growled in response.

His gray eyes ignited. "I could tear you apart so easily, *malyshka*," he said, that word taking on a whole new understanding now that I knew what it meant. I trembled once more, and he pinched my nipple. "Arms up."

I did right away, and I sagged when he let go of me and left the room. He disappeared into his walk in closet, and the moments in which he was away were agonizing.

What's he doing?

I was dripping between my legs, and even more so when Maxim came back with a belt in his hands. He was still completely naked, his cock solid between his powerful legs.

I studied him as he closed the distance between us and gasped when he secured my waiting wrists to the bedpost. He wasn't gentle about how tight he made the belt. If anything, something wild hit his eyes the tighter he made it.

"Now that I have you like this you don't move, all right?" he stated, admiring his work. He smiled a little. "I'm going to explore you, but while I do you don't move. Not a fucking inch, you understand?"

"I understand," I said, making sure he had his consent. I was curious what he'd do, but thought he'd start with kissing me. I was dying for it so I quaked a little when he passed over my mouth and went straight for my neck. His nose touched down, his breaths heavy.

He was smelling me.

His mouth parted along my neck while he did, something

so animalistic about it as he drank my scent in. I did the same with him, unsure if I could even stand tall with how glorious he smelled. It was so lethal, his wild scent.

Kiss me.

He wouldn't, making me wait while his teeth dragged along my pulse. My eyes closed, and I jolted a little when his teeth dug into my neck. It wasn't hard, but scared me.

He scared me.

He was so powerful and could hurt me so easily in this vulnerable position. I kept trying to put that out of my mind though. Sex could be…hard for me, but I was trying to release control.

"I smell it, you know? Your apprehension. Your fear." His hand closed over my throat, squeezing slightly. I was reminded what little power I had in this situation, and my eyes closed tight for a different reason.

Relax.

I was trying to. I wanted to trust him, but it was so hard for me.

"It's so fucking beautiful, baby girl," he said, his fingers easing beneath the hem of my nightgown. His fingers ghosted along my thighs. "I'm going to lift this up."

He didn't until I nodded again, and I was so lost in the moment. I was lost in my head and trying to let go.

It was hard once I noticed his stare.

He'd bunched my nightgown up over my head. It was secured at my wrists, but once it was, he didn't touch me anymore. He simply stared, and the wild look in his eyes had transformed into something else.

Madness.

His frown was deep, his eyes full of rage, and it took me only seconds to realize why. He noticed the soft scars on my chest, the ones I usually hid with makeup or clothing.

He must not have seen them when he watched me shower.

I didn't know if his camera was too far away or what, but clearly, he hadn't seen them. He obviously hadn't seen them when we were both at the pool with Polly that day, but that was intentional. Whenever I was in a bathing suit, I used makeup to cover them up.

Maxim's expression was murderous when he touched one, and right away, my body locked up, instinctual.

No. No. No.

I honestly forgot about them in the moment. Forgot my history and he allowed me to do that for a second. He wasn't now, and I felt so vulnerable under his intense stare.

"What is this?"

Especially when he asked me that. I didn't want him to see that part of my life. I didn't want *anyone* to see, which was why I'd learned how to cover the scars up. I'd gotten really good at using makeup tutorials over the years.

Apparently not good enough.

"Someone hurt you," Maxim surmised, and I did allow a tear to fall. I didn't want to look weak, and I knew I did in that moment. His eyes narrowed. "Who?"

"Let me out of this." I jerked, feeling as if put on display. My scars didn't define me, and I didn't need his fucking sympathy. "*Now.* Get this thing fucking off me, Maxim."

He wasn't, and the murderous look in his eyes intensified. "What is this, Sia, and who did it? Tell me who I need to kill. I'm fucking serious."

Oh, now suddenly he was my savior? He who treated me like garbage when we first met? I jerked in the bindings. "I mean it, Maxim, let me out of this."

"Sia—"

"Red." The safe word blared from my lips.

I couldn't do this.

I couldn't, and I was fucking stupid for thinking I could. I was too damaged, too...

My arms were lowered in seconds.

Maxim didn't make me wait. He was being serious about my safe word, and right away the belt was removed and my arms lowered. He even fixed my nightgown, but once I was covered, I didn't stick around for anymore conversation.

I might just cry.

I'd show how weak I really was, but Maxim didn't allow me to go far. In fact, I only made it a few steps before his hand cuffed my arm, but he didn't jerk me around.

He was gentle.

The touch was almost timid and as vulnerable feeling as I was. "*Malyshka.*"

The word melted through me and did make me feel soft, weak. His other hand cuffed my arm, and when I didn't turn around, he added a little pressure.

"Tell me what happened," he said so gently behind me. I didn't know he was capable. "We'll just talk. Please, can I see?"

My immediate thought was *hell no*. *I* didn't even look at my scars which was why I covered them up.

Why does he care?

He sounded as if he did, this brooding man who'd showed me nothing but cruelty. I didn't want to feel vulnerable in front of him but something had me nodding softly.

I turned around instinctively. I couldn't look him in the eyes. I didn't want him seeing my scars, but I didn't want to *see him* observing my scars even more.

God.

My heart racing, I lifted my arms. I knew this would make it easier for him, and I couldn't bear him asking me to show him.

Gratefully, I didn't have to.

Maxim took the initiative in that moment when he guided my nightgown up again. This time, he took it off, and I shuddered, but not from his touch. I was completely exposed to him now.

I was raw.

I was in so many ways. I waited for the questions. I waited for the *pain*, and he turned me around with a guided hand. I still kept my eyes closed.

Maxim said nothing, so quiet. He touched a space below my collarbone, and though I opened my eyes, I stared at the floor.

Again, I couldn't face him.

"A cigarette burn," I said before he could ask me. I swallowed. "A gift from one of my foster dads when I drank his apple juice. I didn't know it was his."

Apparently, that gave him license to hurt me. He was, admittedly, one of the bad ones, but unfortunately not the worst.

Maxim was still so quiet. So much so that I opened my eyes. I couldn't read his expression in that moment. He was just as bare as me but not nearly as vulnerable. His jaw moved. "A blade?"

So much control was in his voice when his thumb outlined the cut on my shoulder. That one was easy to hide beneath my bra strap.

I was sure he knew all about the scar a knife could make. It was a kitchen knife in this case. I glanced away. "One of my foster moms had a drinking problem."

His hand covered it, and he couldn't blanket his expression when I finally did meet his eyes. His voice had held control before, but his face wasn't in that moment.

He was pissed.

I'd seen Maxim angry, but the fiery rage which held his handsome features even struck me. It wasn't directed at me, obviously, but I still felt it.

He pivoted me around without words, and when his hand touched my back, I knew he found more. I released a breath. "Cooking grease. Another awesome foster home."

I guess I deserved to be punished for being hungry. I'd only asked for food.

But sometimes that was all it took.

I'd seen lots of cruelty over my lifetime. I'd endured, but I was suddenly feeling all of that again. I was with each scar I had to revisit under Maxim's stare. There were a few more, and the last one Maxim addressed was the cut above my eye.

"A dog," he said, and I was sure he'd seen that one before. I didn't hide it.

I nodded. "It happened quick. Only a few stitches."

The anger burned hotter in his dark eyes, and eventually, he left me. He returned once again from his walk in closet, but this time, he was covered. He wore one of his silk robes and had another in his hands.

He dressed me, the material so large and warm. The silk glided over me and hid those hideous scars from my past.

"But you're not scared of them," Maxim said, that control back in his voice. He tied the robe's belt around me. "You and Polly... You're not scared."

I wasn't, shrugging. "It's not the dog's fault his owner was an asshole."

This was true and not all of my foster parents were assholes. Some actually gave a shit, but I was never in those long. The good ones were good for a reason and genuinely tried to help kids. In fact, they helped as many as they could which was why I never got to stay. There wasn't room and...

Maxim's hand slid along my jaw, and instead of turning away, I melded into his touch. Moments ago, I wanted to leave. My scars didn't define me, but I did feel ashamed by them. I was ashamed that someone so powerful could see what I allowed to be done to me. I knew I was young at the time. I knew I'd been a *kid*, but being around Maxim made me feel some kind of way. I always wanted to be strong in front of him. Always.

He guided me to look up at him, his expression so tender.

Once more, I wasn't sure he was capable. I mean, he hadn't even kissed me before.

He did now.

My feet actually lifted off the floor. I was on my toes from both surprise but also how soft and inviting his mouth happened to be against mine. Control was there too, intention. He was holding something back, and I didn't want him to.

I pressed on now that I had him. I wanted him to kiss me. I wanted him to push the memories and the pain away from my past, but eventually, he stopped. He held me back, his hand bunching the robe at my thigh.

"I want to carve out the hearts of anyone who hurt you," he said, my own heart picking up its beats. His nose brushed mine. "I will if I find them. I'll track each of them down and—"

I didn't want to talk about those other people, those monsters. I didn't want to relive my past.

I just wanted him.

So badly. I *needed* him to force those memories away, and when I kissed him again, I showed him that.

He growled in response, both my thighs in his hands when he drew me against his cock. He was so hard through his robe, solid, powerful.

"If we don't stop, I'll be inside you," he said, and I wanted that too. This was so shocking to me. Intimacy was hard for me when it wasn't just sex.

This wouldn't be just sex.

This was Maxim, and there were *feelings*. At least on my part.

"Please," I nearly begged him. I was begging him. I unbelted his robe. "Please."

The noise from his chest rumbled into mine. He pushed his hands into my curls, and soon, we were on his bed. We were on that handsome material, and I was beneath the most dominant man. I should be terrified in this moment, but I wasn't.

I wasn't at all.

Maxim's hand ventured to the belt on my robe. He slid it out, wrapping it around his fist, and in response, I lifted my arms. I thought he'd tie me up. He had before so I was surprised when he tugged my hands down.

He made me fist him instead.

My hand full of him, I gasped, the man so solid, so firm. I almost couldn't hold him in one hand, and his mouth touched mine.

"Not tonight, *malyshka*," he said, tossing the belt. With it gone, his hand formed around mine. He made me fist him harder, faster. He bit my mouth. "Tonight, it's just this. You and me. Nothing else."

I didn't know what he meant, but I shuddered when he ripped my robe open and proceed to nibble small bites on my chest. He drew my nipple into a warm mouth, sucking, laving, and I instinctually opened my legs. The noise from Maxim's lips was feral, and his sucks stopped when he started licking down my body.

He ended up between my legs.

His nose parted my folds, and at this point, I was bucking, my back curled as I wriggled. He hadn't even done anything yet, but with him there…

"You're so pure," he said, kissing me there. How was it possible he was so tender, gentle. He nipped at my sex. "So sweet."

But I wasn't pure, not at all. I'd had sex before but that wasn't the first thought that came to mind when he said what he had.

You're damaged goods.

This was something I knew, and Maxim clearly saw with all my scars. Not all scars were on the outside though, and I felt myself lock up a bit with my thoughts. I tried to block things out of my head, memories, but it was hard sometimes.

The damage was done.

Again, I was damaged goods, but something about Maxim's soft kisses had me relaxing. I eased into his mouth over my sex, his kisses tender, sweet.

"You're so lovely, *malyshka*," he said, and I felt that way in the moment. Maxim's gray eyes had changed upon peering over my sex. They were darker, and his nose touched the air. The lust in his eyes had me melting, and when he slid a digit inside me, I felt my back bow to new levels. He groaned. "So fucking perfect."

Another word that didn't describe me at all, but I blocked out inner thoughts. I just let myself feel in the moment. Maxim's fingers as they tunneled inside me…

Maxim's tongue when he licked me.

He guided my juices out of me, and my toes curled, fighting the orgasm that was on the brink. I didn't think I could last, and when he forced my legs apart, I knew he didn't want me to. He wanted me to give in.

"Give yourself to me," he said, my thighs over his shoulders. His fists were gripping my legs so hard I knew I'd have marks in the morning. He licked my clit. "Let go, baby girl."

And that was it. I did, vibrating over his mouth. The fire burned deep in my core, and I couldn't hold back.

I let go.

I released it all, completely exposed to him, and Maxim didn't stop licking until I was done. If anything, he stayed longer. His kisses and tongue cleaning me up and being so soft. It was like the care of his hand, but he used his mouth instead.

It felt so nice.

I felt *cared for*, and I had no idea that was possible with him.

But didn't I?

He'd protected me before. He made me feel safe, and the fear only hit me when he guided his robe off and hovered above me. His mighty body encapsulated me, dark tattoos covering so much of his body. He was perfect, down to the length and thickness of his engorged cock.

I pressed my hands to his abs, trying not to be intimidated. This was the source of my fear, and tingling sparked between my legs when he had me fist him once more. His gray eyes ignited, something wild and animalistic ringing them. Something told me he was doing all he could to contain himself.

He was so capable of breaking me.

He could in so many ways, and if he knew all of them, I knew he'd stop this. He wouldn't want anything to do with me.

"Open for me," he said, parting my legs again. I didn't think I was ready so soon, and I did feel myself lock up right after he put a condom on and was at my entrance.

I hadn't expected it.

I physically felt myself shutdown but not because I came before.

Don't do this. You're okay…

It was hard for my body to believe it sometimes. Even though *it'd been years*, I still got in my fucking head. It didn't happen all the time but often enough where I knew the signs.

You're okay. You're okay. You're okay.

"*Malyshka?*"

Maxim's word brought me out of my head, and even more so when his mouth touched mine. My body went languid, burned.

Yes.

My hips rose, lifting to meet his, and I didn't realize I was moving with him until the roughness of his thighs were meeting mine. He tunneled deep, his cock reaching me at new depths. He fucked me slow and each ministration brought me to the present.

It brought me to him.

Maxim squeezed me to him, his kisses, his...fucking so intentional. This wasn't just flesh. This was connection, and normally, that did lock me up. I usually had to put myself somewhere else mentally when I was with someone physically.

I couldn't help it.

That wasn't the case right now, and though Maxim started slow, he picked up hard and fast. Tears pricked my eyes but not because I was in pain. It was because emotion was hitting me in new ways. I wanted to feel this.

I *was* feeling this.

I felt every inch of this man. Especially when he made me look at him. He forced my curls away from my face, kissing my cheeks.

"Come for me, baby girl," he said, his words gritted, and though his thrusts were hard they were so well controlled. Like he was holding back. Like he could do more. His mouth touched my ear. "Let yourself go."

I didn't know how he knew I was holding something back, but with his prompt, I once again allowed my body to give into his and what he was doing to me. I came in a violent shudder, and he continued to pump inside me. He did until he reached his own high.

Maxim flooded the condom, his dick vibrating inside me, and the whole time he looked like he was biting one of those rubber balls without the ball. Like he really was trying to control himself.

I kissed his mouth, both of us holding back. I had a feeling he was doing so because he could hurt me. This sex seemed very vanilla compared to what I knew about him, what I assumed about him.

His eyes opened once I did, and he gave in too when his

hands fisted my shoulders. He grunted as he emptied himself, and the next thing I knew, I was in his arms. He was kissing me everywhere but my mouth. It was so intimate. It was so normal, and I wondered if he was doing that just for me. To make me feel good. He spent the most time at the wounds I usually covered up. Like he was caring for my scars both internal and external.

And maybe he was.

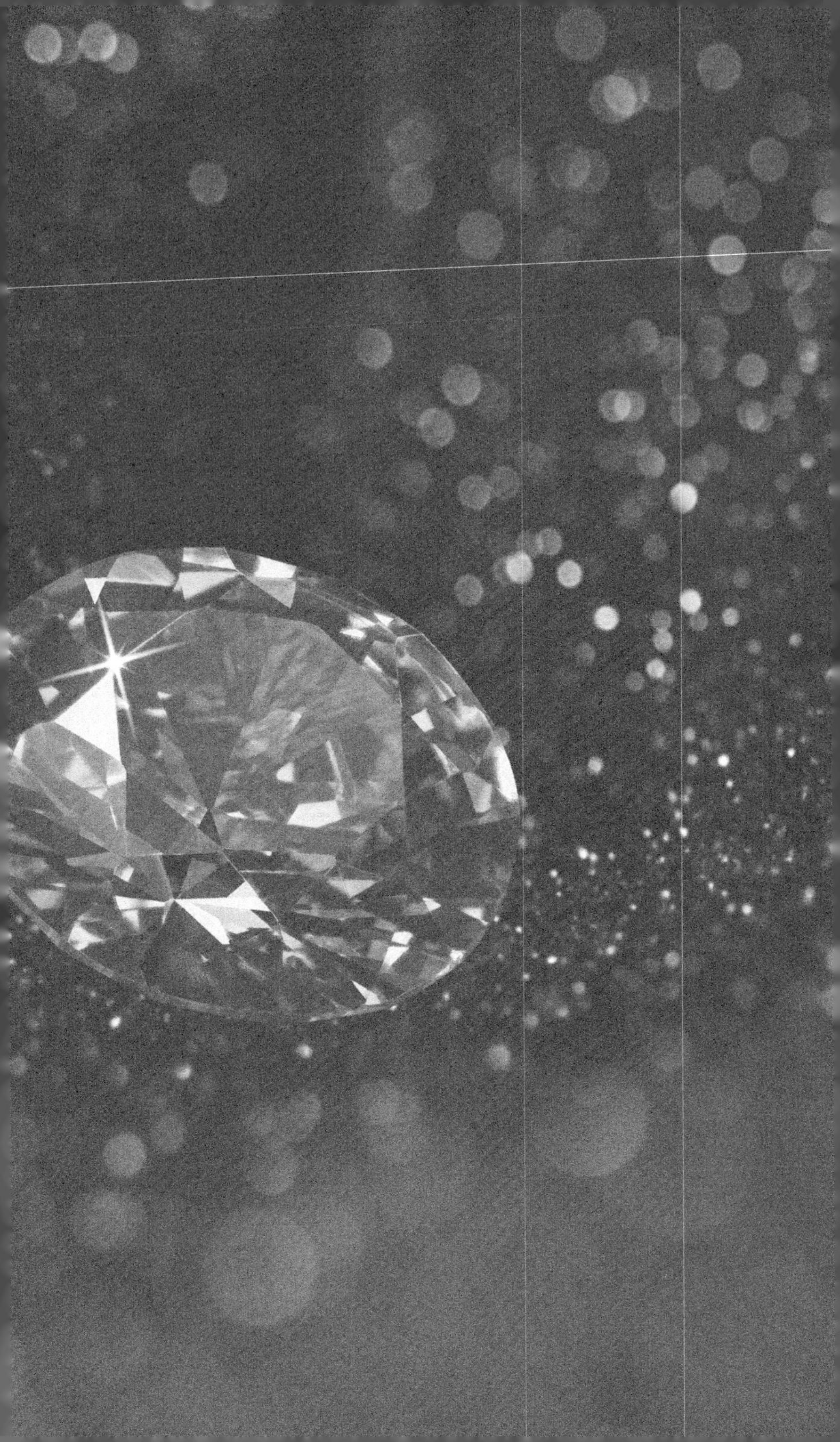

CHAPTER TWENTY-THREE

Sia

I woke up, and it was light outside.

And I was sore.

It'd been a while since I had sex, and I pressed my legs together.

I wonder if he knew.

Maxim might have. Everything about me probably came off as young to him and inexperienced. I turned over, expecting to find him, but his large bed was empty.

And cold.

His spot was almost frigid, and I sat up. There was no fire in the fireplace. It'd been on as we'd gone to sleep.

I waited a moment, thinking maybe he just went to use the bathroom or something, but that couldn't have been the case. His spot was cold.

Anxiety hit me a little bit, and I waited, just lying there for a moment. Eventually, I chewed my lip and got out of his bed. I ended up sneaking my way back into my own bedroom.

I didn't want to run into Lettie.

I realized how wrong all this was, sneaking around behind my friend's back. The worst part was that hadn't even been my main concern when I'd gotten up. It'd actually bothered me more that I woke up in a man's bed, and he'd been gone. I looked like some young pathetic girl in his sheets, and that bothered me a whole lot more than Lettie's thoughts about me sleeping with her dad.

I didn't know what that made me. At worst a terrible friend, and at best, well, a terrible friend. Even still, I couldn't avoid the sick feeling that overcame me that Maxim left me in his room. He left me alone in a cold bed, and my mind couldn't pull away from that.

I have to get Polly.

She was my priority, my job. She hadn't gone out since last night and needed to be fed and watered.

My nightgown was crispy under my robe. It'd dried weird and had been laid out with a robe on a chair. I noticed it when I'd initially gotten out of bed, and I was in such a hurry to get out of Maxim's room I hadn't realized it'd been laid out for me to find. This was most certainly Maxim's doing before he left the bedroom that morning.

Is he at work?

It'd drive the dagger deeper if that was true. Like I really was just some young fuck to him who he probably only screwed to get out of his system.

You threw yourself at him.

I did because it felt like we had a connection. Hell, last night had felt like a connection. I couldn't get out of my head how caring he was, how gentle, when he was normally so prickly.

That circulated my brain the most after I'd gotten dressed and came downstairs. I managed not to run into anyone along the way, but it was still early. Lettie might still be sleeping since she went out last night.

You're a terrible person.

Again, this I knew, and it was even worse that what I'd done behind her back hadn't even been worth it. Maxim hadn't been there when I woke up, and I was so in my head that I was startled when I came across Sophia. She was cleaning the downstairs banisters, and I nearly clipped her.

"Good morning, Sia," she said, not paying me too much mind, and I was glad. I was starting to feel so ill.

I greeted her but for some reason I didn't keep moving. I stopped. "Did Mr. Petrov already leave for work this morning?"

I really was an idiot and almost didn't stay for her answer.

She glanced up. "I think he's out with Polly," she said, and my mouth parted.

Polly…

Not believing it, I thanked her, then headed outside. The day hit my eyes, and I shielded them, unprepared for it. What I really wasn't prepared for was Polly with Maxim who were both sprinting on their way back to the house.

Maxim was covered in sweat.

Naked from the waist up, he jogged with Polly beside him. He had a set of earbuds in, his tatted torso glistening as he pumped his arms. He noticed me because Polly did. She immediately tugged at her lead to head toward me, and when Maxim spotted me, he pulled an earbud out. Something warm hit his gray eyes when he did, and whatever that something was sent me in just as much of a tailspin as it had last night.

Fuck.

This guy… This man really had me gone. My face immediately flushed, and I distracted myself with Polly when Maxim unclipped her. She came right to me of course, and I buried my face in her fur.

"It's an early start for you today, huh, girl?" I normally didn't have her up this early but was going to get her up today.

"She was trying to get ahead of me this morning during our run, and I was the one who woke her up," Maxim said, light laughter in his voice. His attention drifted to me. "Did you sleep well?"

Beautifully until I realized he was gone.

I didn't admit that of course. I stood. "Pretty good, yeah."

Rocking on my heels, I suddenly found myself awkward in front of him. This was ironic considering what happened last night and how I'd come onto him.

Maxim approached me in the next moment, and I rubbed my arm. Needless to say, I was completely aware of him as he got closer. His masculine scent quickly engulfed me, and he got as close as he could without drawing too much attention to us. There were several people out tending to the Petrov property, and normally, I wasn't so aware of them.

I was now since Maxim kept his distance. I was sure he was aware of his staff too.

"I hoped so," he said, again only looking at me. "I wanted you to sleep so I took Polly out for you. She's fed and watered. Tired."

Suddenly, I felt really silly for thinking he'd just left. Especially since he'd done something so sweet.

Really awkward now, I chewed my lip. "Thanks."

"Of course."

I had no idea where we'd go from here. I mean, it wasn't like we could deny what happened between us last night.

I didn't want to deny it, anyway.

I wasn't sure how he felt, and there was still that considerable distance between us. There was also the fact that I was his daughter's friend.

"I'd like it if we could spend the morning together," he said. I blinked, and he smiled. "I texted Lettie this morning. She stayed the night with her reject of a boyfriend."

I'd laugh at what he said, but then I mulled over what he was asking me.

He doesn't want this to end.

I didn't either, and though I didn't like doing this without Lettie knowing, I wasn't personally ready to go there just yet. I wasn't sure how to address that obvious elephant in the room.

I guessed that was what made me a terrible person again because the butterflies hit me before my next statement. "What did you want to do?"

My thoughts immediately went to more sex. Especially because last night didn't appear to be what he normally did. He also mentioned the vineyard to me. That he'd run me down, punish me. He'd been jealous of the guy I'd danced with last night. Actually, that dance was what sent me running. I hadn't wanted to be with that guy, and he'd come onto me after the dance.

I'd obviously backed away from that situation, and my stomach flipped when Maxim drew in even closer. He was still at what was considered a normal distance between two people talking. He clearly wanted to keep things discreet, just like me with the Lettie situation for the time being.

"I'd like to bathe you," he said, his voice low and almost timid, shy. The notion was crazy since he was so dominating. His head tilted. "I didn't get to do that last night since we fell asleep, and I'm sorry about that. Aftercare is very important to me, and I'm not happy I wasn't able to give that to you."

I wasn't sure what to say to that, but my body certainly wanted that. I burned at the thought of having his hands on my flesh again.

I nodded, forcing anything else out of my mind. I didn't want to think right now.

I just wanted to give in again.

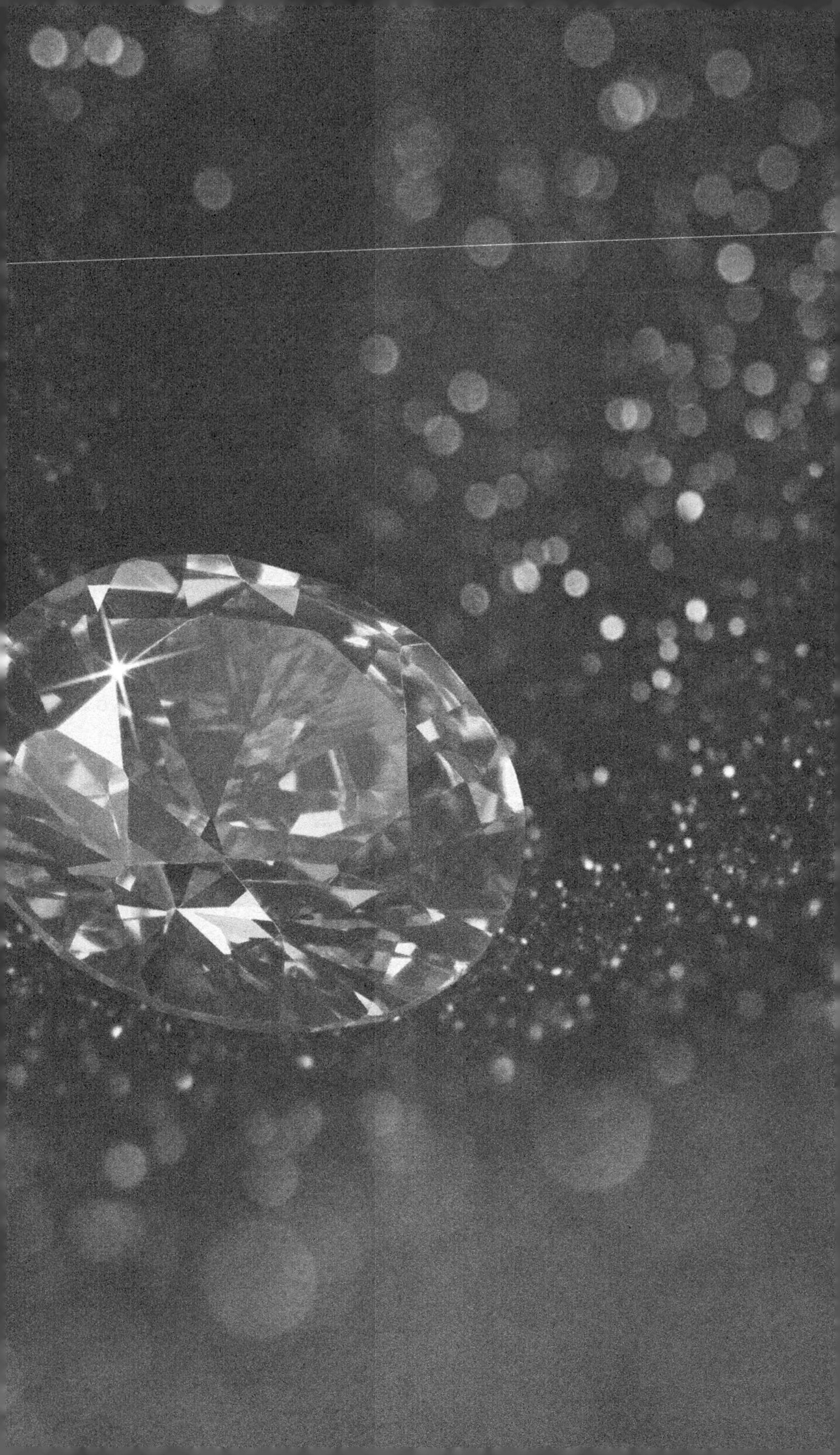

CHAPTER TWENTY-FOUR

Maxim

"So um… Should we talk about Lettie?"

I'd gone into a flow state, my hands on Sia. I bathed her, and her warmth in my hands brought out something carnal in me.

Especially seeing her scars.

I hadn't been able to properly see them on the cameras I'd placed in her room. The footage must have been too far away. I'd also seen her in a bathing suit but missed them then as well. I figured makeup or some other kind of concealer must have been the culprit for that. She clearly didn't want people to see them.

I ran the water over her flushed shoulders, trying not to think about the people who hurt her. I fully intended on looking into each individual who could have ever laid hands on her.

"Maxim?"

Trying to stay present, I focused on caring for her now. I

wet my lips. "I spoke to her briefly this morning. I wanted to confirm her status, I suppose."

Normally, I'd be annoyed she was wasting a rare visit at home with some douchebag. Everything with Sia distracted me though. She seemed to be the only thing that could distract me.

This made her dangerous, and though I was aware of it, I couldn't help the draw I had to her. She was as addictive to me as the spilling of fresh blood during my work. I enjoyed my work. It kept me busy. It kept me in control.

Being with Sia tested this daily, but again, I couldn't resist for some reason.

I felt this harshly as I ran a washcloth over her body. Seeing each scar of hers up close tested me in new ways. This girl had clearly been through a lot.

"She's another reason I got up," I admitted, and Sia turned. I nodded. "Probably best she not see you coming out of my room. I wanted to get ahead of that. I called her after seeing she wasn't home this morning."

This had been what Sia was really addressing with her question about Lettie, and it disgusted me hearing myself say how proactive I'd been about keeping my daughter in the dark.

It was almost as bad as what happened last night and what was happening now. I shouldn't be bathing a girl nearly half my age, her soft ass against my cock...

But I was so hungry for Sia Reynolds. Her taste awoke the demon inside me last night and forced me to lie to my daughter this morning. I told her nothing about what happened last night between myself and her friend.

I watched what I said play across Sia's face. Her nod was curt. "I see."

I braced her shoulders. "I'm not sure how to handle this."

I wasn't. I should have been the responsible one last night, told her no. I could have stopped this at any time, but I'd chosen not to.

In Sia's silence, I continued to bathe her. I watched goosebumps form on her brown skin, her breaths ragged. Tiny shudders moved her delicate shoulders. I sighed. "You're just so young, *malyshka*. I probably should have been more responsible last night."

The words barely left my lips before she turned again. A frown overtook her full lips. "So now you're looking at me like a kid?"

"Hardly." That was the last thing I saw her as. I shook my head. "I just mean…"

"I know what you meant. I'm too young for you, right? Sophomoric?" She started to get out of the bath, the water sloshing.

I got her by her shoulders and returned her to my lap.

"I just mean too innocent." That was putting it mildly. My expression hardened. "You're too pure to be with someone, well, someone like me. A man like me."

My fingers ghosted along her cheek. Doing so was both dangerous and foolish because I wanted to do more.

So much more.

The way she reacted to my touch only sent the urge into overdrive, but I resisted. I allowed her to meld into me but did nothing more. Her eyes opened. "I've been through plenty," she said, and as if to emphasize the point she glanced down at one of the cigarette burns on her shoulder. She covered it with her hand. "Seen plenty of shit."

She obviously had, and I forced down my anger again. I covered her hand. "I know you have, but you don't know who I am. I'm also not a big fan of lying to my daughter."

I wished the lie was my biggest reason for staying away. I honestly didn't know what Lettie's reaction would be but I did know my daughter and I had a great relationship. We had an open one, and if I explained the situation to her, she'd be shocked but would ultimately come around. Would the situation be ideal for her? No, but she'd listen and would be receptive. She would because we communicated and respected each other. She also loved me and knew I wouldn't jump into anything lightly. She knew I wouldn't if something didn't matter to me…

If I didn't care.

My jaw moved. "It's just not a good idea."

Sia really didn't know the type of man I was and wouldn't. She didn't need to.

"All due respect, Maxim, you don't know who I am," Sia said, surprising me when she turned the tables on me. "I don't like lying to Lettie either, and if things continue between us, I won't support that, but as far as who you are and who I am, you really have no idea. I've already been corrupted and it was long before you so you couldn't possibly do more."

She'd no doubt been through a lot. I mean, the evidence was there in my hands.

I stroked her arm. "Sia…"

I wasn't able to put the barrier between us up the way I wanted to when she turned around, straddled me.

I growled. "*Malyshka…*"

Sia knew exactly what she was doing. She was testing the limits of my control. Especially when she stood in front of me. The water dripped from her tiny curls. Her snatch was so wet, her smell lethal…

Fuck.

I was gone when she put a leg up on the tub. She exposed herself right in front of me, and I closed my eyes. My hands fisting her ass, I buried my face between her legs. I did nothing more. I didn't trust myself.

"Please, Maxim," she begged, and that was all it took for me to spread her legs, for me to drink from her sex and pretend I was any kind of man who should be taking anything from her. I dragged my tongue between her pussy lips, tasting how pure she was, how perfect. I made myself forget that she wasn't the only one who had scars. I wouldn't let her see my own, refused to.

I barely saw them myself anymore.

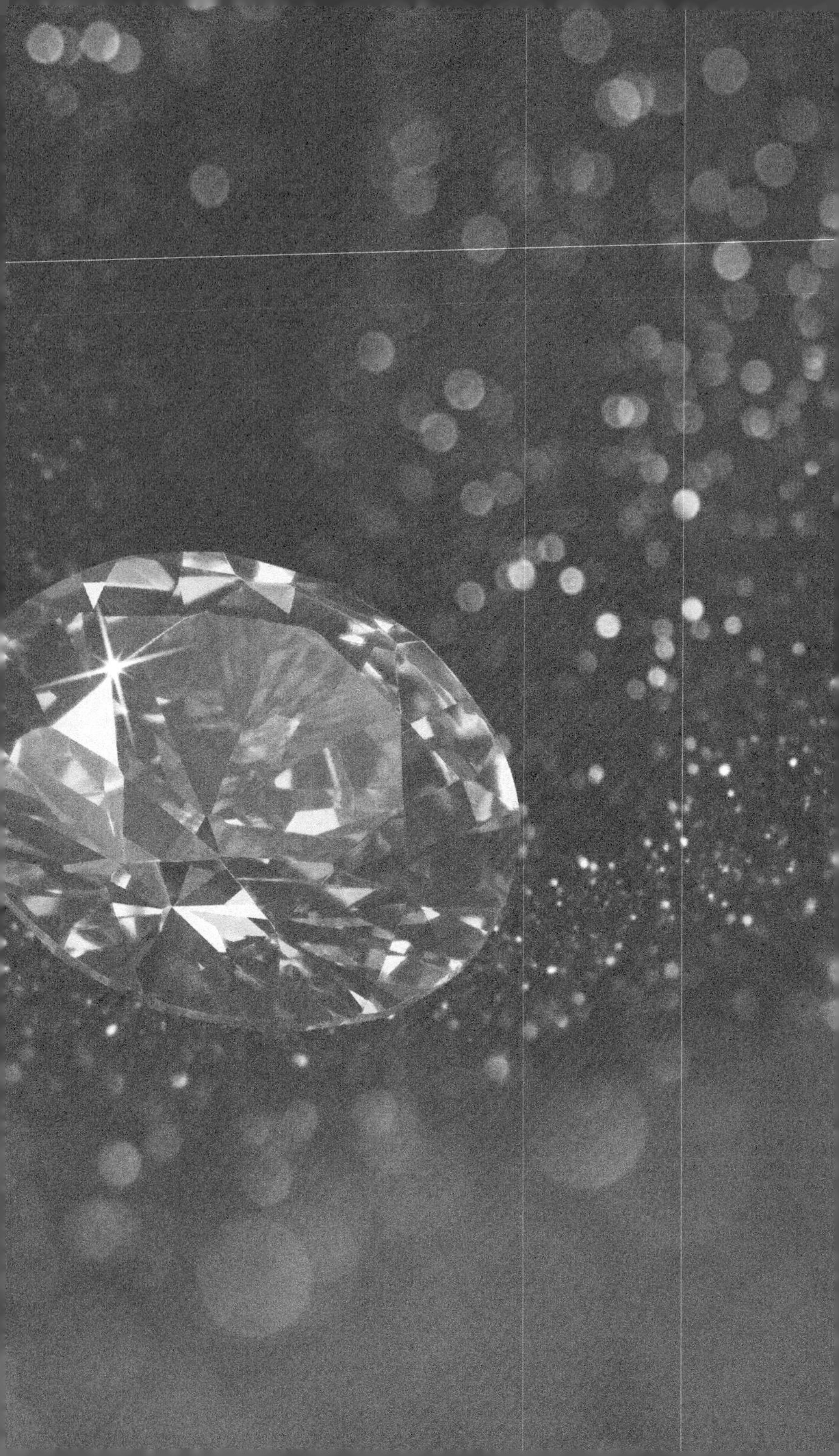

CHAPTER
TWENTY-FIVE

Sia

Lettie came home late afternoon, and when she did, Maxim acted like last night never happened.

Like what happened in his tub never happened.

I wasn't surprised I suppose. He had said I was too young, too innocent. The innocent thing wasn't true at all. He said I didn't know him, but he didn't know me either, what I'd gone through…

He also said he didn't want to lie to Lettie, but that was exactly what he did once she got home. I guessed I couldn't get on him for that because I went into friend mode myself once she arrived. I listened to her about how school was going and even ate lunch with them when their staff put it out.

I wasn't sure what else to do.

"You're just so young, malyshka…"

I guessed I was for thinking anything could happen between myself and my friend's dad.

Maxim basically used Lettie as a buffer the entire weekend

before she headed back to school. There wasn't a moment when he was around that she wasn't, but I couldn't really be mad that he was putting her first.

I mean, she was his daughter.

That I got, and I felt so guilty about what happened too. Lettie had been nothing but nice to me.

I wish I could get her dad out of my head.

Monday came and I found my chores already done for me. Maxim had once again taken Polly out and fed her. He was gone of course, and this time, he had gone to work. Sophia told me.

He really is avoiding everything.

I did feel young in that moment. I felt young and naive for getting wrapped up with him, for having *feelings for him*, and even though I understood him not wanting to mess around behind Lettie's back, I couldn't help thinking about what he said before. He called me pure, but I knew exactly what I was doing when I came onto him in his pool. I wanted to be with him that night.

In fact, I craved it.

Maxim led me to believe a danger followed me by being with him. I obviously knew he lived a dangerous and deadly life. The unknown of that used to scare me, but for some reason, it didn't now. Now, I found myself wondering more about who he was.

I should have let everything with him go. He'd been clear he didn't want to pursue anything, but something had me searching on my phone about things that happened when we were together. I'd also seen things *before* we got together. He'd brought women around, and there'd been some curious things.

My searches involved things like chasing, hunting. He talked about taking me out into the vineyard.

"I'd run you down, then fuck you raw for letting that guy put his hands on you..."

My thighs squeezed together as my search came up with terms like *predator* and *prey*. Maxim obviously was into certain kinks and sometimes Maxim's behavior was animalistic. He'd smell me or bite me.

"You don't know who I am…"

He was like that when I'd seen him kill as well. Something almost primal overtook him. Like it made him alive.

Like it invigorated him.

"You don't know who I am…"

So much darkness was in this man, and it really should bother me. I had a history with my own darkness, *people* who not only hurt me but did what they could to break me. I'd succumbed to it in the past. I'd been *weak*, but that wasn't who I was now. Something Maxim never had been was one of those people. He'd always protected me.

And I was wet.

My searches only invigorated me. I found out more and more about predator and prey, and that seemed to be who he was both in the bedroom and out. He was a dominant.

He was a hunter.

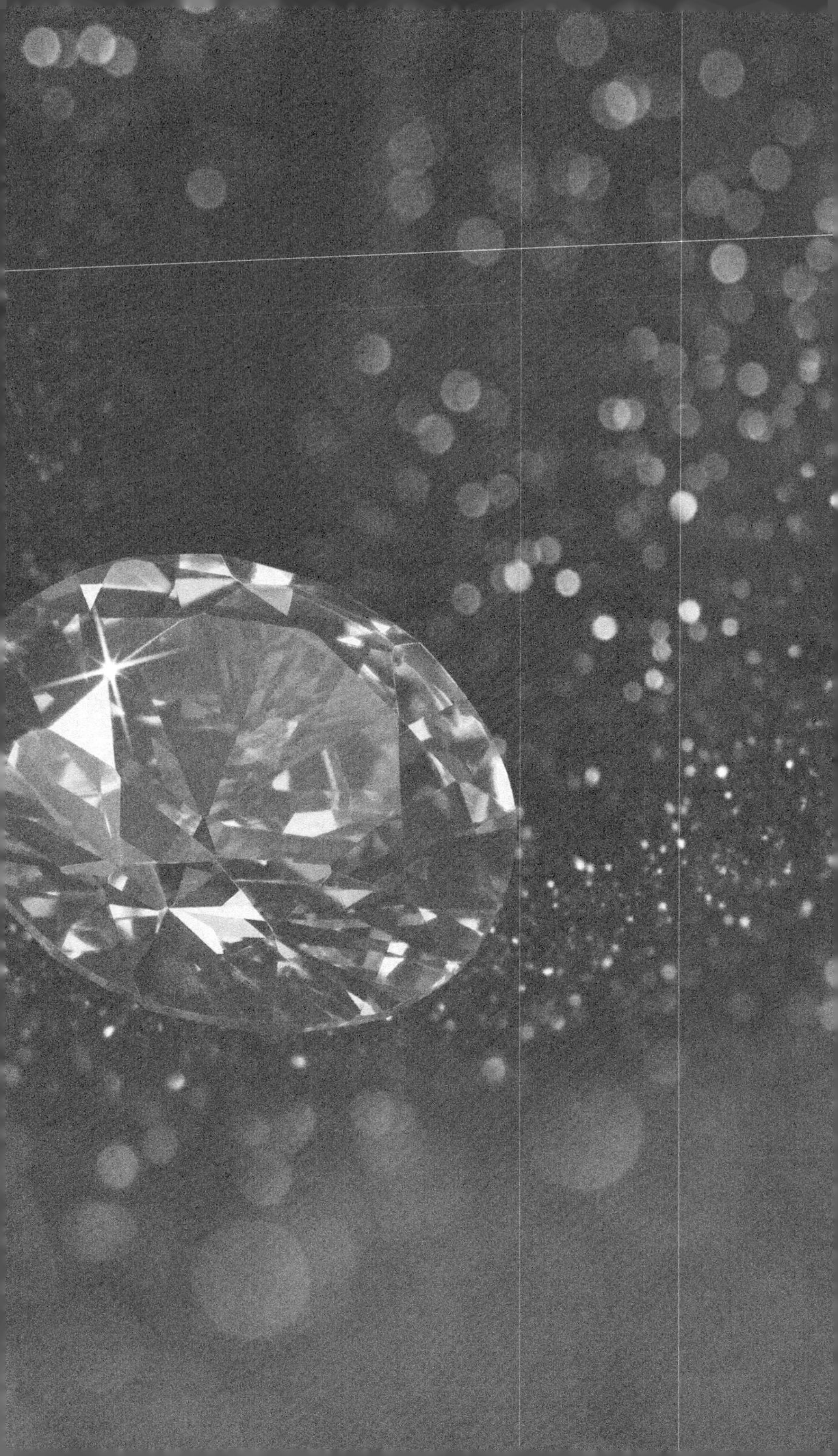

CHAPTER
TWENTY-SIX

Maxim

"What do you mean she's gone?" My hands were in a frenzy in front of Val. I signed to her while I had my phone to my ear.

I called Sia right away after Val told me she was missing.

The phone ringing unanswered in my ear, I didn't like the look on Val's face. Val's jaw tightened. *"She's just gone, Boss. I don't know. I was just notified."*

"By fucking who?" I wasn't even signing at this point, too fucked up and borderline panicking.

I was panicking, and when Sia didn't answer, I tried calling her again.

"Sophia noticed she wasn't around," Val signed, looking panicked herself, and she didn't panic. She held a strong fear in her dark eyes, worry. She never worried either, and that didn't help mine. Val swallowed. *"After she noticed, she contacted me, and I requested a full search of the grounds."*

"And?" I was leaving my office at Peters & Burg.

Val quickly signed beside me. *"They didn't find her which is why I'm alerting you. The security at the house said it was like she vanished."*

Not possible. That wasn't fucking possible. There were too many people around. There were too many who worked for me that kept tabs on her. I had an arsenal looking out for her.

I had an arsenal to keep her safe.

I informed Val I was heading home, and she was right behind me in her car. I made calls along the way, speaking to literally everyone who worked for me or had interactions with Sia on the regular.

Why the fuck did I leave her?

I needed a moment. I needed *time* to figure out what should happen next in regards to her. It was obvious I shouldn't have slept with her. I definitely took advantage of her and the situation. I was in a position of power when it came to her. Not to mention she was my daughter's friend.

Seeing Sia and Lettie together only added to that guilt. They were friends, and that was fact. Even if Lettie was receptive to a potential relationship I may or may not have with her friend, things between Sia and I shouldn't have happened.

I needed time to figure out what to say to her, which was why I immediately put distance between us. I felt temporary space was necessary yet here I was losing my fucking mind about her.

I peeled into the house way too fast. In fact, I nearly hit my gardener but left no apologies when I finally parked. I even left the door of my Mercedes ajar when I left it.

As soon as I got inside the house, I barked for a house meeting. Word spread fast and I had everyone who worked for me downstairs in seconds. That was a lot of fucking people, and I was sure more than one had an idea about what was going on between myself and a twenty-year-old girl.

I mean, they worked for me.

I wasn't naive. A few of my staff (or more) may have

noticed Sia and I getting closer, but it wasn't their job to have opinions. The same went for Val who joined me as I informed everyone to comb the grounds for Sia Reynolds. Val, too, kept her opinions to herself, and after my initial order, she took charge. She got a formal search party going right away even though this probably had already been done.

I didn't care. They were going to do it again, and while they searched, I called Sia. She didn't answer no matter how many times I tried. In fact, after my initial calls the phone went straight to voicemail. Like her phone was shut off or dead.

I didn't know what that meant except that I couldn't track her. When Val got her phone at the wireless store, I instructed her to put a tracker on it. I wanted to know where Sia was at all times, and my head of security hadn't asked. She probably assumed the paranoid fuck in me wanted to know where she was.

Not that I was obsessed.

I *was* obsessed, my shirt open and panic in my veins. Eventually, I stalked my property myself. I was a good tracker, but there was no trace of Sia anywhere.

It was as if she'd actually vanished.

I wouldn't let myself entertain the thought or even think about how many enemies I had. When one took as many lives as I had over the years that was a given. People stayed the fuck away because of who I was and the organization I belonged to. I was Bratva and people didn't fuck with that shit, but someone or *someones* could be stupid.

God save them and everyone they loved if they chose to fuck with me.

My phone flashed, and since I had it permanently secured to my hand, I lifted it.

There was a text.

Unknown: I'm in your vineyard. Come alone.

What the fuck?

Me: Who the fuck is this?

The text message came from a number I didn't recognize, and without saying a word, I headed toward the closest closet I could find in my home. After punching in a few codes, I gathered some knives. They were ones for carving.

They were ones for ending life.

I strapped half of my best tools to my chest, then tucked a gun in my back pocket. I doubted I'd use it.

I didn't need it.

Me: You better tell me who the fuck you are, asshole.

I sent the text while I headed toward the vineyard. I still had people searching the property for Sia, but I instructed them to search other areas. They were to stay away from the vineyard no matter what they heard.

My texts went unanswered. Whoever this was left me on read, and I went into hunter mode. I blacked out. Someone was on my fucking property messing with me.

Messing with what was *mine*.

Instinct told me this person had Sia or had something to do with her disappearance. The bloodlust charged hot in my veins, and I was actually salivating by the time I got deep into my vineyard. I could taste blood. I fucking craved it, but before I could do something about it my phone rang. It was the unknown number, and I immediately answered.

"Who is this?" my voice was rough and charged with that same bloodlust. I gripped the phone. "Whoever you are trust and believe I will end your life and anyone you hold dear to you if you've hurt…"

I couldn't finish the words. I couldn't finish the thought.

My eyes narrowed. "Show yourself to me."

At this point, what they said didn't matter. The end result today would be death reserved for whoever fucked with me and mine. She was mine. Sia Reynolds was *mine* whether that was appropriate or not. She'd given herself to me the moment she stepped into my home.

A breath was on the other end, a light breath, an airy breath.

Had a woman taken her?

Women sounded different on the phone, less aggressive, less intense.

My eyes narrowed further. "Who are you?"

"I know your secret."

I blinked, heart charged, racing.

That couldn't be helped when I heard her voice.

My throat thickened. "Sia..." I wiped away all emotion, focusing. "Sia, have they hurt you?"

And what was this about a secret?

The seconds in which she didn't speak had my mind reeling, but I stayed patient. I waited.

"I know what you're into." She swallowed hard into the line. "I found it. I know your secret."

I didn't know what she was talking about. My hand gripped the phone. "Sia—"

"I also know about the footage. Of me?" Her breath was harsh. "I know you've been watching me."

Alarm bells rang off in my head, and soon, I wasn't thinking about someone hurting her, harming her.

Had she left me?

"You..." I started, my mouth dry. "You know about the cameras?"

I had been watching her. I had been *getting off* to the sight of her.

"I do," she said and thoughts of her leaving on her own accord, leaving *me,* came to mind. Had she been disgusted? Had she left and no one had taken her?

This wasn't the worst, but it almost felt that way. The lining in my throat thickened to massive levels. "Sia..."

I honest to fuck didn't know what to say and her leaving me probably was the best solution. It was for her, and if I'd been stronger, I would have had her leave after things crossed the line. I would have set her up handsomely of course. Financially, she'd want for nothing.

"Have you left me, *malyshka*?" I shouldn't have asked her that. It was an idiot thing to say, but it couldn't be helped. Before this call, I believed my greatest fear was one of my enemies taking her.

Not this.

This had me terrified. I had no control here. She'd taken it, and I felt powerless.

"Is that what you want?" she asked and anxiety almost sounded laced in her voice. Like she was worried about my response. "Because if not, I don't mind being chased. I don't mind being hunted."

What the fuck?

"Because that's what you're into, right? Your secret?" she continued. She huffed. "I looked it up. You're into predator and prey right? It's your kink."

I blinked. "Baby girl, I don't know what you're going on about, but you need to let me know if you've left me because I'm losing my fucking mind."

"I haven't left you, Maxim," she said and the relief that hit me was unnatural, foreign. Her leaving me shouldn't make me or break me.

But it would. My life had changed now that she was in it, and the fact that she wasn't leaving brought all senses back to me.

Especially when she said what she did next.

"I want to be hunted," she charged on, and her voice was breathy, nervous. This conversation was sending her to places beyond her comfort zone, but all it did for me was pump blood into my cock. A moment ago, I thought I'd never see her again, but now... She sighed. "I wanted to be hunted by you. I know that's what you're into."

"I know your secret."

She started the conversation with those words, and now,

this whole situation was taking on a new perspective. She'd gone missing and her absence led me to the vineyard. It was getting dark around us. It was *only us*, and that had been because of her. She said to come alone.

She hadn't wanted anyone around.

My dick steel, I massaged it to keep the growth at bay. "You want to be hunted, *malyshka*?" I questioned, my voice gruff. "You want me to hunt you?"

She said she knew my secret.

Naughty girl.

She was naughty. Though I hadn't exactly been discreet about my vice. I brought women around in the past, and there had been signs.

Her looking it all up after the fact had me gripping a bush at this point. I was afraid I'd blow my load in my pants waiting for her to speak.

"I don't mind being pinned down," she said, and I dizzied, maddened. "I also don't mind that you've been watching me. I've known about it for a while. I was under your desk one day when you... Well, when you got off."

Fuck.

My hands were shaking, and I didn't fucking shake. If she was here, I'd strip her bare. I'd bend her over and fuck her in every dark and depraved way I could until I broke her.

I'd punish her.

I'd punish her for breaking me and keeping this secret from me. I'd punish her for being naughty and encroaching in my space. I allowed no one to get the jump on me in my life.

"I just wanted to let you know it's okay," she said. "It's okay that you're into those things, and it's more than okay that you've watched me. I... Well, I want you."

My demon had been awake most of this conversation, but now, it was going to a place where only it existed and Maxim Petrov was taking a backseat to it. It was *taking over* and... I shook my head. "Sia, listen to me. I become a different person when I hunt. I hunt to break, and I don't want to hurt you."

I really didn't. She was *fragile*, and I didn't want that.

Sia Reynolds had a history. People in her past had hurt her, and I wanted her shielded from more darkness.

That was all she would get when it came to me.

I knew in my heart of hearts this was the real reason why I put distance between us. It wasn't age, and it wasn't even Lettie. I didn't want to put Sia through more trauma.

"I'm strong, Maxim, and I can handle it."

She was saying this now, but it was so easy to just say. I glanced down. "Sia…"

"I just ask that you always look at me," she said, surprising me. It was straightforward, firm. "I like to know what's going on. Always look at me and make sure I can see you."

Surprised again, I didn't respond right away. It was rare anyone new to my lifestyle was so forthcoming. Usually, women bent over backwards for me and didn't know what they were signing up for. They gave themselves to me completely and disregarded their own needs. It was a turn off, and I'd rejected partners for such a thing.

But Sia didn't do this. This young girl was completely aware of her limits, and I found my breath moving huskily into the line. "You want to know what's going on," I said, my cock harder, fuller. I massaged it. "Tell me what else you need."

I shouldn't be playing these games with her. I shouldn't be entertaining this at all but…

"Just that," she said, and I shook my head.

I brought the phone closer. "You need to be specific with your limits. It's so important, *malyshka*, because once we start… Once I start hunting you, I won't stop. I won't if you scream. I won't if you *bleed*. If fact, the sight will only make me more crazy so you need to be fucking certain of your limits."

Admitting this to her should scare her. It should drive her away, but the response on the other end of the phone was the same as mine. She continued to breathe heavily, and my demon fully unlocked.

I went *feral*.

"That's all, Maxim. Just let me know what's going on. I want to be aware of everything."

My chest rose. "I will do that. And you'll always have your safe word if things get too intense."

My mouth was watering waiting for her response, and for a second, I wasn't sure if she was still there.

"It's jellybean," she said, her voice raspy. "Now come find me."

The line clicked off, and I barely blinked. I just reacted, and suddenly, the vineyard became less of a place that produced wine and more my hunting ground.

She's here.

How I hadn't known that before baffled me. Sia's scent was in the air. It was now that I wasn't too blind and worried to be aware of it. She was everywhere, like she'd run through this whole place.

Perhaps she had.

She'd tried to make this hard for me, but she didn't know me. She didn't know who I was and the things I had done. I was the executioner and capturing prey came so easily to me. I always found what I sought out.

Always.

A crackle of leaves sounded behind me, and I pivoted, grinning. She was close.

I hunkered down, my eyes closed.

She gave herself away in seconds.

My eyes shot open, and right away, I went into a full sprint.

I knew exactly where she was and the adrenaline pumped through me like a bullet heading toward its mark. Each sound she made through the vines led my path, her scent like a beacon drawing me directly to her. I found her standing between two grapevines, and that was the first time Maxim took over and the demon took a backseat. Sia was naked before me.

Completely naked.

I was in awe of her as she stood in the moonlight, confident and bare as the light touched her brown skin. Her curls were wild in the night, her flushed tits moving up and down rapidly. She'd been running too.

I didn't approach her, did nothing but stand before her like a man given a precious gift. It was only when her eyes directed toward my hand that I realized I had my knife. In fact, her brown eyes flashed in that direction.

The knife was instinct and sometimes I did make my partners bleed. I liked the smell on my blade, the taste, but I put it away and studied Sia. She made a step after that, like she'd run, and I held up a hand.

"Don't." My voice was rough, and my dick was so heavy I thought it'd snap off. "Don't run, *malyshka*."

It was a rare moment she had me as myself, but she shouldn't test me. The demon could take over at any time.

He *was* taking over. He was with each heavy breath she made and her smell that lingered harshly in the air. The scent wasn't just her natural fragrant aroma but the one she made between her legs. In fact, that scent was *everywhere*. Testing me...

Sia darted off, and the hunter inside me erupted. The knife came out again, and it was at her throat when I eventually caught her.

It hadn't taken long.

She'd panicked, and I was fast. I got her by the arm, and all too quickly, I brought her to the ground. I brought her beneath me.

And once there, I didn't stop.

I had her arms behind her, her thigh braced in my hand when I jerked her roughly across the leaves. She cried out, and it ended up being that to first break her skin. She got caught on something on the ground, and I touched my blade to the cut.

It was beautiful.

I let her see the blood. I actually pushed it to her lips so she could see how magnificent it was. She bled beautifully, and instead of being scared by that, her tongue darted out.

Fuck.

She licked the blade clean, and I lost my shit. Soon, I had my tongue down her throat, the two of us tasting something that was normally repugnant and doing something so depraved. I was wild at this point, but the whole time I let her see what was going on. I wouldn't put her on her stomach. I'd keep her with me.

I'd keep her for-fucking-ever.

These thoughts were dangerous but so was what we were doing. Eventually, my blade was forgotten, and I forced her legs apart. Her glorious scent hit me in copious waves, and she screamed when I pulled my cock out and ripped inside her. I still kissed her, tasted her blood, and she ended up tasting mine when she bit my lip.

Dangerous, little one.

I held her back by her throat when she did that, flicking her tongue with mine as I fucked her into the ground. Her breast in my hand, I squeezed, her tits so beautiful and rosy in the moonlight. This woman was a goddess.

"Maxim, fuck," she called out, but she didn't say her safe word. She just let me fuck her, her eyes rolling back, and it didn't matter how many thrusts I made I couldn't get deep enough.

"So fucking tight, baby girl," I crooned, and her eyes closed when I squeezed her throat harder. She choked a bit, but I didn't stop until her breaths labored to the point where I thought she'd pass out. I knew that point, but she most likely didn't.

Even still, she didn't tap out, and my thrusts went to new levels. I wasn't doing things the way I normally did. Usually, there was a discussion. Hard and soft limits were discussed, and there were definitely contracts. They were to protect everyone, and I couldn't remember the last time I took a partner raw, bare.

This wouldn't be the last time.

Sia's body was my haven, my precious girl to take, to love. I wanted to break her as much as I wanted to put her back together.

"*Malyshka...*" I spilled inside her, coming like a man desperate. I was desperate, and her snatch squeezing around me only made me milk her long after we both came. I needed her essence. I needed her close. When it came to my prey, I always wanted to break them.

But somehow it was me who ended up being broken.

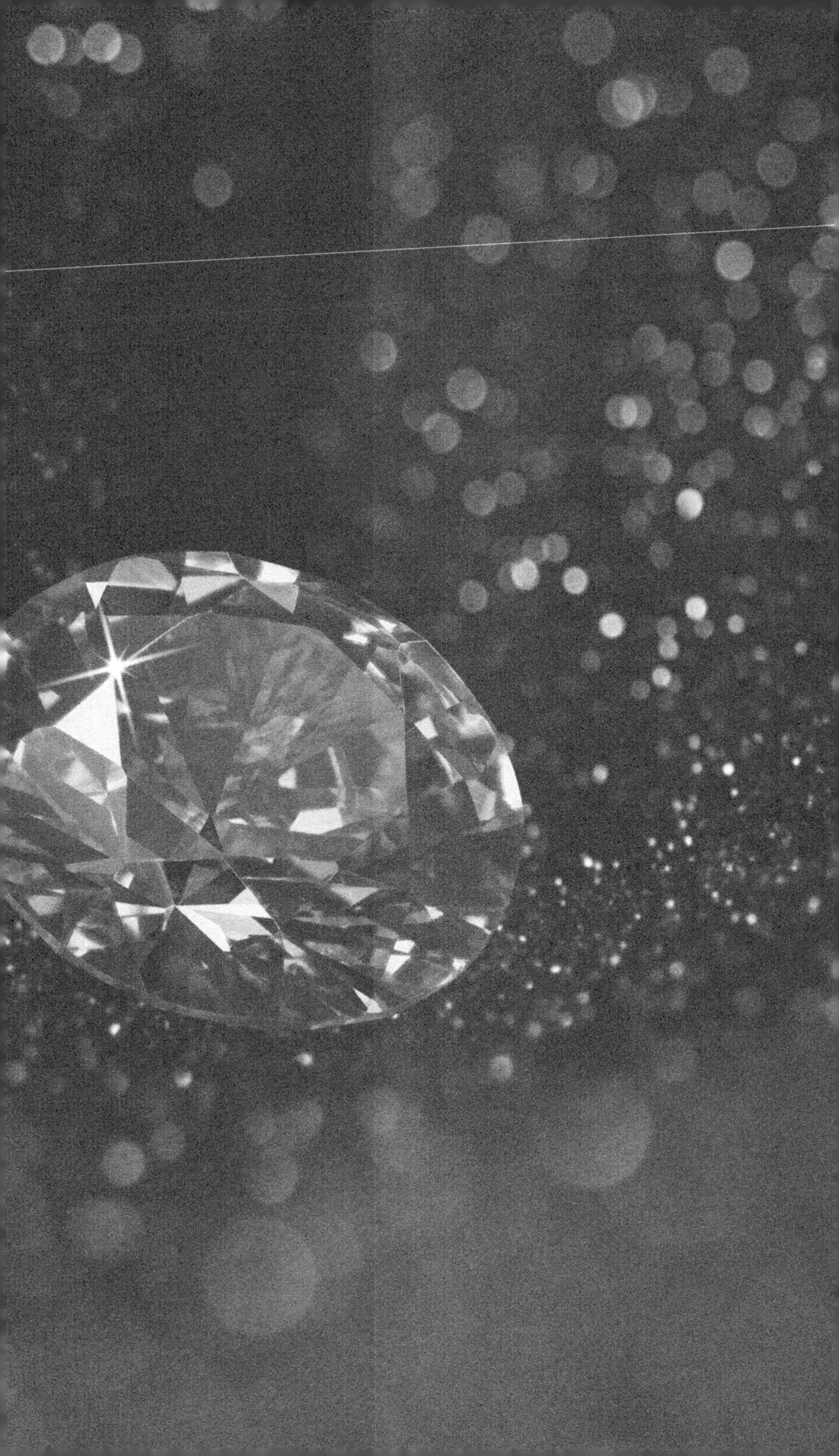

CHAPTER
TWENTY-SEVEN

Sia

Why was I...smiling?

It felt weird to, and I honestly wasn't sure if I would after I decided to approach Maxim.

But I was.

In fact, I couldn't *stop* smiling. Especially when I studied Maxim beside me. We laid in the vineyard for a bit after he'd taken me, and I hoped I did everything right. The internet could only tell me so much, and being with him in that way had been different than I expected. There'd been choking involved.

There'd been blood.

I hadn't really minded either, which was crazy, intense.

I wonder what that means.

I didn't think too hard about that with his arms around me now. We were in his large bed, and he kissed me until we both relaxed into sleep. We'd taken a bath first, and there'd been aftercare. He enjoyed washing me and loving on me. That was so different than how he'd been outside.

I really couldn't stop smiling. Especially since we had spent so much time in the bath. Maxim had said aftercare was very important to him, and he emphasized that again when we'd been in his tub. I'd never felt so cared for after he brought me into the house. He let me wear his shirt and everything.

My fingers grazed the dark hairs on his forearms. His hold on me was tight, steadfast. I tucked tighter into his embrace, and last night, I wasn't sure about how I'd feel when I decided to try out what he was into. The anticipation of it all actually terrified me.

But once we'd gotten started...

Texting him had been thrilling. I'd read all about scenes on the internet. I figured I'd try that out by pretending to go missing, and I'd been exhilarated when Maxim played along. Honestly, I never felt like I had so much power. He hunted me, but *I* felt empowered. I got him to unleash a part of himself that was truly, well, himself.

And it'd been on my terms.

The grin was permanently plastered on my lips. Pivoting in his arms, I wanted to kiss him but didn't want to wake him up. I was only ninety percent sure he'd go for something like last night with me. He'd been trying to pull back, and though I got the Lettie thing, I didn't want him to retreat because he thought I'd be scared about who he was. He had a dangerous job and lifestyle yes, but if his darkness went deeper than that I wanted to at least put it out there to him that I was open to whatever that dark side was. I'd definitely gone out on a limb last night, and I was grateful I had.

I settled for playing with his dark hair instead of kissing him. He looked so peaceful as he slept, and I was pretty sure I scared the shit out of him last night by going missing. I knew I had actually because he had to make a few calls once we got inside the house. He'd snuck me into his room, then called his staff. Apparently, they'd been searching high and low for me.

It was crazy how in the beginning he acted as if he hadn't cared for me. The urge to kiss him really snuck up on me now, but once more, I resisted. I wanted him to sleep, and he seemed to, deeply. He didn't even move as I played with his hair.

He breathed in so deep as I did. Like he enjoyed that even in his sleep. I only let myself play for a few more moments before getting out of bed. Light was starting to appear through his window, which meant it was almost time for me to take Polly out.

I ended up putting on one of Maxim's shirts on the way out. We'd both gone to bed naked. He'd taken me again there. We had sex the regular way this time, and it hadn't been nearly as fun as outside.

I tried to think about what those thoughts meant as I grabbed a fresh pair of Maxim's boxers to put on with the shirt. Outside wasn't only fun, but there were so many things in my head I wanted to try. I was so new to all this, but I was intrigued with everything I discovered on the internet. I was so open, and I did wonder what that meant. I'd never really been physically rough with any partner I'd been with, and the prospect of that should completely horrify me.

I couldn't help it with my history.

My thoughts continued to wander as I went outside with Polly. The house wasn't awake yet, which meant the grounds were eerily quiet when I took Polly out. We did a long walk so I could think and get some fresh air. That ended up not being good enough because after I returned Polly inside I wanted more time. I decided to head out to the Petrov vineyards to get that, but as soon as I was there, I heard a crack in the leaves.

"Hello?" I backed up. I suddenly wished I hadn't already taken Polly inside. There could be animals or...something. My hands curled. "Hello—"

A hand covered my mouth from behind. It silenced my word and my scream, and I bucked.

At least, I tried to.

The world tilted, my vision clouding, blurring. I didn't like being approached from behind and certainly not grabbed from behind. A panic attack on the horizon, I attempted to fight through it with a scream, and it audibly hit the air when I was tossed on the ground.

Pain instantly lanced my kneecaps, but I wasn't on them long. A heavy force grappled me from behind, and I screamed again.

Oh, please, God, no.

I scratched at the earth, trying to scurry from beneath whoever was on top of me. I ended up flattening from the weight, and the panic really set in.

This can't be happening. This can't be...

But it was, my nails digging into the earth. A blade touched my neck at one point, and I knew I was calling out, screaming. Tears rushed my eyes, and I thought I was going to vomit. My panic literally brought chunks and bile up my throat. Whoever was on my back was going to hurt me. They were going to do terrible things, and that I knew in my heart.

My fight or flight couldn't be helped. It didn't matter that the person brought my arms behind me or even when they kicked my legs apart. I had to fight. I had to *try*, but that was made easier when the weight on my back suddenly left. The force on top of me had rolled off, and I turned around.

I blinked upon seeing the dirty man on his side. He was covered in brush and appeared greasy. He was also heavily tattooed from his face to his hands, and I realized I recognized him from the bar the night I ran away from the Petrov house. He was the man who'd hit me.

The one Maxim silenced.

He wasn't looking at me currently. Now on his back, he

scurried away with terror in his eyes. He got on his feet, but the moment he ran in the opposite direction, a blade lodged into his back.

Maxim hit him next.

He forced the man down to his knees with a single blow, another blade in his hands. He used it to stab the man in his ribs, and his eyes had changed. They'd gone darker, and when he twisted the knife, the man's eyes beneath him changed too. They went white, blank.

Maxim didn't relent. He twisted and twisted his blade and didn't stop until the man fell forward beneath him. He collapsed, but even after that, Maxim didn't stop. He took out another blade and shoved it into the man's throat.

I covered my mouth, the blood rushing from the man's wound over Maxim's hand. The force had splattered blood all over Maxim's face, but he hadn't blinked. If anything, his eyes had gone just as vacant as the man's but in another way. It was like he'd left his body too and became something else. Changed.

"Maxim?"

It was like my voice brought him back and all the blood faced me when he did. His dark hair was coated in it, his tanned skin. He wet his lips, and I flinched when he let go of the man. I think that had just been a natural reaction to the body, but the moment I had, Maxim cringed.

"Are you okay?" he asked me, his voice rough, unsure. The statement didn't hold his normal confidence, and soon, he was looking at the man, at what he'd done. He faced me again. "Sia..."

"Yes, I'm fine," I said, getting my thoughts back. I nodded. I was shaking but not because I was scared. I mean, I had been scared before, but now it was adrenaline.

Even still, Maxim put a little distance between us. He stared at the body again, but then, he was looking at me. He nodded. "Good, I..." He fingered his hair. His jaw moved. "I woke up, and you weren't there."

I wasn't. I'd gone for a walk. I nodded. "I took Polly out, then went for a walk."

His head bobbed twice in acknowledgement. He stared at the ground once more, but this time, that'd been because of me. There was a man dead before us, and I couldn't help it.

Maxim's lips thinned. "I don't know how he got in. I'll have to speak to someone. I was looking for you and came across him following you."

This was clearly revenge of some kind, and it made sense after what happened at the bar.

I couldn't help staring at the body. I mean, it was *a body*, and though I'd seen him kill before, it was still foreign to me. *Maxim* was still foreign to me. Who he was, was still different to me, but he didn't scare me. In fact, the opposite.

I had a feeling that wasn't how he perceived my reaction. A tension wrinkled his brow, and he backed up. He put more distance between us, but before he could do more, I moved.

He watched, his observant gaze on me when I not only approached him but pushed my arms around his waist.

Maxim sucked in a breath. He didn't hold me back right away, and his blades were still in his hands. He swallowed. "You're okay?"

I was more than okay. My fingers curled into his shirt. My head moved to nod against his rapidly breathing chest.

His head shook against mine.

"Use your words, *malyshka*," he said, and that term of endearment rolled through me. It was like an ethereal warmth, a haven. His breath went rough. "You're okay?"

Pulling back, I looked at him. He scanned my eyes and so much worry was in his. Did he fear I had been scared by him? That I judged him for what he'd done? I could never. I pushed my fingers into his hair. "I am fine. I'm good. I swear."

Maxim sagged in that moment. If it was from relief or something else I didn't know, but whatever the case, he finally held me back.

He even dropped his knives.

Maxim held onto me with the force of a man who needed something. Like I was *his* version of an ethereal warmth.

Like I was his security.

PART TWO
A NEW DAWN

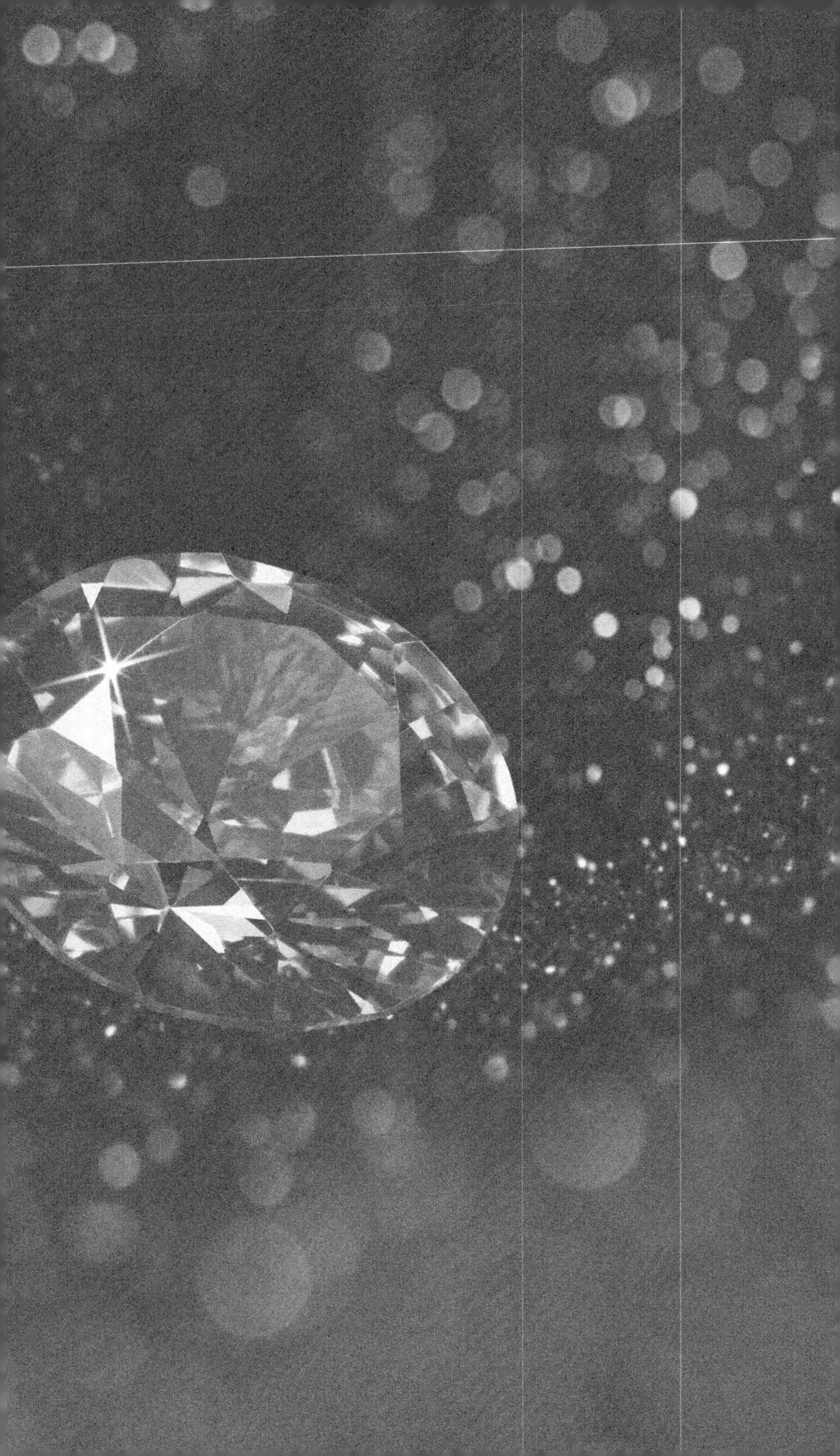

CHAPTER
TWENTY-EIGHT

Sia

The next few days were kind of a blur. Actually, the next few *weeks* were. Maxim spent more time at home than he did away.

He spent the time exploring me.

Really, we explored each other. Maxim had some interesting kinks, and well, I was open. I made sure he knew that when he had me sign a formal contract. I had to detail exactly what I wanted. Maxim said this was necessary so no boundaries were crossed. He had his own limits too but not many. The main one was contraceptives. He swiftly got me on birth control after finding out I wasn't on one. We also got tested since we failed to use a condom at least once when we'd been together. I wasn't pregnant, and we both got tested for everything else too.

He'd apologized profusely that we hadn't used a condom. He said that was outside of character for him, but that just made me more wild that he couldn't hold back. We certainly had some fun sexually the weeks following our initial hook ups, but we didn't do any more stuff in his vineyard. This wasn't because I didn't want to though.

Maxim had people everywhere on his property, and though I didn't want to keep what we were doing a secret he had concerns about our relationship getting back to Lettie. When he said that, I worried I might be his shameful secret, but he said that wasn't the case at all and surprised me.

He wanted to tell her about us himself.

He wanted to do this in person during her next break, and I wanted Lettie to know too. I didn't like lying to her, but the thought of doing so worried me. Maxim and I were fucking. It was fun, but I didn't know what we were. Did I want it to be more? Sure, but I wasn't quite sure how that would work. I mean, Lettie was my friend and what would that make me being involved with her dad? I also didn't know what her reaction would be to me *being with* her dad.

The whole situation was just weird and complicated but what *wasn't* was my connection with Maxim. It was hot, and it was exciting. I looked forward to being with him every day.

I was addicted.

I felt like he might be addicted to me too. Like stated, he spent more time at home than away. It'd been so much in fact that he did start working more at the office. He was trying to spend more time doing that so I'd been surprised after I returned from a walk with Polly one day and found him in his office. He usually didn't come home until late, but it was mid-afternoon.

He wasn't alone.

A man sat in the corner of his office. Maxim had the door open so I could see him well. The man had a hand on his knee, his skin pale and his hair long and dusky. Honestly, he looked kind of like Professor Snape from Harry Potter. He was a rather thin man with a serious disposition.

And the tattoos…

He had a ton of them just like Maxim. They crept out of the neck of his dress shirt, his legs crossed. He was chatting with Maxim, who was sitting on the edge of his desk. He nodded as the man spoke, but both men stopped talking when the thin man noticed me at the door.

I gripped Polly's lead, the man's stare so intense. His head cocked, he stared at me curiously, and once his attention was on me, Maxim's pivoted in my direction too. His gray eyes honed in on me just like they had that day he'd been in his office with those other people. The difference was he smiled at me this time. A noticeable glimmer of warmth also crinkled his eyes, and that made my stomach flip.

God, he was too good at that.

I turned to butter in front of him, and it took Polly fussing beside me to break me out of the Maxim trance I was in. Even still, I might have stayed longer, but suddenly, my vision was cut off from the two men.

Val.

She was in the room too. She eased in front of the doorframe, and I gathered she must have been standing beside the door.

She smiled too before nodding at me. She closed the door after, and I felt kind of silly for staring into what was obviously supposed to be a private meeting.

Me: Sorry. Wasn't trying to be nosy.

I shot the text off to Maxim after returning to my room. I still only had a few contacts so I had to double check I sent the text to the right person. I was paranoid about sending something to Lettie by mistake and almost had a couple times.

Maxim's text message bubble surfaced quickly after I texted and that surprised me. I hadn't expected a response right away since he had company.

Maxim: It's fine. No big deal.

Maxim: And I don't recall giving you permission to expose your neck.

I could almost hear the grit in his voice, the arousal. Maxim tended to like my neck. He liked biting it and pressing a blade to it. I think it got him off seeing his knife touching the vein beneath my skin, but he never did more than that.

Well, he didn't unless I made him.

I may or may not have leaned into his knife a few times. I couldn't help it seeing his reaction to the blood. His pupils always dilated, and he licked me clean every time. That got *me* off and led to some of the most awesome sex we had.

I was turning into someone really interesting since we'd gotten together, and every time we played, I found out more and more about myself. I discovered my own limits and loved that I got to test Maxim's power. I wasn't used to having that a lot in my past.

Me: I don't recall saying I care. *tongue out emoji*

So I liked being a brat, which was something else I found out about myself. This wasn't surprising. It had always been fun to test Maxim, tease him. He liked so much control.

Maxim: It's nice to know how brave you are with some distance between us.

I could almost hear that in his voice too, and my face warmed, my thighs clenched.

Me: What are you going to do about it?

Maxim: You'll see once I'm done with this meeting. Now be a good girl until then, or I'll take it out on your ass.

I hoped he would.

Snickering, I tossed my phone on the bed. It flashed again, and I immediately picked it up.

Lettie: Hey, friend! How are you?

The smile fell from my face, but I responded quickly. I always did.

Me: Good. How are you?

Lettie's text bubble popped up, and I waited. She would probably want to chat for a little while and always did. God, I hated lying to her.

But what choice did I currently have?

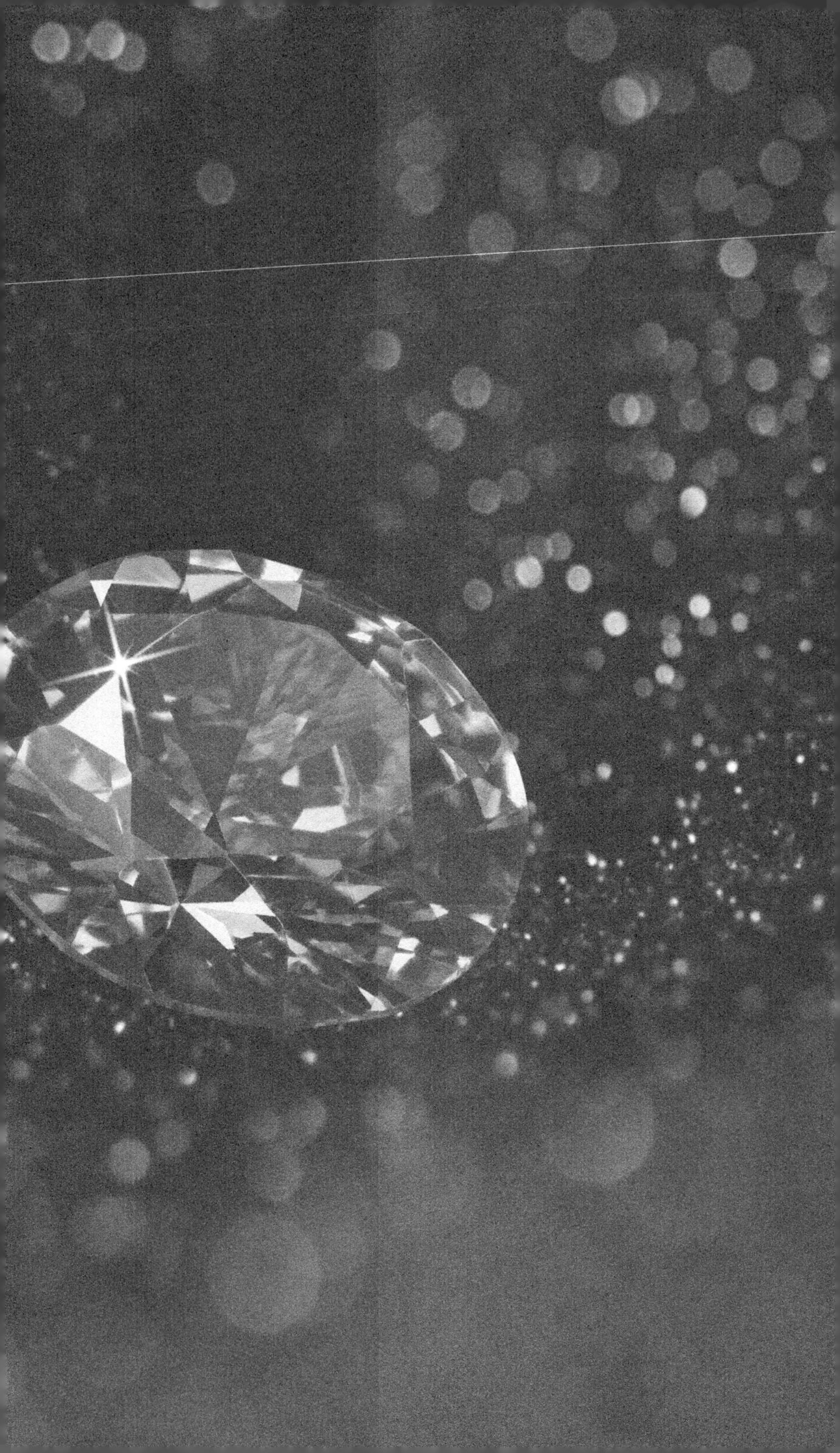

CHAPTER
TWENTY-NINE

Maxim

"I apologize again for what happened," I informed Natan outside of my office. Val held the door open for me, and I nodded at her. I faced Natan. "What happened at my home shouldn't have."

For many reasons, it shouldn't have. We handled things in different ways in the organization, and I acted rashly.

Though not unjustly.

If I had it my way, the man who attacked Sia—*my Sia*—would have been carved from the inside out. A swift death wasn't justice enough, and I think I'd only made it quick because of Sia.

I knew that was the case, but I still worried that night after I disposed of that filth in front of her. I feared Sia's judgment I supposed, but once again, she surprised me. She hadn't been disgusted by the bloodshed.

She hadn't been disturbed by me.

I braced my hands, sighing when Natan nodded at me. He was known as *pakhan*, the leader of the Bratva here in

Chicago, and he hadn't been upset when he found out what happened in the vineyard.

"I'm just glad you told me," he said, putting on his sports coat. Sophia had it ready for him when I guided her in. He nodded at her, and after putting it on, he tugged down the sleeves. "The man never should have entered your home, but then again, you should have told me when he initially attacked your member of staff."

I didn't like calling her that, but I had no other way to explain her to him. At least, not in a way my adoptive father could understand. Sia was so young.

My jaw shifted. It wasn't like that didn't happen. Especially in my world, but things were complicated. At least with me. Sia was my daughter's friend, so yes, that complicated things. Whatever Sia and I were wasn't anyone's business. It wasn't anyone's but Lettie's, and I would be talking to her about it the next time she was home. This wasn't a conversation I wanted to have over the phone. My daughter and her approval meant the world to me. She and I were all each other had.

At least, that was how it used to be. Before Sia...

I did do things I didn't normally do when it came to her. Things like silence one of my Bratva brothers for hurting her instead of going to the *pakhan*. Natan would have handled things in his own way, but I never let him.

Again, I acted rashly, emotionally. These were my sins, but my father was understanding. He placed a hand on my arm. "You're fine. Just, next time, you talk to me. He might not have come back for revenge had you done that."

I acknowledged this, bobbing my head once. With a gesture of my hand, I started to walk Natan out, but he stopped me.

"I actually have a job for you," he said, reaching into his coat, and when my brow lifted, he raised his hand. "I'd never ask unless it was important."

He knew my protests before I voiced them. I didn't do jobs on location anymore: hits. I didn't like who I became when I did. I became obsessed with the job, the bloodlust...

What I did now I had more control of which was why I earned the right not to be one of the Bratva's hitmen anymore. We had underlings for that, others who hadn't earned the same right as the *pakhan's* son.

Though getting back into the field unsettled me, I took what Natan pulled out of his jacket. It was a photo, and I immediately blinked at the image. I glanced up. "But he's just a boy."

He wasn't a child but a boy nonetheless. He wore an academy uniform, his hair curly and his skin light brown. The tone reminded me a lot of Sia as well as his smile. It was innocent, young.

This kid couldn't have been more than seventeen, which was why I think this affected me so much. He was too close to my daughter's age.

"Do you know who he is?" Natan questioned, and when I shook my head, he studied me. "His name is Andre Duncan. At least, on paper. In actuality, his name is Andre Novikov."

Instantly, my head shot up.

My body went numb.

The photo nearly dropped from my fingers, and I had seconds to recover before Natan drew closer.

I decided to speak before he could. "How is this possible?" I asked but kept my voice even.

"Because I obviously can't trust those who I thought I could," he said, studying the photo beside me. "Now you understand why that traitor Ilya had to be eliminated."

Ilya's voice sounded in my head suddenly. He'd pleaded with me in his final moments.

"Maxim, please no... Natan made a mistake..."

"You didn't make a mistake, then," I stated. The words tasted like gravel in my mouth, but I played it off. I made myself sound unaffected. "He said as much as he pleaded for his life."

Before I had my people beat him like a piñata. He said he just couldn't do something and mentioned a little boy.

Christ.

The dread hit me then. So many thoughts fired back at me but not one did I allow to play across my expression. I couldn't with my adoptive father here.

He studied me again. "The Bratva makes no mistakes. *I* make no mistakes," he said, his voice callous, cold. I was usually the same way. It was necessary in the organization. "Gratefully, not all of our people are as foolish as Ilya. Someone found out he was hiding the boy and reported that to me. He was keeping him at a boarding school in Switzerland or some shit."

Natan never lost his cool.

But when it came to the Novikovs…

He was easily triggered by that topic, and I was the same. Nikolai Novikov was responsible for the murder of my father. He killed my dad, *his doctor*, because he couldn't save the man's wife. He was a man of bloodshed and greed, and Natan had just as many tales regarding his heavy hand. The Novikov Bratva had to end in Chicago…

So the rest of us could rise.

I stared at the photo in my hands, my swallow hard.

"And I thank you for what you did that day. To Ilya?" Natan placed a hand on my arm. "I hoped that traitor's death would coax whoever was helping Ilya keep the boy safe to come forward. We received a tip Ilya was helping the boy, but we didn't exactly know where the kid was being kept. Ilya was questioned, but even after his betrayal was found out, he wouldn't reveal the truth."

The lining in my throat thickened. "And his death helped revealed the truth? The boy's location…"

This was obviously true, but I asked anyway.

"Yes, though not without struggle. I had to make a statement so Ilya's family was also tortured. I had to make it known to anyone who may be helping that traitor what would happen if secrets were kept from me."

I gripped the photo. "He had a wife and child."

He was me, just like me.

My father didn't have to vocalize that torture meant elimination. He took out Ilya's family.

Again, he made a statement.

This too was normal in our world unfortunately but such savagery regarding a man's entire family was rare.

Natan's hand moved to my shoulder. "I had to, son, and doing so got us the information we needed."

He knew how this affected me. I had a kid myself…

Going for one's family to gain information wasn't outside of the norm in our organization but such tactics were more common under the Novikovs. When my father stepped in as *pakhan*, he made it known the Bratva didn't do any unnecessary bloodshed.

The torturing and killing of Ilya's family felt unnecessary, but I didn't vocalize this, and I wondered why he didn't ask me to torture Ilya myself for information. The fact he hadn't made me grip the photo in my hand more tightly.

"Why are you asking me to do this?" I asked but, again, kept my voice even.

"Because you're the only one I can truly trust to handle something like this, son," he said, and my head lifted. "Take care of it please and do it quickly. He is a boy and doesn't need to suffer for the sins of his father."

And yet, he would die anyway. The punishment always fit the crime, and in this instance, this boy was paying for his father's sins.

Like the rest of his family had before him.

Sia

Maxim was filling a bag for some reason. He was *packing* and moving in quick time. The only reason I knew he was packing at all was because I happened to catch him in the middle of it.

"Maxim?" I questioned, and he crossed in front of me. I mean, he barely noticed me at all until I stood in front of him. "Are you leaving?"

"I have to go out of town," he stated, then proceeded to cross in front of me again when he grabbed a t-shirt off the bed. I'd never seen him so frantic. He'd taken a shower, then immediately started doing this. His shirt was open, and his hair was still wet. He glanced up. "I uh, it's for work. I have to leave for work I mean."

"Okay." I sat on his bed and watched him scurry around for various items. Socks. Toiletries.

Normally, I didn't come into his room before bedtime, but I hadn't seen him all day. He never came to find me after his meeting ended, and I did see the guy he'd been speaking to leave earlier. He pulled away in a car with blacked out windows, and I watched him from the window of the library.

I went to find Maxim after that, but I was told by Val that he was in his office making calls all afternoon. It wasn't unusual for him to work from home, but what was unusual was how frantic he was. He seemed frazzled and completely unnerved.

I placed my hand on the bedpost. "When will you be back?"

"Not sure."

"Like a day or…"

"Most likely longer." His bag was packed, and he zipped it. He also didn't look at me.

My head cocked. "Will it be more than a week—"

"I said I'm not sure, Sia."

Having been snapped at, I closed my lips.

Maxim did too, and the last time he'd snapped at me had definitely been before we were fucking. He pushed his hair back with a sigh, and I got off the bed and started to leave the room.

He cut me off.

He placed his hands on my face, strong, warm hands. He didn't apologize to me, and for some reason, I didn't fight when he brought me forward.

He kissed me, his lips just as warm and encapsulating as his hands on my cheeks. Maxim was never a man of words. He wasn't generally tender either but this kiss and his hands on me were.

"I'll try not to be long," he said, his finger wrapping around one of my curls. He scanned my face. "Usually work trips don't take long, but I don't want to get your hopes up by giving you a timeline."

Yeah, I didn't like the sound of that. Especially since he'd had a meeting today with a guy who looked more than ominous.

"Is what you're going to do dangerous?" I asked, thinking about the unsaid thing in the room. As far as we both knew, he ran funeral homes where he sometimes *eliminated* people. I still didn't know why, and of course, I never questioned.

I was smart enough not to.

I wasn't sure what I expected him to say in response to my question. He'd been quite vocal in the past that I didn't know who he was. This obviously wasn't just in the bedroom. He was a different person outside of this house, and I just accepted it.

I had to.

I thought his openness about the more secret things in his life might have changed, though, considering we'd gotten closer, but when he picked up his bag and placed his hand on my cheek, I knew that it hadn't. He didn't say anything right away, leaving us in silence for a moment.

He wet his lips. "You text me if you need anything, okay? Val's been informed to look after you while I'm gone."

As suspected, he didn't answer or even acknowledge my question. I folded my arms. "So you're not going to tell me if what you're doing could get you hurt. Nice."

"*Malyshka*, I think you know I can't."

Actually, I didn't know that. I mean, could he still not trust me? Really?

He guided me to look at him. "Just wait for me, all right? I'll try to be back as soon as I can."

That wasn't good enough, but I guess I didn't have a choice but to accept what he was telling me.

He kissed the top of my head before letting me go, and I had a sinking feeling in my chest as he allowed the door to close behind him. I was pretty sure Maxim was in the mafia, and maybe him keeping things from me was less about trust and more about keeping me out of danger. Regardless, I was here and was a part of his life. At least in some capacity.

I felt like the guy I was seeing was going off to war or something, but at least the partner of a soldier in the military knew what they were in for. I had no idea what Maxim was doing or what he was about to do. I had no idea if he could *get hurt*.

And that fucking terrified me.

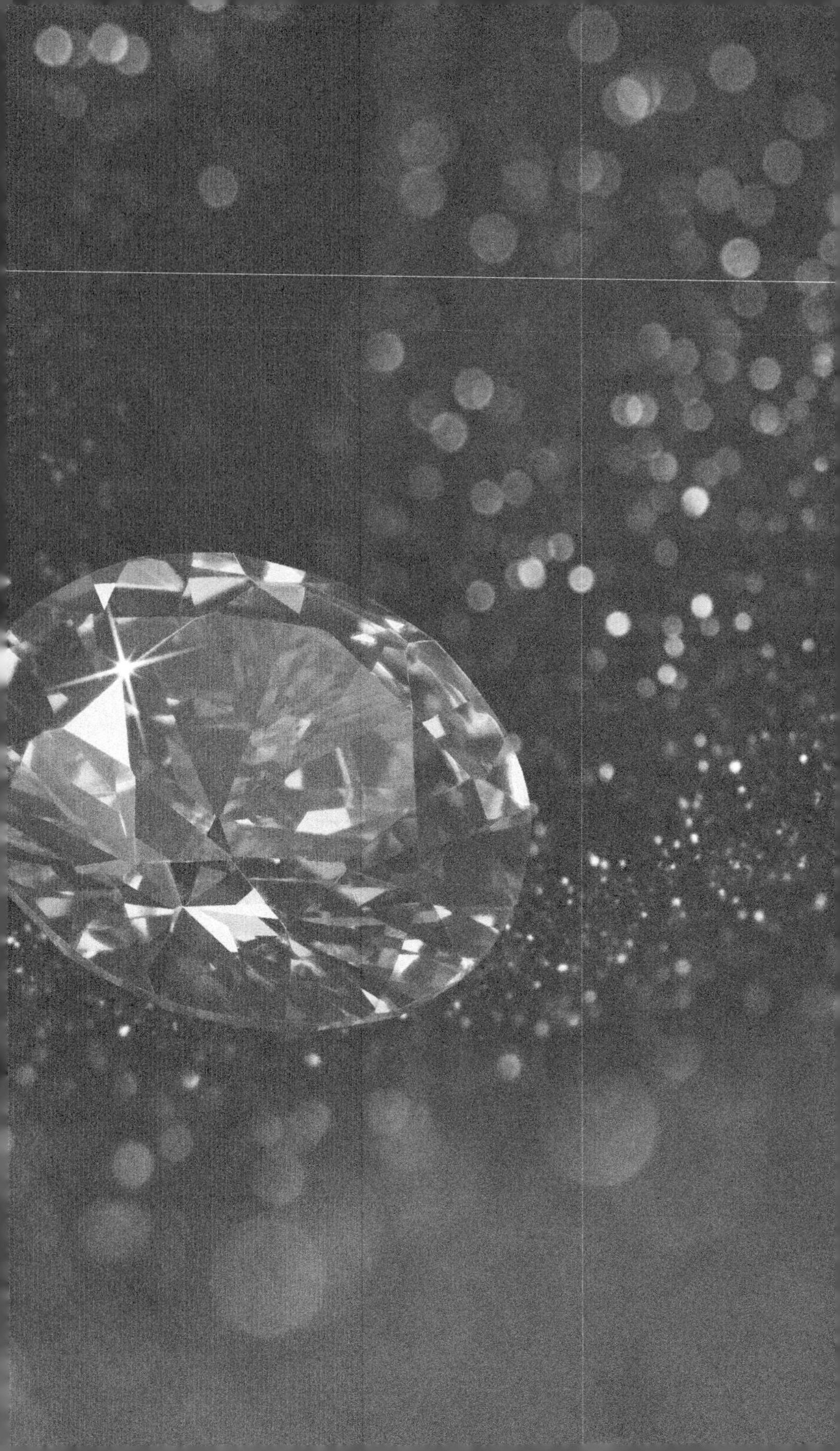

CHAPTER
THIRTY

Sia

Maxim was gone longer than a night. Than a week.

And he rarely texted.

He called even less, and sometimes it'd be days before I heard anything at all. Usually, I just checked in and asked how he was doing.

All I got in response were canned answers. He said he was busy and still working the job he was on. It was nice hearing from him, but he wasn't telling me anything at all.

"Malyshka, *I think you know I can't.*"

I didn't like how he sounded before he left and definitely didn't like how he sounded *after* he left. He never sounded carefree anymore during our sporadic conversations. He sounded serious and certainly didn't tease me. I never liked that, but once the teases were gone, well, I missed them. Now, Maxim sounded like he had when we first met. He came across as overworked, stressed.

And I didn't like it.

What I liked even less were when the calls and texts

stopped. Like they just *stopped*. I'd message him something, and there'd be zero response. Eventually, I started asking Val if he was okay. I was worried and needed to know, but each time I inquired, Val assured me she'd heard from Maxim, and he was fine. I was relieved when she'd tell me this, but why wasn't he telling me that himself?

I was starting to ask Val about Maxim's status too much, and I knew when she started looking at me funny. One day, she looked on the cusp of asking me why I kept asking so I broke down and texted Lettie. I was also tired of Val's canned answers.

Asking Lettie had been a mistake though. I wasn't weird about my line of questioning. I didn't want her thinking Maxim and I were involved before he was able to talk to her, but I did ask if he was normally gone for extended periods of time surrounding work. When she said not usually, I really started freaking out, and I could tell she did too when she started texting me and asking for more details. I didn't have those details, but I was able to assure her he was okay in the end. Her worry had stopped then but mine hadn't.

Something wasn't right about all this, and my gut told me that. Maxim appeared borderline panicked before he left and definitely frazzled. That wasn't normal at all, and I was thinking about that one day when I got Val's attention in the kitchen. She'd pretty much been staying at the house. Apparently, Maxim had wanted her to watch over everything while he was gone, but I had a feeling that was mostly for my benefit.

"*Val?*" I signed. She taught me her name and quite a few signs. I'd been a sponge for them. I really wanted to be able to communicate with her, and I could tell she'd been happy I was interested.

Val had been peering out the window, but she left it. She'd been doing that a lot since she got here, which didn't make me feel great. I never used to catch her doing that. I'd obviously been attacked, but my attacker was dead.

This made me think about Maxim. Things didn't feel safe here anymore, like they used to, but I worried less about my own safety. If people were after Maxim, I didn't know what I'd do. I didn't know what I could do.

"Can you teach me to fight?" I signed to Val, and her brow lifted. I wasn't sure if that was because of the request or the sign. I had to spell out the word *fight* since I didn't know it. *"I'd like to fight. Can you teach?"*

I spelled out the word again, and she smiled. She waved at me before showing me the ASL word for *fight*.

"Thank you," I spoke the word while signing. She nodded, then took out her phone. I watched her type a response, which wasn't uncommon. We normally did a combination of signing and texting. This was because of me of course. I wanted to be able to speak with her dominantly in ASL, but I was still learning.

"Why do you want to learn to fight, jellybean?" her phone screen said. She started calling me *jellybean* after seeing how many I ate since she'd come to the house more. I'd been stressed a lot with Maxim gone, but I found comfort in the nickname. Actually, it always made me laugh. Val typed again. *"You just want to learn for fun?"*

Not exactly. I swallowed. "I don't want to be here feeling helpless." I chewed my lip. "I hate feeling helpless."

I was only partially honest with Val. Yes, I did feel helpless being here. Especially after being attacked, but I felt useless as well. What if the difference between me being able to help Maxim or not came down to my ability to defend myself? I knew that sounded silly, but that was how I felt. I wanted to be able to take care of myself, yes, but maybe I could help him too in some way.

This did sound silly, but I wasn't just going to sit around

and do nothing. Not when he was out there doing God only knew what.

"*I can help,*" Val signed before helping me make tonight's salad. I didn't like Sophia making me dinner every night like I was royalty, and I really didn't like eating by myself. Val ate dinner with me most nights when I asked. I made my own meals, and she helped sometimes like this.

"*Help me fight?*" I signed. "*Or help me with dinner?*"

"*Both.*" Her eyes warmed after her sign, but then her expression fell. She typed on her phone before showing me the screen. "*I'm sure you felt helpless when that man attacked you, and you should learn some basic defense maneuvers. I can teach you that. No problem.*"

I was grateful for the help but didn't dwell on what she said. It was probably best she thought I just wanted to defend myself. She'd probably find it silly that, if it came down to it, I'd want to help Maxim too. It probably *was* silly.

I just didn't care.

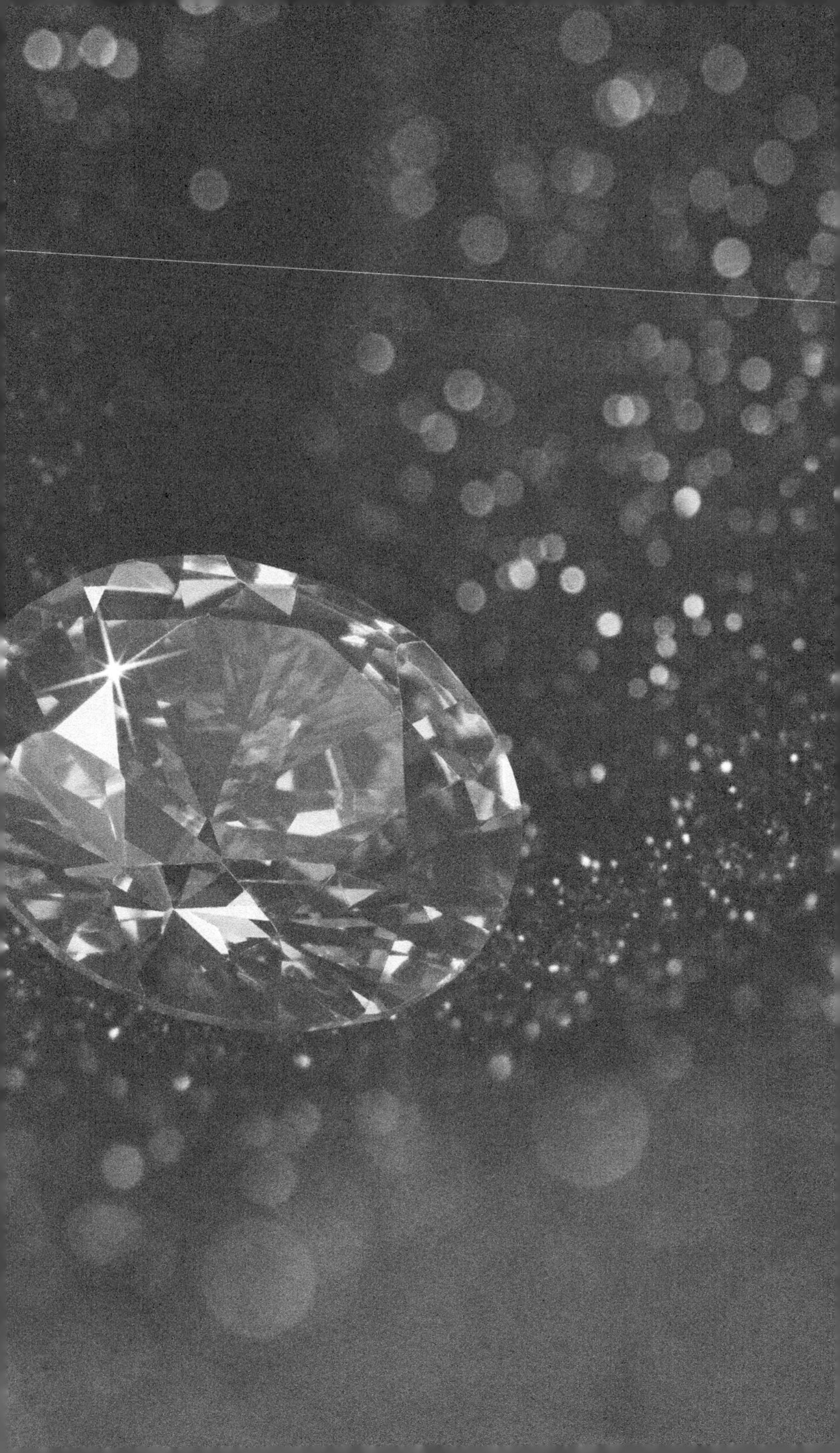

CHAPTER THIRTY-ONE

Maxim

Home was welcome after days upon days of tracking, searching.

I'd been gone over a month.

I felt the weight of all that time away. It rested in my back and shoulders.

It dwelled in my hands.

Upon entering my house, I shut the door and was immediately accosted by a hound.

Polly.

I lowered to her level and rubbed her behind the ears. It seemed the pup missed me. I also noticed she'd been allowed to wander freely in the house while I'd been gone.

Not minding that, I smiled at her. "Where's your mother?"

Sia had become her mom since she'd been here. Really, Polly had become our dog child.

I laughed at that thought, and of course, Polly didn't answer. She scampered away, and in her absence, I unbuttoned my shirt, winding down. I glanced around. "Sia?"

I had no idea why I called her randomly. I hoped she was nearby in the house I supposed.

I was desperate for her.

I'd kept her at arm's length for the past month. This was mostly for her protection. I turned into someone else when I was on a job, and I didn't want her to see that.

I felt so heavy from the person I'd been for the past few weeks. I just wanted to forget that person. I wanted a warm bath and Sia in my arms.

Having not heard Sia's voice, I asked about her as I passed various staff. No one had seen her recently, and I ended up checking her bedroom.

I cracked open her door but found nothing but a made bed. I headed to my room in the off chance she'd be there, but when she wasn't, I called Val.

"Welcome home, Boss," Val signed through my phone screen. She appeared to be in the gardens, and I assumed she was patrolling my property. Her head tilted. *"Your trip was successful then?"*

She already knew the details. I kept her in the know about everything as things happened.

"You already know how everything went," I signed back. I figured she was just making conversation or something. In any sense, I wasn't trying to make small talk right now. My eyes narrowed. *"I'm looking for Sia. Have you seen her?"*

I tried to make what I said sound casual. I instructed Val to keep an eye on Sia, but I told her to do that with everything around the house and my businesses. I wasn't at the point where people needed to know about Sia and me. I wasn't until I told Lettie, which I obviously hadn't had time to do since I'd been away.

A lot of things had been put on the back burner due to this job. It hadn't even turned out exactly how my father wanted. My mark had been tipped off and ultimately had gotten away. I informed Natan of those details, and he already had people trying to track the kid down. They'd find him, and once they did, I'd be ready to complete my mission.

I'd make myself.

The last month had been long and hard, and even though I hadn't been able to complete one mission, I'd been able to succeed in another. It took me weeks to find someone else, but I had. I'd been looking for another mark. One that had evaded me once before but I hadn't allowed that to happen again. I took care of what needed to be done this time, and because I did, I could rest easy tonight.

Everyone in my life could.

I didn't normally leave open loose ends, and the Bratva never did. I had one that haunted me for a long time, but now, I'd made amends. I hadn't been weak this last month. I finally did what I needed to do. I buried that error from my past figuratively and literally.

Val was signing with someone else, someone who called for her attention in the background. I called her name, waving through the line, and she nodded. She checked her Apple Watch. *"It's Monday, right?"*

"Correct." I was in my office now and sat down. *"Where is she?"*

"At class I believe."

I sat up. *"What are you talking about?"*

My head of security was still distracted. Someone else was talking to her now, but when I barked out a grunt, they both stopped signing. The gardener Val spoke with scampered away, and Val faced me. *"I mean, she's at class, Maxim."*

"I know what you said, but Sia isn't in school so she can't have a class."

"She wasn't in school, but she is now, so she does."

What the fuck?

Val's brow lifted before she signed, *"You didn't know?"*

"No, I didn't fucking know," I grunted. *"Where is she going to school?"*

"Prairie Hill."

Hearing the name of the local community college, my head cocked. *"Since when?"*

"For a while now," Val signed. *"You haven't talked to her?"*

Not as much as I would have liked and especially not toward the end of my mission. I couldn't have the distraction, and again, I hadn't wanted her to see me when I allowed my demons to take over. I became the monster within.

This was necessary but not something I needed her to see. I lost control sometimes, which was why I didn't do jobs anymore. I got off on the bloodlust and who I had to become to be the executioner. Avenging my father and what happened to our family had been priority.

"Who's with her?" I asked. I wasn't happy Sia was away from me and the house, but I suppose I understood. I'd been gone a long time and hadn't expected her to be twiddling her fingers when I came back. Even still, her being gone didn't sit well.

Especially when Val said what she did next.

"I had Gleb take her to class, but he returned to Peters & Burg," Val signed. *"He'll come back and get her when she's done—"*

"You mean to tell me she's at school by her-fucking-self without a chaperone?" I hadn't even bothered signing. I was up and out of my chair, and Val was waving at the screen.

"She is. Gleb used to wait for her, but she said that wasn't necessary."

Sia said like she had a fucking choice. I pointed a finger at the phone. "You were supposed to have someone watching her at all times. She doesn't get a fucking choice!"

I realized how I sounded, protective and crazy. Especially when Sia was just supposed to be a member of my staff.

I didn't care, and I'd address this shit after I went and got her. I was already grabbing my keys, and Val was still signing.

"Sia is cool on her own, Boss. I've been working with her and believe me when I say she knows how to hold her own."

I wasn't listening to what she had to say, too enraged, too betrayed. I specifically asked Val to protect her. I passed off the urgency of my need for that before. Sia had been attacked so that had been easy. Now, I just looked fucking crazy, but again, I didn't care.

"Just tell me where she is. Her class schedule or whatever," I signed, already outside. I opened my car. *"And we'll have words about this. I specifically gave you instructions regarding her protection, and this wasn't it."*

"I'm aware but you already handled the brother who attacked her, Boss, and word through the grapevine is Natan settled any kind of tensions that may have resulted from that. Your house is fine. That includes Sia."

I was aware of that too. Of course, I was. My adoptive father put out a veil of protection over me and mine after what happened at my home. He calmed the storm, but any logic of that was gone at the present.

I didn't think clearly when it came to Sia, which was why I forced her out of my mind for the past month. It wasn't just because I didn't want her to see my demons. The fact of the matter was I had a semblance of control over them when she wasn't in my head.

But I had zero control when she was.

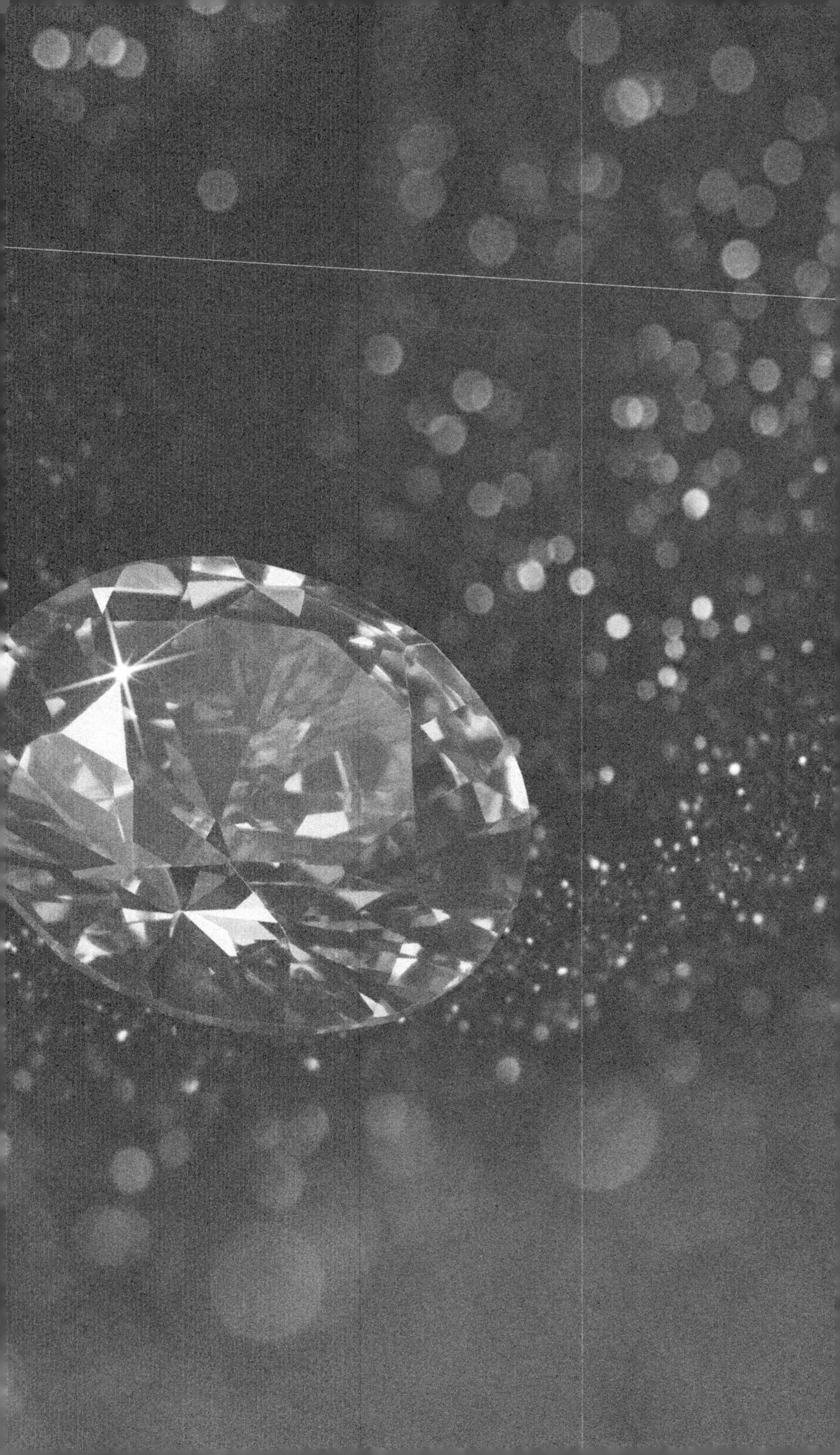

CHAPTER
THIRTY-TWO

Maxim

I was unimpressed with Prairie Hill's campus, or rather how *open* it was.

Sia was here? What was Val thinking?

Grunting, I sped too quickly through the parking lot and nearly hit a few people. I'd blame that on the fact that it was dark and not that I was zooming through the campus like a madman.

I parked my car in front of a random building, and when I left it there, security rolled up and tried to say something to me.

They thought better of it when I glared at them. They backed off, and I stalked the sidewalks toward the building mentioned on Sia's class schedule. Val texted it to me.

I stopped in my tracks shortly into my hunt. As it turned out, Sia wasn't that hard to find. It helped Prairie Hill's campus was 90 percent white, but Sia just stood out.

She couldn't help herself.

Her thick curls bounced on her shoulders during her

stride, her books to her chest. She appeared like a college student in a sweatshirt and jeans, a flush to her cheeks while she played on her phone. She was distracted by it and strode right past me. I caught a whiff of her then, so soft, sweet.

Seeing her and drinking in her scent quite literally froze me where I stood. I became a man entranced and unable to be moved. I wet my lips. "Sia..."

She hadn't gotten far away from me. She froze in her tracks too, turning around slowly. I'd been enamored by this girl just walking past me with her attention buried in her phone so the moment she made eye contact and parted those full lips...

Those lips and I had a history, our bodies the same. Mine woke up right away, blood pumping its way through my veins in a charged heat. It settled right between my legs, so much repressed emotion and passion instantly reinvigorated at just the sight of her. I hadn't let my thoughts of Sia Reynolds come to pass while I'd been on the job. They were dangerous thoughts that would have kept me from my mission. They would have kept me in a place where I hadn't been able to leave her or worse take her with me. They would have put her in danger and distracted me.

Well, that was all back now upon being in front of her, and when I took a step toward her, she proceeded to take one back. I wasn't surprised by this reaction. I hadn't seen her in a while and... "Sia."

She blinked but not as if she hadn't heard me. In actuality, her expression read awe. Like she couldn't believe I was standing there in front of her. She swallowed. "Max—"

She ended up cutting herself off. She did before she rerouted and walked away from me as if I hadn't spoken. She didn't get far of course. I was fast and cut her off.

I got her scowl then, and when I reached for her, she pivoted away. This was to be expected too, but it didn't stop the lightning rod of fire that ripped through my chest.

"Sia—"

"What are you doing here?"

I blinked, not expecting this question. My jaw moved. "Why are you running from me?"

I got a laugh in response, a loud boisterous laugh that made quite a few of her fellow students stop and take a look at us. I growled at them all, and they eventually kept walking.

I faced Sia. "I don't believe I said anything funny."

I got she might be angry. I left her for a while, but she shouldn't be running from me.

"Oh, you definitely said something funny." She stepped to walk away again, but she was small and I wasn't. It took merely a step to cut her off, and she bared her teeth. "Move."

No one commanded me. I didn't move, and when she attempted to, I got her arm.

She worked it away. "You're unbelievable. You know that? You've been gone for a month, Maxim Petrov. A month in which I only knew you were alive because Val was telling me you were."

I had stopped responding to her calls and texts toward the end of my mission. Her contacting me was making it hard to do my duty so I had to disconnect, cut off.

It wasn't something I was proud of but it'd been necessary. I dampened my mouth. "I told you I was working."

This got another one of her boisterous laughs, and my eyes narrowed. Sia Reynolds was never one to hold back her sass, be a *brat*. If we were in the bedroom, I'd punish her. It was our dynamic, and normally, that shit did something for me, but not in this moment.

I was sympathetic to her anger though, or at least, I understood it. I pocketed my hands. "I also told you I'd be back, which I am now. I'm here, and I find out you've not only started school, but you're here by yourself without an escort."

I was fine with her starting school and even encouraged it in the past. What I didn't appreciate was her doing so without security. Not to mention, she just didn't tell me she was enrolling.

You did cut her off.

Whether I had or not, she could have mentioned that detail. I would have seen it in a text or she could have easily had Val relay that information to me.

"Because apparently, I was just supposed to sit around and do nothing while you ghosted me."

"That's not what I—"

"You know what, Maxim? Fuck you."

Her bite was back and tenfold when she pivoted away from me. I expected a degree of her anger upon coming back. Of course, I did. *I did* leave her but maybe a part of me thought she'd be better than, well, me. I was an asshole but no matter how frustrated Sia was with me she'd always been a light through my darkness. She'd been a place I could go to and seek solace.

I needed that after so many weeks on the job. Shit had gotten *dark* while I'd been away and a big reason I'd been able to push myself through it was because I knew she'd be there once it was all said and done. I'd never been one to need a lifeline but after Sia came into my life…

Her presence changed me and her walking away had me grabbing for her again. Oddly enough, I was too slow. Actually, I wasn't too slow.

She was just quick.

She dodged my grab with the finesse of an assassin and even held onto her books. Their position in her arms didn't teeter, and after she evaded, she held up her hand as if ready for combat.

What. The. Fuck?

She just stood there in a fighter's stance. Like she was about to kick my ass, and I blinked again. I tipped my chin at her. "Where did you learn this?

Hell, where had she learned to dodge the way she had?

I pivoted, and she did with me, all while holding the same fighter's position. This wasn't amateur. She'd been taught something. Clearly.

Her jaw moved. "Val," she said, finally easing up, and I did recall my head of security telling me she taught her a thing or two. Sia sighed. "Now, let me pass."

I pulled out my knife instead. Well, at least one of my knives. I handed it to her. "Can you do something with this?"

I was curious now what Val had taught her, and it turned out to be a lot when Sia not only gripped the blade but threw it. She sent it through the air in a whoosh, and it landed not far away from us.

She sent a Coke can by the trash can flying, and when I strode over to it, I found my blade through the center of the logo.

Damn.

So, I'd been hard when I saw this woman again. Damn hard but now, my shit could split fucking *wood*. I turned around, and Sia merely shrugged.

"I can do enough," she said simply, like a badass. I certainly hadn't left her in a position to defend herself, which was why I'd left a fleet around to protect her.

Apparently, she didn't need it.

She'd obviously taken her fate into her own hands, and I was so awed I did allow her to move away from me. She mentioned something about Gleb picking her up but that wasn't happening.

"Actually, I'm taking you home," I said. I returned my knife to my jacket, and that had been a feat. The urge to take that knife and spill her blood was there after what she did, taste her…

I wasn't the only one who enjoyed our blood play. I wasn't the only one who enjoyed a lot of the things we did both inside and outside of the bedroom. This girl had been an enigma to me. I'd found partners on kink apps who weren't as open as she was.

I hadn't known what to make of Sia when we first got together and still didn't. She seemed to surprise me more and more every day, but what wasn't surprising was her reaction to being told what to do. Her jaw clenched, and she looked like she wanted to take my knife and slit *my* throat.

"I'll take the bus," she started to say, but there were no games when I cut her off this time.

Nor when I had her jaw in my hand.

I didn't do this forcibly. I could have and something told me *she* could have maneuvered her way out of such a hold. Neither one of us chose to do something we could have easily done, and I certainly noticed that on her part.

I also noticed the tremble in her delicate mouth and the way her complexion shifted from tan to one with a slight rose tint. I still affected her. I was in her head.

My thumb hovered above her mouth. "You can be mad at me all you want. Fuck, I don't care if you talk to me at all, but you are coming with me. I'm taking you home, and that's not negotiable."

It wasn't, and I didn't dare move. I didn't know what I'd do if she submitted to me or denied me. Either choice might have me bending her over.

She jerked her chin out of my hand, and though she may have done so with a little pout, she didn't put distance between us. I took that as her answer.

The drive home with Sia Reynolds beside me was a tough one. There were a million things I wanted to both ask and tell her, but I chose to do neither. I kept a brick wall up just like I'd done when we'd been apart. I wanted to know how she spent her time away from me, and why she chose to go to school. I wanted to tell her how much I missed her but opted out of conversation entirely.

She did the same.

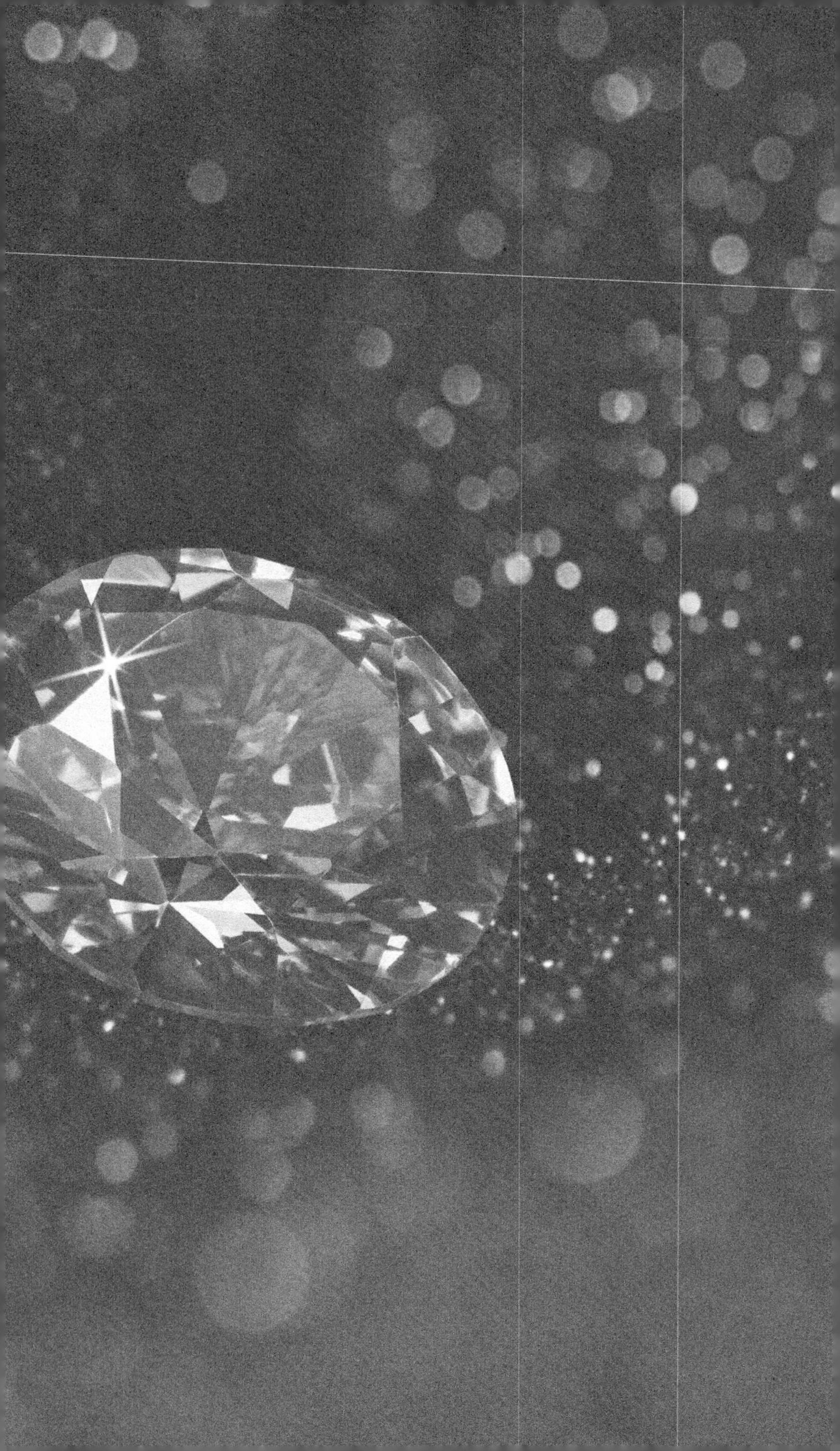

CHAPTER
THIRTY-THREE

Sia

The next morning I'd been surprised to find Polly already fed and given water.

She'd even been walked.

How did I know? She wasn't jumping at her crate the moment I entered the room. Actually, she had the look of a satisfied dog, and one glance at her food and water dish confirmed she'd been cared for already.

It didn't take a rocket scientist to figure out who'd done it.

Something told me Maxim Petrov's love language was acts of service, but it would take more than that for me to overlook how he left me the last month.

Even still, being around him again…

Seeing him had been unnerving. It was even worse being in close proximity with him in his car. I hadn't been close to him in a long time. I hadn't smelled his husky scent or felt him around me. His aura had been powerful like it always was.

It felt like he'd been away so much longer than he had.

The constant dull ache I had in my chest while he'd been gone let me know how much I missed him, worried about him. He'd taken a big part of me with him when he'd suddenly up and left, and when he came back, that crevice hadn't been easily filled. We were in the car for a while and said nothing to each other the whole time. The same occurred when we got home, but that had been because of me. I hadn't even told him goodnight before I went to *my* room by myself. I just left him, nothing but anger and resentment in my veins.

There was a fair amount of anxiety too, that stemmed from being around him and not knowing what to do with that. I had a lot of anxiety while he'd been gone. I had the urge to use, but I hadn't. I hadn't even gone for my jellybeans out of sheer stubbornness. The urge to use and default to disastrous ways was definitely there, but I wouldn't let him being around take me there.

Maxim Petrov didn't control me.

Of course, that was easy to say when we weren't in the same room together. He was downstairs in his favorite chair at the dinner table after I checked on Polly. He was there reading a newspaper as if nothing had happened. His bulky frame was in a white dress shirt that labored at the buttons, his tattoos on full display down to his knuckles. He was the quintessential hot dad with his paper in front of him and his readers on, his dark hair slick and intentionally messy.

I tried not to look at him when I entered the dining room and would have backed out had he not lowered the paper. He targeted me with those gray eyes, and it took me a moment to realize the table had been filled with food. There were silver trays with danishes, fruit, scrambled eggs, and other various breakfast items. Basically, he had a buffet in front of him.

I waltzed right by it all, trying to ignore the fact there was a place setting opposite of him. It was empty and the only other one on the table.

"So you're going to ignore me, *malyshka*?"

He really was arrogant, wasn't he? He always had been.

Even still, that hadn't stopped his effects and the fact that my legs felt a little jelly again upon hearing him call me that nickname. I wouldn't let myself succumb to that though and entered the kitchen. I poured myself some cereal.

It was hard focusing and allowing those corn flakes to enter my bowl when, suddenly, my presence wasn't the only one in the kitchen. I instantly became aware when Maxim entered. It was like he sucked up all the air in the room, his energy too big for it.

"Malyshka…"

He wasn't on me, but he might as well have been, his voice rough, husky. He drew in close, and that did surprise me. He'd wanted to keep our relationship under wraps until he told Lettie about us.

Even in the car, he hadn't been this close. In fact, we felt just as far away from each other as we'd been when he'd been gone. That wasn't the case now as he pivoted. His hands were suddenly on either side of me on the counter, caging me in. The box of cereal froze in my hands, my breath picking up.

"Sia…" He breathed my name right along the shell of my ear and hot lava blazed down my neck when he drew in my scent. He sniffed me wildly, feral like he did sometimes when we played. He never did this in public either. He always put distance between us.

No one was around us now, but Maxim always approached proximity with me with caution. He wasn't now, and I wondered if he was having a hard time fighting it. If he wanted me as much as I wanted him in all his time away…

His hands braced my hips, but instead of giving into him I found myself pulling away. I couldn't do it. *He* couldn't do this. Not after he left, hurt me…

He watched me slide my bowl across the counter, then the opposite one when I pivoted. He drew those tatted fingers through his inky locks, a sigh on his lips.

He shook his head. "You're really not going to talk to me?"

That was him last night, wasn't it?

I put the cereal box down. "You really think taking Polly out this morning and getting Sophia to make that breakfast out there is really going to fix things?"

Clearly, that other place setting was for me. At least, I assumed it was.

Maxim frowned. "I made it."

"What?"

"*I* made it for you. Breakfast?" He folded his burly arms. "Spent all morning on it. I wanted us to talk and eat together. I missed you, *malyshka*. Desperately."

My throat closed up. That was hard to hear. It was hard like a sock in the chest, and my throat heated when I shook my head. "And again, that's supposed to fix things?"

"It was supposed to be a start. Yes." He eased closer, but I backed away.

"I don't have time to talk, and I definitely don't need you to do my job. My chores? Last I checked, everything to do with Polly is my job. I'm your employee, remember?"

Sheer stubbornness had these words flying out of my mouth, and I certainly hadn't missed their effects on Maxim. He winced like I struck him with a hot poker.

"You haven't been just my employee in a long time, Sia," he said, but when he crossed the room *I* winced, cringed. Maybe I hadn't been his employee, but the way he'd treated me once he left made me feel worthless. Like I was just some object he could use then throw away when he didn't need me. Where was all his thought and care when he'd been ignoring my text messages and calls? People who missed each other didn't do that.

"Sia—"

I couldn't even look at him. I gave him my back, and eventually, abandoned my cereal all together. I'd rather go without it today. In fact, I'd rather starve than be in this room one more minute with him.

He called after me again when I left, but I didn't care. Maxim Petrov couldn't just charm his way back into my life.

It just wouldn't work this time.

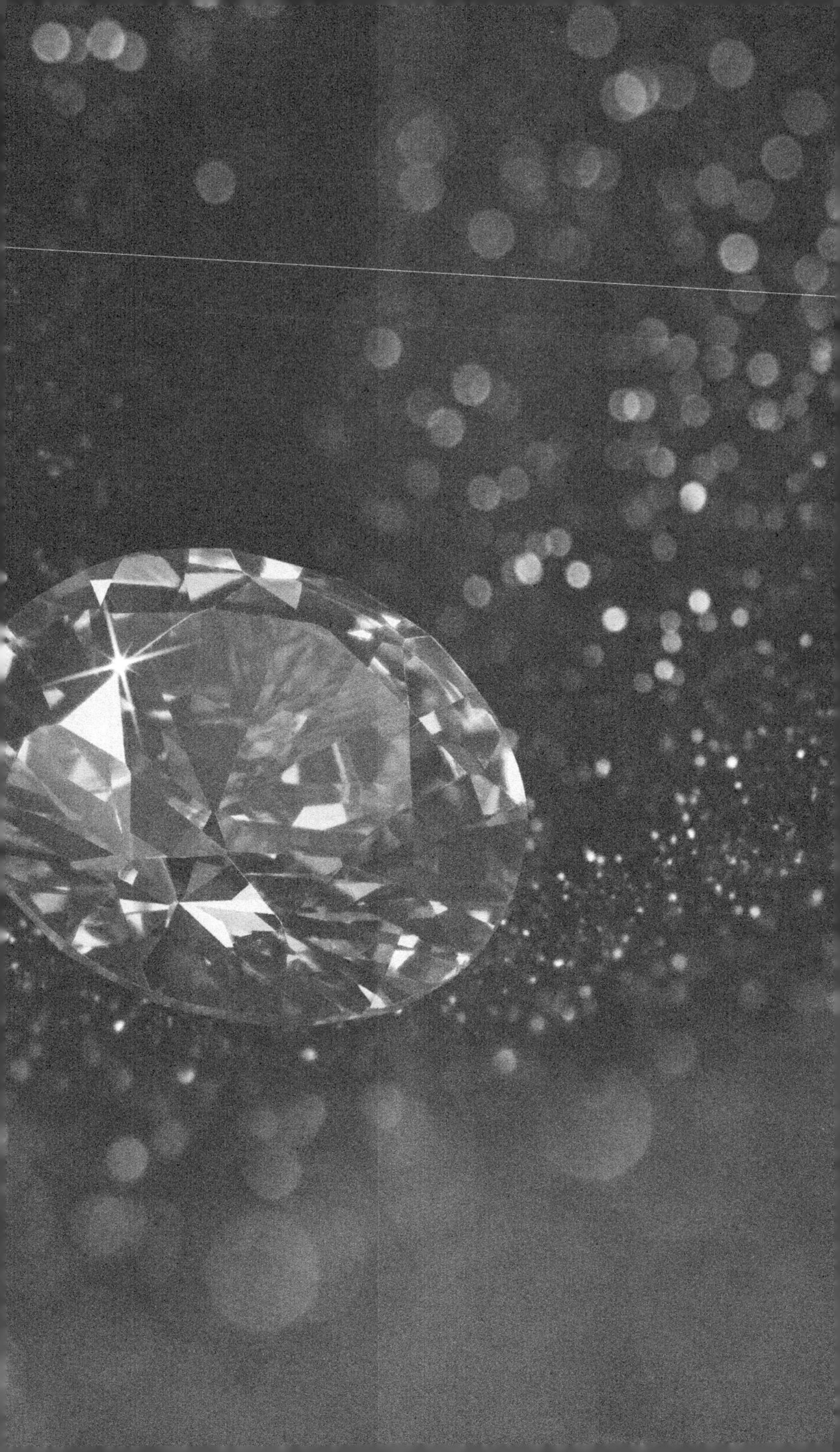

CHAPTER
THIRTY-FOUR

Maxim

Sia had a social life…

And I didn't like it.

I came home to find my house filled with *people* one night, people I certainly didn't authorize in my home. Especially when I came home to spend time with Sia.

I'd even brought her flowers.

I put them away upon finding her in my library, again with *people* in it with her. There were a couple of girls and guys who all appeared to be her age. They lay on my polished floors, books in front of them.

Annoyed, I left the room, a growl on my lips.

I tossed the flowers on the kitchen table when I spotted Val in there. She had a clipboard in her hand and looked to be going over security protocols like she did sometimes.

She spotted the flowers, looking at them curiously.

"They're for Sophia for the dining table," I passed off, not needing her to question me. We already had weirdness between us after she allowed Sia to go to school by herself. I

later spoke to her about that and had been glad I'd been able to keep my temper in check.

Val may or may not be specious about Sia and myself. If she was, she never mentioned anything. It wasn't her business to mention anything, but I wasn't trying to make our relationship more obvious by scolding her more than necessary for not looking out for Sia. I came at her professionally when addressing the issue with her though I had every urge within me to release Val from my staff.

That was how crazy Sia Reynolds made me. Val was one of my most trusted and Sia triggered actual thoughts to remove Val from her position.

Grunting, I lifted my hands to sign. *"Who are those people in my library?"*

"You mean Sia's friends?"

"Sia has friends?"

Val's primary focus veered to me at that point. She'd been going back and forth between signing and studying her clipboard which she'd placed on the counter. She lounged against the countertop. *"I believe it's her study group. It's Friday night, right?"*

"Correct, but I don't believe I authorized people to just be in my house."

"All due respect you weren't here to authorize, Boss," she eyed me, her sign a bit flippant. I supposed she was still annoyed I'd scolded her. She hadn't taken it lying down but that was Val. She stood firm on her position that Sia was safe and could handle herself.

I saw that first hand, but I didn't fucking care. Had I been here she wouldn't have left my sight.

Laughter hit the room then, chatter. It appeared Sia and her "friends" were done because soon they were passing the kitchen.

I watched them all laughing, the guys in the group way too close to her.

One fucker even had his arm around her.

The only thing stopping me from *stopping that* was Val and the fact the guy removed his arm before they all headed outside. I watched the group reconvene in the back gardens through the kitchen window, their books still in hand.

They obviously all knew my property well and immediately took seats out there. I had stone benches, and they sat on them, the sun setting around them and *my* vineyard behind them. Sia had people out there like this was fucking holiday break.

"What is she studying?" I asked, passing off my glare in that direction by heading to the fridge instead. I got some juice and chose to pour it in front of the window.

"Biology, I believe." Val's full attention was still on me, my head of security way too observant. Her arms folded. *"I believe she wants to be a vet."*

I knew she wanted to go into the medical field. She must have decided she wanted to work with animals. There wasn't much about Sia on paper I didn't know.

The same went for her body.

The few weeks in which we spent time together felt like eons ago. I nearly mourned them now.

But leaving had been necessary...

I told myself that, and it was true. What I had to take care of *was* necessary and not just for the safety of my home and my daughter. It was for Sia's well-being too.

It was for *our* well-being.

The only world in which she and I could be together required me to leave and take care of my business. I had taken care of it and now we had a chance.

I drank down the juice in my glass. I ended up drinking the whole bottle, my eyes on the back gardens the whole time.

"Anything I need to know, Boss?" Val was beside me now, but her stare was outside. She made it brief before facing me.

I put my glass down.

"Make sure they don't leave that area," I barked while signing. "And if they come inside the house, they don't go anywhere but the library. I don't want them anywhere else in the house."

I left the room before Val could respond.

I didn't think what I said required a response.

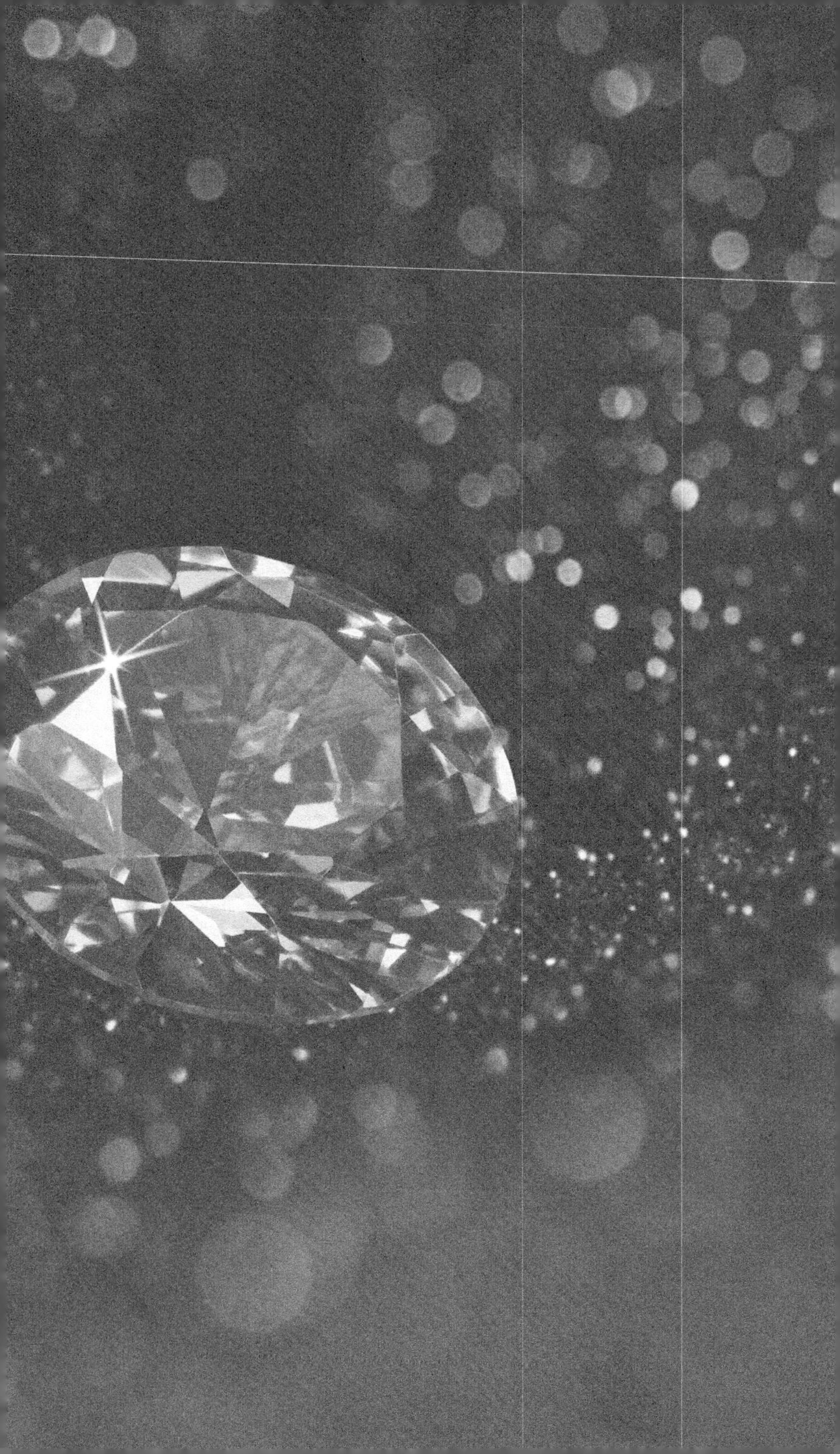

CHAPTER
THIRTY-FIVE

Sia

Being around Maxim was…unnerving. I'd gone out of my way not to be around him, but he definitely made himself known.

He had a tendency to linger, leer. Especially when I brought people over. Apparently, I wasn't allowed to have friends while he'd been away.

As far as I was concerned, he *still* wasn't here, and that was one hundred percent his fault. He left, and I knew he was working, but he didn't have to cut himself off from me. It was like I meant nothing to him.

Maybe you don't.

This was a fear and a thought I wouldn't let myself entertain. I did that and I got too in my head.

I also didn't acknowledge his continued presence around the house which was far more now than before he left. It was like I saw him everywhere and at all hours. Often, he'd look on the verge of trying to make conversation when we ran into each other but then I'd go the other way. It was easy to do in his large house.

I thought he'd get the hint, *leave me alone*, but then, his gestures started. Every morning he was at the breakfast table with an expansive breakfast. There'd always be two place settings, and he'd be waiting at one. He didn't even eat before I came into the room. He'd just be sitting there with his paper, waiting.

I always ignored him and though he stopped taking Polly out in the morning, he was always hanging out with her. I'd catch him playing with her or taking her on walks after he got home from work.

He even took her swimming.

He didn't swim with her, but he did let her play in the lake out back. There was one further out on the property. Polly would swim while Maxim read a novel out there, his smile subtle on her. He probably was only hanging out with her more for my benefit, but I couldn't deny how happy *they both* looked.

Nor how happy it made me that he was hanging out with her.

Things were actually the way they should be now. I'd trained my employer's dog and now my employer had not only a handle on his pup but seemed to enjoy spending time with her. He laughed with her, and whenever he spotted me, he gave me a wave. He hadn't given up trying to talk to me.

I told myself his gestures didn't matter and each wave I ignored and interaction I avoided made that easier.

My evening classes became my saving grace.

Deciding to go back to school wasn't easy for me. There was *nothing* easy about going back, but at least I knew Maxim wouldn't be there. I could take a breather from life at the house.

I hadn't wanted to go back to school initially, but with all the free time I had after Maxim left I figured attending classes in the evenings wouldn't be a big deal.

No, it wasn't one.

Shortened semesters had opened up in the fall, and once I got the instructor line up, I decided to give it a shot. I should be able to do what I wanted to do, and Maxim was right about one thing: I needed to start if I planned to graduate anytime soon.

My nights were quiet since I started school, and gratefully, without the brooding Russian god. I also started to make friends so time in class was really enjoyable.

I saw lots of familiar faces when I arrived to my class that night and took my same seat. Things were easy in my night classes and quiet.

Which was why this new arrival caused quite a stir.

A man strode into the classroom, and he was well over the age of your average freshman. This wasn't uncommon with night classes, but what was had been the attention he got.

All the girls started immediately whispering when a tattooed god sat next to me instead of my friend Seth. We weren't besties or anything, but we were the same major: biology. One didn't necessarily have to pick a lane at community college, but it was smart for the associate's degree. I planned to use that to transfer to a school that had a good vet program.

Seth would be forced to find a new seat considering Maxim sat next to me.

What. The. Fuck.

What the fuck indeed. Maxim Petrov... *My* Maxim Petrov folded his bulky body into a seat normally reserved for guys and girls a fraction of his size. He wore black down to his leather shoes, a messenger bag on his arm.

"What are you doing here?" I whisper-screamed, trying not to *actually* scream. Maxim placed his bag down and was currently lounging in his seat like him being in my class was a normal occurrence.

He sure acted like it was. He pulled a laptop out of his bag and everything, nearly acting as if he hadn't heard me when his back touched the seat. A waft of his masculine scent hit me, his aftershave sharp, spicy...

He's not your Maxim.

He's not, and he finally regarding me when he lounged back. A lot of "who's that" whispered around me, as well as a few giggles from fellow classmates.

Jesus.

I mean, I had to give it to them. He *did* look great today. His black button up revealed a sliver of his sculpted chest. It was chiseled, brawny. His head cocked in my direction. "I'm sorry, were you speaking to me?"

It was still jarring to speak to him. I spent most of my days ignoring him.

He was being cheeky and knew good and well he heard my question. Even still, he played the part, his dark eyebrows dancing.

My God, he's...*flirting* with me.

He totally was, his arm on the too small desk and the flirting might have gone further had not Seth walked into the room a second later. Upon spotting a large man sitting in his seat, he took a step (or two) back. We didn't have assigned seats or anything, but we all generally sat in the same seat. It was just routine, really, to sit with your friends.

Seeing my attention was on someone else, Maxim angled in that direction. He had his glasses on tonight too which made him look like a sexy daddy.

He is a sexy daddy.

Uncomfortable now, I shifted, and Maxim folded his arms in Seth's direction.

"Is there a problem?" he asked Seth, the cheeky smile

wiped from face. He pointed to the seat Seth stood in front of, the one *Maxim himself* currently sat in. He eyed Seth. "I'm new to this class, but I wasn't aware people claimed seats outside of high school."

What the fuck?

Maxim waited for a response, but Seth's attention passed over Maxim to me.

Maxim frowned. "Why are you looking at her? I spoke to you so you should look at me."

Right away, Seth did, and I wanted to scream.

Apparently not wanting any trouble, Seth lifted his hands. He nodded at me before finding a seat in the back of the room, and Maxim was snarling by the time he shifted around in a desk that really was too small for him. He looked like Goldilocks in the baby bear's bed.

"What are you talking about this is your class?" I whisper-shouted again, but the arrival of our professor had me looking up. He gestured that it was time for class to begin and Maxim reached into his messenger bag once more.

He pulled out a textbook.

Needless to say, my jaw dropped.

He was serious about taking this class and opened his laptop beside the book.

"I mean I'm taking this class, *malyshka*. That's what I mean by this is my class," Maxim said, crossing his legs. He waved toward the front of the room. "Now, you better pay attention to our professor."

I had no words, and our professor didn't even appear fazed by the new arrival.

"I take it you're the new student," he said to Maxim, and when Maxim nodded my eyes bugged out. The professor nodded back. "Welcome to Biology 101, Mr. Petrov."

Maxim thanked him, then glanced my way. He did so only briefly before sitting up straight...

As if he was about to take notes.

With the chaos of the new arrival passed, everyone else began to do the same. Everyone but me that is…

And it wasn't because I couldn't find my pen.

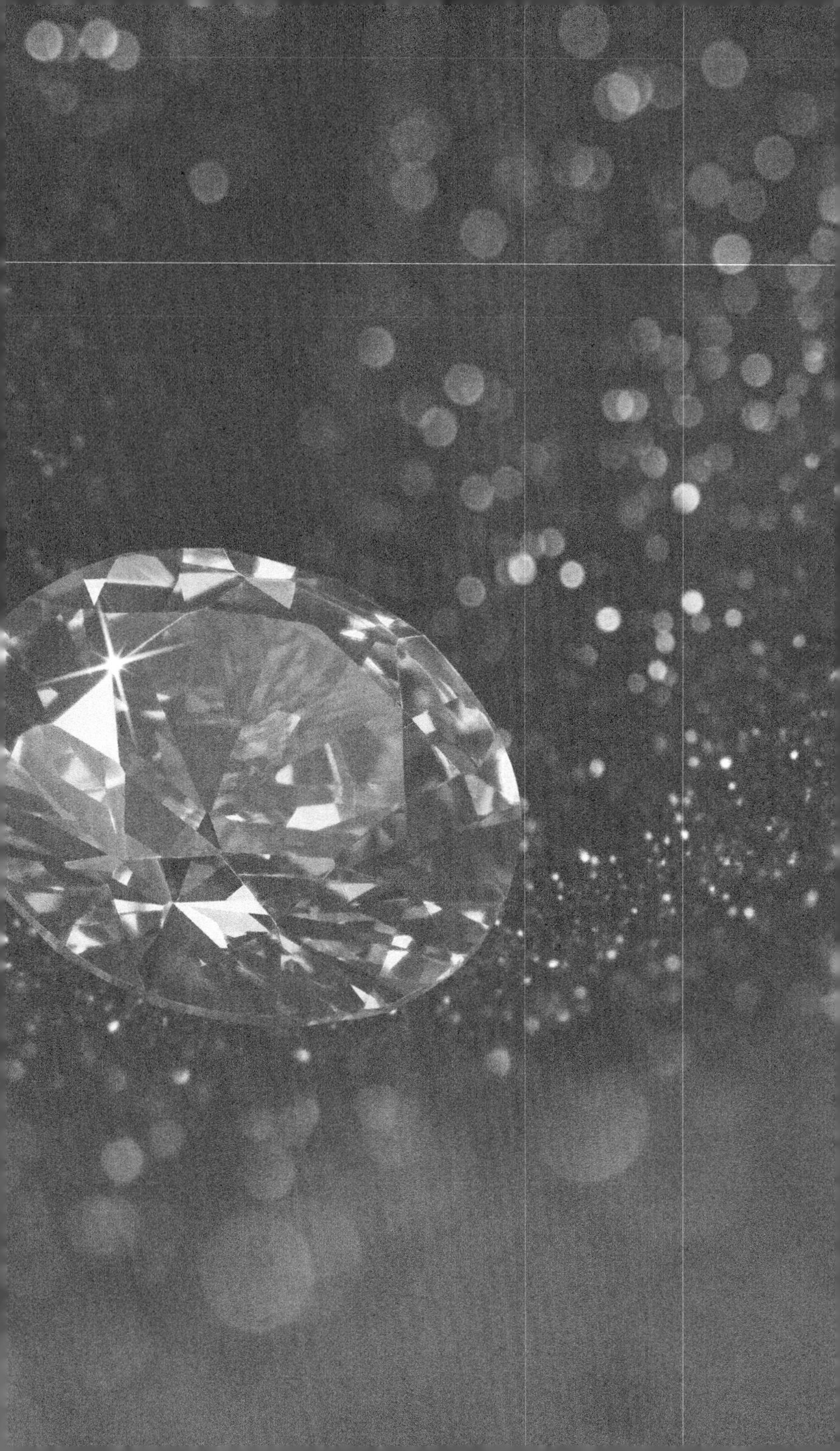

CHAPTER
THIRTY-SIX

Sia

So um, Maxim wasn't joking about attending school. In fact, he was in quite a few of my night classes. When I asked him about it, he said it was for his biology degree.

What. The. Fuck.

As it turned out, he wasn't joking about that either. He attended every night session and even weaseled his way into my study group. It couldn't be helped considering I had my group at my house.

Which was his house.

It was his house, and I hadn't even asked him to be in the group. *My friends* had and what was ironic as fuck was Seth had become his complete fanboy. Maxim had scared the shit out of him that first night of classes, but it didn't seem to be the case after that.

I think Maxim being brilliant had something to do with that.

It was something the whole class saw rather quickly. Maxim was the first to raise his hand and command the room.

He was just as comfortable there as he was directing his staff at home or at work.

I had no idea when he found time to actually go to work since the majority of his time seemed to be with myself, in my classes, and with *my* friends.

Even still, I tried to ignore his presence most of the time, but that was obviously hard. Maxim commanded any room he was in. The girls giggled all over him when in conversation either with him or about him, and the guys in my classes wanted to just chat with him. If anything, for his brilliance. He was very intuitive when it came to the biological sciences which shocked the hell out of me. He was such a violent man, dangerous…

But he seemed to be smart too, and I caught sight of him in the funeral home's embalming room one day. Another thing I'd been doing during Maxim's time away was trying to earn my keep. I knew I was his paid employee, but I was also eating his food and just playing with Polly all day. I needed something outside of school so I asked Val if there were any jobs at the funeral home. I thought being around Dr. Barinov would be nice, and well, I knew for a fact Maxim wouldn't be there.

At least, he hadn't been.

He was there now. Though, he wasn't every day. Often, he was just surveying his staff and the general operations of the business, and though I'd chosen to work at one of his funeral homes that had less traffic, he still came around sometimes.

He was around today, and his hands were in his pockets as Val signed to him. He hadn't known I was in the room sweeping at first but not for long.

Those steel gray eyes hit me like a ray gun, and once they were on me, they stayed.

Jesus.

He *still* affected me, his attention lingering during the majority of his conversation with Val. *She* was actually working and hadn't noticed his attention veered during her signing.

I certainly had, my head down while I continued to sweep. It didn't matter I didn't look directly up at him. His masculine scent filled the air and warmed my blood without the contact.

I hate this.

I really did but continued to sweep. I decided being in the same room with him was too much so I made the decision to take my sweeping to another room.

I stayed quiet in my little corner for a while, sweeping, but eventually, Val came in. I waved at her, and she waved back even though she was in the middle of a conversation. The conversation gratefully wasn't with Maxim, but he wasn't far behind her in his own conversations. He had a pack of men with him in suits. He was nearly always surrounded by others when I saw him. Like at school, he was constantly commanding attention and people listened.

I could see Maxim and his group from behind the dark caskets I was sweeping under. I was used to that by now, caskets and death around me. It seemed to always follow me since I ended up in Maxim's world.

Eventually, I made it over to Val who had ended her conversation and was now writing something down. I stopped sweeping. "Does Maxim have any degrees?"

I would normally sign to her, but still didn't know a ton. I learned new ones every day but my confidence with what I did know wasn't always there.

Val, of course, understood, and when she looked up, she had a frown on her face. I assumed due to what I said.

I shrugged. "Just wondered." I mean, he was really smart in my classes. Like really smart.

"*A few,*" Val signed, then took out her phone. She typed on the screen for a second. After she finished, she showed me, and I nearly dropped my broom.

"*He's got a degree in applied mathematics,*" the screen displayed. After swallowing, I started to say something, but then Val took the phone back.

She showed me the screen again. "*Then there's his master's degrees in both electrical and aerospace engineering. He also has a doctorate in physics.*"

"Physics?" I croaked, and Val nodded before typing again.

Good God, there's more.

There *was* more, and she typed for a while before showing me her screen once more. "*Mmhmm. He's done some studies in psychology too. Oh, and I believe he also has a film degree. He likes old films.*"

She then put her phone away like she literally told me nothing of note.

He has a degree in film too? What the actual fuck?

If this man didn't already surprise me, he certainly was now, and I couldn't help looking in his direction once more. He'd moved on to another part of the room with his group, and though they were speaking to him, his attention had again veered to me.

Maxim's nod was subtle in my direction. It was like me being there meant nothing, and this was just a normal casual occurrence for us.

It blew my mind how he could just do that. He was constantly there. He was always around me and in *my* world but at the same time gave me space. He never forced conversation with us but constantly made himself available. Like he just wanted to be around me or something.

I refused to believe that and certainly didn't let my heart go to that place. If I did, I felt something but it was hard not to with this new information Val gave me. Maxim was basically brilliant and definitely didn't need to go to community college.

He's going to school for you.

Val lifted her hands. "*Why do you ask, jellybean?*"

It took me a second to realize she'd been *watching me* watch Maxim.

Her eyes narrowed. "*Sia?*"

She'd given me my name in sign language, something she said her community did. I'd loved what she came up with. She did a soft flow of her hand around her face for my name.

"*Just wondered,*" I signed, spelling it out, and she smiled. I defaulted to the alphabet when I didn't know something, and Val waited patiently until I finished. "*Do you know where he went?*"

Val cocked her head, her expression curious, and I stopped signing.

I chewed my lip. "When Maxim was gone, do you know where he went?"

I didn't want to actually know where he'd gone. I guess in a weird way I just wanted to know him. I wanted to know something about him, *anything*, and he certainly wasn't very giving with himself.

I wanted to know why he cut me out of his life.

Of course, Val couldn't answer that in a simple question, and obviously didn't know what I actually meant. Her expression was more than confused now, and I felt silly for asking. Before Maxim left, he'd wanted to be private about our relationship. He'd wanted to talk to Lettie about it first.

I wasn't sure that would ever happen or even if I wanted him to at this point, and I didn't want Val to know about us for my sake now. I didn't want to acknowledge what we had. It hurt too much.

Val typed on her phone once more, and if she knew anything about Maxim and myself, she didn't let on. She simply showed me her phone. "*I have a feeling you know I can't tell you that.*"

She was always professional when it came to her boss. Even with me despite how close we'd gotten.

Nodding, I looked away but glanced back when she waved her hand in front of me.

She showed me her screen. *"But I can say it was the last place he wanted to be and the last thing he wanted to do."*

I was shocked she told me that much. She could be just as secretive as Maxim and never did expose any part of his life.

She did today for some reason and exchanged a glance between Maxim and myself. I once again looked over at him, and this time his focus had returned to his group.

It was something I noticed before making myself sweep another room.

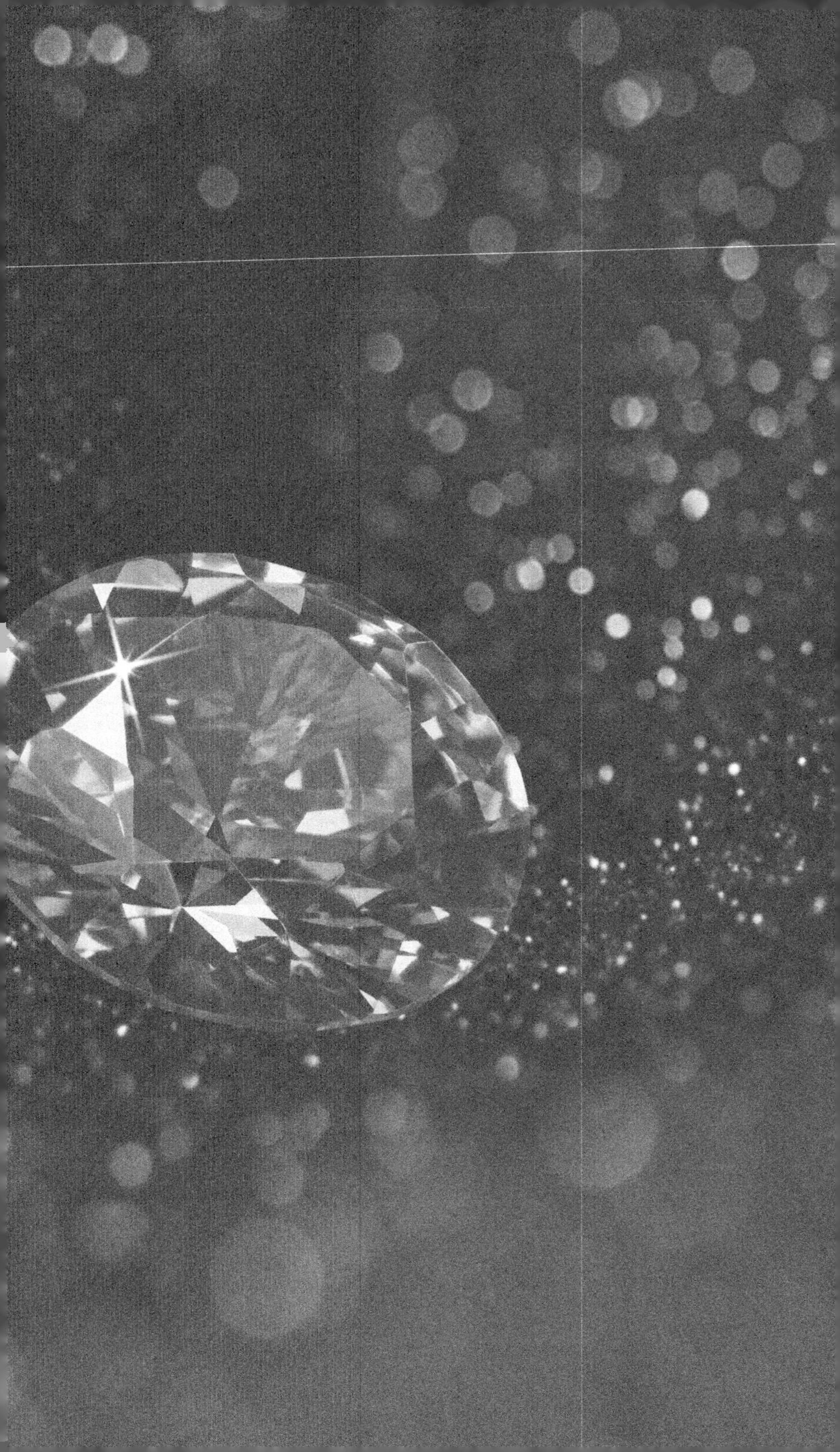

CHAPTER
THIRTY-SEVEN

Maxim

So Sia's friend Seth was a fucking idiot.

I smirked and continued to pretend that I found anything he said interesting. He'd been prattling on for the past hour, and I allowed him to.

We were best friends after all.

He believed he was mine, and I sat back, putting up with this guy. He had a tendency to enjoy hearing his own voice, and visions of my blade cutting it off hit me more than a few times since I joined Sia's study group. I'd convinced them to start meeting at the campus library now. This was more appropriate and not in my fucking house.

Seth grinned. "Am I right, Max?"

I fought my hand from reaching for my blade. Tack on another tally for the annoying things this fucker did. My name wasn't fucking Max. I grinned through bared teeth. "Right, sport."

I smirked again at his excitement from the nickname. Leave it to this idiot to think calling him things like *sport*, *scout*, and *buddy* were anything beyond demeaning. I was placing him beneath me, and that was easy to do since he was a right idiot.

In all honesty, I hadn't been a part of this conversation with him for pretty much the entire hour.

My attention was on Sia.

It often traveled to her during our study sessions, and currently, she scanned some of the shelves in the library.

I watched her from my position across the room, my sight and full awareness on her gorgeous ass. She had a little skirt on today, one that rose each and every time she reached for a book. It exposed her caramel-kissed thighs, and I fought to keep myself from staring too long.

Today, I decided against fighting temptation. It was rather boorish listening to Seth, and when he looked to be on the verge of calling me Max again, I got up.

I spared his life today, heading over to Sia. I quickly came across her on a stool as she reached for a textbook, and fuck if I was letting her do that.

"Eh, let me," I said right before she could grab it. She could fall and hurt herself.

Her dark eyes landed on me as the book passed in front of her, and I watched her full lips pout when I gave it to her. Her expression screamed annoyance at me. Like I had the audacity to help her.

This seemed consistent with the way she looked at me all the time lately.

"Thanks," she said, tucking the book to her breasts. She never exposed them, always covered. It wasn't like the nightgowns she used to wear for me, her body exposed, her neck.

I kept my focus on the book. "No, problem, and that's one of my favorites."

I didn't spend a lot of time reading textbooks in my spare time, but Gray's Anatomy was one of my favorites.

Sia smirked.

"I'll bet," she said, and when my head cocked, her eyes lifted. "Val said you've done this school thing quite a few times. She said you have a few degrees."

My head of security had spoken about me, but I didn't show my annoyance.

I merely nodded. "Over the years I've found I rather like school."

"Really?"

Again, my nod was curt. "I've had a lot of spare time while being in the organization."

This was completely true, and especially once I proved myself to Natan. I basically got to choose whatever lane I wanted within the Bratva. This included my own hours and how I wanted to spend the majority of my time outside of the business. Something told me the amount of time I had on my hands had nothing to do with Sia's next response though.

Her full lips parted. "The organization?"

I propped a shoulder against the bookshelves. "The Bratva, *malyshka*."

There. I said it, but she already knew. I assumed for a while she knew I was in organized crime.

I just never said it.

Those words were out there now, and Sia's next response consisted of a lot of blinking. This wasn't surprising.

"Maxim..." My name left Sia's lips when I eased close to her, and her sweet smell filled my nose. It was always mouth-watering, and God did I want a fucking taste. Her dark lashes lifted. "What are you doing?"

I was going to fuck her in the middle of a community college's library. I was going to *taste* her and was going to do so paces away from her study group and that fucker Seth. I didn't care. I stopped caring.

She was so close.

All she had to do was give me an inch. I cared about that

inch—her submission—for some reason. I wanted to earn the right to have her when I was never a man of patience. I wanted to be patient with this little one.

My fingers barely grazed her flushed cheek before she was sliding clear from the space between me and the bookshelves.

"We have class soon," she stated to my back, and I stayed put against the bookshelf. If I moved wrong, *breathed* wrong I would fuck her and something told me a quick fuck wouldn't let me back into her life. She was making me work for this shit, work for her, and I didn't do that. I took what I wanted. I obtained, but in that moment, I gave myself several seconds.

They proved to be enough when all I did was follow her back to the study group.

―――

I studied Sia from her usual seat in class later that night. Her idiot friend Seth had wised up the first day I attended classes and permanently relinquished his seat for me. This allowed me to sit right next to Sia, but that proximity certainly didn't give me any advantage. She continued to ignore me night after night and class after class.

"Sia?" I questioned, wishing for her to just *look* at me. The plan was to allow her to come to me, to immerse myself completely in her life but allow her to come the rest of the way.

I wasn't patient tonight though. I needed to hear her voice, her acknowledgment.

I wet my lips. "*Malyshka?*"

She emanated a chill from her desk and what I wouldn't give to redo some time and rewrite past actions. I had duties to the Bratva. I had duties to myself and my daughter. My priority was keeping us safe which was something I'd been doing for nearly twenty years. I didn't regret leaving Sia, but I did regret what that absence caused. It caused this: her not trusting me and closing herself off from me.

I whispered her name again. She peered over at me, but her focus redirected to that fucker Seth when he raised his voice.

"Professor has ten minutes before we all leave," he announced, pointing at the clock at the head of the room. He laughed. "It's like a rule."

I hadn't even realized Professor Langston was late, but I didn't fucking care. I leaned closer to Sia. "*Malyshka*, you can't possibly ignore me forever. You live with me."

But the girl was damn sure trying. She wet her lips, and my cock jumped that she might tell me off, that she'd say *something* to me and when had I become this person? I didn't need anyone. Lettie and I didn't need anyone...

Tell my soul that, and I almost called for her again but stopped when someone entered the room.

"All right. All right. Settle down. I'm here now," the man said, and I growled at another interruption.

I decided to check myself in this instance but only because I was trying to respect Sia and the reason she was here, *school*.

The man who entered the room didn't look much older than me, and eventually, I faced him and finally listened to him introduce himself. Apparently, Professor Langston was out today, and this guy was the stand in.

He settled a messenger bag on the front podium. "And I'm sorry that I'm late. I'm not used to night classes and was told about this placement about an hour ago."

The man announced himself as Professor Handler, and that he normally taught this class during the day. Because he did, he could easily keep us on track with Professor Langston's schedule, but I stopped listening when I noticed Sia.

She'd gone flush.

A deep red tint hit her brown cheeks, but that was only

the first phase before the color completely drained from her face. The muscle inside my chest kicked like one of Peters & Burg's hearses charged into me. I touched her arm. "Sia?"

She didn't respond when she normally would have. She'd give me her sass or ask me what I was doing touching her in such a public way. I probably shouldn't be beyond the intimacy of my home, but that didn't stop me from doing it. I heard from Seth she told their group that she was staying in my house because she worked for me.

Professor Handler opened his laptop. "I want you all to begin by pulling out your textbooks and turning to page—"

Our substitute professor stopped speaking, and when I really took him in I quickly noticed he was just as red as Sia. His hands were also gripping the podium, his eyes blinking wide in my and Sia's direction.

I eased my hand off her, and I also noticed he wasn't looking at me or the fact I touched her. He was just *staring* at her, and she was staring at him...

Like she knew him.

It was like they knew each other, and rather quickly, the professor was redirecting his attention to the room. He cleared his throat. "I'd like you to turn to page three hundred and ninety-five please."

Like good students the class went for their books, but my focus stayed on Sia Reynolds. She was the only one who didn't reach for her book.

She ultimately never did.

We were in the car later that night when I spoke Sia's name again. And, like in class, she didn't hear me. It took several times before she even looked at me.

Since she refused to have security with her at all times I

took her to and from class personally. This wasn't negotiable, and though she didn't like it, she put up with it.

She didn't have a choice.

She didn't, just like she didn't when it came to this conversation. She could ignore me all she wanted during our drives but not tonight.

She knew that guy.

What I didn't know was how and why she reacted in such a way to his appearance. She'd adverted her eyes from him the entire class, and after his initial notice of her, he kept his focus on anything else and *anyone* else. It took effort not to notice someone, and I knew that firsthand.

Sia had her arms hugged around her, holding herself even though there was plenty of heat in the car. "What do you want, Maxim?"

A response, good.

My eyes narrowed. "You know our substitute. How?"

I was never one to beat around the bush, and at my directness, her small shoulders locked up again.

Mine did too, my entire body ramrod straight. I knew Sia. I knew her body.

I knew her discomfort.

She was giving it to me in bounds, and I wished for her to deny she knew this guy. It was obvious she did. She shrugged. "I barely know him."

"Barely?"

Her nostrils flared, and her lip curled in a way where I thought she'd tell me off. Again, her shoulders lifted. "I used to work at his vet clinic."

"And?"

"And he was a terrible boss. He was a dick but lots of people have terrible bosses."

She was right. Lots of people did, but her reaction to him (and him to her) wasn't normal. My jaw moved. "*Malysh—*"

"Drop it, Maxim," she gritted, and if she was trying to fool someone into thinking this guy was simply a bad boss, she was doing a poor job.

Sia stayed quiet the rest of the way home, but I watched her after we got there. I also checked the cabinets.

It was the first time she'd taken jellybeans out of them in weeks.

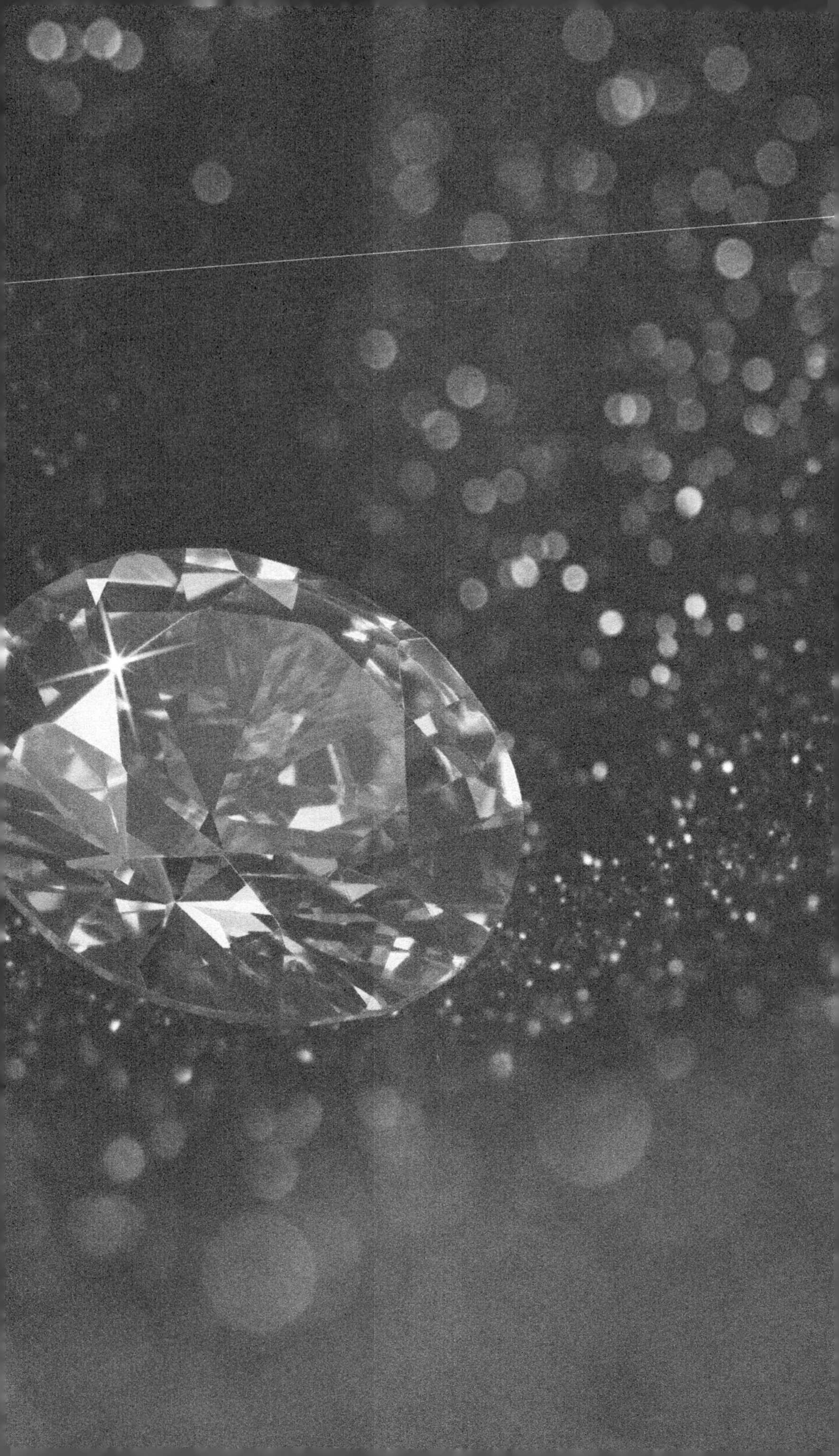

CHAPTER
THIRTY-EIGHT

Sia

I threw up that night, violently. In fact, I was so sick I sent word to Sophia that I wouldn't be down for dinner.

I couldn't face Maxim.

I couldn't face anyone, and he came by my room later that night. I'd been scared at first that he'd just barge his way in, but he didn't. He knocked. He respected me, and when I told him through the door I missed dinner due to my period he gratefully hadn't stayed long.

What a cop out.

Was I aware I'd chosen the weak way out to avoid him that night? Yes, but I didn't have the strength to speak to him.

I was too busy throwing up.

I had nothing left by the time I peeled my eyes open the next morning, and the only thing that got me out of bed was Polly. I took her out, got her fed and watered, then she came back with me to my room. We didn't leave all day. We barely left for two days.

And Maxim was gone.

I'd gotten word from Val that he'd been called out of town on business and wouldn't be around the house. He hadn't even said goodbye, and I didn't know how to feel about that. He'd done nothing but insert himself in my life for what felt like forever and now that he was gone I should be relieved.

I should be.

I shouldn't feel frigid. Like I was two seconds from breaking knowing he wasn't near. I hated that he'd filled a void once he'd returned from his last trip, and it hadn't mattered that I was pissed off at him.

The only thing good about him being gone was that I could avoid school for the rest of the week without him questioning me. I couldn't take the risk that Professor Handler would be there.

I'd been so stupid.

Of course, I knew that running into him was a possibility. I knew that he taught at that community college, but I figured I could avoid him by taking night classes. He was a daytime professor like he said, and I should have been able to avoid him.

You're so stupid.

I felt ill every night I thought about him, and it was only Maxim's return the following week that made me finally get ready for school when it was time. Maxim would ask if I didn't go, so I was at his car at the usual time.

"Mr. Petrov is at Peters & Burg tonight, Miss Reynolds," Jonathan, Maxim's gardener, said. He smiled at me. "I've been instructed to take you to class myself this evening, if you're ready."

Jonathan was one of Maxim's larger gardeners, and I didn't miss the nine millimeter strapped to the man's hip when he opened the door for me. Pretty much all Maxim's hired help was strapped though. I guess it came with the territory regarding Maxim's business, his life.

I guess Maxim was done playing pretend regarding

school. He'd obviously had no interest and was only going to prove something to me.

I wasn't sure what, and I hated that my heart did something when Jonathan told me he wasn't around tonight. The only reason I found out Maxim was home at all was because I wasn't sleeping lately and saw him roll in around three this morning.

His Mercedes had crept up the driveway, and I cracked opened my door with bated breath when he walked past my room. His head had been low, his hands deep in his pockets, but he hadn't stopped. He kept walking right on past my room. He said nothing.

I guess he really was playing pretend, and I was too. I'd been pretending in my own way, and I think for a very long time.

I nodded at Jonathan, feeling haunted when he took me to class. Seth quickly got me updated on what I'd missed in class when I texted him from the car that I was coming back tonight, which was how I found out Professor Langston was still gone. Apparently, he was on paternity leave because he and his wife adopted a new baby.

This was great news of course, but it also meant our biology class had a temporary professor placement. The very thought made me sick. The placement could still be Professor Handler.

I lingered outside of the biology department after Jonathan dropped me off. I didn't dare go inside but I needed to at least be on campus until my classes ended. Word might get back to Maxim that I didn't go.

I didn't know why I cared about that, and eventually, I decided to move away from the biology department buildings entirely. I thought I'd burn some time by going to the library or something, but I pulled a huge idiot move when I let Seth and our study group pass me.

"Sia, hey!" Seth said, and I silently cursed myself. I

shouldn't have been anywhere near the biology department if I didn't want to see anyone I knew. Seth grinned. "So glad you're feeling better. You're on your way to class, right?"

I wasn't, but I didn't have a choice now.

Smiling, I nodded at them all and headed back toward the biology department with them. I felt more ill with every step and thought I'd faint by the time we all made it to our room.

I sat in my usual seat with shaking legs and ignored the fact that Seth approached Maxim's seat.

"You know when Max will be back?" he asked, looking like he wanted to place his bag down on the desk, and I tried not to cringe that he shortened Maxim's name. I didn't know why that bugged me.

Probably because it bugged him.

I wasn't dumb. I knew how much Seth and his sunshine energy pissed Maxim off. Maxim Petrov was a dark cloud and anything bright and sunny was seen as a threat. They were a violation that needed to be upended.

I told Seth he could sit there of course. Maxim wasn't coming back.

I'd been lost when Seth continued to speak to me. I was lost in my head and couldn't focus at all. It wasn't until he mentioned Professor Handler's name that I came back to the present...

As well as something else he said.

"Yeah, I guess they found his body over the weekend," Seth said, and I had to do a double take. Surely, I hadn't heard Seth right, but then some of our other friends chimed in and crowded around us.

"The news said it was a homicide. No leads, and it sounds like it was gruesome," Georgia, one of our other study group members, said. She shivered. "The news didn't give details, but some influencers I follow got the tea. They said Professor Handler was castrated. His *hands* were cut off, his eyes and tongue carved out... I couldn't believe it when I heard it."

Our group was abuzz, and my swallow was hard upon hearing what she said. My ears sparked hot. "His tongue?"

"Yeah, and like? What the hell?" Seth got his books out right around the time another professor came into the room. He announced himself as Professor Spears, and that he'd be taking over for the rest of Professor Langston's paternity leave.

No one was really listening though. The room was just as abuzz as our group. Seth shook his head, his head low in my direction. "Someone out there is really fucking sick to do that to him."

You should agree with him.

"Yeah," I said.

You should nod.

I did that too, and my short responses seemed to be enough when Seth redirected his attention to the front of class. Eventually, our new professor got everyone to quiet down when they were clearly talking about a murder.

"Someone out there is really fucking sick…"

Sick was a grown man who preyed on children. *Sick* was when someone seemly kind brought a young girl into his home and pretended to be her savior. He pretended to save her from the system by giving her a safe home with him and his wife. And also sick was someone who snuck into that young girl's room every night for a year…

He did until she made him stop.

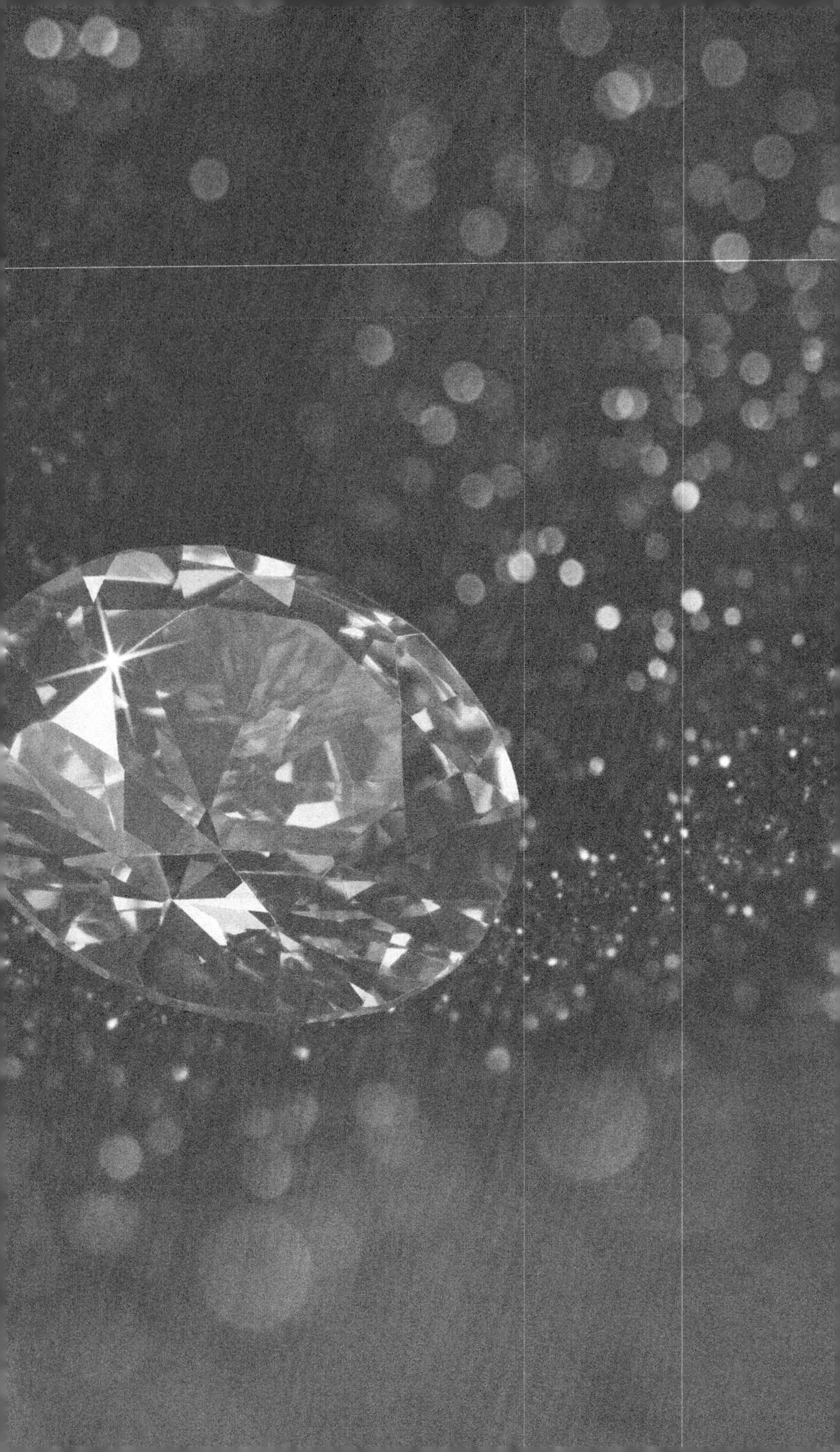

CHAPTER
THIRTY-NINE

Maxim

"Are you sure you're going to be okay? I can always come home, Dad. You know that."

My daughter was apologizing for choosing to spend her winter break with her friends in Bali instead of coming home for Christmas. She wanted to see more of the world, and she shouldn't apologize for that. I fought hard for her to have that.

I smiled strong in front of my daughter. We were on Face-Time, and she seemed happy. She appeared to be on the beach, and I didn't see any men with her in the background that I'd have to strangle. "Of course I don't mind, love. You have fun."

Again, I fought hard for her to have that.

My finger traced the desk in my home office as my daughter continued to tell me about the great time she was having so far in Bali. It seemed she'd done a lot even though she'd only been there a few days, and things at school had gone really well for her this semester. Her grades were great, and she was dancing her best. I knew the latter for a fact since she sent me videos from time to time.

I was glad to hear her say it though, and that her teachers were pleased with her dancing.

"How's Sia been?" she asked me. She frowned. "I feel like I don't hear from her much since she started school. Do you know how her semester's been?"

Of course, my daughter knew Sia was in school. They were friends. Of course, she knew about Sia's winter classes. Of course.

I leaned forward. "She's been fine, love, and I never thanked you for hiring her."

That sole action changed the entire trajectory of my life. My daughter would never know that though. There was a time I thought she'd know, but my month away had ultimately resulted in transitioning my life in yet another direction. It was one where Sia and I ended up on opposite ends. There were always ripples when one made a choice, cause and effect. There was balance to the world.

Always.

My daughter's smile warmed. "That makes me so happy. I knew you two would get along. Sia's great."

She was great, but unfortunately, I wasn't such a great man. I broke her in the end, her trust.

Malyshka...

I listened to my daughter talk for another hour, and that was easy to do. I loved hearing her happy and listening to her joy kept me off the thoughts in my own mind. It kept my thoughts of *Sia* and everything involving her away. She was somewhere in this house, but I'd never felt so far away from her.

I was weak when I opened my laptop later that night. I supposed I just wanted to see her. I clicked onto my Sia Cam, and there she was.

Nearly naked.

The instinct to close my laptop had me gripping it. Her privacy shouldn't be violated, but the fact that she wore a towel made me hesitate. It made looking at her not as forbidden.

These were things I told myself as I watched the flush across her brown skin. She was about to shower, the mist around her, and I knew this was her shower time.

You're a terrible man.

I was, my guilt heavy, a burden. I didn't feel guilty for many things. In the world I lived in and the job I had, there was no guilt. There were actions, and there were consequences. There was no gray, but getting involved with her had been a mistake, and it was one I couldn't take back.

No matter how much blood I shed.

My chest felt caved, and I started to close my laptop, but I stopped at the sight of dark eyes. Sia stared directly into the camera.

She stared at me.

Of course, this was what my dark fucking heart wanted to believe. She did know I had a camera in her bathroom so this was possible.

Malyshka?

Blood charged my cock when she started touching herself. Her fingers dipped beneath her towel, and eventually, her towel fell off her flushed body. It pooled at her feet and revealed her brown nipples and cunt, the hairs on her snatch curly and dark.

I sat back, unable to fight when Sia's fingers picked up with vigor between her legs. She could have been pleasuring herself innocently, but she did know I had this camera in her private space. She *knew* I could be watching her at any time.

What are you doing, malyshka?

She was playing with me, teasing, and my hand eased over my dick. The fucker hurt in my pants, and I couldn't help it.

You really are terrible.

How else could I explain what I was doing? I shouldn't be giving into this, her, but I was.

Because I wanted her. I wanted her so deeply and viscerally, and the feeling pulsed worse than the pain charging my cock. It hurt because I knew I couldn't have her, *shouldn't* have her.

Sia spread her legs for me, and before I knew it, I had my hand down my pants. I jerked off, our ministrations the same.

Fuck.

We both said it at the same time, her mouthing it through the screen while cum splashed my abs. My shirt partially opened, I allowed the jets to stream, and it was as if Sia knew.

It was as if that'd been her intent.

She continued to stare at me deeply through the image on my screen. She didn't put her towel back on. She didn't even shower. In fact, she turned the shower off, then left the room. She'd done all that because she knew I was watching.

She'd done all that for me.

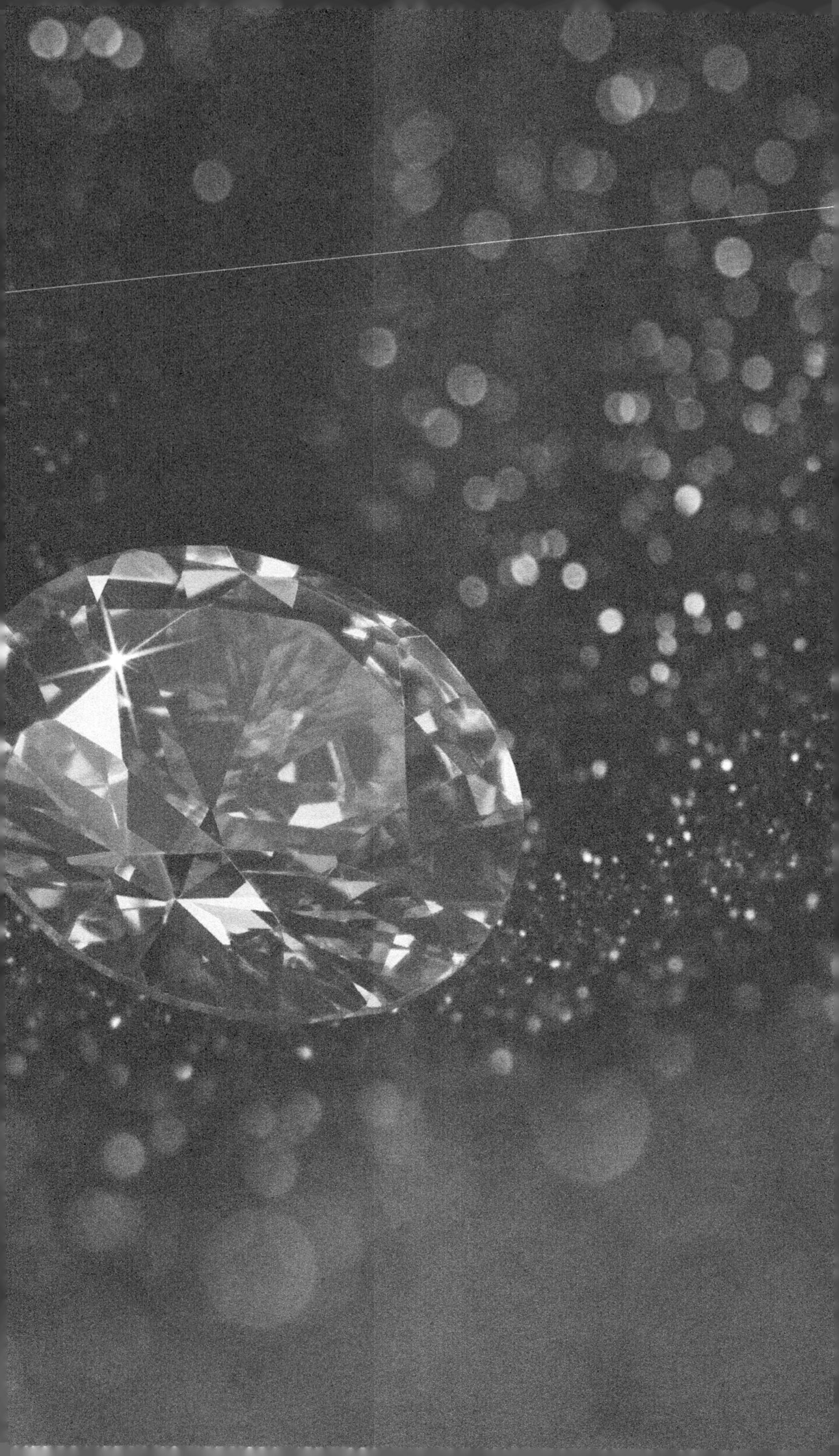

CHAPTER
FORTY

Sia

I was naked when Maxim eased into his bed that night. I hadn't gone back to my room and didn't want to.

I was shivering.

Anticipation struck a deep shudder within me, but no fear. There was absolutely none and couldn't be.

"*Malyshka...*" The bed dipped behind me, his proximity close but not close enough. Maxim drew in a breath. "*Malyshka*, let me inside you."

He was asking for permission. Even now after the display in the bathroom. He knew I wanted him. He knew *that I knew* he could be watching me, and even if he didn't, I was currently naked in his bed. Despite the obviousness of the situation he was still asking for consent.

Because he was a good man.

I knew bad men. I knew them well, and no matter what Maxim did or how harshly he did it, he could never fall under the umbrella of the dark and depraved. He was dark yes, but not once had I ever felt anything but safe with him. It was why I'd given him my body so many times.

My need for him physically brought numbness to my body. If I didn't have him inside me soon, I thought I'd actually die. "Maxim..."

I reached for his face in the dark, shadows passing over his chiseled features. He was fully clothed and hadn't even taken his shoes off. He wouldn't unless he had that consent.

I gave it to him when I reached back, fisting his cock through his pants. He growled oh so hard before crushing our mouths together in a way that made me hate myself for denying him so long. I'd gotten scared. I'd gotten *lonely*. I felt like he betrayed me by giving me a part of himself, then taking it away.

But he hadn't. Truth of the matter was I didn't know why he put so much distance between us for so long. Maybe he had his own fears about commitment, but he'd done nothing but try to remedy that with me *for weeks*. I mean the man went to a fucking community college with kids half his age just to be close to me, clearly.

He had gotten close. He'd gotten close and deep, and then there was what had me in his bed now. Maxim Petrov showed his love through action. He didn't have to put it on a billboard to let me know how much he cared about me.

"Sia..." His tongue dipped into my mouth, his hand between my legs. He brought my arms up, cuffing them with a firm hand before affectively pinning me beneath his weight. "I can't stop. Please tell me to stop."

I wouldn't. I refused, and I knew why he'd want to. I had a feeling he knew so many things about me and not just how to work my body.

"No way in hell," I said, deepening the kiss and widening my legs. I thrust my hips up, and he growled so hard I felt it in my teeth.

"Goddess," he breathed, kissing the word down my jawline, my neck. "My angel."

He felt like mine.

A noise escaped my lips when he pinched my clit, then rubbed it. Two fingers drew back and fucked me while he did it, and I nearly came for the second time tonight.

"Fuck, Sia. Fuck." Our mouths were fused, his clothes finally off when he shed them one by one, and when he finally let me have him he was just as naked as me.

His body was so hard, solid. He was like a mural of danger and dark ink, and I kissed so many of his tattoos.

The sound he let out was feral, primal. He brought my legs up and eased himself inside me, deep. He didn't wear a condom, but I didn't care. I was on birth control.

"Maxim…" I shuddered beneath him, wanting this for so long, to feel close to him again. "I need you."

It was so hard for me to admit that I needed anyone. I'd survived for so long on my own, but all I wanted—truly wanted—was someone in my life I could trust. I wanted to be able to give myself to someone else and know they wouldn't use my vulnerability against me.

"Sia Reynolds, you have no idea of my need," he said, the words humming against my neck, and I gasped. He kissed the space beneath my ear. "If you knew how bad I wanted you, it'd scare you, *malyshka*. I need all of you in every way you can give."

I gasped again, wanting that too. I wanted to be needed but had been too scared to let myself go in the past.

I wasn't scared now, pumping Maxim's cock while he milked my sex. We were a sea of limbs and sweat, and the taste drove fire through me. His taste brought me to life, and once I had that, felt that…

There was no going back for me, and I had a feeling the same went for him. He roared when he got close to the edge, but I was long gone before that. The fire hit low in my belly, and my walls squeezed so freaking tight around him.

"Sia..." He dragged my name across my lips with so much control and not once did he not let me see him. He always kept me facing him. He framed my face. "My baby girl."

I panted, getting way too emotional, but I couldn't help it. I felt safe, so incredibly *safe* and someone like me didn't get that. I didn't get to bask in the safety of the world at all, let alone with someone else.

I guess that was another gift he gave me.

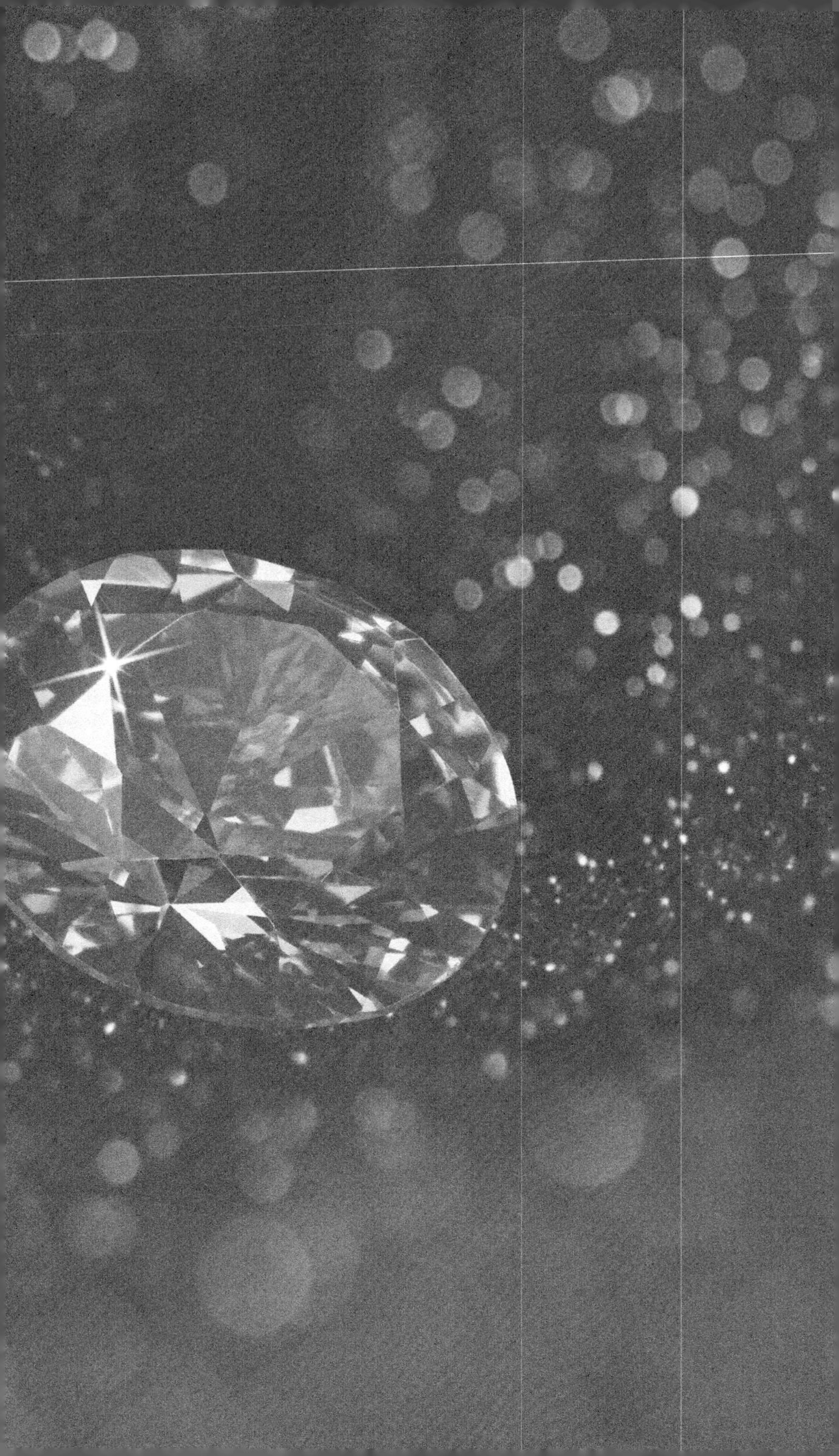

CHAPTER
FORTY-ONE

Maxim

"It was you, wasn't it? Professor Handler... It was you," Sia said, her small body curling up against me.

I was happy to have her in my arms in that moment because at the sound of that *fucker's name* I know I would have annihilated shit. I know I would have *killed* something or someone.

In fact, I already had.

I held Sia closer, saying nothing. I drew fingers down her warm skin and focused my attention on that instead.

"Maxim?"

She didn't want me to respond to her. She wouldn't want to know the truth. Sia turned on my chest, her arm rested firmly against my heart. I didn't want her there...in my heart, but she was woven so intricately inside me. My soul couldn't differentiate hers from my own.

"It was you. Everything that happened to him," she said.

She didn't sound frightened by what she clearly uncovered, but she had seen me take a man's life before. She'd seen me do it more than once.

I squeezed her arm, choosing my next words carefully. I feared going mad talking about this topic. Someone hurting her... My eyes narrowed. "Why did you let me take you so rough, *malyshka*? Do those things to you..."

Why did she let me have her? Touch her. I shouldn't have, and she should have told me about her past. Had I known I never would have—

Her hand touched my face. The warmth reached the darkest parts of my soul. Her head shook. "You're not him."

Him...

I growled. "You should have never let me take you in such a way. All the things we've done sexually. The vineyard..." My jaw moved. "If I had known, things would have been completely different."

I never would have touched her. I never would have put a claim on her after knowing what she'd been through.

The fucker who hurt her had sung like a canary.

He had after he pissed himself, and the vomit came after I cut off each one of his fingers. I took a digit for every one he'd placed on her.

And it still wasn't enough. It could never be enough.

"Maxim." She made me face her in that moment, her touch guiding me. Her mouth turned down. "You're not him. You're not that monster."

I was a monster. Just a different kind. My hand ran down her wrist. "He touched you."

He did, *nightly*, and she'd been a child. He said the abuse went on for a whole year until she stopped it. She set the fucker's house on fire, and he only let her go because his wife wanted Sia out of their home. She was a 'problem child', his wife said.

I wanted to kill her too. I wanted to slaughter anyone who'd ever hurt her or wronged her. Sia had been thrust back into the system like a problem when some fucker had abused her. She put her trust in someone only to have the trust violated…

Then, when she should have had allies after the abuse, she got trapped in a flawed system. I knew her records. Juvie had been Sia's punishment after the fire when all she had done was try to defend herself. The drugs had obviously come later, and who could blame her?

It was a miracle she was alive.

I cradled her closer and would fuse her to me if I could. "He touched you and got away with it." And yes, I ended him. The fucker more than deserved it, but death wasn't enough for him. My heart charged harder. "He's the reason for the drugs."

He was the reason she had a drug problem.

It all made sense.

That asswipe was the reason for everything wrong in her life, and she didn't even have to tell me. I knew darkness in my world, and there was always a reason for an action. Something happened, and there was always an equal and opposite reaction.

This was my own life: my own darkness the reason for my entire being. My family was taken from me too young, and I did what I had to do to avenge them. I continued on my father's legacy, but only after I took care of who wronged him.

My mother had been first.

A money-hungry opportunist, she used and abused my father before leaving him and going onto the next. My father wasn't a wealthy man, but she took everything he had before abandoning him and our family.

She paid for that, my first kill, but the most important one came years later. It came after Natan found me and offered me a better life. He discovered a screwed up kid and helped him overcome the corrupt system that landed him there. My father was *murdered* after all he'd done was give his life to a family. The Novikovs. My dad was their family doctor and was killed himself after Nikolai Novikov was done with him.

Nikolai Novikov was rotting in the earth now thanks to my blade. That was where he belonged, and Natan, the rightful *pakhan,* was now head of the Bratva in Chicago. I loathed any and all kinds of corruption. I loathed when people took advantage of others for their own selfish gain.

Sia's abuser was lucky all I did was carve him to pieces.

"I tried school once before," she said, gratefully taking me out of my thoughts. They were headed to the darkest of places and not so easy to come back from. She placed her head on my chest. "I tried community college before. It didn't work out."

"Because you saw him." Once more, she didn't have to tell me. "*Malyshka…*"

"I," she paused, sniffing a little before rubbing her noise. Her eyes were red, and she closed them. "I didn't know he taught there. I actually thought he was still practicing. When I'd been a kid, he was a vet. He taught me so many things. He…" She shook her head. "I saw him, and I couldn't handle it. I went on a bender and dropped out of school after the first week. I'd never even tried drugs before, but I couldn't deal."

And why was she expected to? She wasn't.

My mind spun with thoughts, the urge to kill in my fingers. I incinerated that fucker's body in the end. This was one of the usual ways we got rid of bodies at Peters & Burg, but usually the body was dead before that.

He hadn't been, and the sounds of his screams were a symphony to my ears. The flames claimed the last remains of his life, but now, I was wishing for an even slower death. One that involved animals and feeding.

She trusted this man, and now, I knew why she was so good with animals. Why she loved Polly and tried so hard with her. For me.

There was no reason kindness should be in Sia's heart. Not when it'd been so betrayed.

I let her go, and her eyes narrowed in response. I sat up. "Why did you let me touch you?"

I hadn't been gentle with her, or even kind, the majority of the time we'd been intimate. It wasn't my usual way.

"Maxim?"

My head was in my hands, but I faced her. She addressed me and deserved respect, but it was so hard to look into her brown eyes. There was so much innocence there even though someone attempted to steal it.

She shook her head, a wash of curls skating across her shoulders. "Anything you did I wanted."

"Sia—"

"No." Her voice radiated in my bedroom, the flames from the fireplace flicking off the flushed tones of her skin. She was beautiful, so goddamn beautiful. Her fingers wrapped in my hair. "You have always been clear with me. You've respected me, and you've always asked for consent. You never took anything from me."

But didn't I? My chest felt caved in, and once more, she made me face her. She pressed her forehead to my temple. "I feel... I feel powerful with you. Like I have control. *I* have control, and you've given that back to me. You always have. You always make me feel safe, Maxim."

She was wrong. I didn't give her anything. It was her who took it back. I closed my eyes. "I'd never forgive myself if I hurt you."

"You didn't. You never did. You are safety to me. You make me feel so safe, Maxim. *I've always* felt safe with you."

"You know nothing about me, *malyshka*," I finally faced her, no longer taking the coward's way out. "You know nothing about the man I am, or the things I've done."

She'd only seen a fraction of my darkness and had no idea what I was capable of. My soul was coal black and hers was pure white like fallen snow from my home country. Snow was so beautiful in Russia, just like her.

"I do know you." Her lips were warm against mine, soft, and, weak again, I didn't fight them. She pressed harder. "You showed me who you are. You've shown me so much love."

It was her who showed me love. She'd done the impossible.

She managed to love a monster.

There was no place in my life for so much goodness. Good things died in my wake, but here she was. She was giving herself to me when she got on my lap, and I spread her legs that night once more. I wanted to be someone she could love.

I wanted to be someone she deserved.

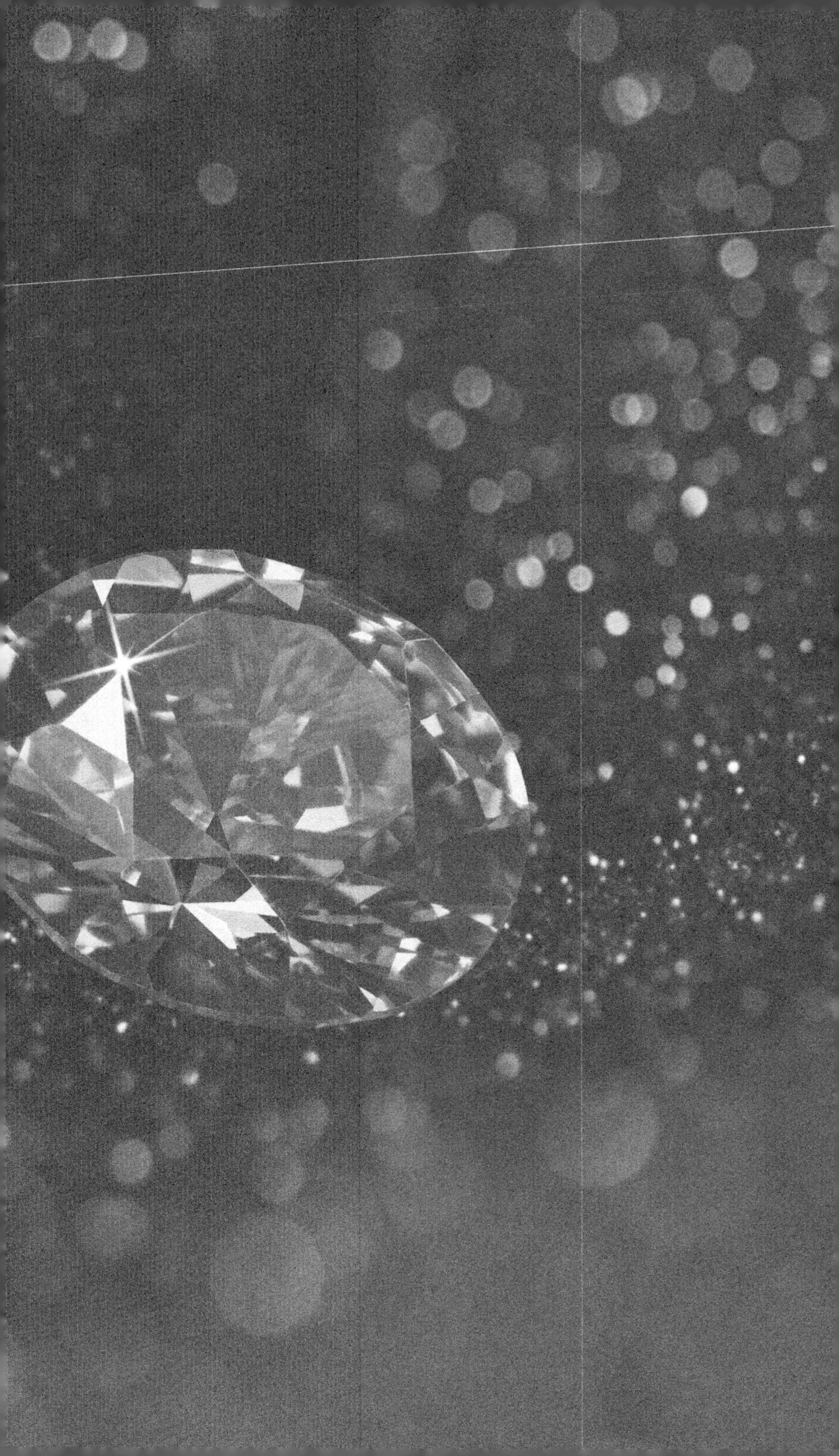

CHAPTER
FORTY-TWO

Maxim

Sia's arms wrapped around my waist as I made her food. I think she was still surprised I knew how to cook even though I'd made her full meals before with my own hands.

Seeing me in the act firsthand delighted her, and I could tell whenever she pressed her cheek to my arm and grinned. Something as small as making her homemade mac and cheese for lunch brought her joy, and I'd taken every opportunity I could to cook for her in the past week. I'd taken seven days off, unheard of, and Val believed I'd lost my mind.

She hadn't questioned it though and did well running things while I was away. In fact, I'd barely checked up on her and the ongoings of Peters & Burg. I passed things off and held faith everything was going by my standards.

I considered this the Sia effect and the feeling I got when she moaned around a spoonful of something I gave her. It warmed my blood in the same way it did when she took my cock, and she'd been taking a lot of cock lately. I basically shutdown my house in the past week. I gave my household staff *paid* time off with the sole purpose of being able to fuck Sia Reynolds on every available surface in my home. Sophia thought I lost my mind too.

I hadn't though, and the privacy created a little utopia for Sia and me. We needed the time, and I owed it to her after taking so much of that away.

"When will we do another scene?" She was eating ice cream on the kitchen counter after lunch, her gloriously smooth legs crossed. She wore nothing but one of my old t-shirts, and the erotic vision had me wanting to drizzle that Rocky Road down her shapely legs and lick it from in between her toes. She grinned. "Can we do another soon?"

I was eating ice cream out of a half gallon and depositing it in my mouth with a wooden spoon like some barbarian. Once more, this was the Sia effect. She had me doing things I hadn't done since I was young. I smirked. "Scenes, huh? What do you know about doing any of that?"

"The internet told me. Well, YouTube." She kicked her legs, then proceeded to fit the entire wooden spoon into her mouth to get the ice cream. If she wasn't careful, I would be eating that ice cream off places on her body. Or *out* of places. Her head tilted. "That's what they're called, right? Scenes?"

Miss Sia Reynolds believed she knew my kink, but the internet didn't have shit on what I was into. Placing my ice cream down, I wrapped a hand around her throat. "The internet can't teach you what I'm about, *malyshka*. But yes, they're traditionally called scenes."

Her delicate throat bobbed under my hand. Her eyes flared, and her quick panting let me know she might just want me to eat that ice cream out of places after all.

"Anyway, it's too cold for that. To go out to the vineyard I mean," I said, releasing her and leaving her hot, burning. I liked to tease her just as much as she enjoyed being my bratty girl. I smiled. "Wouldn't want you getting sick."

"We could always do one inside."

"Inside?"

She nodded, spreading her legs like a dirty girl...my naughty whore I'd turned out this week. Fuck, she'd turned me out, and we'd have to scrub this place *fucking down* by the time we were ready to come up for air from each other.

Sia was trying to play a game with me, teasing me just as much as I teased her. I hitched a hip against the counter. "Let me guess. The internet told you that too."

"Yep."

She was spending too much time on the internet, and she used her little toes to pull me toward her. She put her foot right between my legs, beneath my cock, and her eyes flashed by what she clearly felt.

"*Malyshka*..." My voice was gravelly, my hand behind her neck. "I'm happy to fuck you anywhere you want in my home...the regular way."

We'd played together before, but I always turned into someone else.

And if I hurt her...

We had played before, but that was before I knew her history. She said the things we did empowered her, but I was still hesitant to jump right back into things. She frowned. "I don't mind doing those things we did. Actually, I really fucking like them."

I could tell she had, and I smirked again. My thumb touched her mouth. "I liked them too, but I play because I enjoying breaking. I'd want to break you, *malyshka*, and I couldn't have that. I turn into someone else when I play."

That was the point of it. Hunting controlled my demon and tamed my bloodlust. I'd uncorked a genie in my thirst to avenge my father, and that hadn't stopped just because his murderer was ten feet under. Breaking something into submission kept my demon in check. That and the work I did at Peters & Burg.

I didn't want to become a tyrant like Nikolai Novikov. I

killed for honor and justice and anything else *did* turn me into that fucker and monsters like him.

A smile escaped Sia's full lips as she looked at me. She pushed her warm hands into my shirt and slid it off my shoulders.

"I'm not fragile, Maxim," she said, but wasn't she? My dirty girl was so delicate. She placed her hands on my face. "But I feel like you know that."

I did, which created a vast paradox in my mind. Sia Reynolds wasn't easily broken. I'd tested her yes, but then there was her history. She was stronger than anyone should be at her age. She'd been through hell and back and returned with a sword, shield, and victory.

"You can't break me," she continued, her warm lips chasing heat across my tattoos. She started at my shoulder, moving on to my bicep and chest. "I want to play."

My growl was feral. I guided her off the counter, then bent her over it. "Use your safe word."

My next instruction was for her not to run. She was to leave the kitchen calmly, and I'd wait five minutes before hunting her.

I ended up finding her in thirty seconds. Sia's smell filled this whole house, but there was no where she could hide where I wouldn't find her. Even still, I let her think she was getting ahead of me. I chased her several rotations around the house before we ended up back in the kitchen on the floor.

I shoved her t-shirt up, and she fought me in a way that had my dick *steel*. I kept her on her back, remembering her limits, and since she didn't use her safe word, I proceeded to pull my cock out and shoved it inside her.

She fought then too, bucking, and I nearly blew my load within seconds of being inside her.

"Sia, *fuck*." The demon flared to life inside me, my mouth on one of her dark nipples as I fucked her wildly. "Take me like a good fucking girl, baby."

"Fuck you," she shot, but the scene was over when she rocked her full hips up. She met every one of my thrusts, taking it deep like a good girl. "Maxim..."

And there was my sweet Sia, my demon physically tamed when I kissed her sweetly...

Then made love to her.

This hadn't happened before. My hunts never turned into...*this*. Normally, once I let myself go to that place there was no going back.

"Sia..." I kissed her hard, filling the condom with a sharp thrust. Sia's walls closed tight around me, and I milked her while we both came down from the high.

"Yes." The word escaped her lips as I kissed her, and I was inside her so long. I didn't leave and was hard-pressed to do so.

My mouth warmed her stomach after, her pussy. I spent some time there licking her tiny curls before tugging her shirt down and pressing her against me. We lay on the floor together, both our hearts beating fast.

"Is that what you meant when you said the internet can't teach me what you're about?" she asked out of nowhere, facing me. Her curls were everywhere, wild and beautiful. She touched my face. "Because you'd want to break me."

It had been what I meant, but I never told her the reasons why. There was so much she didn't know about me.

But I wanted her to.

"I torture and kill for the organization," I said, and when she didn't interrupt me, I continued. "I enjoy bringing justice but didn't always have control. Play and what I do at Peters & Burg keeps me in check."

It was important she knew this. It was important she knew me.

Sia didn't say anything for a long time, and I worried what I said was too much for her.

But then, she kissed me again.

She tugged my belt loops and something unleashed inside me. Something wild that made me hotter than I'd ever been for her. She held no fear being this close to me, and her reaction to what I'd done to that bastard who violated her had been the same. She wasn't scared and hadn't distanced herself from me.

I didn't know that would mean something to me. For someone to see me more than as the face of a man in the dark. I pressed my hand to her face, bringing her beneath me. I think I was in love with Sia Reynolds.

I'd fallen with no safety net.

I took her two more times on the kitchen floor before she was laughing beneath me. She had me laughing, both of us in fits like we had no care in the world. She made me feel free and how funny that was for a man like me.

I got my clothes arranged before making her a semblance of decent. She still had nothing on but my shirt, but she was covered enough.

I peeled myself off her mid-kiss. I wanted to bathe her. We both got distracted after our play, but I intended to rectify that now.

I had Sia sighing when I pressed a final kiss on her neck, but she wriggled away upon gazing over my shoulder.

"Oh, my God… *Dad?*"

I swung around and stared directly into the eyes of my kid. Lettie stepped back, her hands in the air, and I wasn't surprised since she just found her father in a comprising position.

But then, she saw Sia.

I had to say it took my daughter a second. Her focus had been on me at first, but upon spotting Sia beneath me… *Sia in my shirt* beneath me, she dropped everything in her hands. She had several colorful bags that appeared to be Christmas presents.

Fuck.

"Holy fuck, Sia?" Lettie pressed her hands to her face, then her eyes. "Holy fuck. Holy fuck. Holy fuck. Holy *fuck*."

My daughter's choice of words could use some work in front of her dad, but I wasn't focused on that at the present. Lettie left the room in a panic, and I started to go after her, but didn't want to leave Sia.

She waved me off. "Go." A sharp panic flashed across her pretty face, and when I didn't move, she pushed me. "Go, Maxim. You need to go. She needs you."

It was clear I needed to talk to my daughter, but she wasn't the only one who needed my attention. Sia appeared physically ill on my kitchen floor, but she wouldn't let me tend to her when she nudged me.

Why the fuck hadn't I told Lettie about us?

I was regretting that now, caught between two halves of my heart. Sia made me leave the one half in the kitchen, my stomach tight each and every step I made away from her.

"Holy fuck, Dad. Holy fuck!" Lettie was flailing at this point. She was in the foyer freaking out and was still in her coat and gloves. She waved her arms. "You and Sia? Holy fuck."

"Calm down, Lettie." I understand she found me with her friend, but Sia and I were both adults. I raised a hand. "Just calm the fuck down and take a second."

I had no idea why she was home, but if she intended for her arrival to be a surprise she'd accomplished that feat. She started to speak, but the floor creaked, and we both turned around.

Sia.

She had Polly's lead in her hands, gripping it. She was against the wall in the foyer like she was trying to sneak through the room and take Polly out, and nothing about that surprised me at all. Polly was comfort for her, and that was clear whenever I watched them together.

I held out my hand. I wanted her to seek comfort in me as

well, and the tightness ensnaring my chest relaxed when she decided to come closer. She and Polly made their way over to me, and it was like a tether eased in its tautness. Like we were connected on a visceral level. It was one I'd been denying for a long time, but I wasn't anymore.

"Wow." The word came from Lettie, watching at the point Sia took my hand. Sia and I had been distracted with each other until she said that. Lettie put her hands together. "This is serious."

My daughter knew me. I didn't bring women around really as I never fucking dated. I fucked with no attachments only. I didn't see the point of doing anything else considering the world I lived in. Anything loved could be taken away.

It appeared Sia Reynolds was worth taking the risk for more.

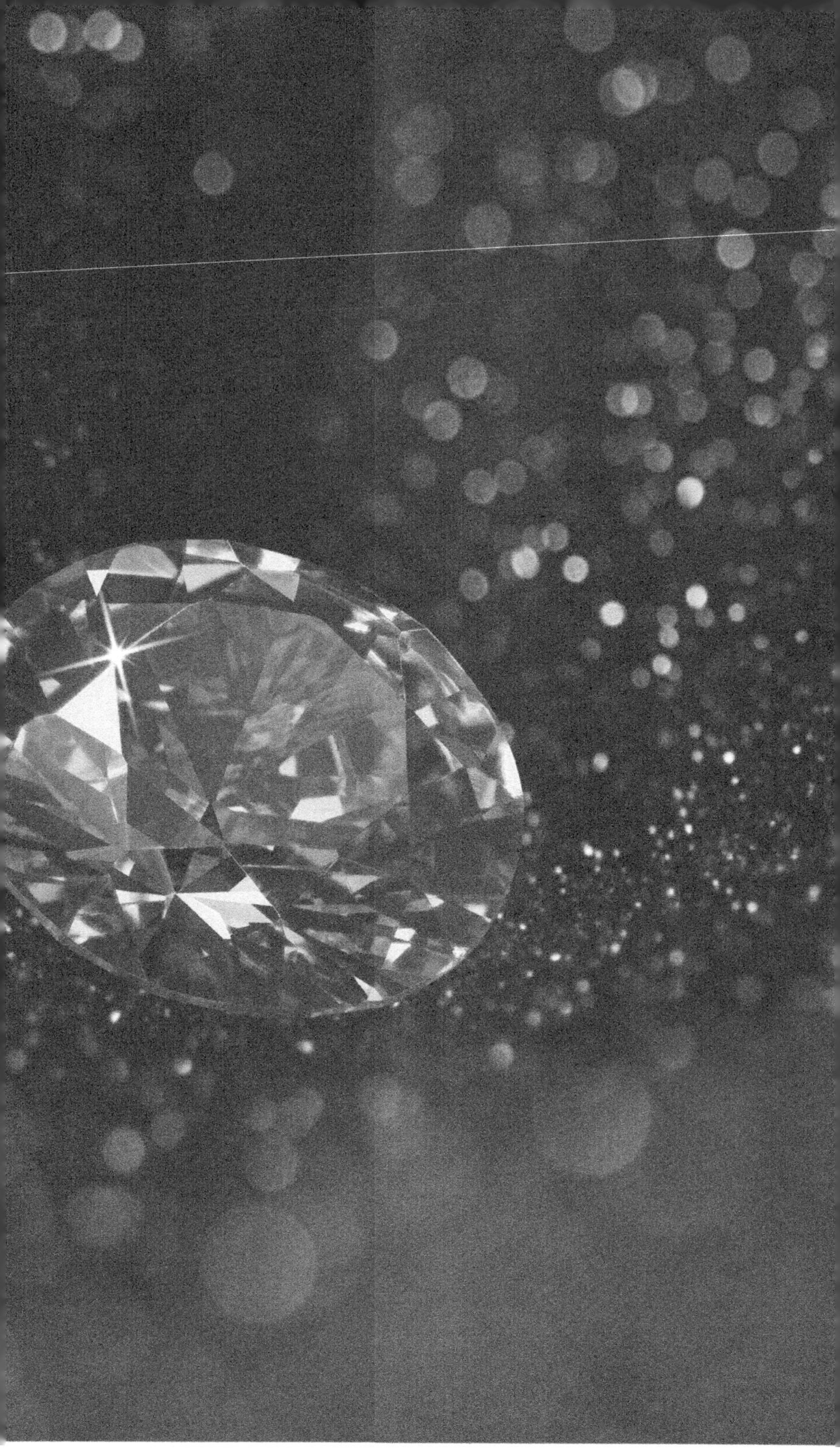

CHAPTER FORTY-THREE

Sia

I let Maxim explain everything to Lettie. It didn't feel appropriate any other way.

Fucking hell.

We both lied to Lettie, but *he was her dad*. He could lie to her.

I was supposed to be her friend.

I was a friend who kept something big from her after she'd given me a home and a job. This whole thing felt shitty, but what made me feel shittier was that I was hard-pressed to regret my actions. I regretted the lies and the omission about our relationship, but I didn't regret falling in love.

Love.

It felt like too weak of a word after finding out what Maxim did for me. He removed a monster from the world *for me*. My foster dad had been a specter over my entire life for so long. He dictated every action, every thought, for years and just when I thought I'd be okay he reappeared. I'd been trying to get my life together by going to school, but like when I'd been a kid, he stole that away. That fucker took more than my innocence.

He took my entire life.

It took me so goddamn long to come back from everything with him, and the last time, I'd spiraled so bad. That cop I hit? I actually saw *Handler's* face. I'd been drugged out of my mind and saw my abuser.

It'd been so bad.

Who knew where I'd be if I hadn't gotten arrested. Who knew what I'd be if not for Lettie, then later, Maxim. Maxim may have been a grumpy, violent man, but he never once didn't show me who he was. He didn't pretend to be one thing, then turn into someone else, and he always *always* made me feel safe.

In so many ways.

Maxim Petrov made me feel powerful, and I finally felt in control of not just myself but my body. I made the rules, and it was Maxim's job to listen and respect them. It was something he'd always done for me, and my wishes and personal boundaries were so goddamn important to him. He never touched me unless I felt safe, and I felt like I'd finally regained control over my life.

I felt empowered.

Maxim's discussion with Lettie was long, and she didn't say much. She just listened. Eventually, Polly tugged on her leash to go outside, and I used that as an opportunity to give them some space. Lettie did need to speak to her dad, and she probably couldn't be candid with me there.

I hadn't wanted to leave Maxim. Somehow, I'd allowed this grumpy and violent man to completely bind me to him. I knew that because as soon as he'd gestured me into the room initially I hadn't wanted to leave. I wanted to trust in him and the situation. I wanted to trust that things would be okay.

I wanted to trust *him*.

I *did* trust him, when I didn't trust. He gave me that back too, and I didn't know how much I needed that. It was by sheer will that I allowed myself to separate from him in the end. Polly was tugging to go out, and though Maxim didn't look like he wanted me to, I did leave. He had an expression weaved amongst his handsome features that let me know I wasn't the only one privy to the draw between us, and maybe I wasn't the only one receiving power between the two of us.

"Wow, Dad. Just wow." These were the words I heard Lettie say after I came back into the room. Maxim and Lettie were in the living room. I'd crated Polly, and Maxim and Lettie hadn't seen me yet. Lettie's head tilted. "Yeah, I uh... I don't know what else to say."

She'd said something similar before, and again, she hadn't said much before I left.

Maxim had his legs crossed on the couch, and the light from the fireplace set a glow on his face. He'd started the fire shortly after we moved the conversation to the living room.

His expression was serious.

"I love her, Lettie," he said, the embers from the fireplace crackling in the distance, and my lungs squeezed. His head tilted. "I haven't told her yet, but I do. It just kind of happened. I'm sure she can agree neither one of us went looking for it."

I did agree.

He loves me.

I didn't mean to eavesdrop and maybe that was why the universe intervened when I knocked over a decorative dish full of polished marble. The rocks skittered onto the floor like my jellybeans would, and Maxim and Lettie instantly gazed up from their conversation.

Fuck.

My first thought was to back away on instinct, but once again, Maxim put out his hand for mine.

Come to me, malyshka.

I could actually hear his deep voice inside my head, his

smile on me. He never used to smile a lot, but it seemed that was all he'd been doing lately. He hadn't left the house all week to work, and I hadn't just seen him smile during his time off. I heard *him laugh*.

Maybe he wasn't so grumpy anymore.

He took my hand, and Lettie, well, she was beaming. She actually had her hands to her mouth like her dad and me were the most adorable thing ever, which was very surprising to me. I hadn't known how to interpret her lack of responses before.

"Lettie?" Maxim weaved his hand in mine, but he stared at his daughter. Lettie dropped her hands, and the next thing I knew, she was nodding.

I had no idea what that meant, but my heart certainly leaped into my throat when suddenly, Maxim was no longer sitting on the sofa...

But dropping down on one knee.

Holy fucking shit.

I didn't know what to think. I was kind of losing my mind, and Maxim's smile didn't leave. He wasn't one to do it much so the expression was rather quaint, but that was what I think made it so handsome.

Wow, I really am in love.

This guy's *smile* danced butterflies in my stomach, and my belly only danced more when he kissed my hand.

"I want to ask you something, and I know it might feel sudden..." He gazed back at his daughter. She had her thumb up this time, and something about all this felt pre-thought out.

Oh, my God. Is he really going to...

"I also know your age. You're just starting life and..." His expression turned serious again, and my heart somersaulted when he brought me closer. His mouth warmed my hand. "*Malyshka*, a life with me would be nothing but dark."

It was the vulnerability of what he said. He hadn't asked

anything of me yet, but it felt like he had. Like a life with him wasn't one at all.

I couldn't breathe, but he had to know a life with him wouldn't be far off from where I'd been headed before him. I'd gone through so much before we got together, *my life* dark.

"You've only just been introduced to my life, but people can't easily come out of it," he explained. "That's just not the world I live in, Sia, and though I wish I could offer you something different that's not my reality."

His fingers traced a freckle on my wrist, and when he warmed my hand again with his lips, I died a little because I knew what I was going to say to whatever he asked. It was a death and resurrection. I was leaving behind who I was for something better.

"It's hard for me to ask you to sacrifice life as you know it," he continued, frowning. "And I feel selfish for asking, but there really isn't any dating in my world, Sia. That's just not how it is, and though I feel like a selfish fuck I..."

I decided to get on the floor with him at that point. I needed to. I needed to be close to him.

He pushed his big hands into my hair, and I felt him *everywhere*. The intense shiver I felt down to each one of my toes, and I shuddered despite the warmth in the room.

His fingers brushed my cheek. "Sia, please be mine. Be mine in every way. Be my wife, *malyshka*. I need you."

Lettie let out a little noise behind her hands, and with her smile, I had a feeling this really was okay with her.

"*Malyshka*?" Maxim was waiting on me, and I understood what he said. It was a dangerous world he operated in, and even though I didn't know a thing about it, I could imagine people didn't come and go easily from his life. Once they were there, they were permanent, so there was no point in wasting time.

He saw me as permanent.

This really did feel crazy. I mean, I was only twenty, but

then again, it didn't feel so crazy. I smiled. "That depends. Does Polly still have to stay in her own quarters?"

I was obviously toying with him. The answer was yes to his question. It was fuck yes, but I couldn't help being a little bratty.

Maxim's eyes instantly darkened and something told me I'd be paying for my sass a little later. I could only hope. He eyed me. "*Malyshka*, the damn dog can stay in our bed if you say yes."

Lettie had a little bit of a cringe when he said that, but I didn't blame her. This would be an adjustment for her and me.

I had a feeling her dad's happiness outweighed all that though, and only one person looked happier when I finally did say yes. That person was obviously her dad, but then again, he had nothing on my smile. He really did see us as permanent, and my own reality hit then. I didn't just trust Maxim Petrov with my body.

I trusted him with my entire soul.

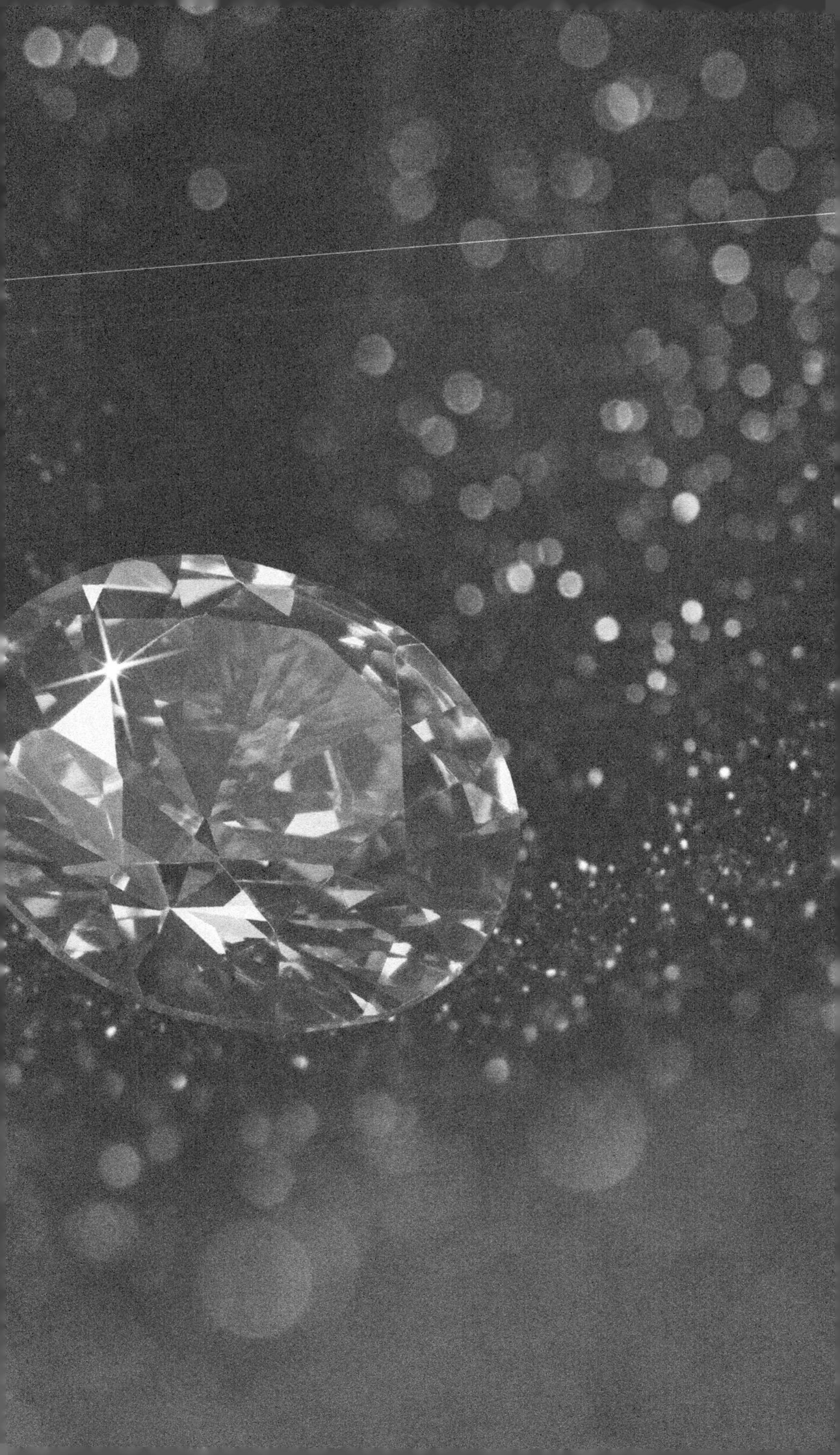

CHAPTER
FORTY-FOUR

Sia

So apparently this wedding was happening really soon. Lettie proposed holiday nuptials. Holidays as in *this* holiday. She didn't trust her dad not to elope after she returned to school (her words). I guess Maxim really wasn't into pomp and circumstance, and the last time Lettie tried to throw him a birthday party he bribed her not to with her Jeep. This totally sounded like him, and neither I nor Maxim fought her on her plans to spearhead the whole thing.

It made her happy.

Anyone could tell that as she deep-dived into appointments and ordering holiday arrangements. Before I or Maxim knew it, Maxim's home was filled with enough wedding garb to make a party planner piss his pants in glee. We didn't need one with Lettie at the helm, and she'd definitely put a sizable hole into Maxim's bank account. His black card was probably on fire with how much she had him swiping it.

And he did. He did every time and, not only that, he came

to each and every appointment and was actually adamant about his attendance.

"Girl, I've never seen him act like this," Lettie said, scanning some fine crystal at a small boutique in the city. She was registering Maxim and me for gifts and was very serious about it. She glanced between the crystal vases. "This is like the third store, and he's still here."

Her dad was still here. Again, he'd been adamant about attending any place Lettie or I went. I thought it was for security. I mean, he'd been pretty freaking crazy about that when he found out I started school and had no one with me, but he'd called Val to come with us today. His head of security went to every shop we did so Maxim wasn't needed. He could work, but he wasn't.

Mind you, Maxim didn't look particularly thrilled to be here doing all this, but he was here and mostly present. He and Val were signing over by the shop's doors. Any place Lettie or I went into Maxim and Val shut the place down so Lettie could have her attack of it, and I tried not to watch them too much after I caught tidbits of something they signed at the first shop.

Maxim had asked Val to be his best woman for all of this. He'd asked her and actually smiled when she signed back she would. It'd been an intimate moment and one I wasn't quite sure I interpreted completely. I was still learning my signs, but I was pretty freaking sure that was what happened.

Lettie only confirmed it.

Lettie *did* know her signs, and she saw that exchange between her dad and Val too. It'd been another time she said she'd never seen her dad act this way, and I think we were all surprised Lettie was here and we were doing this. I guess Lettie had come home early from Bali to spend Christmas with Maxim and see me. She'd said that. She'd actually said that. Somewhere along the way this girl and I had developed a friendship beyond a temporary community service stint, and though she'd been surprised by all this, she'd been supportive. Val had too, and honestly, her *lack of surprise* by Maxim's and my relationship had surprised me. I guess we hadn't been too great at hiding it.

I studied Maxim, now in a handsome gray suit. It hugged his muscular build sinfully, and I tried not to stare *again* if only for Lettie. She was supportive, but I didn't want to make things weirder for her than they already were.

"I haven't seen you like this either," she said, noticing my stare, and my face shot up in fucking heat. She laughed. "It's like you're alive. It's like *he's* alive and," she paused, staring through a crystal vase she picked up. She smiled before putting it down. "He lights up when you're in the room, Sia. I mean, it's my dad so it's more like a strong flicker, but there's light."

I glanced his way. His signs were very expressive with Val. He even made a joke and nudged her, which was crazy. The man didn't *joke.*

He had light.

I did too, and I couldn't deny that even if I wanted to. I felt like I was on a cloud even before he proposed.

"It's nice to see," Lettie said, smiling a little. She scanned a goblet. "I'll admit that I didn't know how to feel about all this, but there's no denying, well, all this. Besides the fact that he can't leave you alone for a second it's just all over him in general. He loves you, Sia, and you clearly love him."

I did. Though, ironically enough, I hadn't told him yet. We seemed to be doing everything backwards, him and me. I overhead him tell Lettie he loved me, but he hadn't said it either.

It honestly kind of made me laugh internally. Maxim and I were so backwards, but we just made sense. I played with my hands. "I know this is all weird." It was for me too. I mean, she was my friend first. I pushed back my curls. "It honestly just kind of happened, Lettie."

I heard Maxim say the same thing to her, and though she'd said she was cool with it to both of us, I'd yet to pull her aside. Part of that had to do with the fact that Maxim was so close, but I wanted to. She deserved that.

"I know," she said. "And I am happy for you guys. If you make my dad happy, then that's who I want him to be with. I want you happy too. You deserve that."

I found out she knew all about my history. Maxim had told her, and I said that was okay. I wanted her to know. We were about to be family, yeah, but Lettie and I really did have a friendship. I cared about her.

"But I will say calling you my stepmother would be weird so..."

"Oh, please God *no*," I said, waving my arms, and borderline cringing. She laughed, and I did too. I smiled. "We're friends."

She hugged me. "Closer, Sia Reynolds. Much closer."

I felt the same way, and when I told her that, I think it choked us both up. No way would I ever be considered this girl's stepmom, whether legal or otherwise. But friends? Great friends? I'd take that.

She rubbed my arms. "Good. Now that's settled, let's finish up and see about getting both of us dresses," she stated before scanning a final vase. She winked. "Maybe we can convince my dad to go stalk someone else for a minute because he is *not* coming wedding dress shopping."

Did she know her dad? I had a feeling she'd be hard-pressed to convince him to go somewhere else.

Even still, I decided to let her try, and I was happy for these moments we had together. I didn't have a lot of people in my life I considered family. In fact, I had no one before her and Maxim. I'd been alone for so long, and I think I convinced myself that was okay. I think it had to be.

It was nice things no longer had to be that way.

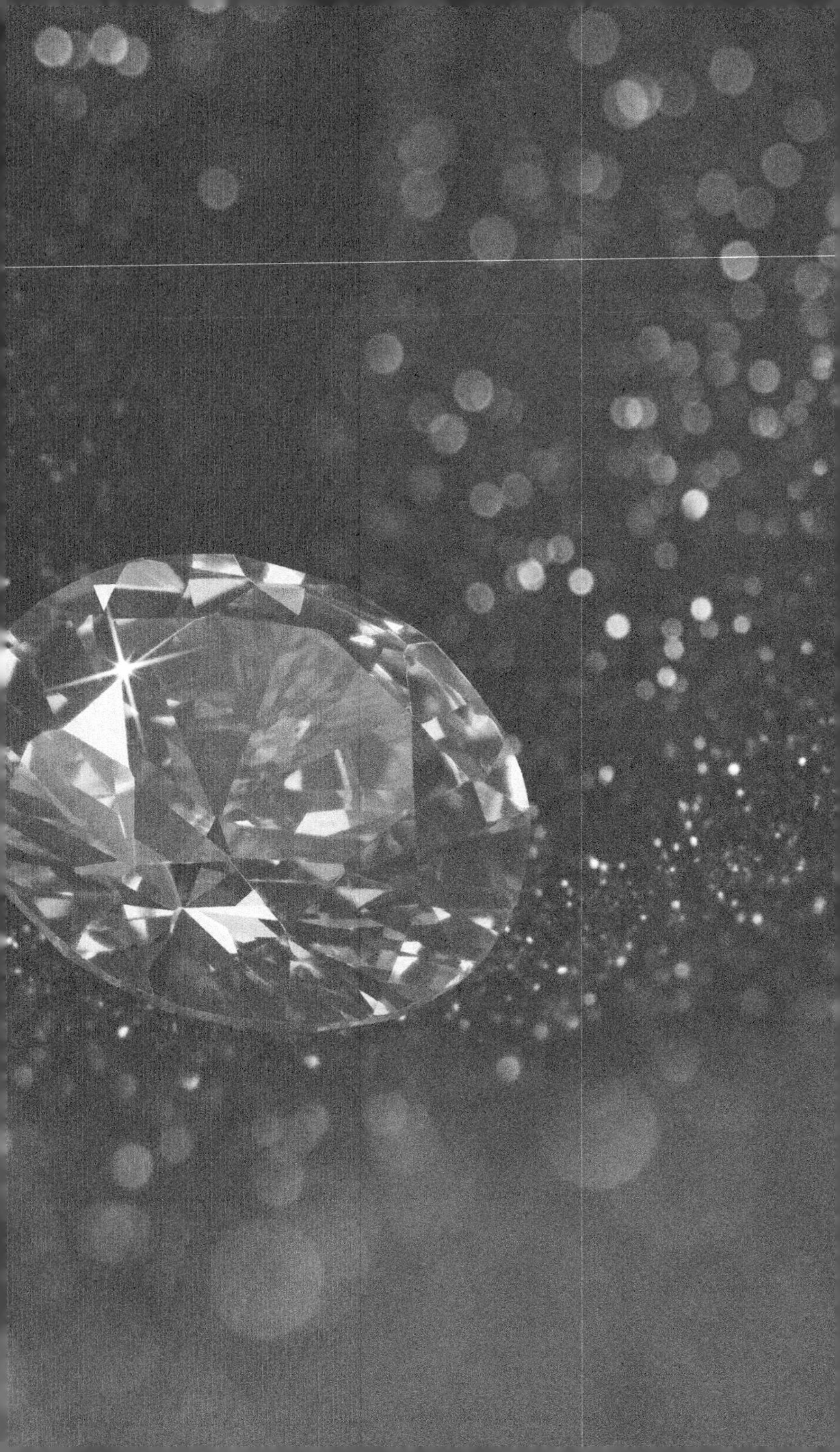

CHAPTER
FORTY-FIVE

Sia

Lettie and I were able to get Maxim to go away for dress shopping, but when it came to Val? Nothing doing. Maxim's overprotective nature when it came to me (and his daughter) wouldn't stand for that, but I think Lettie and I were okay with the decision in the end. Val certainly had her opinions, and it'd been nice to have another eye.

Was this all really happening?

Honestly, it kind of felt like a bit of a dream, but, even though things were moving quickly, they did feel right.

The manor when we got home looked…different. Actually, this was an understatement. For starters, none of the lights were on. It didn't need it with the adornments of flickering candles and soft light. There wasn't a stretch of the floor where there weren't candles, and I had to avoid the tea lights so I didn't accidentally kick anything over.

"Holy…" The word left my lips as my dress bag was taken from me. It took me the better part of three hours to decide on a wedding gown, but that was mostly due to Lettie and Val. My tastes were too simple as far as they were concerned.

The whole day had been fun and kind of felt like I had family. I had people who cared that I looked nice and, well, just cared.

"Told you she'd like it." This came from Lettie, the one who'd taken my dress. She'd spoken the words to Val and Lettie had her own garment bag in her arms. She was my maid of honor. She grinned. "Dad's in the dining room."

I swung around, my brow lifting. I pointed to the room. "You knew he'd do this to the house?"

"Why do you think we kept you out so long?" Lettie peered over to Val who laughed. She was in on this too? Val placed her hands on my shoulders.

"Have fun. He tried real hard with all this," she signed to me, and this really was a set up. I didn't know what it was a set up for, but I got an indicator when I did head into the dining room. At least, I thought it was the dining room. The actual dinner table was missing, as well as the chairs.

They'd been replaced with pillows.

They were a handsome red and more of those candles were around. The small set up in the center had a wide berth, and I supposed I wouldn't be guessing where I was eating dinner tonight. There were two gold domes in front of the crimson pillows and place settings on either side. The main attraction was Maxim though, who brought out two golden goblets.

And fuck did he look handsome.

He didn't even have to try, though he had, and I never thought I'd see him in a *sweater*. He had it bunched above his thick forearms, his tatted muscles on display. His inky hair was in a tousle, and he smiled warmly at me upon approaching me.

"Sparkling cider," he said, handing me a glass. I suppose

even if I was of legal age to drink he knew I wouldn't. His hand folded behind my neck. "*Malyshka.*"

That was all he said before kissing me, his mouth so warm. His tongue brushed mine, and I thought I'd melt where I stood.

"What is all this?" I asked him, breathless. His nose brushed the tip of mine, and I did go weak in the knees.

"Call it a bit of a do over." He acquired my glass after I took a sip, then placed both his and mine down to help me out of my coat. I felt not as dressed up as him in my leggings and tank, but, with the way Maxim looked at me after the coat was off, I didn't care. He gave my shoulder the briefest of kisses before following down to my chest, and I wavered more than slightly before he pulled away.

"I'm not much for romance, but even I know you deserve much more than what you got from me in the past, Sia." Using my coat, he made a makeshift blanket for me. He helped me sit with one hand, and when he joined me, he put both my hands in his. He kissed them. "I'd give you everything if I could."

I had no idea what he meant until he opened up a third dome. I hadn't seen the other one between the two place settings.

Maybe because it was so small.

I thought maybe this would be dessert to whatever was under the other domes, but *dessert* looked a little different than a black velvet box.

Holy fuck.

He snapped the box open too, and each candle's warm light flickered off the diamond inside. It was an oval shape with black stones around it.

I said nothing as he took it out.

"This is what I hope to be the start of us. A true start of a life..." He smiled a little, as if to himself. His gray eyes flicked in my direction, so steely and intense. He took my hand. "A lifetime."

I waited, but he didn't put the ring on. He just held it and my hand.

He kissed my fingers. "That is if you say yes. If you say yes to us and yes to me. I know I'm a complicated man from a complicated world, but I'm asking you for that. I want you to choose me, Sia. I want you to have me like I want to have you for a lifetime and more if I physically could."

Those words and the ring were still between us, and I realized what this was. He said he wanted a do over, and I guess when I initially said yes to an engagement it hadn't been like this.

Oh my God, he's proposing.

He was, formally. His lips turned down. "This is the proposal you should have gotten, baby girl. I love you and want to spend the rest of my life with you."

I didn't really know love before. I'd felt so much pain, but had wanted love, yearned for it. I wanted to belong somewhere, and I wanted to belong to someone. I may be stubborn like him and acted like I didn't need anyone, but I did.

I did, so much.

I must have been crying because Maxim's thick fingers glided across my cheek.

"Happy tears?" he questioned, an uncertainty in his voice I'd never heard. He smiled a little. "Or did I botch this up badly?"

He didn't know how good he did, and I kissed him.

"I love you, too," I said, then told him yes. I'd give him a million yeses if I could.

As predicted, not much talking happened after Maxim's proposal. I mean, after that proposal I was hard-pressed to do anything besides kissing and getting completely naked with him.

And he looked like sin.

He smelled like it too, and I had little to no excuse to keep my hands off him after Lettie texted she'd gone out. She said she was visiting her boyfriend, but I had a feeling she'd just been trying to give us some privacy. She was so cool about all this, and I wasn't sure I'd be if things were the other way around.

"Sia, fuck." Maxim eased his full length inside, the two of us in his big tub. We'd had some play time around the dining room before completely *not* eating. He chased me around a little bit before fucking me in the kitchen.

Twice.

Now, he was fucking me in his bathtub, and even though I was sore as fuck, I needed it. His groan was deep and gravelly as he took me, and the bath water sloshed so much there was nearly as much water on the floor as in the tub. He sucked my nipple. "Fucking perfect, so sweet."

He kept calling me that. His sweet and his baby girl.

I pushed my fingers through his inky hair, fucking him hard from above, but Maxim was never one to give up control easily. He turned the tables on me, and soon had my curls coiled around his thick fist.

He fucked me from behind with his powerful hips, smacking me flush against the tub. I trusted him to have me in this position now, and when he came with a roar, the call I let out easily tested the sound barrier.

"Oh, my God," I said, my eyes rolling back. A low chuckle rolled into my back from behind.

"As long as you know who I am," Maxim stated, arrogant as fuck as he laced our fingers together. He kissed me between my shoulder blades. "I love you, sweet girl."

I felt so warm, loved, and definitely did again when he took me to bed. We didn't fuck again, but we cuddled, which seemed even more intimate. I studied the ring he gave me while he kissed my neck softly.

"Was I too rough tonight?" Maxim asked in the dark. His thick fingers laced with mine. "You're not sleeping. Are you sore?"

I had to smile to myself that was why he thought I was still awake. I lifted my hand, showing him why my attention was stolen. The faint moonlight in the room caught the large diamond in the center.

"I wish I'd been able to give you my grandmother's ring, but unfortunately when my mother left it went with her," he said, his voice changing a little. It went gruff, agitated. He pulled me in close. "You would have loved it. It was beautiful."

This ring was beautiful. In fact, it was freaking gorgeous and more than enough.

"I love this one," I said, no words out there for how much I loved it. I brought his arms tighter around me. "It's perfect."

I never recalled him speaking about his family before. Just him and Lettie.

So much I didn't know about him.

He said that to me of course, that I didn't know him, but I knew what I needed. I knew his heart, and that was the most important.

"You deserve something more perfect," he said, kissing my naked shoulder softly. He hugged me close. "But I was glad I was able to give you this. It's not my grandmother's ring, but it's a fine replacement. I was never able to retrieve it after everything with my mom."

"Everything?"

"She's gone." His voice changed again, deep again. "Anyway, I don't want to talk about my mother. We can talk about literally anything else but that wretched woman."

He sounded so cold talking about her. Maxim readily had

a chill in his voice when talking about nearly everything, but this was slightly different, darker.

His hold on me got stronger as well, his body tense. I didn't know my parents. I'd been in the system longer than I could remember, but for all I knew, I could have an equally rough history with mine.

I just didn't know.

I was so young when I'd gone into foster care, and I didn't even have birth records. I'd been dropped off at a fire station when I'd been three. At least, that was what I'd been told.

I didn't have any memories at all from back then, but that made sense since I was so young. My first memories were in an orphanage. I just always recalled being alone.

"How about your dad?" I asked, hoping that was a lighter topic, and I was granted relief with rough laughter.

"Certainly a better topic," he said, making me smile too. I could hear it in his voice when talking about his dad. "My father was an immigrant."

"Russian?"

"Yes." He probably assumed I knew with what he'd called me. "He, myself, and my mother came over to this country when I was very young. Because of that, I'm not fluent in the language. My father was kind though. You would have liked him."

"Would have?"

"He's gone, *malyshka*. Passed," he stated, my heart suddenly sad. "It's just Lettie and me here, and she didn't get to know my father either. He died before I even hit puberty."

How sad for him. How sad for her. "Can I ask how?"

"You can." He played with my fingers, and even though I couldn't see him behind me, I envisioned him studying our hands. He stretched them out in the light. "He was murdered. A hit from inside the organization and by a man he trusted. My father was the man's family doctor."

Oh, my God.

I turned around in his arms. He'd spoken coldly about this too, but so deadpan.

He brushed hair out of my face. "Don't be sad for me. My father was avenged. I made sure of it."

He said a lot without saying it. Like he knew how his dad was avenged and maybe even took part.

I tried not to let that freak me out. He'd mentioned something about justice before, and the few times I'd seen him hurt people (with the exception of the first) he'd done it after they hurt me. He seemed to operate in response to action, and though that didn't justify it, I did get it.

This man and his dark world... I found myself seeing it not so black and white, but in shades of gray. I studied his eyes. "You're in the organization even though it hurt your father?"

"The man who murdered my father was in charge, but after his reign, a man who I consider a father stepped in. He changed things. Made things better." His hand moved over my hip, squeezing. "I owe Natan my life. I owe him everything. He raised me after my dad died."

"Is that the man who you met with in your office? " I asked, remembering he had a couple meetings I'd stumbled upon, but only one had a man who Maxim seemed to answer to. Maxim had been leading that first meeting I saw, and that had been obvious. The men crowded around him like he'd been in charge, but in that other meeting another man held Maxim's attention. Maxim sat before him respectfully like the other guy had been in charge.

"That was Natan, yes. My *pakhan*." His tatted knuckles grazed my lips. "But you should probably sleep now. Sleep and no more questions."

"Why?"

His digits brushed my eyebrows now, my lashes, until my eyes closed. "Because it might affect me if those brown eyes change when looking at me."

I opened them. He thought something he said would change how I looked at him? He had to know it wouldn't. I already knew a lot of the things he'd done. He'd showed me. I wrapped my arms around his neck. "You've already showed me who you are."

"You don't know the beginnings of who I am. Nor do you know my middle or end, and I hope you never will. I spare Lettie from the details, and I intend to protect you too." He brought my head forward, kissing my brow. "Now sleep."

He brought me into his mighty embrace as if summoning the close to this intimate conversation. He shared his heart with me, and he didn't do that a lot.

I dragged my fingers across his arm. "Did Natan ask you to do something? I mean, back when you left suddenly."

Maxim's big hands braced my arms. He said nothing, just murmured for me to sleep when he kissed the back of my head. I was sure his boss had asked him to do something. And whatever it was had changed things.

It'd made things different.

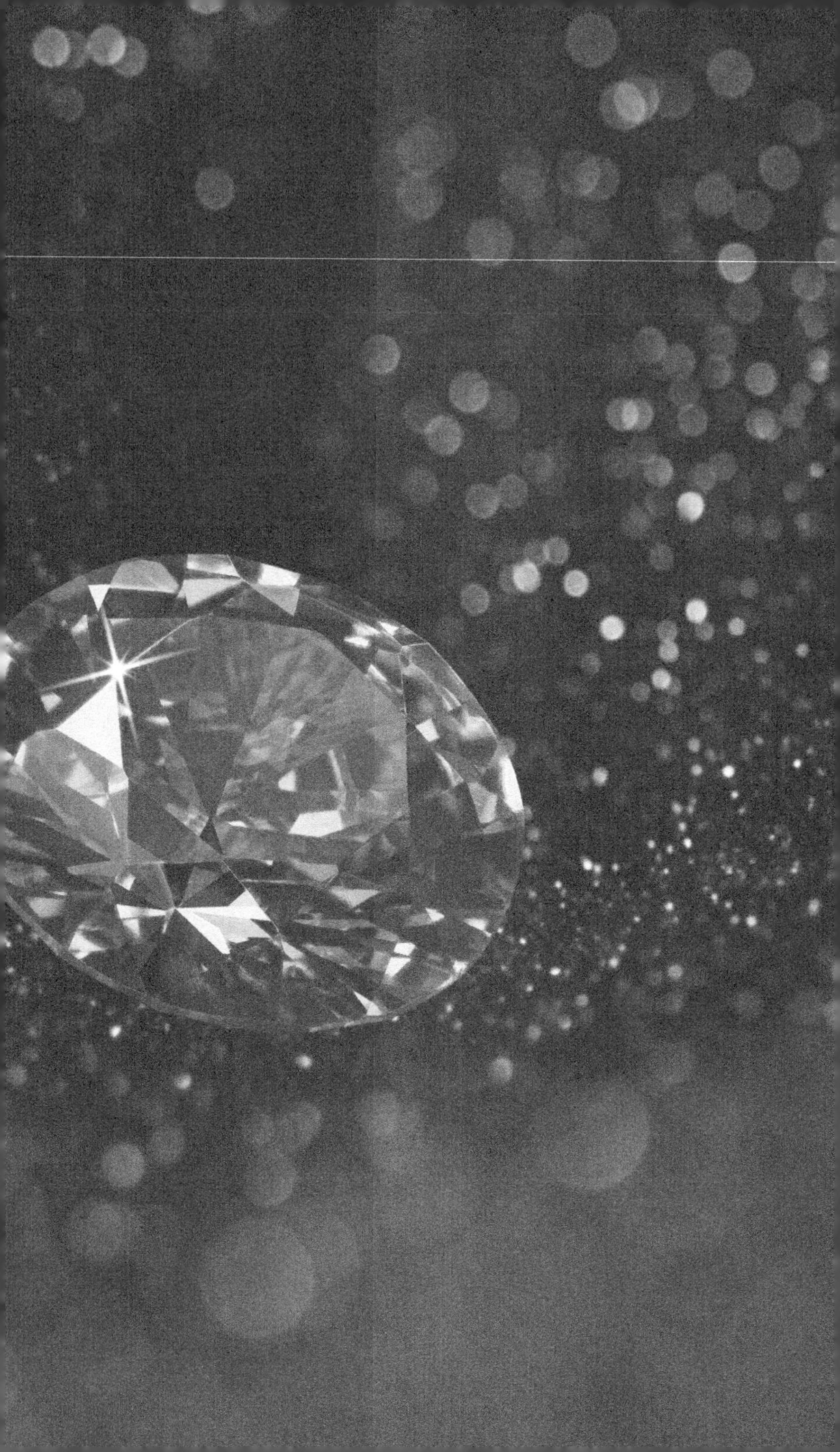

CHAPTER
FORTY-SIX

Maxim

I was going to have a talk with Sia. There were certain details about my life that I wanted her to know, but that she couldn't. They were dangerous for her, yes, but I also didn't want her affected by them.

She'd been understanding so far, but I wasn't lying that I didn't want to see those dark eyes of hers affected. They would be if they were exposed to some aspects of my life. It'd be natural and well, I couldn't have that. There were some things that needed to be pure and stay that way. They were things *I needed* to stay grounded. I'd never be on the right sight of the light. I'd seen too much. I'd done too much, but there were still things I wanted to come home to. Things like Sia and her beautiful soul.

I was a selfish man, and I knew that. Sia Reynolds kept me a little bit human, and I couldn't help but yearn for that.

"Sia?" I reached for her on the bedsheets, still groggy from sleep. I cracked my eyes open. "Sia…"

Her side of the bed was cold, the fireplace out. I'd gotten up in the middle of the night to turn it off.

Stretching, I sat up and saw a note on the pillow.

Lettie and I took Polly out for a walk. We'll be back later. Sleep in.

Sia and I typically took Polly out together, lately.

How much had changed.

There was a time in my life where the last thing I felt I needed was a dog, let alone a companion. My life had too many complications to have a woman in it, and I had far too many enemies to allow for something like that. Sia Reynolds changed the fucking game for me whether I wanted it or not.

The fact that Lettie had been so open to having Sia in both our lives only solidified Sia's place in our family. She belonged with me, and that was where she'd be.

I took my Rolex off the table, studying the time. I didn't know when Lettie and Sia left, but the property was big and they could be gone for a long time. Especially if they trekked through the vineyards like Sia and I enjoyed doing with Polly sometimes.

I smiled to myself. What a different man I'd been. I used to be what one would consider a workaholic. Now, I couldn't have enough time at home with Sia Reynolds beneath me. My hunger for her stoked the beast within, but I chilled the fucker down with a cold shower that morning. I made it quick, wanting to have breakfast ready by the time Lettie and Sia returned.

Again, what a different man I was. I wasn't quite sure I even knew my way around the kitchen until Sia came. I picked up a few things from Sophia over the years so I could cook for Lettie on occasion. She liked my Mickey Mouse pancakes, and I always put chocolate chips in them for her. She was a bit too old for those now, but she might find that fun since she was home, and I was sure Sia would enjoy them. What woman didn't enjoy chocolate?

Once more, I chuckled at myself. I was actually excited to head to the kitchen and didn't balk at all the things my daughter had filling my house. She had wedding stuff everywhere, but that didn't bother the anal fucker in me. These things only meant my tie to Sia would be permanent soon, and that was something I needed.

I wasn't surprised to see Sophia in the kitchen when I came down, but what threw me was the appearance of another. People weren't just in my fucking kitchen without authorization, or at least without me knowing about it.

Natan didn't need authorization, but it was unusual to find him there. He wiped his mouth with a napkin. "Maxim. Good morning."

My strides slowed. Sophia appeared to have made a spread of toast and jam for him. He ate it at the center island in the middle of the kitchen on a barstool. My hand touched the island. "Good morning. Did we have a meeting? I'm sorry if I..."

I was going to say missed it, but I didn't miss things. Especially when it came to him and double when it came to him in my home. My adoptive father didn't need an appointment, but I always knew if he was coming.

"Oh, no. We didn't," he said, watching as Sophia placed a cup of coffee before him. She avoided his eyes when she did, then mine when she passed me. It wasn't unusual Sophia did that to Natan. He could be intimidating, but when it came to me she always had her head raised. Natan sat back. "You didn't miss an appointment and pardon my intrusion today."

He didn't have to apologize, but this was different. I'd given him notice I wouldn't be working this week, and that was going to be longer now. Sia and I planned to wed before Lettie returned to school, and after that, I had my own plans to extend that time off further. I wanted to give her a proper honeymoon, amongst other things.

"I hear you're getting married," Natan said, and something unsettled in my core. I hadn't purposely gone out of my way *not* to tell Natan about the engagement, but since I hadn't he shouldn't technically know about it. I never said anything. Natan grinned. "And to the young woman who's working for you. Sia Reynolds. Correct?"

I wasn't sure who told Natan this, and though it wasn't secret, I hadn't told anyone but Val. Of course, my staff knew but word in my house didn't leave it.

"Yes," I said. Again, my upcoming union with Sia wasn't secret, but everything happened so quickly. I honestly hadn't been able to tell Natan, but I planned to once everything settled. He would be invited of course, and Lettie would see to that. I nodded. "Yes, I am. It all happened really fast."

It had all been a fucking whirlwind, but the best ride. Natan's head lowered. "Then I believe a congratulations is in order."

His next move was to pull out a cigar for me. This was a generous gift as he only smoked the best Cubans. He had two, one of which he lit before handing me the other.

"Thank you," I said, but decided not to smoke it yet. It was too early in the day for me. "And sorry I didn't tell you about the engagement right away. Like I said, it all happened really fast. Lettie is planning the wedding. We plan to have it before she goes back to school in the spring."

"Well, that is fast," Natan continued, focusing more on his smoking cigar than me. He studied the smoke. "But how happy of an occurrence. Again, congratulations. My son deserves to be happy."

I appreciated that, but I still didn't know why he was here or how he found out about Sia and me. It was the latter that kept my eyes on him. It was rare I didn't know things, and though I wasn't required to know all of Natan's ins and outs, I did when it came to me. I lifted a hand. "Would you like to move to the study? We can talk. Catch up."

He was obviously here for a reason.

"Mmm. Yes." He gestured for an ashtray, and Sophia came quickly with one.

Her head dipped quickly out of the kitchen after she gave it to Natan, and I opened up my phone.

I texted Val.

Me: Can you contact Lettie or Sia and tell them to take Polly out by the lake? They took her for a walk, but I want them to stay out of the house for a while.

Val: Sure thing. Everything okay?

I wasn't quite sure.

Me: Natan's here.

"Maxim?"

Natan was waiting for me by the door, and I put my phone away. I lifted a hand with a smile. "After you."

He knew his way around my home and nodded, allowing me to follow after him. I was sure him being here was just my paranoia. I'd been having a lot of paranoia lately when it came to him.

Probably because I created a reason for it.

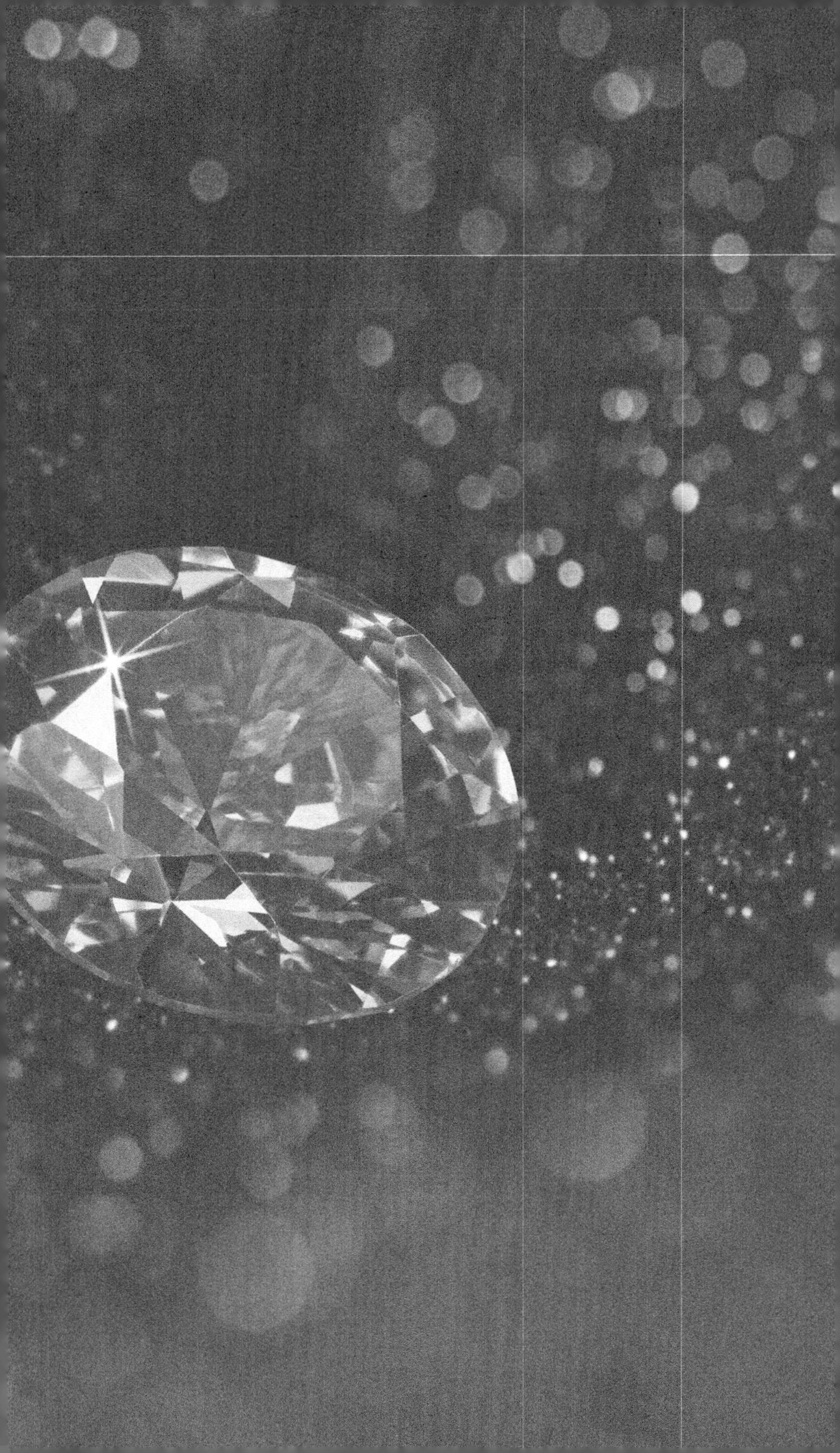

CHAPTER FORTY-SEVEN

Sia

Val: Maxim says he wants you and Lettie to head to the lake. I probably should give you some bullshit excuse about why, but the fact of the matter is you're about to marry him so I believe you're able to handle real talk. He wants you and Lettie to stay out with Polly longer. His boss is at the house, and he doesn't want you there. Don't tell Lettie though. He wouldn't want her to worry. Just go to the lake and wait for my report.

Val's text gave me pause, but I didn't let that show.

Me: Should I worry?

I didn't understand why I should. I mean, Maxim said his boss was like a second father. Unless, his boss had some bad news...

Val: I'm not sure.

Val: I'm on my way to the house. Just take Lettie to the lake and be discreet.

I didn't know what excuse I'd use. It was cold enough to see our breath outside. It was winter for fuck's sake.

And I was worried. The unknown made me worry, and the fact that the man I was about to marry was in the mob. He also hadn't wanted to tell me anything, and that really made me freaking worry. I lifted my head. "Hey. Why don't we take Polly to the lake?"

Lettie had been directing Polly back to the house. She adjusted her coat. "You sure? It's kind of cold."

We'd taken the long way through the vineyards. Polly had her snow boots on, and Lettie and I had been chatting. It'd been nice, but it was cold so we'd been trying to head back. I shrugged casually. "Yeah, I like us just talking and stuff."

I didn't like lying to her, and though I did enjoy talking, I wouldn't normally linger out in the cold.

Lettie, as open as she was to adventures, didn't question it, and I smiled before leading the charge. I took Polly, and Lettie followed behind me.

She adjusted her scarf around her head. She had it wrapped like a Hollywood starlet over her pale locks. She squinted. "Hey, I think that's Ivan."

Lettie waved a hand to a man who was already by the lake. It was him and a couple other guys, and they all had serious dispositions about them.

They were also big as fuck.

They wore ankle-length wool coats and hats. They all turned, and the one in front lifted a hand in our direction. I assumed that was Ivan, and when Lettie started to head toward him, I touched her arm. "Hey, um, I'm not sure we should go over there."

I didn't know those men, and then there was Val's warning. I just didn't feel comfortable, and Lettie laughed.

"It's cool. I do," she said, rubbing my arm. "They're my goddad's guys. They're good."

Was her goddad Maxim's boss? That would make sense since Maxim said Natan was his second father. Even still. "Lettie—"

She started sprinting toward the men before I could finish, and I had no choice but to follow her. I kept Polly with me, close, and tried to stay close to Lettie too.

"Hey, guys," she said. She hugged the one she called Ivan, and though he hugged her back, he studied me. It wasn't a pleasant stare either. It was one of scrutiny and made me feel like I wasn't wearing any clothes.

Like he was looking through me and not at me.

I really didn't know what to make of it. Especially when he told Lettie she needed to go back to the house.

"Natan wants to see you," Ivan said, and that didn't sit well. Again, I didn't know this guy, but I did know Val, and she told me not to do that. Something felt off with this whole situation.

That confirmed when the guy put his hand on my friend.

Ivan got her shoulder, *forcefully,* and proceeded to direct her to the house. She asked what was going on, and when another guy went for me, I reacted.

I kept my whisper to Polly low, but she heard it. I said *get,* and she bit the guy's ankle before he could grab me.

"God. Fuck!" the man roared, and Polly took him down. I'd been training her for defense little by little after the day I was attacked outside Maxim's manor.

Polly growled at the man once he was down. She kept him there when she got his clothes, but my heart leaped in my throat when Ivan suddenly pulled out a pistol. He directed it at Polly, and Lettie grabbed him.

"What do you think you're doing!" she shrieked. "Stop!"

Ivan wasn't going to stop and both Lettie and I saw that. Lettie hit at his hand, and he shoved her to the ground. She screamed, and the guy's distraction gave me an opening.

I kneed him right in his balls. Polly still hovered over the guy who tried to hurt me, and after I got Lettie up, I whistled for Polly.

She came right away, and I ran with her, taking Lettie with

me. Thrown, Lettie was flailing, but she picked up her pace quickly.

I think that had something to do with the heavy footfalls behind us.

"Stop!" Ivan shouted, and Lettie and I turned but didn't stop running.

Pop. Pop. Pop.

Gunshots. Ivan fired three shots in the air, and my stomach rolled. I nearly tripped but kept on my feet and both Lettie and Polly continued to bolt with me.

"Stop right fucking now." Ivan shot in the air again. Polly barked. "I don't want to hurt you!"

I didn't believe that fucker, and neither did Lettie, whether she knew the guy or not. She grabbed me, directing me and Polly. Polly was barking until I told her to stop, and Lettie and I disappeared into the vineyard. We didn't have much coverage since it was winter, but Lettie appeared to know where to go.

"Come on," she whispered, our footfalls crunching, but the men behind us were too. "Dad has a safe house out here."

Of course he did.

"Lettie!" Ivan called out, and we both nearly yipped when another gun shot hit the air. Lettie and I both went into survival mode, our heads low and sprinting fast. I was very impressed by her, but I shouldn't be. This was her father's world, and she understood it. At least to some extent.

I thanked God for that, and even more that she was aware of what to do in this situation. She found the safe house quickly, which happened to be in a shed within the seemingly miles upon miles of dormant grapevines.

Lettie didn't even have to unbolt the door. She headed inside, and once we were in there, she typed in a code on the wall. A slat in the floor opened, a metal one that lead to a staircase.

"Come on," she whispered again, and I quickly followed.

Downstairs was completely different than upstairs. Upstairs it was just a beat up old shed, but downstairs it looked like the Pentagon. There were monitors and buttons everywhere, and after Lettie typed something into one of them, the slat above closed.

The room went dark.

But then Lettie called out *lights* and every light in the room flickered on.

This really was a safe house. There was an entire wing outside of the computer room, but I didn't have time to explore when both Lettie's and my phone went off.

"It's Natan. My goddad," she said, looking like she was going to answer it. She thought better though, and I blinked when she destroyed her phone against the wall. She swallowed. "He could be tracking it."

Smart.

Lettie gazed around, her eyes wild. "Why did he send people out here like that? I don't understand—"

My phone was still going off, distracting us both, and I almost destroyed mine too. Almost.

Maxim's name on the front gave me pause, but only for a second until I answered. "Maxim?"

The line was quiet. It was with the exception of my breathing.

But not for long.

"To whom am I speaking?"

I recognized the voice even though I'd only heard it once before. I'd only seen him once before too. My mouth parted. "This is Maxim's phone."

It was, and he should be answering it. Not this guy. Not his boss.

My throat squeezed, and an alarm hit Lettie's eyes. I think it was an alarm we shared. In fact, if I was looking in a mirror I was sure I'd see the same degree of fright on my face.

I put the call on speaker phone.

"This is Maxim's phone," Natan said. "I have it, and now, I need to know to whom I'm speaking."

"Natan. What's..." Lettie's eyes flashed when I waved my hand for her not to speak. Something was going on here, and whatever it was didn't feel like it was good.

I mean, his men shot at us.

They didn't shoot at us per se, but they'd let off rounds to alarm us.

"Lettie, my dear. Is that you?" Natan asked, his voice just as ragged and gravely as it'd been that day at the house. It was like he gargled nails on the regular, and his face came into my mind. He had lengthy black hair and was thin. He also had just as many tattoos as Maxim had, and his were faded in a way that reminded me of prison tattoos.

I might not have been far off.

"Natan, what's going on?" Lettie questioned, her voice high, worried. She swallowed. "Natan..."

"I know you're in the safe house, Lettie," he said, and we both faced each other. "But you aren't in any danger. I would never hurt you, dearest."

She said nothing, waiting like me.

"That being said," Natan continued. "I'd like both you and your friend to come to the house—"

"And why is that exactly?" I asked, definitely not doing that. "Where's Maxim, and why are you calling from his phone?"

There was silence on the line for a second, but only a moment.

"Because you obviously picked this call up and not my own from Lettie's phone," he said, calm. He was so fucking calm, and I didn't like this shit. At all. "And hello again. You clearly aren't going to tell me who you are, but I think I have an idea. You're Maxim's fiancée and congratulations to you. I was just telling him that back at the house."

Lettie was wavering, and I was too. I didn't know her reasons, but they were probably similar to my own.

"Where is he?" I asked, and Natan laughed. *Laughed.* It was a low laugh. A harsh one.

A cruel one.

I didn't know this guy from Adam, but he was freaking me out, and Lettie was grabbing my arm. Even though this man was supposed to be her goddad, a person who claimed he would never hurt her.

"I have to say you probably wouldn't care so much about him if you knew who he was," Natan said. "What he's done..."

My eyes narrowed. Maxim had done a lot of things. I stood tall. "I know the kind of man he is."

"Do you?" It felt as if he was patronizing me. Like I was a little kid, and he was teasing me. "I don't think you do. Not really. In fact, I'm pretty damn sure you have no idea about the man you're about to marry. If you did, you'd want nothing to do with him."

Lettie's face was red, and mine was hot. Like, lava hot.

"You know, I didn't used to be in charge around here," he continued. "For a time, I worked under someone else. A tyrant, and it was your Maxim who aided me in my position. Want to know how he did, Sia?"

I didn't like my name on his lips, and I refused to answer. This felt like a game, and I wouldn't.

"Well, I'm going to tell you anyway—"

"Have you hurt him?" I asked, refusing to play *this* game too. "I swear to God—"

"He helped slaughter an entire family," he said, continuing as if I hadn't spoken at all. As if I didn't fucking matter. "An entire legacy. He did that for me. Helped me rise."

I knew about that. Well, sort of.

A family...

Maxim said he got revenge against the man who killed his

father, and after he had, Natan took over. He never mentioned a whole family though. Did that family include a wife? Children?

I had to say I didn't want to know the answer, and anything he'd done I needed to talk to him about. I didn't need to talk to this man. I swallowed. "Is Maxim okay?"

"You're still asking about him," he said, and Lettie was shaking beside me. I was too, and we held each other. "Like I said, you wouldn't if you knew."

"Knew what, Natan?" Lettie's voice shook as much as our bodies did.

"You're both going to come to the house, Lettie," he said, as if she hadn't spoken now. "This doesn't have to be complicated. In fact, it can be very simple. I want to discuss a few things with your friend Miss Reynolds, one of which is what to do about her fiancé now that I've confirmed he's betrayed me."

I gripped Lettie, and she gripped me back. She shook her head. "Betrayed?"

"Yes, my darling," he said, and the audacity he had to call her that. He was clearly holding her father hostage. "For you see, the family he aided in eliminating was our very own Miss Reynolds'."

The phone slipped from my fingers and hit the floor. A piece of it broke off, but I still heard what he said next. Lettie and I both did.

"Come to the house, Miss Reynolds," he stated. "Or should I say, Miss Novikov."

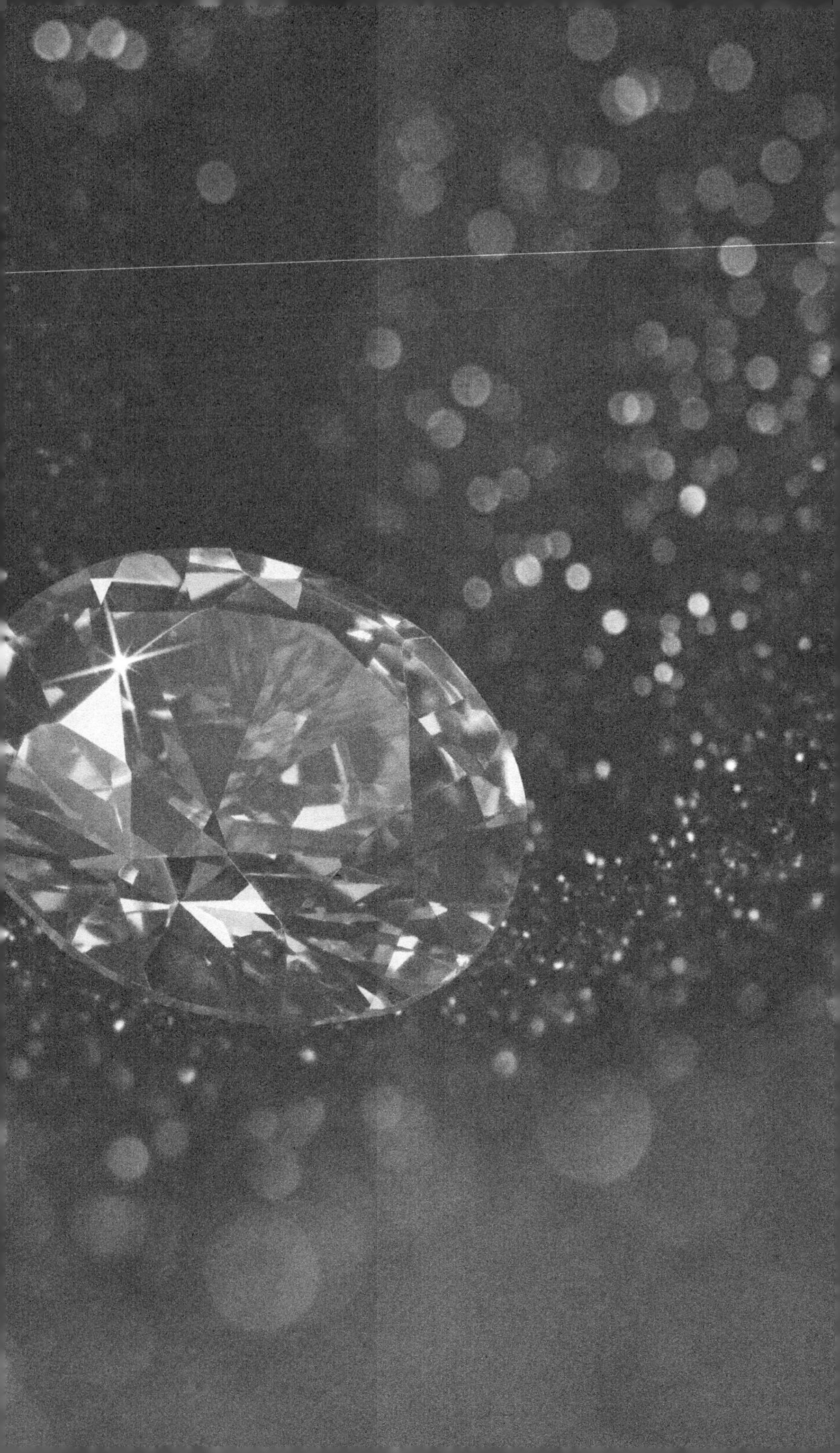

CHAPTER
FORTY-EIGHT

Maxim

Val and I gazed up as another entered the room.

The air left my lungs.

Oxygen from the room completely disappeared when I saw Sia. She was wearing a sweater around her tiny frame, her arms bunched up, her gaze wary. Her dark eyes locked on me, and I did something stupid in that moment. I left Val's side and the men I used to call friends, brothers. One had taken my cellphone earlier and given it to Natan.

I'd plotted his death after he'd done that. I'd plotted everyone's in this room outside of Val who'd come in shortly after Natan had been acting peculiar. He escorted me into my own office where he already had men stationed.

My cellphone had been taken not long after.

"Sia..." I had no weapons on my person, but I had hands. I had hands and the drive of a man who'd been fucked with.

The men guarding Val and me had no time to react before I was halfway across the room. Sia was within my reaches when someone called for me to be restrained, but that wasn't needed in the end.

Because Sia stopped. She didn't come to me. In fact, she *backed away*, which made me hesitate. I had the briefest iota of hesitation, but it'd been enough for someone to grab me.

Natan came out of the shadows.

He'd gone off on his own after acquiring my cellphone and refused to answer my inquiries about what was going on.

Instead, he had me restrained.

He did that to me, then Val, and I'd been doing recon on the situation ever since. I'd been deciding which action to take next and who to kill once I did. Make no mistake: I was in this room and this situation by choice. Val and I both were. Especially when I heard word that Lettie and Sia had made it to my safe house. There'd been whispers amongst the brothers that my daughter and another girl had made it there. My girls were safe and, until I could make them safe further, I didn't act.

Not until I knew what the fuck was going on.

I growled. "Natan—"

"Do you not recognize her, son?" My adoptive father was circulating Sia, his gaze peering over her. "I suppose you wouldn't, would you? The last time you saw her she was what? Three?"

I didn't know what he was goddamn talking about, and I was about to act if he kept *looking* at her. I never questioned Natan the man, but he was fucking with me and mine. I growled. "What are you talking about?" Before he could answer, I glanced at Sia. "Sia?"

She wasn't looking at me for some reason. The floor was suddenly her fascination...

And she cringed when I said her name.

It was like me calling her hurt her for some reason, and I didn't understand. Natan's head tilted. "I told her who you are, Maxim. Who you are to her."

I didn't know what game Natan was playing, but I was tired of fucking playing it. "I don't know what you're talking about."

"I think you do." His hands gripped the desk, his expression stern. "After all, you lied to me for nearly two decades about her."

Two decades...

I really didn't know what he was getting at, but two decades was sticking out in my mind. It was a very distinct period of time, and one I knew well as of late.

It'd been one I'd been trying to run from.

For all those years, I'd avoided correcting a mistake, but now I had. I spent damn near a month doing so. It'd been a month away from my family. My Sia.

"You're going to have to be more specific," I said, and he would. The things he was saying didn't make sense, and my *pakhan's* eyes darkened.

"You take me for a fool, Maxim." He went behind my desk, appearing to be the king of *my* motherfucking castle. He sat down. "But I think you and I both know I'm not one. How else would I have come to be in my position? You know as you helped me rise."

I had helped. I served him loyally up to this point.

Almost...

I didn't speak, and the only reason I continued to breathe, remain calm, was because I had to. There was too much at stake. Especially with Sia here. "Natan—"

"Why is it you think she can't look at you, Maxim?" Natan frowned in Sia's direction. "Why it is she can't bear to look at you?"

What had he done to her? Said to her? "Sia?"

Eyes still on the floor, Sia hugged her body as if she was cold, and I was about to act. I was about to move and take her away.

That was until Natan said what he had next.

"She's the spitting image of her mother Keena, but her eyes," Natan paused, as if for dramatic effect, "Her eyes are all her father. I should know the eyes of my enemy well, and you do too Maxim. After all, you watched the life leave them after you killed him."

Dread hit me, and Sia cringed again. Her jaw locked so tight, and I shook my head. "Keena…"

The word left my mouth lightly. I hadn't heard that name in a long time.

This didn't make sense.

"Tell me, Maxim, did you kill her father in front of her?" Natan came from behind my desk. "Did you let him suffer in front of your fiancée?"

I had no words for Natan, too busy staring at Sia who, once more, wouldn't look at me. There was no way she was who he was insinuating, that she was a child of…

"Nikolai Novikov," he said, his chin lifting, and I blanched. Val did too. She was watching this whole thing, and this was a name she probably hadn't heard in a while.

That name was burned into my memories for a lifetime though. The man killed my father.

And so I made him pay.

It'd been my biggest accomplishment, an achievement to avenge my father. I shook my head. "You believe Sia is…"

"Anastasia Novikov, yes," he said, and my mouth parted. Val's did too. Natan put his hands on the desk. "But I don't just believe it, son. It's true, so don't lie to me and tell me it's not. *Don't lie to me* and tell me you didn't betray me for all these years. Just look at your fiancée, Maxim. Fucking look at her!"

He spat every word, and I was looking at the woman I loved. Apparently, I hadn't really looked at her closely.

How could this be?

I hadn't looked for the features of Keena Novikov, or the dark eyes of the man who took my father. I'd only seen the eyes of the woman I loved in Sia. I saw her beauty and passion.

I saw her heart.

Natan was mistaken, and, swallowing, I broke my gaze away from Sia. She wasn't looking at me anyway, and I needed to maintain composure for what I planned to say to my adoptive father next. "Anastasia Novikov is dead. She was killed by Ilya—"

"Ilya Titov." He mentioned the full name of my deceased Bratva brother, the one I'd killed via his instruction. Natan claimed Ilya betrayed him, and I didn't ask questions. I didn't question and didn't need to. The word of the one who led us was good enough to damn one of our own, and I'd trusted Natan completely. We all did. Natan wet his lips. "She wasn't in the car that day with her brother, sisters, and mother. She escaped the bombing. Something Ilya recently admitted."

My chest locked, tightened, and for the first time during this conversation, Sia gazed up. She stared at Natan in the horrified way one would look as if they learned they had an entire family...

And lost them all in the same day.

Her eyes even got glassy, but this wasn't true. This wasn't. I swallowed. "Natan..."

"She was sick, Maxim. Stayed home with her father who you were assigned to kill," Natan continued, and the room got so silent with his words. "So you see how this looks, son? Because you did show proof of Nikolai Novikov's death, but you failed to mention his daughter was at home with him during the kill."

Finally, my girl looked at me. *Finally*, she saw me, and I didn't want her to see. I didn't want her to see my reaction to the devastation in her eyes, the hurt and pain I saw in response to Natan's accusations. Seeing her this way *destroyed me*, and I didn't look away from her as I said, "It's true. Anastasia was there, but I took care of her."

I had. I might not have that day, but I did. I corrected my error.

I protected my family.

My thoughts traveled back to that day, that kill, and I was hard-pressed to forget it. I had a little girl at home myself during that time, a baby. Lettie had been dropped on my doorstep by her deadbeat mother. She hadn't told me I had a child, and after she left me with our daughter, she split. I hadn't seen her since and didn't need her. We'd done fine on our own.

I saw my little girl in that child who'd been there the night I'd been assigned to kill her father. Anastasia had been older but I saw Lettie in her.

"Dropped off at a fire station when she was three," Natan said, pacing around me now, circulating. "With no memory of hardly anything."

That was because she'd fallen.

I'd been shocked to learn Nikolai's child was there that night and the only reason I had was because I heard her cry.

She'd been upstairs.

I could only imagine the sound of her father hitting the ground had woken her. She'd been in her crib and when I found her, she'd been on the floor. Like she'd crawled out and tried to get to him or see what the noise was. Either way, she'd fallen, hit her head...

"*Natan,*" I urged, watching Sia visibly pale. *It's not true, malyshka.* "Anastasia Novikov is *dead*. I may have let her go that day, but I took care of her. Recently, I took care of her."

I didn't know how he knew all this. About what happened with the fire station, or that Anastasia had memory issues when I dropped her off.

I traveled far to get her to safety, as far as I could away from the reaches of her father's sins and the hand of Natan. A kill order had been out for her whole family, and though I never agreed with slaughtering women and children for the sins of a monster, this was the reality. The Novikov bloodline had to end for the Brotherhood to start anew by order of *my* father.

But I couldn't do it that day with Anastasia. She was so young. Just a baby with round cheeks, dark eyes, and these little curls. She'd had chubby arms just like my baby had at the time. My Lettie.

"Her orphanage had her under a false name. Probably because she couldn't remember hers," Natan continued as if I hadn't spoken. It was as if he didn't care that I had spoken. His expression went hard. "Though she wasn't far off. It wasn't widely known her parents shortened her name. Called her Sia."

Sia…

"That was probably the only name she could pull from her memory," Natan continued. "The last name *Reynolds* the system most likely gave her. Anyway, I know that *you know* she was placed in an orphanage. Your head of security let me know you were looking into children's homes recently, ones who had girls who fit Anastasia's description and were dropped off there by fire station representatives during that time."

I glanced at Val who paled. Her look said everything.

I didn't know.

She wouldn't know. I hadn't told her anything and her reporting to Natan would have been normal. She probably would have even done so casually, not knowing *not* to. She'd never betray me. Even for Natan.

"As it turns out, there were two girls who were dropped off during that time who matched the description," Natan said, which I didn't know. Val searches I had her do hadn't resulted in much. In actuality, it'd been my searches that found who I was looking for and there'd only been one girl. One.

"Natan, you're right. You're right about everything from

the fire station to my search regarding the orphanages." It'd been a proactive measure, a loose end I had to fix, and one Ilya's death did prompt me to correct. He was the other side of the kills that night and seeing him put in front of me as meat to slaughter let me know I needed to fix things. Our sins could always be found out, and I wasn't going to let that happen. The fact of the matter was Anastasia Novikov may have been a toddler at the time of my mistake, but she wasn't anymore.

I studied my fiancée, still pale in front of me. My throat thickened. "And I don't know how you've come to this conclusion about Sia, but I assure you she's not Anastasia Novikov. She's not because I spent a month recently hunting Anastasia Novikov down."

Sia's head jerked up, her eyes narrowed.

I swallowed hard. "I took care of her, and if you need proof of death, I can give that to you. I made a mistake that night with Nikolai, Natan. He had a little girl not much older than Lettie at the time and I..." I glanced away. My jaw clicked. "I found it hard to take care of her that night. I'd been weak back then, but I'm not now. As it stands today, Anastasia Novikov is dead by my hand."

She hadn't suffered, her death quick. She was working at a seedy bar, and she had no other family or children.

There was no one to miss her.

Of course that didn't make it any better but taking her life had been easy in the way where I knew her death would save those I cared about. There'd be no end of the terror Natan would inflict if he knew a Novikov was still alive, and though he loved my daughter, he would take her from me. He might not kill her but he'd take her, and she'd be at the mercy of him and the system of the Brotherhood.

Then there was Sia.

He would hurt her. He would have and would have thought nothing of it. She meant nothing to him.

Anastasia's bullet to the back of the head had been quick. It'd been mercy. Natan would have done worse, and after it was done, I disposed of the body via the proper channels. I did acquire proof of death and DNA for safekeeping though. I'd done it as a safeguard, and apparently, I'd been right to do it.

I always wanted to protect Sia from the specifics surrounding the darkest parts of my life, and it wasn't easy for her to hear this news. A gasp touched her full lips, and I wasn't surprised. The people she'd seen me hurt in the past she'd witnessed reasons for, with the exception of one.

Sometimes if a death was justified it made it easier for one's mind. It made it easier *for her*, but this wasn't the same as those other deaths. Today, all she did was stare away from me. She saw Natan's executioner today.

She saw the monster.

"You killed the wrong girl, Maxim."

I wasn't able to dwell on Sia's reaction. I was too busy shooting my attention over to Natan.

You killed the wrong girl…

"Like I said, there were two," Natan said, and my heart raced. "A DNA test confirmed it wasn't her."

I couldn't even fathom what he was saying. What he was saying couldn't be right.

You killed the wrong girl…

Natan put a hand out. "The woman in front of you—*your fiancée* is the real Anastasia Novikov, and she was right under your nose. I'm sure if you test her DNA you'll find the same. I had a member of your household sneak a glass with her prints. She is the true Anastasia." His eyes went cold. "She is the true daughter of our enemy."

Our enemy.

This wasn't possible. The things that had to take place for this to happen…

The fate and happenstance.

My daughter finding Sia and later her coming to work for me had to happen. Then there was what happened after. Sia Reynolds had completely upended my life.

She allowed me to fall in love.

I didn't know this was possible, and this woman did the unthinkable. She *changed* me. She...

A hand folded on my shoulder. It was Natan's, but I was staring at Sia. She looked so much like Keena, her mother, but she did have her father's eyes. She had *my enemy's* eyes.

Malyshka...

A gun was handed to me. My father jerked his chin toward Sia. "You can correct your error, my son. You can do right by me."

I could correct my error.

"Kill the daughter of our enemy," he said in my ear as if he were the Pied Piper. "Finish the job you started almost twenty years ago."

Twenty years ago I'd been a broken man, a broken *boy*. I had so much pain and my father had healed me. He allowed me to seek justice for those who hurt me. Sia's father took my dad from me.

I raised the gun, and Sia stepped back. This whole time she'd been watching our exchange with tears in her eyes, a mixture of hurt and betrayal on her face. I had become the same monster her father had become to me. I took her father from her, and that wasn't lost on me.

The irony made me hesitate, but I swung the gun towards Natan, and when his expression went merely grim, I was surprised. I found no surprise on his face at all.

Only sadness.

His head lowered, and he watched as I moved in Sia's direction. He watched me place her behind me. I shielded her from him.

I made my choice.

I loved this woman and, vendetta or not, no one was taking her from me.

"We're leaving," I said, watching as Val crossed the room with me. She made her choice too. I eyed the room. "I'm taking Sia, and you're letting me, father."

He would. There was no debate.

Val got Sia's arm, and I didn't miss how Sia locked up. I didn't think it was because of Val though. All this was just too fucking much for anyone. Sia and I might not be able to come back from this, but *we'd handle this* outside of this room and without the Bratva's eyes on us. We'd do this away from Natan.

My adoptive father watched as Val, Sia, and myself backed away.

Natan shook his head. "You take her, Maxim, and her brother dies."

We all stopped on a dime, and Sia shook after what Natan said.

Natan nodded. "I have her brother, and I will kill him if you take her."

Sia looked at me, a new ring of terror in her eyes, and I was sure that terror matched mine. Natan had sent me on a task recently, but it hadn't borne fruit. He sent me to kill a kid, and that kid happened to be Anastasia Novikov's brother.

Sia Novikov…

My fiancée did look like him. Though, I'd only been given a docket of photos. *How had I not seen this?*

"You sent me to kill him." I resisted the shake in my hand. I held steadfastly to the gun, even as I received another horrified look from my fiancée. I ignored it, keeping my gun aimed at my father. "You sent me to kill that boy."

And I would have if I'd found him. I would have had to as commanded by the *pakhan*.

"I wanted to see your reaction to the request," Natan

stated, frowning. "I wanted to see your reaction to Ilya's deceit and also see if you'd admit your own."

So he knew. He knew this whole fucking time I'd lied about Anastasia Novikov being alive.

"I also wanted to know what you'd do after I asked," he said, and I grimaced. "You did seem like you intended to execute my order, but I question now if you'd actually have gone through with it. Your betrayal today with Miss Novikov tells me that."

I said nothing and was well aware Sia's eyes were on me. The tears had hit her chest now, but she wiped them away quickly upon seeing I saw them. She was locking herself up. She was locking herself away…

And she was doing so from me.

Again, I wasn't sure if we'd make it back from today, but her trust in me had to be low priority at the moment. I couldn't deal with anything else until I knew she and Lettie were safe. I assumed my daughter was still at the safe house, and I was going to get her after I got Sia out of here.

"It was a good thing I held onto him for safe keeping, and I do have other plans for him. Plans that will keep him alive," Natan continued, then studied Sia and me. "The son of my enemy could be a good tool. It could be a tool I'll utilize, but only if you make the right choice, Maxim. Give me Miss Novikov, and I might consider forgiving you."

My father was bullshitting. So many of my Bratva brothers were in the room and the minute I drew the line in the sand I knew I was damned. The *pakhan* couldn't forgive. He couldn't because that would make him look weak, and even if he could forgive that wouldn't matter. He wasn't taking Sia from me.

He couldn't have her.

In the next moment, Val and I communicated in the way of two people who didn't need verbal cues. We'd operated together for a long time, and it took nothing more than a look for her to fill the room with smoke. Sia shrieked beside me, and I lowered to the ground with her.

We had to in order to escape the gunfire.

The room filled with bullets, my Bratva brothers firing at us. Crawling, I kept Sia with me. I got an arm around her waist, and she basically flailed when I picked her up. She kicked when I shot out the window in my office. I jumped with her in my arms and landed on my feet. I went running after that, Val beside me.

We didn't look back.

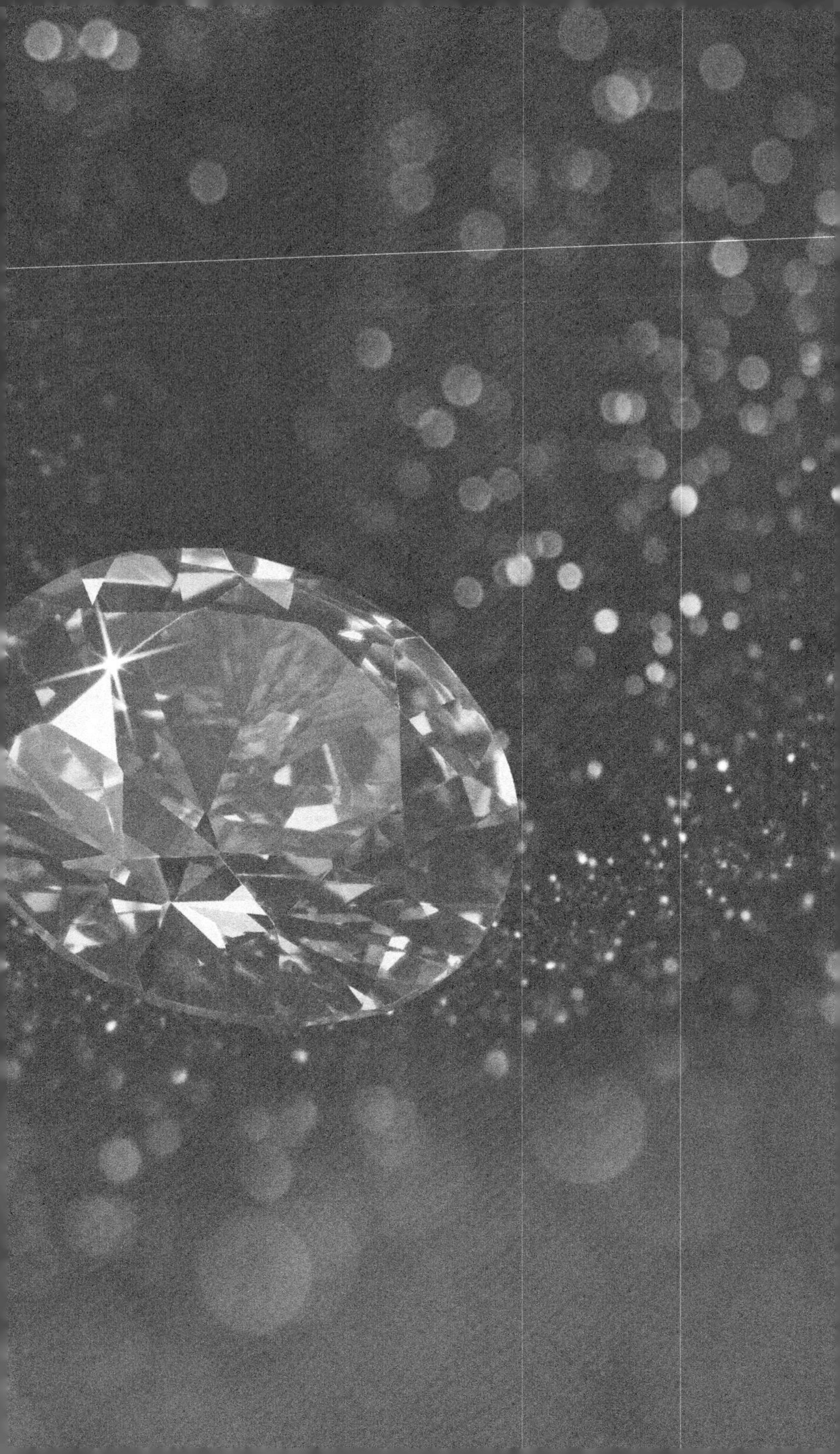

CHAPTER
FORTY-NINE

Maxim

"Maxim?"

Sia's voice was in the back of my mind as I started my Mercedes. I kept cars hidden away for times like this, escape. My garage on the outer most reaches of my property hadn't been tampered with.

We barely got there.

There'd been another shoot out in the end. Natan's men had chased us, but Sia and I got away. I had home field advantage.

Val hadn't been so lucky.

My head of security followed us, but we'd been separated. She told me to go on since I had Sia, but I lost her in the fray. I was sure she was fine. Val knew how to handle herself.

She *would be fine*, and as I put my car into drive, Sia grabbed my arm. "Maxim, we have to go back. Maxim!"

My fiancée's voice was more urgent now, but at least she was talking to me, touching me. I shook my head. "We can talk after I get you safe, Sia."

And going back wasn't an option. Honestly, I had no other thoughts besides getting her out of the area. We had minutes before my father's men caught wind of us, seconds.

Sia tugged my arm again. "Maxim, we talk *now*. Maxim!"

"*Malyshka*—"

"Maxim, they have my brother!"

Her words sobered me, and I finally faced the woman I loved. She had a cut above her right eye. No doubt from the glass as we escaped.

My stomach rolled I had been the culprit of that, and people would pay for her blood that was spilt. This would have to be later. I *needed* to get her safe. I had to.

Sia blinked down tears. "Maxim, they have my brother. We can't just *leave*."

But couldn't we? We could, and I intended to. My daughter was safe, and she knew the escape route to the main roads. I'd trained Lettie on the tunnel system I'd built in the safe house since she was a kid. She knew the procedure. She was to remain there until she heard from me, which she did when I pressed a button on my watch. I was safe, and she was too when she pinged me back on her own smart watch.

I peeled my gaze away from Sia; it was hard to look at her now. She did look so much like her mother.

How could I have missed this?

I was a hunter, tracker, but even I hadn't picked up on her connection to Nikolai Novikov. Sia's mother, Keena, was the second wife to Nikolai after his first had died in childbirth. It was that death that set off a chain of events that affected my entire life. My father was Nikolai's family doctor. He'd delivered Sia's three sisters, and though the last had survived childbirth, the mother obviously hadn't.

Nikolai had taken out that death on my father, and it was something I had to live with even after Nikolai's own death. It stuck with me long after my revenge. How could it not?

It haunted me today, my enemy present in the eyes of the woman I loved. She did have Nikolai's eyes. She really did.

I faced away from Sia, my hand white on the steering wheel. "We have to, Sia. I have to get you safe."

"Maxim, they have him..." So many tears poured down her cheeks, her voice strained. "Please. Please, they have him. They have him and Lettie and Val."

"We're going to rendezvous with Lettie," I said, unable to look at her tears. They'd break me if I allowed them. "I've already contacted her. She's safe, and Val will be fine."

I couldn't guarantee the latter, but my friend knew her shit.

My friend.

She really was. She'd gone with me. She chosen this ride even though this would draw a line for her against Natan. She showed her loyalty, and that shit meant so much.

Val could take care of herself, and the two of us had our own procedures for times like this. We had rendezvous points too, and we'd use them once we heard from each other. We had steps, plans, and things would be okay.

I refused to believe anything else. I couldn't. I'd go mad, and as far as Sia's brother, I had thoughts on that too. I bared my teeth. "In regards to your brother Andre, we'll go back for him. *I'll* go back for him after I get you and Lettie safe."

"Andre?" Her mouth parted. I forgot she hadn't heard his name. Natan never said it, and he was actually her full brother. They shared the same mother, Keena.

I nodded. "I'll go back for him. I promise, but I need to get you and Lettie out of here."

I was only thinking a few moves ahead, and right now, getting her and my daughter safe was priority.

"It might be too late by then," she said, whispered. She hugged her body. "He said he'd kill him if you took me."

Natan did but I also knew my father. He needed this boy

as leverage right now, and if Andre was off the table, there'd be no room for negotiation.

"He won't. I know my adoptive father. He'd need the boy to maintain the status quo. He won't harm him. Not yet."

"The boy..." She whispered that too. She shook her head. "Is that all he is? A kill? A vendetta?" She blinked down more tears. "Is that all I am?"

I tensed, hard not to. "Of course not."

I said this but I'd be lying if I said her statement would have been false mere months ago. Had I not actually known Sia, fallen in love with her, she might have been shrunk down to that. The fact of the matter was she was the daughter of the man who killed my father.

I dared to look at her now and was so frustrated she placed herself in harm's way. She should have never come back to the house.

"Why did you come back to the house, Sia?" I asked, then reached for her. My fingers brushed her arm, but when she winced I pulled away. I frowned. "I won't hurt you. You don't have to be scared of me."

She said nothing, swallowing. "You killed my father," she said, and my throat thickened. "He said you had so I came back to learn the truth. I had to know the truth..."

The truth.

"Why don't I remember anything?" she asked, finally facing me, and the anguish in her eyes, the betrayal, sliced me in half. I'd been physically sliced before, and it felt nothing like this. "I don't remember anything. I remember nothing about my family."

She had been young. I faced the road. "You hit your head on the day of your father's death—"

"You mean *his murder*." Her eyes were red, glassed. "You killed him, Maxim, and then you went after *me*. Someone you thought was me."

I'd done that too. My hand gripped the wheel. "I had to

do what needed to be done. I did it to protect you, *finished the job I was assigned* to protect my family. Natan would have come after all of us. He did."

"And you realize how that sounds?" She sat back in her seat. "You wanted to keep me safe, but you literally killed someone you thought was me. Then there's my dad—"

"He's not." The words came out before I could stop them, her eyes flashing at me. I faced her. "That man didn't deserve you to acknowledge him as your father. He killed *my father*, Sia, for fuck's sake!"

"And what did my mom and sisters do?" She angled forward, her hand shaking when she touched her chest. "What did Andre and I do? You had a hand in all of it, Maxim. *You* and the organization you belong to destroyed my entire family."

We had, and she was right. I kept my focus on the road. "The sins of your father destroyed your family, *malyshka*," I said, and I was weak then. I didn't look at her reaction to what I said so boldly, coldly.

Again, I was weak.

"Maxim…"

Sia's voice came again not long after our drive into the backroads. She'd cried herself into silence, her whimpers against the door. I had to steel my heart against them. I had to in order to get her out of here and get to my kid.

I didn't even have to look at her to know why she called my name. We hadn't been driving long through the labyrinth of woods, and though I knew I only had moments to get us on a clear path, I thought we'd have longer than a few stretches of road.

I was wrong.

Dozens of vehicles blockaded the road ahead, dark Range Rovers with blacked out windows.

"Fuck!" I cut, peeling between two trees. The wheels labored and burned on brush. I darted ahead only for my path to be blocked again. More Range Rovers with dark windows.

Sia grabbed the door when I rerouted again. I think she screamed or at least called my name.

I'm getting you out of here.

I would, even if I had to sacrifice myself. There wasn't a scenario in which the woman I loved would die today.

I would die first.

"Maxim, they're everywhere," Sia shrieked, her voice strained. "Maxim!"

We were forced to stop when we were suddenly surrounded. There was no way to go forward or back...

Only through.

I intended to do that, telling Sia to hold on, but I hesitated slightly when Natan stepped into the road, his hands deep in the pockets of a gray wool coat. His dark hair fanned in the breeze, and I shut off my heart again. There was only one way to go, and I revved up the engine of my Mercedes.

Sia shook her head. "They're going to kill my brother. You have to stop."

I told her he'd be fine, though I couldn't guarantee that. "*Malyshka*, we have to go on. He will be safe."

"You can't *know* that! You can't. You..." She faced the road, her tears falling again. This shit was gutting me, but I couldn't stop.

I refused.

I revved up the engine once more, and the only reason I didn't shift into drive was because of what Sia said next. She screamed it, her voice drumming in my ear.

It did until I listened.

She was panting next to me, crying. She rubbed her eyes.

"If you don't stop all of this and allow the only family I have alive on this earth to die, I will hate you. I will hate you forever, Maxim. *You need to stop.*"

I couldn't see past what she said. I couldn't *not* hear it. She said her brother was her only family.

Which meant she denied anything else.

Despite all the stakes and all that happened between us, I reached for her again, and this time, she shook her head. I wasn't allowed to touch her. I wasn't allowed to have her.

She got out of the car before I could stop her, and there was no shake in her body when she did. She braved that shit out and left the vehicle. She put her hands up in front of dozens of armed men, and I ran after her.

Guns drew. Pistols were everywhere, including my own. Natan had one out as well, and he kept it aimed on Sia.

The blood in my veins turned to ice.

"Natan, if you ever cared about me at all, let this go." I'd never asked for anything from my father. Not a thing. If he could just give me this one... I put my gun away, lifting my hands. "Take me. Let Sia and her brother go—"

"If I go with you, will you stop?"

My eyes flashed, and Natan's did too.

Sia swallowed. "If I go with you, will you let Maxim leave? You don't go after him." She put her hands on her chest. "You take me, and you let him and Lettie go. You leave them alone."

I stepped forward. "Sia—"

"You have my word." Natan snapped his fingers, and all the guns were put away. All but my own when I lifted it. Natan shook his head. "Your fiancée's made a deal, son. It's an admirable one, and you should honor it."

He wouldn't take her. He wouldn't *have her*, and I reached for her arm. "*Malyshka—*"

"I'm not going with you, Maxim," she said, her arm snapping away before I could touch her. She lifted her head. "I don't want to go with you."

She didn't want to?

She blinked back a tear. "Go get Lettie. Get out of here and get her safe."

I would get her safe, but I needed *her*. "Baby, please."

I'd never pleaded with anyone before today, and I already had twice. She couldn't leave me.

And yet, she was.

My father kept his eyes on me as he took the woman I loved. She didn't want me, and that felt colder than the snow on my knees when I dropped to the ground. It started to snow after they left.

Both the world and mine froze around me.

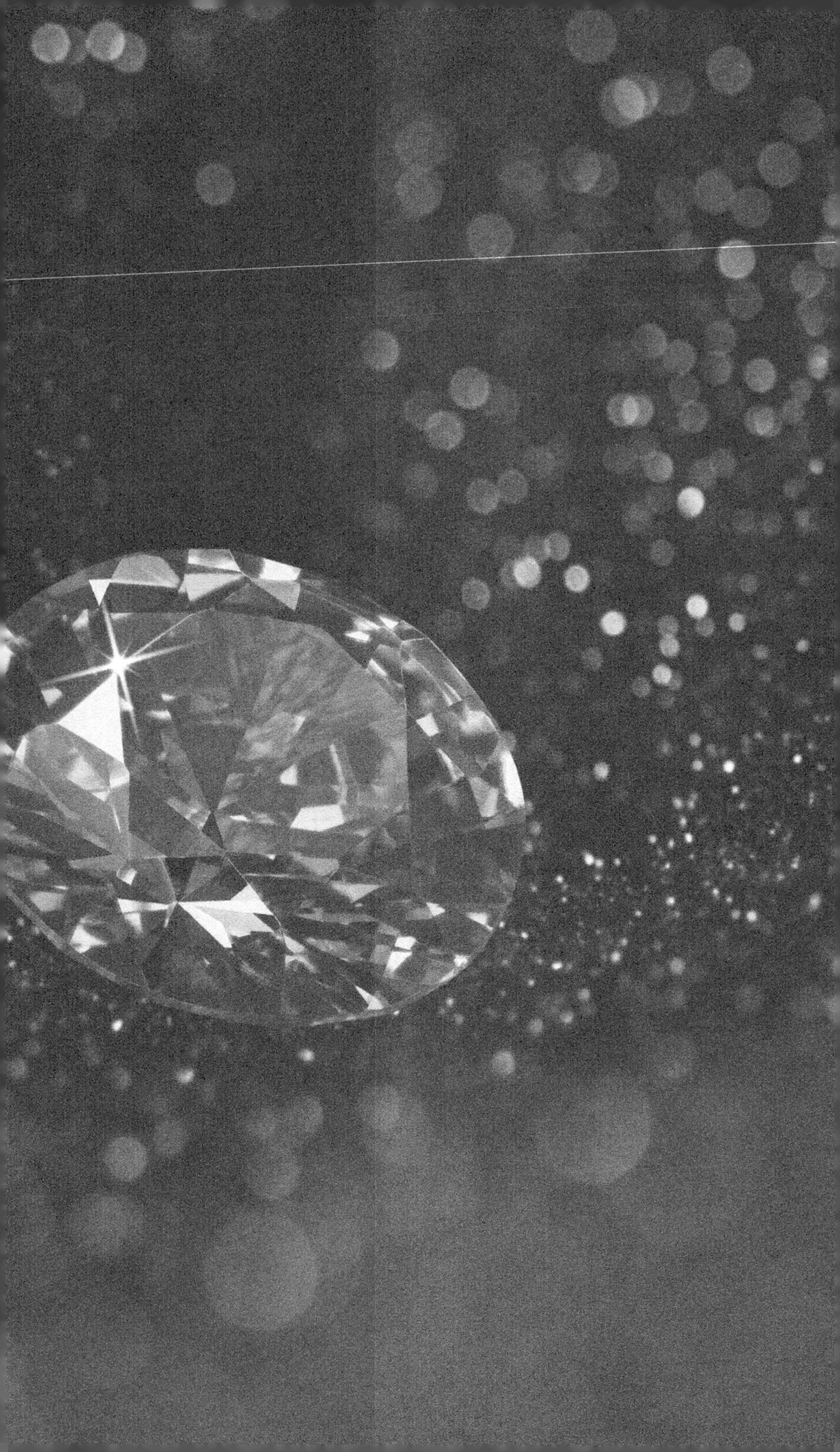

CHAPTER FIFTY

Sia

My phone was taken before I was pushed into a dark room, but not before I sent off a text. It surprised me how long it took for Natan's men to realize I still had a phone.

I stumbled to the ground, my knees hitting concrete so hard that pain shot through my legs like fire. I groaned, but no one gave a fuck. The door slammed behind me, making the room even darker. There was nothing but candlelight in here...

And footsteps.

They were hurried. They rushed in my direction, and the next thing I knew, someone grabbed me. I had no blade, but I had the skills Val taught me. Immediately, I went to shove my elbow into the person behind me, but as soon as I shot my arm into them, the individual let go.

I turned and gasped.

"Val?" I said, making eye contact with her in the dimly lit area. I grabbed her, hugging her and shaking. I was on the cusp of tears, but I wouldn't let them fall.

I wouldn't let them fall.

I braced Val so hard, and she wasn't shaking.

At least, not until I grabbed her side.

Her face screwed up in a deep wince.

My hand came away from her side bloody.

"Oh, God," I started, but she waved her hand. She was wounded on her right side, her dark coat caked in blood. She also had a cut on her cheek like a blade had sliced it. I gasped. "Val..."

I didn't know what part she had in this whole thing with my family. I didn't know if she helped Maxim, but I did know she was my friend.

And she was hurt.

I tried to tend to her, reaching toward her wound but she didn't allow me. She waved her hands, then signed, "*Are you okay?*"

She was concerned about me? I started to reach toward her wound again, but she touched my face. I shook my head. "I'm fine."

I was in the physical sense I supposed.

But all other ways, how could I be okay? I swallowed. "Did you know? About me? My family?"

Did she have a place in it? Had she known who I was the whole time...

Had she helped?

I had so many questions, and Val's frown was deep. "*Your dad was before my time in the Bratva,*" she signed and mouthed most of it. I didn't understand all her signs but her mouthing the words helped. She sighed. "*I'm sorry, jellybean.*"

She was sorry.

I nodded, still processing everything. I'd been given a family, and it was taken from me all in the course of a few hours. I also didn't know where I was. I'd been blindfolded up until a few moments ago, before they shoved me wherever this was.

Suddenly cold, I gazed around. We looked to be underground, but it wasn't sterile-smelling in here like Peters & Berg. It was just dank and dark. Wet. There was dripping coming from above like we were beneath pipes. I faced Val. *"Do you know where we are?"*

I decided to focus on that, and though I didn't know all the ASL signs for her, I spelled out the ones I didn't.

"One of the Bratva's places," she signed, and then completely ignored the fact she was still bleeding. When she noticed I noticed, she waved at me again. *"Don't be concerned about me."*

I couldn't help it, and she cringed when I touched her. I made her lift her jacket.

And all that blood…

My stomach tossed, and I had a pretty strong one lately. I'd developed it considering the world Maxim had introduced me to.

Maxim…

My stomach clenched again if I thought about him. Especially the look he'd given me before I left him and after what I said.

"I don't want to go with you."

It was the only thing I could think of to get him to let me go. I had to go, and seeing Val, I was glad I did. She'd clearly been shot, and with all the gunfire surrounding us during our escape, I wasn't surprised. I touched Val's arm. *"Sit down. We'll fix this."*

I didn't know what we'd do about it, but I had experience with wounds with animals. I could do something about this if she let me.

She waved me away again.

"Come with me," she signed, and though I did, I had no idea why she was concerned with anything else besides her wounds.

But then, I saw him.

Val and I weren't the only two in the room, and as soon as Val and I got closer, the third person came from the shadows. He was a boy in an academy uniform without the tie. The tie was off on a bench, and he played with his hands as Val and I got closer. He was biracial, with curly hair and dark eyes like me.

In fact, he looked a *lot* like me.

I could tell he'd noticed that too, his eyes twitching wide. He swallowed. "Hi."

The word shook, his voice shaking. He was too, and so was I. I didn't have any family. I didn't have anyone to look like me, and we had the same hair and the same eyes.

Our father's eyes.

I knew in my soul this was the case, and suddenly, I was swallowing too.

"Hello." My voice quaked. My mouth parted. "Do you know who I am?"

He nodded, and goose pimples lined my skin.

His throat jumped. "I feel like I do." He put out a hand. "I'm Andre."

Andre.

It was like touching a ghost, shaking his hand, and we both gazed down at our handshake.

"Hi, Andre, I'm Sia," I said, then shook my head. "I guess that's short for Anastasia."

I had no idea that'd been my name. I had no idea.

I guess I hit my head.

I thought with my history in the foster care system I'd already been through so many terrible things. Apparently, I hadn't even broached the surface. As it turned out, my history had already been peppered with tragedy and violence before that.

Andre's had too, and I hated that we related to each other on that. Val studied us during our exchange, her expression remorseful, sad, but also in pain. Holding onto herself, she was clearly trying not to slump, and I grabbed her side.

She let me, and Andre got close too. I nodded toward Val. "She's hurt. Can you help me dress Val's wounds, Andre?"

He blinked in response to my request, but quickly, he nodded. He stepped up. He was brave.

I ended up using Andre's academy jacket to force compression on Val's wound. She was bleeding so much, but that was because it was a clean wound. The bullet had gone right through her skin and out the other side. As far as I could see, it hadn't hit anything major.

There was just so much blood.

Val's eyes started to roll back as Andre and I tended to her, and clearly, she'd been mustering strength to come over to me.

"Will she be okay?" Andre asked me, and it was so weird talking to him. It was weird knowing we had this connection but were strangers.

"I don't know." I didn't want to lie to him. I had no answers. I looked up at him. "Are you hurt?"

"No, I..." He started, then gazed around. "I've been down here a few days, but they've been feeding me and everything. There's a small bathroom over in the corner behind that wall, but no windows or anything."

Which means he looked for escape. I nodded. "And before that? Did they hurt you or..."

Relief hit me when he shook his head again. "No. They moved me around a lot though. Other places like this." He sat down next to Val. We had her laid on a bench. He bit his lip. "Before that, I was at school."

"Do you know who you are? Have they told you?"

I barely knew, but if he knew who I was, odds were he had an idea.

"Yeah." He stared at the floor, a haunted look in his dark eyes. "They told me they killed our family."

They had, all of them gone. We were the only ones to survive.

Maxim…

I wanted to sob. The hate in his voice, his eyes, when talking about my father... He'd killed my dad, and he felt no remorse for it.

"The sins of your father destroyed your family, malyshka*…"*

And so blood was spilled for blood. Sin for sin. My father was a monster for killing Maxim's dad, and Maxim had become the same monster to avenge his. He'd become my monster, and if not for happenstance and sheer dumb luck, I wouldn't be standing here.

If it hadn't been for love.

I acquired the love of the man who hated my father, and I'd somehow gotten his mercy even before that. Maxim had spared me that day he murdered my dad. For a brief time, he had. Until, years later, he killed a woman he believed was me.

It hurt my soul, our history. It was tragic and so fucked up.

"You said you were at school before," I said to Andre, and he nodded. "Did you grow up okay?"

I needed to know. I just wanted one thing to not be fucked up. My childhood was so bad, so much tragedy and abuse.

"Yeah, I was at a Catholic boarding school basically my whole life, but my caretaker never kept from me who I was. He dropped me off at the school when I was a baby and the nuns took me in," he said, surprising me. He chewed his lip again. "I haven't seen my caretaker Ilya in a long time though. He didn't check on me often, but he did come by."

Ilya.

The name was definitely familiar. Natan had mentioned a car bombing. He said I wasn't in the car with my mother, sisters, and brother. Considering Andre was with me now that meant he hadn't been in the car either. Had Ilya saved him? Did he save him like Maxim saved me?

It sure sounded like it, and I glanced at Val. She was lucid but was in and out. "Do you know what happened to his caretaker?"

Andre faced her. He had a hope in his eyes *I hoped* Val wouldn't disappoint, but as soon as she frowned a boulder hit me in the chest.

Val lifted her hands. "*He's gone.*"

I didn't know if Andre knew sign language, but I felt like in that moment, he didn't need to. He had someone who spared his life as well. Natan had mentioned deceit.

And so my brother and I had the same story.

Andre cringed. "Are we going to die, Sia?"

I didn't want to lie to him, and even though things looked bleak, there was hope. I touched his shoulder. "There's help coming. I got a text out to someone. He's going to come."

I destroyed Lettie's phone, but I knew she had a smart watch. I also knew she was supposed to rendezvous with Maxim.

I couldn't take the risk sending him a text. I knew Natan had his phone, but Lettie would have been clear. She could get messages to her watch.

She could get messages to him.

Val tried to sit up after what I said, but I didn't let her. She moved her hands. "*You texted Maxim?*"

"I did. I sent it to Lettie, but she should be able to get the message to him. If she does, Maxim will be able to track my phone. Natan's people only just took it from me before they put me in here." Maxim had let it slip after we got back together that he put a locator on it after I initially broke my phone, and I'd never been happier for my husband's obsessiveness, his jealously and neurosis.

My husband.

My brain had skipped right over the word fiancé. In fact, it leaped right over it.

"I don't want to go with you."

I told Maxim what he had to hear to let me go. He needed to hear these words so he'd let Natan's men take me. I had a feeling they'd take me to my brother, and I'd been right.

I bundled Val up in a blanket on Andre's bench before looking at my brother. "My fiancé is coming. He'll save us."

Because he loved me, and I sent him just the text he needed to see. He'd do that regardless of what I sent him, but I didn't want him to wonder for a moment about my love for him. It'd take a lot for us to move forward after the events of the past, and I wasn't sure we ever would, but regardless, I couldn't turn off my love. Maxim Petrov was deep in my soul, which was why my text message to him said: *Come find me.*

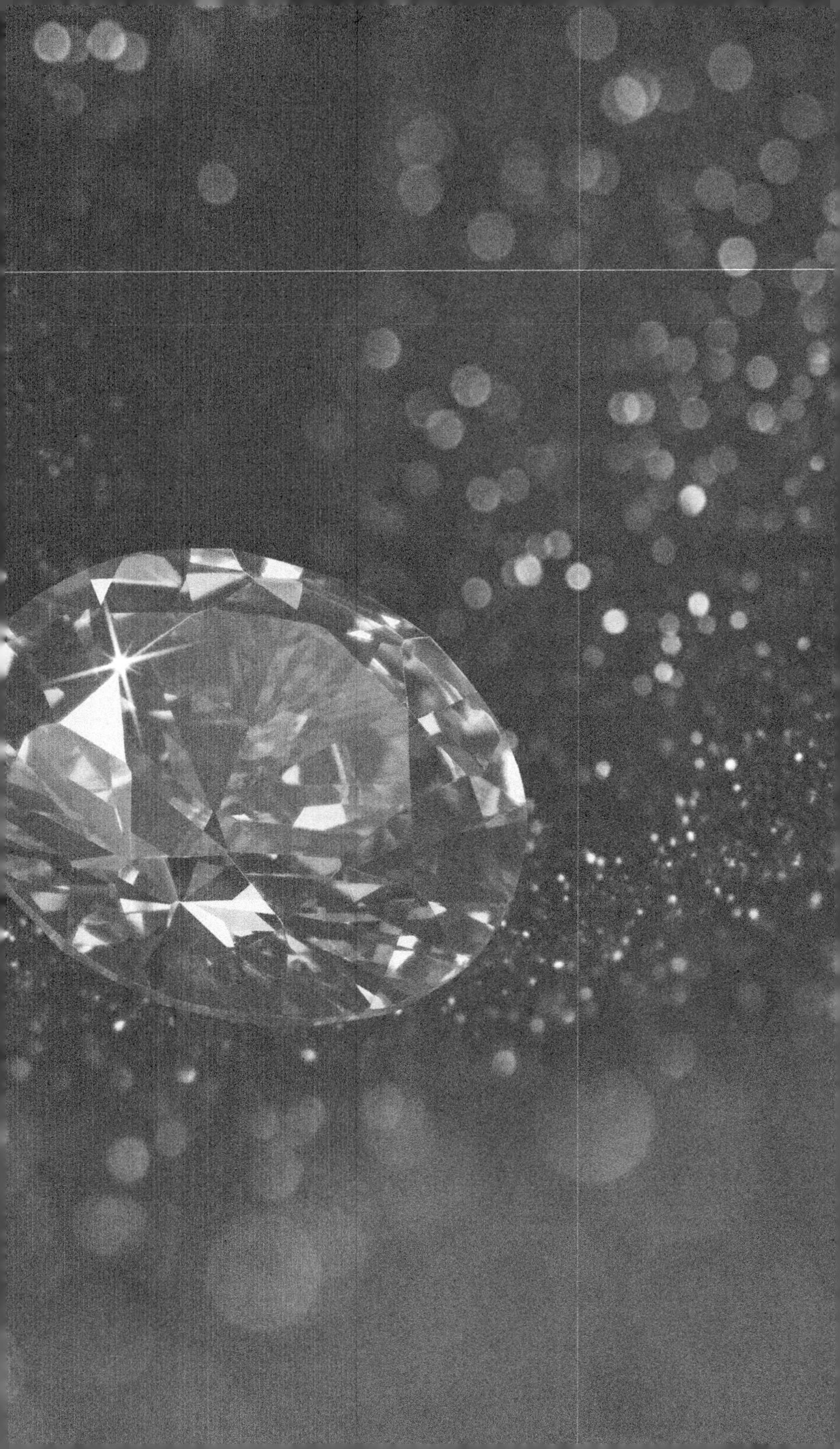

CHAPTER FIFTY-ONE

Sia

It'd been too long. Hours...

And Val was dying.

I'd managed to stop her bleeding, but she needed antibiotics. Not to mention proper bandages. Andre's jacket had stopped the bleeding, but she needed to be stitched up.

"Val?" I touched her face. She was in and out of awareness, and the moments it took her to focus on me scared me every time. I didn't know if she'd just not wake up, and she wasn't being honest about her condition. She kept telling me not to worry.

I knew Maxim would come, and though I didn't know what he was capable of, I had a feeling it was *a lot*. He'd gotten both of us out of a room full of the Russian mob, and we'd both come out with little more than a few cuts and bruises.

It scared me, asking him to come. I didn't want him to get hurt, but I had to put my faith in him.

I didn't have a choice.

Val couldn't focus on me this time when I spoke to her, her eyes closing, and when I gazed at Andre his expression was grave. For someone as young as he was, he was handling this really well.

I guessed I was too.

I couldn't take all this with Val. I got up.

"Where are you going?" Andre popped up, and as soon as he did, Val turned her head. She watched as I went to the door.

I pounded on it. "Hey! Anyone, out there? Hey! We need help!"

We needed to get something for Val, and that included basic human needs. Andre said these people fed him three times a day, but Val needed water.

I banged on the door again, and eventually, I backed up when it swung open.

The guy filled the doorway. He was tatted up to his neck, and some fishtailed around the back and went up to his ear.

I swallowed. "Val needs help. She needs bandages. Antibiotics. *Water—*"

"Boss never gave the approval for any of that," the man grunted. He looked like he wanted to slam the door in my face, but I ran up to him.

"Then ask him." I gritted my teeth. "We need help in here. This isn't fucking right." I surprised myself with my bravery.

The guy's eyes narrowed. "Like I said, he gave no approval, and I ain't bothering him."

This was so sick. Fucked up. I raised and dropped my hands. "I want to talk to him."

"Sia…" Andre stood, fear in his eyes. He shook his head. "What are you doing?"

I didn't know, but I was going to push this. I balled my hands into fists. "This is about me and my brother, right? I'm sure your intention is to kill us and let Val rot, but I'm sure he won't want to do any of that after he hears what I have to say."

This surprised the guy and everyone in the room, including Val. She had no idea what I was doing, and even though I wasn't certain, I did have an idea.

"It would benefit him more if both my brother and I were alive," I said, facing him. It was weird acknowledging I had a brother, but now that I knew I had one…

I looked at the guy in the suit. "I want to talk to Natan."

The guy in front of me cocked his head. He crossed his arms. "You tell me, and I'll relay the information."

I shook my head. "I'll only talk to Natan."

It was the only leverage I had, and when the guy sighed, I had a flutter of hope.

He waved his arm. "Come on then."

I didn't hesitate.

I left the guy at the door and went to get my shoes. I'd taken them off while we'd been waiting.

"Sia," Andre started, but I lifted my hand. I actually did have an idea.

"*What are you doing, Sia?*" Val signed, her movements labored, weak. She also mouthed the words to help me with understanding the signs.

I pushed my feet into my boots. "I'm buying us more time," I said, both signing and speaking. I kept my voice low. "Maxim needs more time."

He was going to come, and I needed to give us all the best chance we had.

Even if that meant subjecting myself to the wolves.

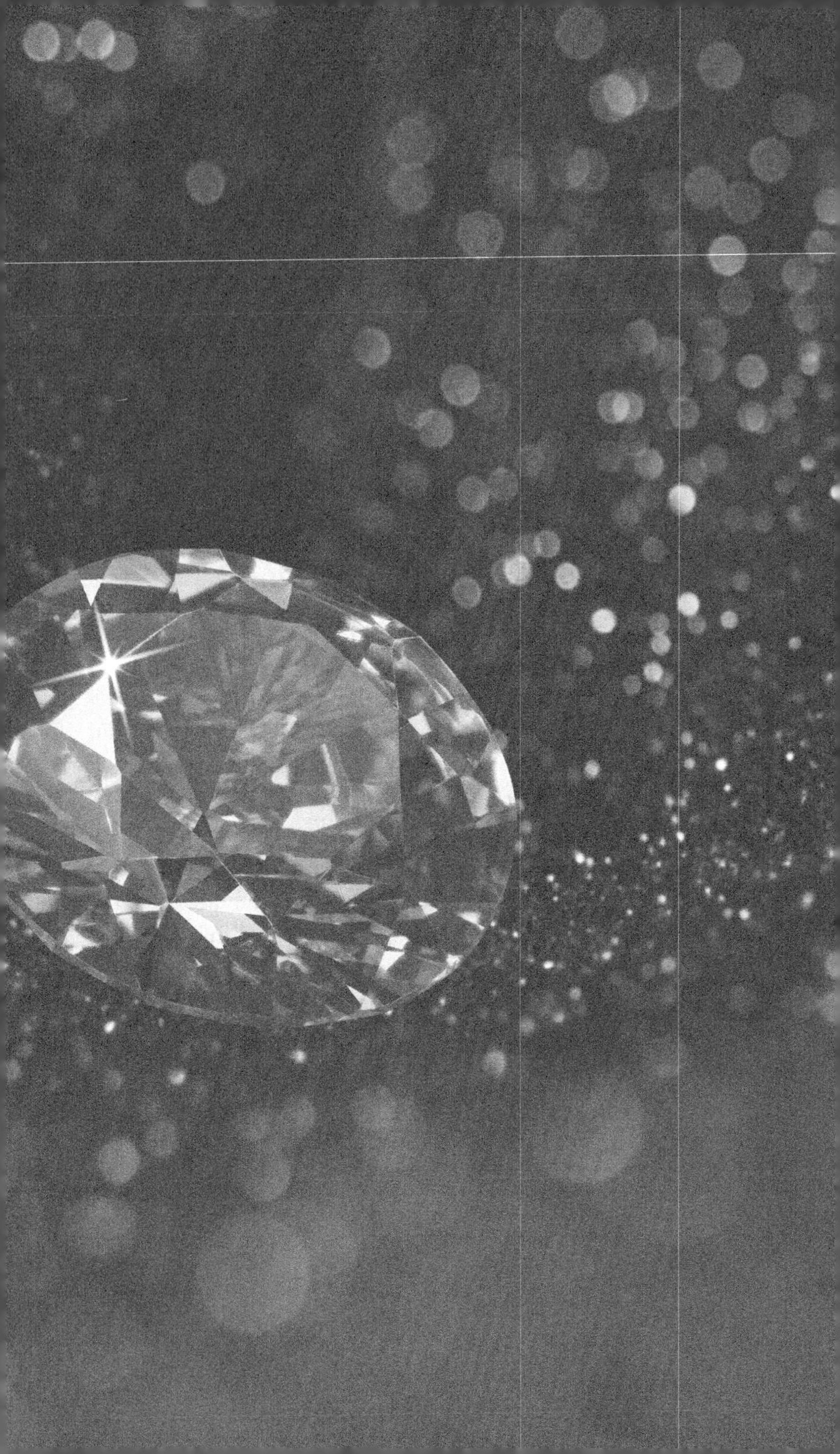

CHAPTER
FIFTY-TWO

Maxim

I was granted a meeting with the heads of the Irish and Italian mobs.

I supposed they were intrigued.

It wasn't every day the son of the man leading the Chicago Bratva wanted to meet, but I was desperate. More than desperate.

Come find me.

Sia's text message was in my head, and though she'd sent it to Lettie, she'd been smart. She knew Natan had taken my phone, so she sent her plea out to where I'd see it. To where it reached me, and my girl had been so smart. I knew exactly where she was, and, odds were, it wouldn't be far from her brother.

What she'd done had been so brave and, out of both of us, she'd been the most level-headed. I'd just been so desperate to get her to safety. Because of that, her brother was placed directly in danger, and I couldn't say I would have done things differently if the shoe had been on the other foot. I was confident I could get to Sia, but that was only the beginning of my battle. Natan wouldn't let me take Sia or her brother without recourse, and my entire family would be watching our backs the rest of our lives trying to outrun Natan. This was a risk I was willing to take, but what I *wasn't* had to do with potential backlashes from the other organizations. We tended not to step on each other's toes, but going against the Bratva's *pakhan* wouldn't be smart.

I needed insurance.

I planned to get that when I was patted down for weapons. I didn't bother bringing any, and if it came to it, I knew I wouldn't need them. I could get myself out of virtually any situation unarmed, but I did leave everything I could with Lettie. We met at our rendezvous point and, currently, my daughter was on her way out of the country. She hadn't agreed with that, but she couldn't be around for what happened next. She took Polly with her; I knew Sia would want that.

The next step was Sia, her brother, and potentially Val, who I hadn't heard from yet. Val never checked in, but in this case, no news was good. If she'd been killed I would have heard about it through my own sources.

"Maxim Petrov." Ronan O'Flaherty, the head of the Irish mob, was an old man with a heavy accent. He had roots in Chicago well longer than the other families in this room. He put his hands together. "I think we're both surprised to hear from you."

My gaze traveled over to the third party of our meeting. Emiliano Costa wasn't a friend, but we were around the same age. Because of that, we tended to see each other at clubs and various social engagements around town. He wasn't technically the head of the Italians, but he currently represented them. He was here on behalf of his father who was currently ill, and that was widely known.

It was also known that his dad was most likely on his last

legs. He'd battled cancer for decades, and it was finally catching up with him in his old age.

"Maxim," Emiliano said as he gripped my hand. It was extra tight and reminded me of our other tie: our kids were dating. Neither one of us was happy about it.

Emiliano let go. "We *are* surprised."

"Especially since it sounds like you and Natan are on the outs," Ronan stated, puffing smoke from his mouth. He stepped over to me and shook my hand as well. We were meeting in the back room at one of his pubs. He pointed his cigar at me. "I'm surprised to see you alive and without a bullet in your head. I know Natan is your father, but you also know how heavy his hand is."

I did, and my adoptive father had ruffled more than a few feathers since he'd taken over after the Novikovs. In fact, Natan was one coup away from starting a war between all the organizations with the amount of bloodshed he orchestrated. Not to mention the mysteriously missing members from both the Irish and Italian organizations. Nothing could be traced back to Natan of course, but everyone knew Natan did a lot to establish power.

And not everyone agreed with it.

I'd been one of those people, but he was my father. I picked and chose my battles when it came to him.

Ronan invited me to sit, but I remained standing. I lifted my head. "I'm going to make this meeting quick, gentlemen."

"I hope so. I'm late for another meeting," Emiliano barked before he began laughing. His meeting probably consisted of a few whores, but who was I to judge? "Tell me why I should be late for you."

"I'm here to make one request." I peered between the two men. "I am at odds with my father, and if I act on him, I'm humbly requesting no interference from either of you."

Both men's eyes flashed, but they shouldn't be surprised by this request. They knew my father wasn't happy with me.

"You want us to do nothing?" Ronan asked, and Emiliano studied him from behind an amber glass. Both men were sitting and peered at one another. Ronan's eyes narrowed. "And why would we ever do something like that? We have a great relationship with Natan, and not doing anything could create conflict."

There were ways in which all the families ran, and to keep order, we had alliances. It kept us all protected. So if I *did* come at my father, that would mean actual war with the Irish and Italians. They'd go to war against me alongside my father's organization.

That wasn't something I was willing to subject my family to, no matter how good or how confident I felt about making us disappear. I didn't plan to kill my father, but I would if it boiled down to it.

I guess I really was his executioner.

He'd given me no choice, and I wet my lips. "Because I know for a fact that two of the youngest members of the Novikov family are still alive."

Ronan stopped smoking, and Emiliano stopped drinking.

I nodded. "They are, and if you do nothing, I will help enact plans for a takeover in which the Chicago Bratva and your organizations can work even closer together."

Ronan was sitting up now, and Emiliano was looking at him. A ring of shock rounded Emiliano's eyes from across the table, and I wasn't surprised. The Novikovs might not have been favored by many when they'd run things, but they did have sympathizers. Many of those were amongst the Irish and Italians, and Natan only made that sympathy stronger when he got so heavy-handed. My adoptive father had stepped on a lot of toes since coming into power.

"You know for a fact there are Novikovs alive?" Emiliano asked, and I nodded. He started to say something more, but Ronan raised his aging hand.

"Even if you do," he said nonchalantly, "but who was the

fucker fooling? His eyes lit up so big at just the thought of taking my father down. Again, my dad had been heavy-handed. "Who's to say Maxim can get the Novikovs to agree and execute a takeover."

"One is my fiancée," I said. Both men looked at each other. "She and her brother have been taken by my father. It was a direct shot at me and one I can't forgive."

"Hence why you don't want us to act if you confront him." Ronan rubbed his trim beard, his nails pulling through white scruff. "I'll tell you what, Maxim. You have something here. If you do as you say and get the Novikovs on our side…"

"No action will be taken," Emiliano stated. "At least by my family." Ronan nodded his agreement. Emiliano faced me. "That is, if you do what you say."

That was one worry I didn't have. Sia knew nothing of this world, and I didn't want her to be a part of it. I'd respect what she'd want to do, but I think we'd both agree neither one of us should be a part of it anymore.

Come find me.

I'd caused her a lot of pain, and though I didn't know our future, I knew she'd have one.

Even if it was without me.

The potential of that made me swallow, but her life, her safety, was bigger than me and my happiness. I would get her and her brother out. After that, whatever she wanted to happen would.

"You won't have any worries," I said, and both men nodded.

"All right, Maxim." Ronan sat back. He put out his cigar, then leaned forward. His eyes narrowed. "You have one shot, and, if I were you, I wouldn't miss."

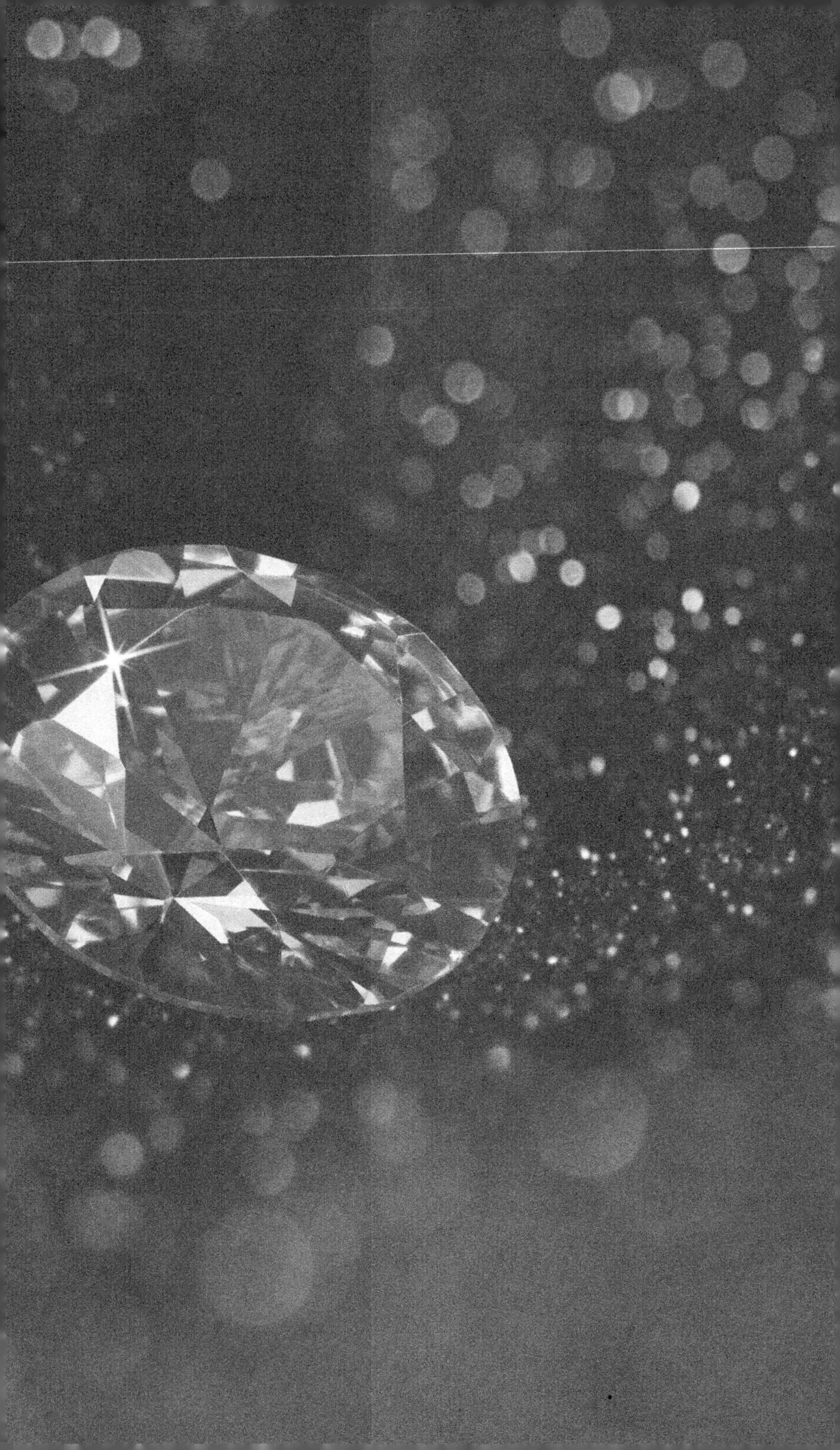

CHAPTER
FIFTY-THREE

Sia

The guy guarding Andre, Val, and me didn't take me to see Natan immediately. I was actually brought into a bedroom. The curtains and sheets were dark. The location unsettled me, but, gratefully, it turned out to be a temporary holding situation.

"Come on," the guard grunted, his cadence as heavy as his accent. Natan had a similar one, and though I'd been searched for weapons before they'd taken me I was searched once more before being brought in to see Natan.

"Miss Novikov," Natan said. He was pouring a brown liquid into a tumbler inside an office that appeared very similar to Maxim's. All dark brick and handsome wood, it had a masculine aura about it. But not once had I felt intimidated in Maxim's office.

I stayed by the door, but was guided forward by the guard with a grunt. I stepped forward, but only just, and was relieved when the door closed behind the guy.

Though I didn't know why. I wasn't safe in this room with

Natan. No one else appeared to be in here with us, but he was in charge of a crime organization for a reason.

Natan showed stained teeth with a wide smile. "I hear you have a proposition for me. Please."

He gestured for me to sit on a stone-colored sofa, and, though I did, I sat on the edge. Natan didn't sit, and as he took a sip from his tumbler, he flashed what he packed behind his black suit jacket. I didn't know much about guns, but he had at least that one.

I shifted. "Yes, I don't think you should kill my brother and me."

I had a feeling that was where this was all headed, considering the lengths he'd gone to kill not just my father, but my entire family. Even still, I wouldn't just roll over and let him do it.

Natan's smirk made him appear more intimidating, and he always did remind me of Professor Snape from Harry Potter. His dark hair was cinched just behind his head, and he was ghost-white. The chalky appearance of his skin tone only brought out all the faded tattoos sneaking out of his black shirt. He tilted his head. "It's nice to know you don't think so, but you've failed to tell me why I'd care about that."

He sucked down his drink, and suddenly, I wished it was poison. *He* was poison, and though I didn't know much about him, I did know that he brought up Maxim. I loved Maxim. I loved him so fucking much, but he had a darkness to him I knew came from only this man. Maxim's darkness I embraced, but I was hard-pressed to ignore what that darkness did to him. He looked like he carried the weight of the world every day.

I had a feeling a fair share of that weight came from a man he'd called a father, and a man who played with his son as much as he did couldn't possibly be a good person. He said he'd tested Maxim by sending him after my brother, and that was just sick, cruel. I braced my legs. "I think you're better off working with us. Utilizing us."

I followed Natan with my gaze, his eyes on the active fireplace in the corner of his office.

"Utilize you in what way?" he asked.

I swallowed. "I don't know anything about your organization but the fact that my dad and my family came into power before yours."

The very talk of it narrowed Natan's eyes into slits, but he allowed me to continue.

"I'm sure there were allies for my family. People who had loyalty to the Novikovs, sympathizers." I shifted in my seat again. "I'm not proposing my brother and I have any part in the inner workings of your organization, but we can work *with* you. Let people know we're alive and you have our support with whatever you're doing."

This was a long shot, what I was proposing here, and as I watched Natan circulate the room, I slipped a hand under my shirt. I pulled out a small piece of wood. It sat just beneath the underwire of my bra and had been easily concealed from the man who searched me.

I'd been hoping for that.

My hand braced around the wood, and I tucked it beneath my legs as Natan turned around. I had a lot of time in that bedroom, and the bedpost proved to be helpful. There'd been a loose piece of wood I whittled quickly against a letter opener on the desk.

Thank you, Val.

She'd showed me more than how to use a knife, and I was grateful for those lessons now. Even still, I didn't move. Natan had a gun, so I just sat quietly. I hoped for an opportunity.

Smart, the man kept his distance, his eyes cold, passive. He sighed. "You know you are so very much like your father," he said, making my eyes narrow. He shook his head. "Always talking talking talking with not much to say."

My lips parted, but I said nothing.

He grinned that ugly smirk again, but then suddenly, he was exchanging his glass for the gun in his jacket.

My hand braced the wood.

"He talked even when he didn't need to," he said eyeing his gun. He didn't point it at me, simply studying it in the fireplace's light. "Had too many plans. Too many ambitions. Too many things he wanted to change."

He flicked something on his gun, and I flinched.

He grinned. "But he was also weak and incredibly naïve. He actually believed that Maxim's father was responsible for the death of his wife. Like anything could actually be done and she could have been saved while delivering Nikolai's child. He so easily believed that. Like his doctor could have done anything at all for her to live."

I blinked, but Natan didn't. His grin merely stretched to sickening lengths.

He wet his lips. "My son is loyal to me," Natan stated, his finger hugging the trigger. My heart raced. Especially when he pointed the gun in my direction. "And I don't need you just like I didn't need your father, little girl."

The sound of the gun blasted through the room, and my heart stopped, the blood in my ears pounding. I saw Natan's smile again as the bullet tore through my skin, and the force shot me back into the couch.

I slumped about the time my vision started clouding, my fist bracing a sharpened piece of wood.

I did it with some of the final few moments of my strength.

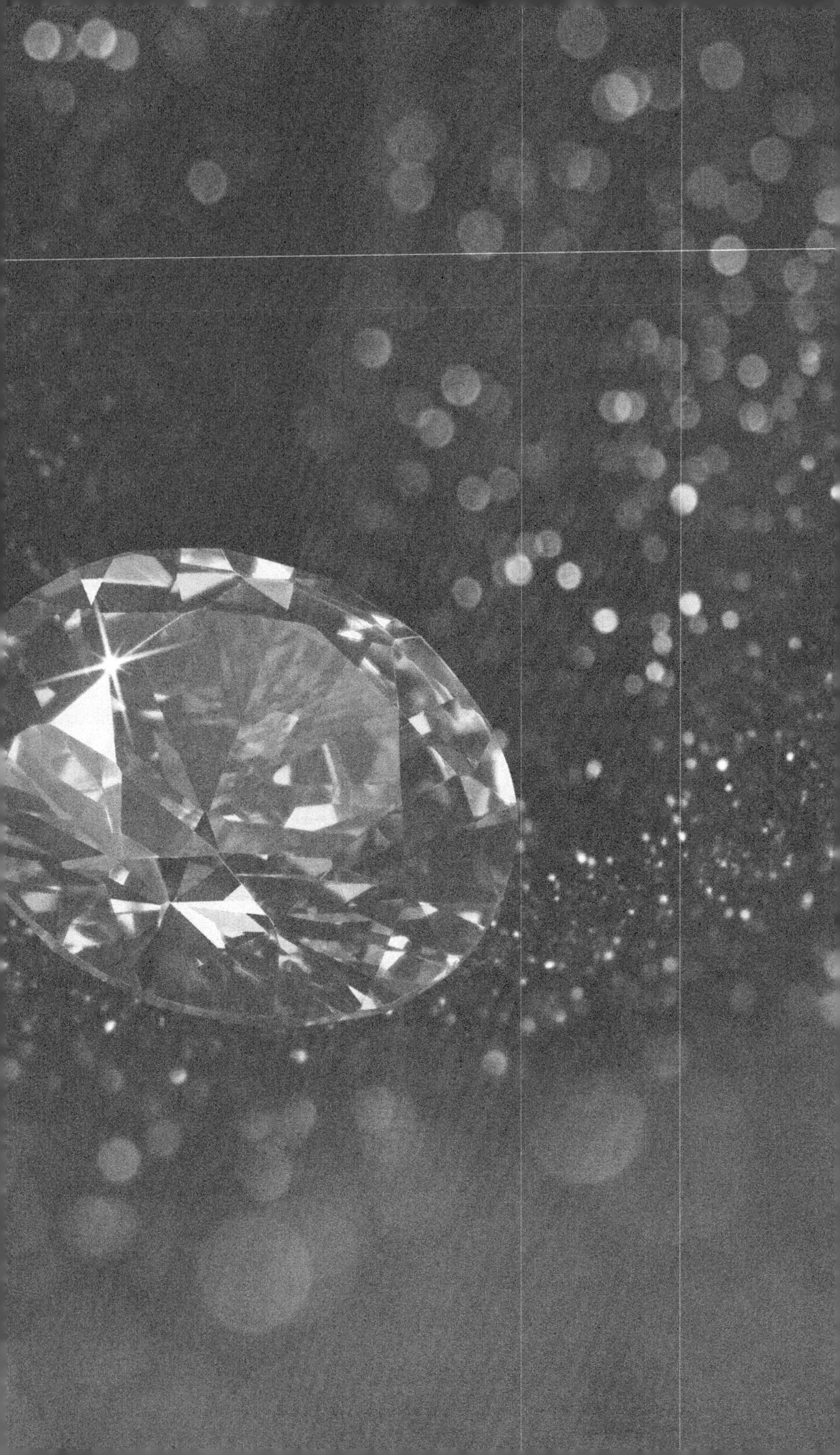

CHAPTER FIFTY-FOUR

Maxim

"You got five minutes, Maxim. If someone sees you, I didn't."

I still had friends amongst the Brotherhood. People I'd saved or done right by.

I nodded at the latest after what he'd said. His name was Sasha, and I'd had him over for dinner more than once.

All that would be gone now. I'd have to leave the country with my family.

I knew where they were holding Sia. Besides being able to track her phone, I cashed in a few more favors amongst the Brotherhood. Friends told me exactly where she was being held, and I also knew her brother was being held somewhere in the building.

I found him first.

He was in a holding cell underground, and though Sia wasn't there, he wasn't alone.

"Val," I signed as I said her name, rushing over. She was laying on a stone bench, and the boy beside her appeared absolutely terrified.

His likeness to Sia was uncanny.

I saw that now that I knew the facts. There'd been similarities in his picture of course, but I just hadn't seen the connection.

I actually had to swallow upon seeing him in real life, and, backing away, the young man hit the wall. He probably didn't know whether I was a friend or foe.

I showed him my allegiance as I moved to study Val's injuries. She was covered in blood, and I pulled in a breath when I lifted her makeshift bandages. She'd bled through a coat and shirt combination, but the bleeding from her wound did appear to have stopped.

"Val," I said, and she lifted her hands.

"*It's just a flesh wound, Boss,*" she signed, her smile wobbly. "*You have to get Sia.*"

"Where is she?" I asked. I was told she'd be in this room. I faced Sia's brother. "Where is your sister, kid?"

He blinked, but, as I attempted to lift Val, he helped me.

"They took her," he said, grunting when we both managed to get Val on her feet. She was one of the strongest people I'd ever known; not only did she carry her weight with a clear fucking bullet wound, she took steps.

"Took her *where*?" I gritted, guiding Val toward the door with the kid. I knew who he was, and he obviously knew that I knew.

"*Natan,*" Val ended up signing, and we had to rest once we got out of the holding cell and against the wall. She lifted her hands. "*She demanded to see him and get help for me. Foolish girl.*"

Foolish indeed, but that was Sia. If Val was suffering, she wouldn't have taken that lying down.

I wouldn't let my thoughts linger on whatever situation she decided to walk into because in that next moment, I was making Sia's brother look at me. I knew he was only a kid, but he was going to man the fuck up today. Val's and Sia's lives depended on it. "Kid, can you hold her weight?"

"Andre," he said, and I nodded.

"Andre, can you hold Val's weight?"

He did, pushing himself under her arm. Val sucked in a large breath again, but I knew she'd be okay. Her wound was a clean through shot, and her bleeding had stopped. She had time.

It was Sia I didn't know about.

Don't think that.

I wouldn't even entertain the possibility of something happening to her, my stomach goddamn tight. Once I knew Andre had Val, I left her to him.

I put a hand on Andre's arm. "I need you to help her get to my car. You follow this hall. Take two rights, and then a left. Your path will be clear for at least five minutes."

I'd cleared it. I cut through anyone who'd been in my way. I hadn't wanted to shed the blood of people I had considered friends, but my father left me no choice.

I squeezed Andre's shoulder. "You need to be strong, okay? I'm going to get your sister. You leave her to me. You get Val to my car. You'll see it right outside, then you sit. You wait."

He nodded. His dark eyes made me cringe because they did look so much like my fiancée's.

"Tell her thank you," he said before I left, and I shook my head.

I told him he'd thank her himself once I saved her.

As promised by Sasha, my path remained clear, and though I didn't know where I was going, my father resided dominantly in two places in his large brick home. One place he liked to dwell was his bedroom.

The other was where I found his body.

I saw him first. He had a shard of wood in his chest, and his eyes were open. He was bleeding out in the middle of his office's floor, and the only reason I didn't take anything else in inside the room was because of the shock of that.

"Maxim…"

If I hadn't seen him, I would have seen her first. Sia was also on the floor, bleeding out…

I rushed over to her, stumbling. She was caked in blood, and I gathered her up, hugged her to me. I touched her face. "Baby, baby. Baby…"

I was shaking, and she gasped when I searched for the source of her wounds. Her brown skin was so pale, ashen.

"I'm sorry," she whispered, trembling. Thinking I found the source of her wound, I ripped her shirt to study it. She winced. "I tried to buy us time. I tried to buy Andre and Val time."

I forced the shake out of my hands, making myself look at the wound. She'd been shot in the stomach, and it wasn't a graze.

I covered it, picking her up in my arms.

"Maxim, I'm sorry. I stabbed him but not before he pulled out a gun."

She did that to my father?

My brave *malyshka*.

She managed to take down the leader of the Chicago Bratva. She did that while shot.

"Don't apologize, baby. Save your strength." I calmed my nerves by tucking her into me. I needed her heat and she needed mine. "Just breathe and stay close against me."

I couldn't really defend either of us with her in my arms, but I'd do what I needed to do.

The woman I loved wouldn't die today.

Andre and Val were in my car when Sia and I eventually

made it outside. Val was in the backseat hunched against the door, and Andre was across from her.

"*Sia?*" Val's hand motions were weak when I opened the door, but she was stronger than Sia. "*Oh, no.*"

"Sia!" The word ripped out of Andre's mouth, and he got out of the car when he saw I had his sister. "Oh, God. What happened?"

"Andre, I'm going to need you to drive, okay? You can drive stick shift, right?" I prayed to a god I never prayed to when I asked a teenage boy this question, and I was granted with a gift when he nodded.

I handed him my keys, then remained in the backseat with Sia. I didn't let go of her, her bleeding body cradled in my arms.

Her frail body trembled. "Maxim…"

"I said to save your strength, baby." I touched her hands, my head shooting up. "Andre, go now."

He did, getting us out of there. I directed him twist after twist through the woods, but I didn't know how I fucking did. I didn't know how I was still here in my body.

"Maxim, it's cold," Sia said, tears pinching out of her eyes. She curled into me. "I'm so sorry."

Why did she keep apologizing? *Why?* It was so brave, what she did. She didn't even know her brother, and she did that for him, for Val.

I hugged her. I hugged her so fucking tightly. "You did beautifully, okay?" I touched my mouth to her forehead, and I realized I was shaking too. "You were so brave. So very brave, *malyshka.*"

"Are Lettie and Polly okay?"

I actually had to laugh she was thinking about them right now. She touched my face, and I touched her hand. "They're both safe, and Lettie's pissed at you for making her stay in that safe room."

No one argued when my girl wanted something.

"Are we going to the hospital?" Andre asked from ahead. We were taking the backroads, but we were clear. No one was following us.

Probably because my father was dead.

I made myself stay stone to the fact. It was either us or him. *Sia* or him. I shook my head. "I have a safe house. We're going there."

I'd tend to Sia's and Val's wounds there, but we had to go quickly.

"Maxim?"

"Baby, I said to save your—"

"Natan told me something," Sia gasped, holding my hand. "It's about your father. Your real dad."

I blinked, my hand threading in hers.

She cringed. "He said he convinced my dad to have yours killed. He tricked him." Her face screwed up again, and Andre glanced back. Sia's lips turned down. "He's the reason both our dads are dead."

Andre's mouth parted, and my chest locked, tight. In the end, I had no time to react to what she said. Because, in the next moment, Sia's eyes rolled back.

My heart stopped shortly after that.

PART THREE
AFTER THE ASHES

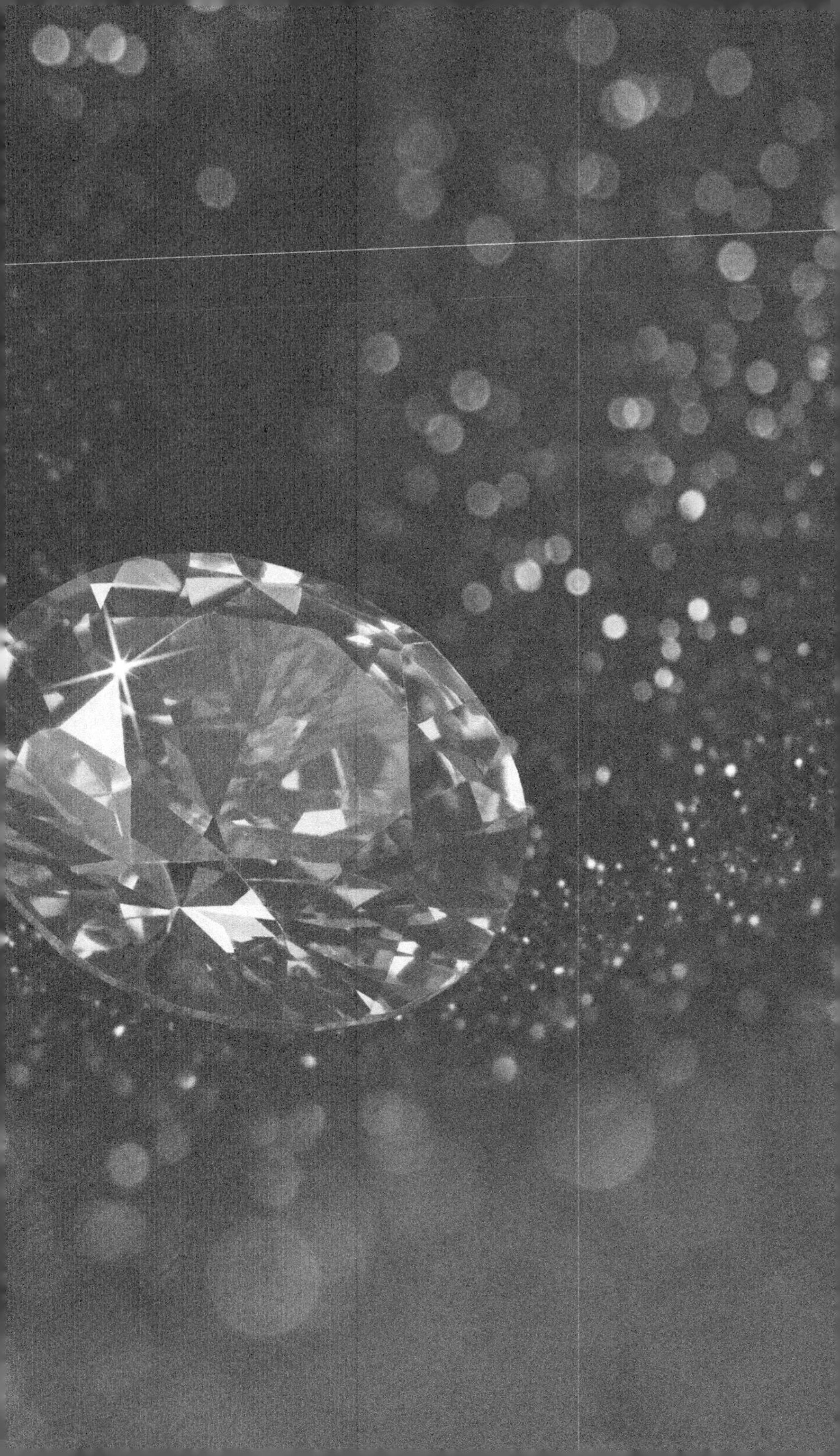

CHAPTER FIFTY-FIVE

Maxim

"I have to say Maxim, you've certainly held up your end of the deal."

I glanced away from the barges at the pier. Guns and various other weapons—both illegal and not—filled them. It wasn't every day I oversaw a shipment, but I did today.

I was restless.

It was Lettie's idea for me to go out, and though she wasn't wrong, I didn't think now was the time. It was a very bad time, but I was urged by my daughter to get some fresh air. I think I was driving everyone in my life crazy these days.

Ronan O'Flaherty stood at my side. The Bratva had been working very closely with both the Irish and Italian mobs. As Ronan said, I held up my end of the deal. He also told me to take a shot once and not miss.

She hadn't.

Sia had made a sacrifice the night of my father's death. She'd gone to him to buy time. She'd been waiting for me even though I was responsible for taking her family away.

The Chicago Bratva and I had ruined the Novikovs, and it was only at the urge of my daughter that I attended Natan's funeral. She told me I needed to be a better man than him, but I think the only reason I actually went was because of Sia. She'd put my fake *manipulative* father figure in his grave...

And I needed to see him lowered into the ground.

Natan had been arrogant that night, foolish. He thought he'd killed the last daughter of Nikolai Novikov, and when he went to check the body, *my girl* delivered the ultimate maneuver that ended his life. She'd done it with a shard of wood.

She was so brave.

So much had come out after that. How the man who'd raised me had groomed me. How I became his lethal killing machine to enact his revenge. Natan's private journals revealed his hate for the Novikovs. Sia's great grandfather had a hand in the loss of Natan's own family.

And he never forgot.

Natan's manipulation began then. He rose up the ranks of the Brotherhood, and ultimately, made the Novikovs his puppets. The Novikovs may have been in charge, but Natan was working the puppet strings. That was until Nikolai Novikov saw right through him. He didn't allow himself to be manipulated and so Natan arranged to take him out. An opportunity rose with the death of Nikolai's first wife. Natan took advantage of the fact that the man was grieving and had Nikolai kill his own doctor.

My dad.

Natan had always admired my father for his skills in torture and death, and Natan also knew the man had a son. He knew he had someone he could groom and developed my skills to help overthrow the organization. He did, and I played right into it. I actually called that man my father.

I was haunted at the funeral, and I made myself steel during the discussions today. I was happy Natan's death brought the Russian, Italian, and Irish mobs closer together. The streets had never been quieter. There was order, yes, but there was also respect. I had righted a wrong and exposed the world to Natan's treachery. I also held up my end of the deal and showed the world that the Novikov bloodline still existed.

I just hated that the woman I loved had to get shot to do it.

"Should you even be here?" Ronan asked me, smirking. We had a respect for each other. I wouldn't go as far as saying we were friends, but we had bonded over a beer or two in the past. He grinned. "Don't you have a baby to deliver?"

There was no other place I wanted to be, but again, I was driving more than one person crazy in my home. I think the final straw had been when I threatened to have all the staff in my home fired because I noticed a chill hit my wife's shoulders.

Lettie: It's about time. You can come back now. *smile emoji*

My breath left as I checked my text. My phone had pinged, and Ronan's grin widened over my shoulder. He must have seen my text message.

He patted my shoulder. "Congratulations."

I couldn't speak.

It was time.

Sia: Where are you? She's coming fast.

She...

My world was continuing to fill with girls, but I'd want it no other way.

I was smiling the whole drive back home. A home birth was my wife's choice. Sia and I had been married almost a year, and it didn't take her long to get pregnant. We fucked like rabbits on the regular so that made sense.

"*Malyshka...*" I said, my mouth dry.

She took my breath away.

Sia's brow was glistening, her brown curls piled up on her

head. The room was hot and thick with a woman's labor, but my wife never appeared more beautiful.

Upon spotting me, Sia reached out for me. Her eyes narrowed. "It's about time. I've been trying to keep her in."

I laughed, which proved to help with my nerves. I hadn't been around for Lettie's birth. Her mother had stolen that from me.

My hand slid into my wife's, a diamond ring and matching wedding band on her finger. We ultimately ended up going to Vegas to get married. Much to my daughter's chagrin.

Lettie was here too, of course. It was her summer break. She was on the other side of Sia's bed, but she got up once she saw me. Lettie grinned. "I'm going to tell Andre it's almost time."

He lived here too, my home a full one during the summer.

I spoke with both my wife and her brother about what they wanted to do now that they were reunited. They agreed that Andre would continue his education overseas. His entire life was there, but he did come home whenever he had breaks. He and Sia reconnected during that time, and she and I visited him too. In fact, the two of us spent half the year across the pond so my wife and her brother could have more time together, and that one hundred percent was able to happen thanks to Val. My head of security watched over things stateside while Sia and I were away. Natan had no family outside of myself, and it'd been left up to me to lead the organization. It was a position I never wanted. I also had no right to have it, but Sia and Andre were young and didn't know this world. I would do what I needed to do until either one of them decided they wanted to have any part of it.

But in this moment, I wasn't the *pakhan*. I wasn't anything but a man who wanted to help deliver his child into the world.

"A girl," the doctor said, the woman aged with warm

eyes. We shopped around a lot for the perfect doctor, one we could trust. She lifted our daughter. "Ten fingers and ten toes. She's perfect, mom and dad."

She was, and I watched, awed, as the doctor handed our daughter off to her mother. Sia squeezed her, tears in her eyes, and the crying, kicking infant was one of the most beautiful things I'd ever seen. I'd already felt real love before. I felt it when I first realized I had a daughter, and again, when I found Sia.

But somehow my heart stretched yet again. It did for this beautiful baby girl with ten fingers and toes.

I pressed my mouth to Sia's cheek. "You did it, *malyshka*."

Sia didn't cry a lot, but she cried rivers now. She'd been through a lot this past year. She'd been bed-bound for weeks after everything with Natan, and I thought I almost lost her that night. I'd come close. So close…

It was hard to remember that time now with so much joy in the room. Sia smiled, and both Andre and Lettie were grinning like fools on the other side of the bed. Sia's brother managed to make it into the room in time, but my awareness of him had been lost upon watching my daughter come into the world.

"Wow, sis. Wow," he said, his eyes shining. He shook his head. "She's amazing."

She was. She really was.

"She's so beautiful," Lettie said, cooing at her little sister. She faced Sia and me. "What are you naming her?"

Sia and I hadn't really discussed too many names, but one had come up.

"Valerie," Sia stated, rocking our child and smiling up at me. She handed off our baby to the nurse to clean up, and my heart went over there too. It did until our Valerie was returned to us.

And I finally got to hold her.

We hadn't told Val we were naming our child after her,

but it felt natural that we were. Our daughter was going to be a strong warrior.

We'd nearly lost Val the same night as my father's death. Luckily, currently, Val was rushing to the house to meet our daughter. I texted her it was almost time on my way over. My head of security was working like a fiend in the organization so I could have time with my family.

She was working like a friend.

I didn't know how I'd been gifted with such abundance in my life. I had copious amounts of friendship and love, and that would truly have been my father's American Dream. I did it for him. I lived for him.

"Thank you, Dad," I whispered at the ceiling as I rocked my baby girl. I kissed my baby's mother after that.

"I love you," she said, and I whispered the same. We both shared tragedy. We both shared loss, but we also both had been able to overcome it. We became each other's family in the throes of adversity.

Together we won.

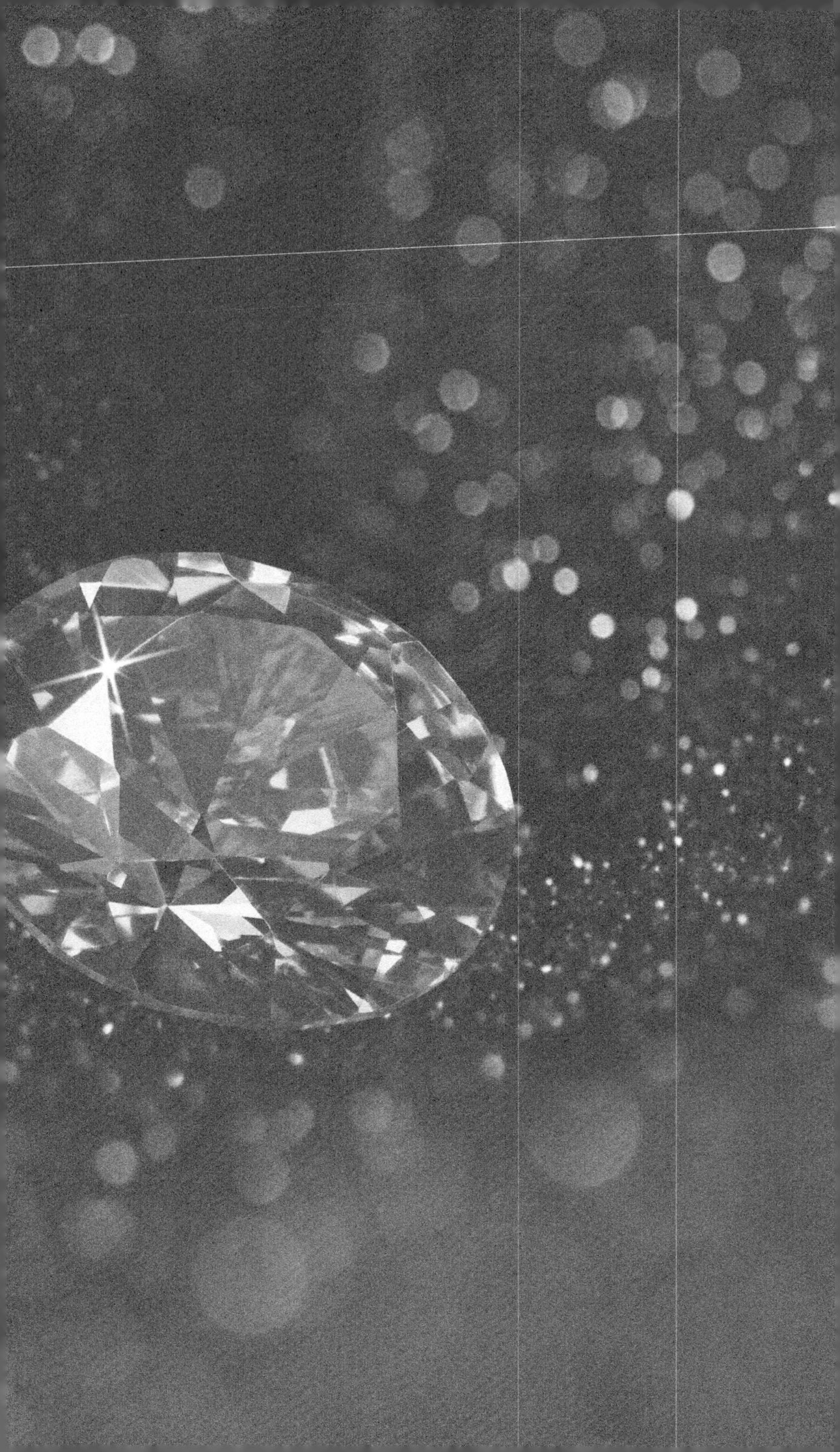

EPILOGUE

Two Years Later

Sia

Andre took Valerie's little hand, my toddler waddling her way across the wraparound porch. I lowered my textbook. "Make sure to hold onto her if you're going into the water."

We were all vacationing on the east coast this year. It was Maxim's idea. We'd just arrived, but I had some work to finish before I could enjoy anything. I was in my last year of my undergrad program and was really serious about getting my degree in animal science so I could pursue my dream of being a vet.

My brother rolled his eyes. "Nah, sis. I'm just going to let her scamper all over the beach and let the ocean take her."

I started to get up. Something I'd come to know about my brother Andre was that he was a smart ass. He was kind of like me in that regard.

Maxim lowered his newspaper. The six-foot-five god was in the other rocking chair beside mine and appeared unusually domestic considering he ran the Russian mob in Chicago. It was a role he never asked for, but he was a natural at it, and in a world where neither my brother (nor I) wanted to lead an entire organization, my husband had been a godsend. Andre and I may not always feel that way about the Bratva, but that was our position on everything for now.

Leading the Bratva may have been a role Maxim never asked for, but he was great at it. The Brotherhood respected him, and I think he felt a duty to right some wrongs. Natan had hurt a lot of people, and though that wasn't Maxim's fault, he didn't care. He wanted to make things right.

And I loved him for that.

His job was very dangerous, but he never put the family in harm's way. He also had Val, and between the two of them, they'd restored what they wanted in the organization. Honor.

I didn't know my father. I didn't know my family outside of Andre, but I had a feeling my dad would have liked that. I'd heard from many over the years that he was a very good man, and now, my husband knew that too. My dad had been manipulated just like Maxim had.

Maxim frowned at my brother. "Perhaps I need to go to the beach with you."

He was so protective of his little girl, *all* his girls. Let's just say our toddler said the word *poppa* before *mama* for a reason. The minute I pushed our baby out she became poppa's little girl.

Before Andre could answer, Maxim was out of his chair. He wore gray slacks that hugged the entirety of his thick legs, and his dress shirt made me want to peel open a few more of those buttons for a peek at his tatted chest. He picked Valerie up, but before he could hit the ground running on taking her, I got up too.

I took our toddler, then handed her off to Andre. I laughed. "He will take care of her."

"Of course, Max. She's my niece." Andre lifted Valerie in

the air, making her laugh when he tickled her little stomach. She wore a jumper over her polka dot swimsuit. He pressed a thumb to her button nose. "My niece loves me and wants to hang out with me today."

Valerie didn't get a lot of time with Andre lately, since he started college. At least when he'd been going to boarding school, we'd been over there with him for some of the year. Now, he was a college student just like me. I worked at the funeral home a lot, but was going to school in between shifts. I didn't *have* to work, but I enjoyed it. Anyway, our daughter rarely saw her uncle, and the two needed that time during our vacation.

Maxim grunted, but he allowed his baby girl to be carted off. He pointed at the two from the porch. "You hold her hand the whole time, Andre. I mean it."

"Maxim." I rubbed his chest, feeling his rapidly beating heart. If Lettie was here, she'd be talking her dad off the ledge too. She and Val had gone to the store to get groceries for dinner tonight. Val often came with us on our family vacations, but it wasn't just because she was security.

Val was family. She was a friend. Something I'd come to know about Lettie was that she was an excellent cook on top of being an amazing dancer. Something told me once she graduated college she'd be a principal dancer at whatever ballet company she saw fit. I grinned at my husband. "You know he will take care of her."

Our little girl had so much love, and, though our family was small, it was large with love.

That was just how we were.

Maxim kept his eyes on Andre and Valerie as they made their way down to the beach, and though Maxim grunted again, who was he fooling? He knew our daughter was in good hands, and he *loved* Andre. I mean, he let the boy call him Max so if that didn't mean something I didn't know what did.

He rubbed my back with a distracted touch, but soon, his attention was on me. "Come. I want to show you something."

After bringing me into our rental house, he brought me into his embrace. He squeezed my ass, and the noise that released from my lips pushed a delicious smile across his.

He licked my mouth. "Not quite what I was going to show you, but maybe later."

I could only hope and got a good handful of his ass as he took my hand again. The brazenness of the act made him grin, and I loved how lighthearted he was now. He used to look like he had the weight of the world on his shoulders. Especially when everything had happened with his adoptive dad. He had so much guilt back then, and it was completely unwarranted.

It'd take a long time for us both to heal. It was a day-by-day thing, and not every day was easy. I still mourned for a life and a family I lost both physically and mentally. I'd probably never have memories of who I used to be but my days were easier with Maxim and our own family in my life. They were made easier with days like this at this beautiful beach house. We were all together as a family, and I had no idea what he could possibly show me that would make me any happier than I was now.

But then, he showed me.

I'd seen the lines on the wall once Maxim moved a bookshelf. The shelf had been covering them up.

Getting close to the wall, I started to ask Maxim what all those little lines were on the wallpaper, but I didn't need to when I saw the names.

The name *Savina* was next to the tallest line, then *Mila*. It was followed by *Lydie*. And at the bottom...

"Anastasia." I hunkered down, shaking a little. The line couldn't have been more than a few feet above the ground, but it was there. Andre wasn't on here, but he had to have been a baby at the time the line for Anastasia was made.

I put my hand on the line.

"I'm sorry it took me so long to find this place," Maxim said.

I turned to find my husband behind me. His hand rested on my back, but he put his other hand on mine on the wall. We covered the name *Anastasia* together. Maxim faced me. "I'm still going through Natan's things. This place came up amongst the properties he acquired over the years. Your family owned it and used to vacation here."

My heart beat so fast.

"Andre already knows this is your family's home. I told him when I found it, and it was so hard for us both to keep the secret from you. To surprise you." Maxim pressed his mouth to my temple. "Maybe you'll be able to feel your family here in these walls."

I blinked down tears, not knowing what to say.

Maxim frowned. "Does being here make you sad, *malyshka*?"

No. In fact, it made me the opposite. I knew virtually nothing about my family, but here they were. My sisters…

I faced my husband, kissing him.

"Thank you," I said, my mouth warming his, and he brought me against him. He swept me up off the floor, our heat melding together. I didn't know how we ended up in our bedroom, but we did.

He pressed me against the bedpost, and I moaned.

He groaned against my mouth.

"The way I want to explore you, my love," he said, working me around. Moving behind me, he kissed down my spine. His hand slid into the front of my jeans, and I rose up on my tip toes. He breathed me in. "I'll have to settle for these stolen moments."

We didn't get to do as many scenes as we did before Valerie was born, but we still had time to play. I pushed my ass against his cock. "Don't go easy."

"Fuck." He bit my ear with a growl. His fingers were in my underwear now, his long digits flicking my bud. "Bend over. I want your ass."

I didn't make it easy. I liked being a brat, and he enjoyed being a brute. He ended up ripping my jeans down and forcing my panties off.

I was rewarded for my bratty behavior with a hard fucking. His cocky, angry thrusts charged in and out of my ass with vigor. He got me nice and lubed up, his hand full of my curls.

"Fuck, baby. You look so good like this." His hands took hold of my ass and my back bowed when he cracked a sharp slap against my right ass cheek. He rubbed my stinging flesh. "Relax, my love. You're in good hands. Your god's hands."

Using my hips, he picked up the pace, and I gripped the bed post. I called out his name. I called for God and all kinds of other things. I called for *relief*, which he so graciously provided.

My ass was raw by the time my walls vibrated. My release gushed down my legs at the same time he emptied his seed in my ass. He ended up pushing most of it back in, and my eyes rolled back so fucking hard.

"That's right, goddess. You don't get to be free of me," he said, working his cum back in, and I nearly collapsed, my release was so hard. I didn't want to be free of him.

In fact, I refused.

Maxim knew I liked a rough fucking. He didn't disappoint, but afterward, he took care of me. We lay in bed after he cleaned me up. He massaged my warm ass cheeks too, and afterward, he held me, kissing my ear.

"Maxim?" I felt like I was falling asleep in his arms, but we couldn't. Lettie and Val would probably be home soon, and eventually, Andre and Valerie would return from the beach.

Maxim didn't say anything, but his kisses were becoming

lazy too. He was there but was clearly dozing off. His soft kisses were the only thing letting me know he was still awake.

I smiled. "Is this real?" Was *he* real, and all this? My life. I hugged his arms around me. "Are you real?"

His kissing didn't stop, and eventually, he was between my legs beneath the sheets. He was on his hands and knees while he worshiped my folds with his mouth. He showed me exactly how real he was and how real all this was.

"I love you," he said, making me come again. My juices filled his mouth, and he groaned like he was the one to come. Like I'd given him the best gift he could have ever received. "I love you so much my beautiful girl. Is *this* real?"

He said something to me in Russian after that, and I pulled his head up. I wanted to see him, his handsome face.

I was rewarded when he surfaced from beneath the sheets. I brought his mouth down to mine.

"I love you," I said to him, letting him know how real this was, how real I was. He managed to give me my happily ever after.

We were each other's.

The end.

ACKNOWLEDGEMENTS

I want to take a moment to thank all my patrons on Patreon for all their support! I appreciate each and every one of you. Thank you so much for supporting me and my work <3

Madison	Valorie B	Bryn M	Jacquelynn R	Coffee Break with Books
Kim P	Ressa	Alexis C	Lisa A	Breanne T
Jessica S	Kymmie G	Sophie E	Ashley R	Aubrie O
Dorothy G	Bibiana	Aiden	Michelle	Mike L
Kimberly E	Gemma	Amie N	Katherine M	
Mariah H	Sophia A	Rosa M	Carrie	
Nashana W	Emily C	Bree B	Dixie	
NeuroSpicyGiGi	Kara G	Christen	Delayne	
brianna a	Violeta W	Lexi F	Kittycat	
Olivia K	CHRISTINE M	Katelin	Becky B	
Kelly A	Katie H	Annalisse G	Danielle B	
Aaron	Emily K	Alex J	Brittany	
Maleny	Elissa C	Melissa	Sara S	
Elle	Peggy S	Schella D	Kristina	
Verrell	Rose-Mari	Lisa G	Tawnya M	
Rosa L	Jasmine J	Amanda S	Rachel	
Tommy59	Emily A	Amandha k	Valarie G	
Lily K	Jessica B	Emi B	Devonne H	
Erin G	Vieve	Paige L	Maria D	
Savanna L	Karina R	abbycadabby	Jennifer	
Maggie M	Taylour K	Malaika M	Kelly S	
Nita	Hissa A	Justice	Mona B	
Melody	Konnie S	Ashley P	Tiffani	
Lexcy D	Katie	Samantha	Red B	
Kelsey K	Kaci L	Grace	Sunni	
April P	Jamiese	Sophie	Tammi	
sherrie l	Brianne	Nikki W	Madison G	
Jessica C	Naomi	Blair H	Amber M	
smileydragon24	Pippa S	Nikki S	Leighton G	
bethany H	Shekinah K	Heather L	Kirsty A	
Adaria M	Kelley M	Samantha	Shaunna D	
Liz	Michaela P	Jess M	Nichole T	
TeeH	Rebecca C	Xen G	Sarah J	
gigi m	Ms. Diamond	Leah R	Carolyn K	

If you'd like to join me on Patreon (and be listed in the acknowledgements page in my next book!) You can join me at the link below:

https://www.patreon.com/edenoneillwrites

Thank you so much for reading SIA! This book would be nothing without the wonderful readers on Kindle Vella. Thank you, guys, so much for supporting this book.

If you'd like to check out more of my work, you can do so at www.edenoneill.com.

Made in the USA
Middletown, DE
07 February 2025